PRAISE FOR *FORGED BY FATE,*
AND FATE OF THE GODS

"This story was absolutely amazing! It's like nothing I've read before...
a complete game changer. You won't be able to deny that Miss Dillin
is a genius."
—Parajunkee Reviews

"A fascinating and artful blend of myth and legend that makes for a
rich story of transcendent courage and hope. Not to be missed!"
— Saranna DeWylde, author of the *10 Days* series

"Inspired! An amazing fantasy world."
—Book Chick City

"I was hooked! I can't wait until the second book comes out so I can
find out what happens next."
—Jeep Diva Reviews

"A beautiful, sweeping story that puts on display the power of every
interpretation of love, and the truth of what can be accomplished when
people choose peace over strife. I couldn't put it out of my mind for
days."
—Trisha Leigh, author of *The Last Year* series

"A unique, hauntingly beautiful story."
—JC Andrijeski, author of the *Allie's War* series

FATE
FORGOTTEN

Fate of the Gods Trilogy
Book Two

AMALIA DILLIN

World Weaver Press

FATE FORGOTTEN
Copyright © 2013 Amalia Dillin

Published by World Weaver Press
Alpena, Michigan
www.WorldWeaverPress.com

Edited by Eileen Wiedbrauk
Cover designed by World Weaver Press

First Edition: November 2013

ISBN: 0615873685
ISBN-13: 978-0615873688

Also available as an ebook.

For Drew the Third, because when I said, "I'm never going to get published!" he said, "Do not make me buy a publishing company to publish your books, because I'll do it, Savage!"

I might be paraphrasing, but it's still true.

ACKNOWLEDGMENTS

First of all, thank you to everyone who read and loved *Forged by Fate*! I can't tell you how much I appreciate all the reviews and support, and I hope very much that you'll love *Fate Forgotten* just as much. Without you, it wouldn't have been possible for this series to reach as far as it has!

Second, I must thank Stephanie Sauvinet for her help with my French. Any errors in this novel or *Tempting Fate*, are mine—and all the credit for the stuff that's correctly translated goes to her, because I'm pretty hopeless.

For help with the Latin in these books, I have to thank Sarah Walker, who has been my Latin mentor since our days together at the University of North Dakota. She's probably forgotten more Latin than I ever knew. (And what I did manage to learn is all to her credit as well.)

Thanks also to Diana Paz, who I hope will see the changes I've made to her favorite character and not hate me for it—and whose advice regarding *every* character I value deeply; and Zachary Tringali, who always says yes when I ask him, "can you just read this one scene for me and let me know if you think it is terrible?" You guys are the best Alphas and Betas and just plain friends I could ask for as a writer, and I'm glad we're traveling together on this road.

Thanks to Emily Hogarth, who sent me my first piece of fanmail for *Forged by Fate*, which TOTALLY made my month, and thank you to Mia-and-the-Zombies for providing me with the good humor to keep going even when writing seemed like the most frustrating endeavor in the universe. Dan Denton receives my eternal thanks for every single one of these Fate of the Gods books, and an extra heap on top of that for being my number one fan before I even knew what I was doing with these manuscripts.

Some other writers I'd like to thank, who have been totally supportive at every turn: Stephanie Thornton, Gary Corby, Vicky Alvear Shecter, Saranna DeWylde, Wendy Sparrow, Valerie Valdes, Cait Greer, Trisha Leigh, LT Host, ST Bende, and Nazarea Andrews—I am wishing you all so much success of your own, and rooting for all of you and your books!

Of course, no acknowledgment section would be complete without a huge, HUGE thank you to my family—from El Husband to my mother, my siblings to my aunts and uncles, and even my cousins. I feel like becoming an author has been an incredible journey, transforming me from child to adult, and you guys have been fantastic companions to have along the way. Thank you, thank you, thank you, and I hope you won't get tired of reading early drafts for me any time soon, because I'm not giving this dream up! Special thanks to: Adam (forever), and the Cousintry, particularly Emi, Mattias, and Con. Your emotional support has been completely invaluable to me.

Finally, thanks to Eileen at WWP for her continuing enthusiasm and especially for helping me to make these books even better than they were when she first read them.

FATE FORGOTTEN

PROLOGUE
Present-Day France

The minute the car was beyond DeLeon lands, Adam stopped and pulled over. He glowered out the windshield, one hand rubbing at his face, the other still on the steering wheel. Damn it! What the hell had just happened? What had he just let happen?

What had he expected Eve to do? Profess her undying love, just because he couldn't control his? He, more than anyone, was aware of her devotion to her husband. To her DeLeon family. Eve would never turn her back on them. Not for him. Probably not for anyone. Not that it was any comfort.

Thunder rumbled in the clear sky, and he swore aloud. Bad enough this so-called god had the nerve to cut him off mid-thought while he spoke with Eve, but now he had to suffer another lecture? He got out of the car and slammed the door shut.

"I'm not on their lands!" he shouted at the thunder.

Lightning made him flinch, bringing with it a flash of smoke, and soot, and memory so strong it overwhelmed his present. He could almost feel the electricity crawling over his skin, as he relived that last moment in the Garden, before everything had been taken from him.

The lick of fire inside his thoughts, burning everything in its path. Ash clung to his skin, and pitch glued his fingers together around the brand. One tree, then another, then another, dropping scorched branches into the dryer deadfall until the flames spread without his help, and laughter ringing in his ears. Adam shook his head, pushing the broken memory away and taking no pleasure in its belated return. He forced himself to focus on the present. On Thor.

The light turned liquid, then solid as the god emerged from the plasma. Lightning strikes always unnerved him. Slowly, it was becoming clear to him why. If Michael had stolen his memory with lightning, leaving him in a field of soot he had not even had the wit to recognize as the Garden itself, at least he had a reason for fearing it. Adam was sure Thor got some sick sort of pleasure out of tormenting him this way; he had seen the god arrive and depart without the display. But no matter how frequently he witnessed it—and his encounters with Thor were far more frequent than he wanted, to be sure—he could not shake the disquiet, could not stop his stomach from twisting into knots at the sight.

He should have known. He should have realized the burned ground was the Garden. But that he would set it alight with his own hands? He still couldn't believe it was true. Not even after seeing the memory in Eve's mind, feeling her honesty, her fear . . .

Thor glared at him, his eyes white with anger as he approached the car. "When you were given your memory, you made certain promises."

"Yes. Promises. And have I broken them? Do you see a baby in my arms?" He leaned against the hood and slipped his hands into his pockets so that Thor wouldn't see them balled into fists. The gods had returned the memories of his past lives, difficult though they might have been to sort through, but they couldn't give him what Michael had taken. His life in the Garden, before he'd woken in the ash was still largely lost, but for the impression of . . . something he still couldn't name. And Eve. He remembered her green eyes, blinking up at him, all innocence and confusion. "Not that any of you can do anything about it when I do renege. And I will. If only to spite you, personally."

"You really think she'll ever let you touch her?" Thor sneered. "Do you think her so weak?"

"Why else are we the only two to be reborn, if not because we're meant to be together?" He shrugged, forcing himself not to glare. Seeing Thor always brought out the worst in him. He made himself smile, instead. "It must kill you to know you can't have her. That she doesn't even know you exist. You're like some neutered puppy, leashed by your father, by the Council."

"For her own good!" Thunder. Always thunder accompanied the god's anger. And a flare of white in his eyes. Thor was about as subtle as a rhinoceros mid-charge. With a visible effort, the god bit back his fury, but his tone was rich with contempt instead. "She is heavy with another's child, and you thrust yourself upon her—while you are married to her sister, besides! You violate her very mind, after she has warned you against it, after I have already made plain the laws which govern your stay within *my* lands. If you dare impose yourself upon her again, Adam, I'll take pleasure in finding a way to make you suffer for it. Rest assured that no power will stop me in that purpose."

Adam ground his teeth. Having been a guest of Thor's already, he knew the threats weren't even remotely idle. It had required a bit of experimentation, but Thor had found dragging him to Asgard or Olympus a convenient way to beat him to a pulp without causing Eve harm. Nor did the angels interfere on his behalf. They had made their distaste clear when they had washed their hands of him at the dawn of time and set him to wander the earth without any of the knowledge that had been his by right of creation. Son of God, they had called him, as he picked himself up from the ashes, his mind as shattered as his body. First Made.

It wasn't difficult to put it together even without his memory, and Ryam's journal had more than confirmed what he'd suspected about Eve. And of course, that the gods had feared he would search Eve out at all had been enough to compel him onward.

"Do you really think I'd do anything to drive her away?" Adam asked, keeping his voice low and even. "When I've only just stopped being a pebble in her shoe?"

"You have sworn yourself to our terms, forsaken Eve for money and power. For the right to remember yourself." Thor's eyes burned so white-hot they were almost blue. "The Council has already considered wiping you and your sister from the earth once, Covenant or no. Do not tempt us a second time; you will not be spared."

"You're not *my* god, Thor. I don't think I'll be obeying any more of your commands."

Thor smiled, the all too familiar war-hammer appearing in his hands. "I was hoping you'd say that."

Adam glanced at the hammer and swallowed. He hadn't done anything to deserve a beating though, and while there was no love lost between them, Thor wouldn't strike at him on earth without reason. Especially not while Eve was pregnant. Still . . .

"You do realize she's in labor? She's probably already given birth to an heir. The next generation to benefit from your personal protection and aid. Shouldn't you be off haunting DeLeons to ensure the right vows and promises are made?"

Mjölnir vanished, and Thor's gaze seemed to lose focus for a moment. "The baby came early." Then his eyes narrowed. "Because of you."

"Damned if I do, damned if I don't. Had I stayed you'd probably be saying the same thing. But I left for her, Thor. Don't forget that."

He opened the car door and got back in, starting it up and pulling away without a backward look. He had better things to do than waste his time fighting with gods who, for some reason, felt compelled to interfere with men. And Eve.

Eve. The only woman who could understand him. Who could ever really know what it was like to live with all those lives in his head. All the wars, all the death; life after life, century after century. The gods spared him no sympathy, but Eve—Eve knew.

Damn it. How had this happened? He had been happy, married to Mia!

Until he saw Eve, radiant with her pregnancy. He cursed Mia for not warning him that Eve was with child. Something inside him had shifted at the sight of her. It wasn't about the godchild anymore. It was about Eve. It was about how amazing it would be if he could share this with her, as Garrit did. To have her mother his own sons and daughters. It was about having her as his wife to love and cherish and knowing death would never truly part them. And neither one of them would ever have to hide their true selves again. He could give her so much more. He wanted to give her everything. The whole world, wrapped up with a bow, to make over in her image.

He had married Mia for fun more than anything, because she had spirit, misguided though it sometimes was, and because he could not stand to see that spirit crushed under the weight of what was *expected* of her. He had learned to love her. To appreciate her. To care about her, perhaps all the more because through him, she no longer need live within her sister's shadow. Just not enough. Whatever those feelings were, they were pale and empty in comparison to what had broken into his heart when he had felt Eve's child move within her womb, his hand pressed against her swollen belly.

"Thou shalt not covet thy neighbor's wife," he said, staring into the patch of highway revealed by his headlights as he snaked through the mountain roads. Of course, he never had cared for the rules. It was an instinct he hadn't ever been able to shake.

But what if she wanted him too?

He had felt her jealousy, when she had first seen him with her sister. He hadn't imagined that. And when she had thought of Paris, or her life as Helen, there was a fondness in those memories he hadn't expected. She had longed for that part of him, whether she realized it or not.

Maybe Thor was wrong.

It didn't have to be this life, after all. If he could only prove himself, his love, they could have an eternity together. And if the angels tried to stop them—if Michael came anywhere near him with that sword again—Adam would find a way to repay the Archangel for everything he had suffered.

No matter what his sin had been, they'd had no right to steal his memory before he'd even begun to live.

CHAPTER ONE
154 AD

"You betrayed us," Sif said. Her voice was cold, her eyes like golden glaciers. She stood beside Odin in the chamber, her hand on his shoulder where he sat on his throne. Frigg stood on his other side, her face soft, sympathetic. Her eyes as warm as Sif's were frozen. From the way Frigg looked on him, with so much understanding, Thor wondered if she had seen some glimpse of his future.

Odin glowered at the floor, his forehead creased. He stroked his beard with one hand, and the raven on his shoulder with the other. He had not spoken yet, though he had emptied this smaller hall, his throne room, of all but Sif and his own wife. Thor wished he had sent Sif away as well. Wife or not, he had no use for her. Not anymore. And she had made it more than clear she had no use for him, either.

He could not understand why she had set herself against Eve. Sif had never loved him. Had lied to him from the first. What difference did it make to her that he had taken another woman to his bed, so long ago? That he had loved another goddess, when she had taken lovers of her own, betrayed their marriage and her vows even before that!

"If speaking honestly is betrayal to the Aesir, then I will continue to do so with my dying breath," he replied.

"Odin made his feelings known to you, Thor. The Aesir were to stand together in this," Sif said.

He raised his eyes to his wife, and kept his face blank. He wouldn't let Sif bait him today. Not now. "Odin made your feelings known to me, yes. And I made clear to him, mine. There was no honor in this, Sif. To condemn a fellow goddess to death without allowing her to speak for herself would have been a grievous wrong. I would have spoken for any of you, any other god, if the circumstances had been different. I did what my conscience dictated."

Sif sneered. "You acted selfishly to save the woman you love."

"The Council made its decision. She is to be left alone."

"Because of you!" Sif stamped a foot as her voice rose nearly to a shriek. "Because of your betrayal! Speaking against your own father!"

"Enough." Odin's voice was soft, but it carried the weight of authority. He looked up at Thor for the first time.

His expression was drawn, and the illusion that hid the dark hole of his missing eye flickered and faded. Thor could not tear his gaze away from the gaping blackness in his father's face. But then Odin shook his head, and he had two eyes again.

"You are no longer bound to me alone, Thor, but to the Council. You can neither dishonor yourself in the task you have been set, nor dishonor us with betrayal. Follow her as you must. Spy upon her. But you are forbidden to know her, to touch her, to have her as your own. Forbidden to reveal yourself to her, as I know you ache to do. This is your punishment. For all time."

Thor felt himself stiffen. It seemed as though Gabriel's promise of reunion with Eve had not taken into account his father's anger. "This is your final word?"

"I will not suffer your disobedience. If you were not my son, I would have you hanged for your disloyalty. As it is, I can only believe your actions are not your own. Go. Walk the earth and observe, as you have sworn to do. I do not wish to look upon you."

Thor ground his teeth. Not his own. Was that what his father wanted to think? That he was bewitched somehow? The truth was far more insidious, whether Odin wished to believe in it or not. For the first time in more than five cycles he had followed his own conscience, his own will, rather than his father's! And his choice had been right and honorable.

But so be it. Thor turned to leave, Sif's smirk catching his eye, though he did not give her even the satisfaction of a glower. He left the hall without another word, ignoring the silent stares of his brothers as he passed through the large feasting hall on his way out. There was little laughter today, no rich scent of roasting meat. Even the hearth fire barely smoked, as depressed as the rest of Odin's hall in deference to its king.

His father had spoken, and he was cast away. At least he would not have to watch Sif flirt and fawn over the Trickster at every meal. And she could hardly take exception to his absence if Odin had ordered it. After so many years of being leashed to Asgard, even so small a freedom as the right to wander the earth came with more relief than sorrow.

But he could not leave quite yet. He went to the world-tree first, kneeling before it as he had once done as a small boy, on another plane, in another world. Another lifetime. He rested his forehead against the trunk and closed his eyes. It had been a long time since he had prayed to his mother for help, for guidance, for anything, and he could not quite bring himself to do so now. Instead, he breathed in the scent of the bark and the sweet smell of the fruit that made the branches bow around him, savoring it all. This much, he would surely miss.

"Thor?" Frigg's voice was gentle as a breeze. A far cry from the shrillness of Sif's tone.

He dropped his hand and rose. Perhaps a step-mother was the next best thing. Frigg had always been kind. She favored her own son by Odin, Baldur, but Thor had never begrudged her that. Everyone loved Baldur.

"I'm afraid my father would not like to see your pity for me, Frigg."

She smiled and raised a hand to his face, stroking his cheek. "Your father loves you, Thor. Do not think otherwise. But we, none of us, can resist the calls of our mothers. It has always been your fate to return to Her, and Odin always struggled with the knowledge that he would lose you."

"My mother is long gone. Gone even from my memory."

"But not your heart." She dropped her hand, and her expression became grave. "You walk the path you must and there is little any of us can do to stop it. Sif will yet have her revenge, but it will be some time coming. I'm afraid you will spend a long and lonely life, Thor, and you will know heartbreak and pain even more intimately than you do now. But you'll also know love. The love of your mother and your sister."

He shook his head, frowning. "But I have no sister."

Frigg smiled again. "Don't you?"

Perhaps her second sight had confused her. There was a reason Frigg rarely spoke of her visions. There had been more than one night that she wept uncontrollably because they had overwhelmed her.

"I appreciate your words, Frigg." Small comfort though they were, he could not insult her. "Thank you."

"Remember them." She studied him for a moment longer, the smile still tugging at her lips. "And perhaps you will remember your mother as well."

He watched her walk away and sighed. The riddles which plagued him were tiring. The angels, first, and now Frigg as well. Would Ra start next? And Athena?

Athena. He plucked two of the Golden apples from a branch hanging heavy with fruit. The tree had always recognized him, had never refused him its bounty, though he had never admitted his ability to anyone. Not even his father. He owed Athena a thank you, and Aphrodite her gift, and he knew it was not just her sister who loved things made of gold, though Athena would never admit to the weakness.

With the fruit tucked between his tunic and his skin, safe and protected, he let the lightning take him from Asgard to Greece, to the olive grove where he had once sat with Athena and begged for grain. He could not go directly to Mount Olympus without invitation, but Athena knew to look for him there when he came to see her. He sat down on the stone bench, worn now with its age, but still sturdy.

Athena?

Here so soon?

He grimaced, though only the trees could see him. *My father could not abide to look at me any longer.*

Ah, Thor . . . She sighed in his mind, and then she stood before him, her pale skin washed with a glow of moonlight. She touched his face. His cheek, his hair, his lips. Her fingers feather-light on his skin. "I am sorry for your pain."

He caught her hand and kissed her palm before releasing it and standing. "I have brought your sister's payment." The golden apple glittered even in the half light, and she took it. He held out the second. "And a gift for you. With my thanks."

She raised her face to his, but her eyes were sad. "Could you not think of some better way to thank me?"

He didn't smile. "If I could offer you what you wanted, I would give it freely. Without asking for any favors in return. But I would not do to you what Sif has done to me, and I wish you would not ask it of me."

"She's still your wife. Even after this." She looked away. "I thought she would have demanded Odin allow her to divorce you."

"She may still. She is much at my father's side these days. I do not think he would deny her anything. But this amuses her, to keep me chained. Odin has forbidden me to reveal myself to Eve. I may only observe her. Look, but never touch."

"A grave punishment." Her jaw tightened. "Was it Sif's idea?"

He shrugged. The hardness of her voice worried him. "I do not mean to hurt you. Giving you my body, empty of love, would be unworthy. You deserve more. My brother Baldur—"

She laughed. "Your brother Baldur is hardly an adequate substitute for you. He would not even think of standing against your father or his mother, no matter what they asked of him. He would not go to the lengths you have for love. And he does not have your spirit. He would never argue with me if he believed I was bullheaded, or call me out when I behaved like a fool. He is too good, Thor. Too kind."

"What would you have me say? I value your friendship. I have no wish to lose it. Not like this. Not now." He had already lost so much. His father's respect. The love of his wife. Eve. Over and over again, he lost Eve. And would continue to do so.

She shook her head, her lips pressed into a thin line. The apples disappeared into a pouch at her waist and the smile she gave him was strained. "I would invite you to my father's house, but Ares is there, and he was quite put out by the Council's decision. It is better if he does not see you so soon."

"I would not dream of imposing on your hospitality." It was something of a relief not to have to worry about keeping himself sober enough during an Olympian feast to avoid any further complications. Dionysus had a way of making one forget his vows. And he had no wish to hurt Athena so cruelly. "Call for me if there is anything I can do for you, Athena. Please."

"Of course." She waved him away. "Don't let me keep you from your duty."

He nodded at her dismissal and stepped back. He closed his eyes and thought of Eve's family, Eve's House of Lions, and took himself from the grove.

§

When the lightning struck, it wasn't a boy who came running, but a girl dressed in the Roman style. They were so much less isolated now than they had once been, and she showed no fear at all when she saw him standing in the field. No more than ten, she looked at him and smiled.

"*Tonitrus!*"

He tripped over the Latin for a moment. Were they that involved with Rome, now? He supposed they must be. In the last century, hadn't the Romans even taken that northern island belonging to the Celts? Britannia?

"*Salvē,*" he said, offering the little girl a bow with his greeting. She had Eve's smile, though that was all the resemblance left.

She seemed delighted. "*Venī mē! Venī!*" Then she took off at a run, back to the large house she had come from, shouting for her mother.

He followed, as she had asked him to, or at least he hoped she had said he should come with her. It had been some time since he'd used this tongue, and he hadn't pulled the language from her mind. Adults had a broader understanding of the nuances of meaning, and he did not wish to make a fool of himself so soon.

A woman stood at the door when he arrived. She studied his face, and he took the language from her while she did so, relieved to know he had translated things properly. "Greetings," he said again. "I've traveled from the North."

"Thor?" she asked.

He smiled. "You know the stories."

"My grandmother told me about you. She told me you gave us the truth about the prophet and our God."

"And your first mother, Eve."

"Yes. And you come when we call for you. When we ask for your help. You bring us rain in drought and sun in flood."

"I promised your people my help, yes. My protection. For Eve."

"Grandmother thought that you loved her."

He laughed, though it made his heart ache. "You're grandmother was named Julia, wasn't she?" The woman nodded. "She had Eve's perception. What's your name?"

The woman smiled, dimpling. "Flavia."

"Flavia is lovely, though I'm sorry that you're not an Evaline. It has been a long time since there was an Evaline in the House of Lions."

"I'm Evaline!" It was the little girl, peeking out from behind her mother's legs.

Thor smiled and crouched down, beckoning her forward. He kissed her forehead and whispered a prayer to the True God. *Watch over this child, and love her family. Give her a good life among her people, a good husband who will not chain her, but liberate her. Give her your Grace, and let her know her duty, her purpose and pass it on to her children.* He promised himself he would watch her, too. "Bless you, Evaline. Wear your name with pride."

"Will you stay with us for dinner?" Flavia asked. "And tell us the stories, our history. For Evaline."

He closed his eyes and looked for Eve. She was far in the east. Within Shiva's power. And her brother Adam was in Rome. He would not be neglecting his duty to stay. And he owed these people this much. To give them their history. He owed Eve this much, if he could do nothing else. At least her family could know him. Odin had not taken that much from him. He opened his eyes. "Your hospitality would be appreciated. Thank you."

Evaline took his hand, and he let her lead him into the house.

CHAPTER TWO
Present

Eve told no one of Michael's visit, striving instead to settle into motherhood without worry. The archangel had made his point, reminding her of her vow, and as long as she kept it, there was no reason for fear. She would never let Adam have her body. She would never give Adam a child. Why bother Garrit with hypotheticals? He worried enough already, besides, and now they had a child to raise together.

Unlike his ancestor, the Marquis, Garrit had no aversion to keeping his children close, nor did he argue with Eve's desire to care for her children personally. He offered to hire a nanny to have on hand during the first few months, but she dismissed the idea before he had time to press the issue.

"If you insist on believing I'll need help, I'd prefer you ask your mother, or your aunt. Family is always better than hired help when raising a baby, but I'm more than capable of caring for one."

"Abby, I'm not questioning your proficiency, I just don't see any reason why you should run yourself ragged and be up all hours of the night if you don't have to. We have the means, why not take advantage of it?"

"Just because you have the means to do something doesn't mean it's the right thing to do. If you don't want to ask your mother, I could always ask mine."

Of course, he called his mother at once. Juliette was happy to be on hand, and she not only agreed to help with the baby, but also to order the household.

"I know how you hate having a staff, Abby, and the fewer strangers around the house bringing in germs the better off you'll all be. I'll take care of things, and Garrit can fight with me over whether or not to hire a nanny, instead of you." Then she smiled. "I promise he'll lose."

The nursery was installed in the next room, adjoining their master bedroom. A remnant of the days when a husband and wife didn't always share a bed, or even a room. And Juliette and René settled back into the house without the least disturbance.

Juliette's first act was to forbid the rest of the family, not already present, from coming to see the baby until he had a few months to settle in.

"The parade of DeLeon well-wishers, family or not, is only going to be a vector for disease."

Eve was relieved beyond measure to not be required to create or enforce that edict herself. "Maybe Brienne will pass along the word?"

Juliette laughed. "Brienne may have the weight of being matriarch behind her words, but no member of this family would dream of intruding on you or your son once your wishes were known. They have too healthy a respect for their Lady Eve. You may yet thank your Lord Ryam for that."

She grimaced. Ryam, she thought privately, had done more harm than good with the information he'd gathered during their life together in the fifteenth century. Would she ever have a DeLeon husband who was not overprotective? "I do prefer a little bit less reverence."

"Those of us who matter already know, my dear, and as a DeLeon in name only, I fully intend to treat you merely as my lovely daughter.

But trust me that the aid of being who you are will make things that much easier on you now. I can't tell you how many people were in and out at Garrit's birth. It was exhausting, and René was no help at all. So proud to show off his son. It was one of the reasons I only gave him the one child. I couldn't bear the thought of going through it all again."

"Ryam was the same. But there was a certain amount of social obligation then, as well. I wonder if half the reason the mortality rate was so high wasn't because of all those people coming in to chuck the children under the chin with their grubby hands." Eve sighed at the memory. "It's so nice that people bathe with regularity now. That was a difficult time to live through. I still don't take indoor plumbing for granted."

"Tell me at least the DeLeon ancestors had the decency to keep themselves clean?"

She laughed. "Oh, they did. It was one of my first acts as Ryam's wife. At least weekly baths were instituted for everyone. More frequent for the family. I was already in trouble with the Church, so I figured I may as well go for broke."

Juliette wrinkled her nose. "That anyone could doubt cleanliness was a virtue, I'll never understand."

§

Alexandre was a pleasant baby, and not only because Eve was so able to anticipate his needs. He rarely fussed without a reason, and he rarely had a reason to fuss. Motherhood had become more routine than instinct over the course of several thousands of years, and Eve had always loved her children. There was something refreshing about listening to so pure and innocent a mind. Something fascinating about witnessing that development from barely conscious of more than her warmth and her milk, to recognition of Mother and Father, to pleasure and love and joy.

Of course, this particular baby was doomed to be spoiled by his overeager DeLeon family. She hadn't realized at first the significance, outside of the continuation of the direct line. Any baby born to Garrit would have been celebrated, but that it was Garrit's child by herself increased this celebration to exultant proportions.

"Garrit, would you please tell your family to stop treating me like some kind of divine being. Anyone can have a baby. And look—his eyes are already darkening. I wouldn't be surprised if you contributed more genes than I did, to this one."

"I haven't stopped trying since we married, Abby. I'm afraid that it isn't within my power, but I'll speak with Brienne again. Perhaps this time will be the charm."

She handed him his son when he rose from one of the large armchairs to meet her. "Your family is going to spoil him into arrogance. This can't go on. No son of mine will suffer from the affliction of pride. Remind them of that."

"They might listen more effectively if you told them yourself." He cradled Alex against his chest, and watched her as she paced the library. "It will be fine, Abby. Even if they do dote on him, we'll raise him properly. And he'll have brothers and sisters to bring him to heel if he forgets."

"For an only child, you certainly seem determined to breed."

He laughed. "I may be an only child, but I was raised with plenty of family. If we don't give him siblings the closest family he'll have are second and third cousins."

"Mia will have children eventually. He'll have first cousins too."

"Hm." He grimaced. "Adam's children, you mean."

"And cousins, all the same, when they arrive." She stopped before the window, letting the sun warm her face. Adam's children would have been her nieces and nephews regardless, though it had never occurred to her before to consider them such. Brother and sister were just convenient terms to describe a relationship that had no equivalent, but even God had named them twins, once. "Twice-over, when you think about it."

"Have you heard from him?"

She shook her head. "Not since he left at Christmas. I really don't make a habit of reaching him, and I have no reason to expect he'll be contacting me anytime soon." Or ever, if those last emotions had been any indication. Adam had seemed resolved, determined not to hurt Mia.

"He didn't even check in on you after the birth?"

"No." She wasn't sure why it rankled her, but it seemed to offend Garrit, too, somehow. "Why would he? I'm sure Mia told him the baby was fine when she got home."

"I would think that as interested as he's been in you, he would express some concern for your physical well-being."

"Oh." That idea hadn't even occurred to her. "No, that wouldn't matter to him, I don't think. He knows I can't suffer any serious harm. Certainly not from childbirth. I will always be well, just as he will, even if I were sick with something he wouldn't worry for my health."

Not that she'd ever been terribly sick, either. Food poisoning, now and again, of course, but she hadn't yet died from disease, in all her years, or even been seriously crippled by it for any length of time. Plagues came and went, but what she caught passed quickly enough, when she caught it at all. Drug overdose was a misery, though, and if she had her way, she'd never take any kind of mind-altering medication again. Those kinds of prescriptions didn't take into account telepathy, or the discipline of mind it took to keep from invading the privacy of the community around her.

"I suppose I should be grateful that he's absented himself." Garrit came to stand beside her in the sun of the window, Alex asleep now against his shoulder.

She slid under his free arm, closing her eyes and reveling in the warmth of family. "Will your family make as much fuss over a girl as they do over little Alexandre?"

"Almost certainly. Alex will inherit the estate, but our daughter will inherit the family. That she's of your blood, too, will make her all the more important to them. The stories tell us that we have always honored above all else our connections to you."

"I'm not sure I'll ever live up to the legend you DeLeons have made of me. I must've been away too long."

He kissed the top of her head. "Then I guess in the future you'll just have to come back to us more often."

"I begin to think I'm more trouble than anything else." It was the first time, really, that she'd ever come back home for love. Every other life, she'd been running away from something, and even in this time, it had only caused the family distress, with Adam hunting her. And now married to her sister. How it must gall them to have to give him hospitality. To be tied to him at all, when they had spent so many years devoted to keeping him away. "Certainly more than I'm worth."

"Don't be ridiculous, Abby." He pulled away from her and forced her to look into his eyes. "I love you. I wouldn't trade this for anything."

"What about for honesty? For a wife who you didn't have to keep things from?"

He frowned, searching her face. "And how many husbands have you had that you could be wholly yourself with? How many marriages allowed you to tell the truth?"

She dropped her eyes to the sleeping baby in his arms, and tried not to think of Thorgrim. Thorgrim who had been haunting her dreams with a frequency that disturbed her. She felt closer to him now, somehow, though he was three thousand years dead. Ever since Michael had come, Thorgrim had felt ever more present. She hoped it didn't mean she was losing her sanity.

"Too few," she finally said, just to stop herself from ruminating along those lines. "Not even a handful."

"Then enjoy it," Garrit said. "Let it be a life you remember with joy, not with guilt for what I might have had with someone else, because I can promise you I would have had just as many secrets to keep, and it's not possible I would've found someone I loved more than you."

She had no trouble believing that as truth. It was impossible not to notice how easily good men fell in love with her, how completely. She shook her head and turned away, disturbed by the thought. Had Adam even had a chance? Was it because of how she had been made that he wanted her so badly? Poor Mia. But if Adam hadn't loved Mia, he wouldn't have left. He wouldn't have wanted to avoid causing her pain or distress. They wouldn't be living together in London now, still married, would they?

"Abby?"

She sighed. There were so many answers she couldn't find. Questions she couldn't ask. Even about herself. "I'm sorry. I guess I'm just tired. I haven't been sleeping well."

"Go take a nap. I'll take care of Alex."

She kissed his cheek. "Wake me before dinner, would you?" But she didn't wait for his answer before she left the library.

As she curled up in the large bed, she found herself wishing that Ryam were still alive, that she could ask him how he'd known of Adam's coming and why he hadn't seen fit to warn her. Ryam she could have shouted at, demanding to know the truth. Beat on his chest with her fists until he told her everything and why he had kept it from her.

It was more frustrating than surprising that while she slept, she dreamt again of Thorgrim.

CHAPTER THREE
Future

§

Adam stepped out of the car, adjusting his suit jacket and brushing a fleck of fuzz from his arm. He had spent the past year traveling the globe with the help of the incredible wealth which had been part of his agreement with the gods six hundred years ago. He smirked to himself at the use he had put it to. Not exactly what they had meant it for, was it? Then again, he hadn't behaved the way they had wanted from the start.

He waved his driver to stay and set off on a leisurely stroll down the sidewalk. It wasn't exactly the best part of Montreal, but it wasn't the worst either, and some of the most interesting shops sprung up in these in-between places. He loved antique stores and second hand shops. Not as a collector, but because he found that the oddest things brought back memories of times long past and longer forgotten. Not that he would find anything for sale that would bring back the memories he wanted most. Somehow he didn't think there was anything material left in the world from Creation, aside from himself and Eve.

He frowned, staring into the window of a small tobacco shop. Once cancer had been cured, smoking had come back in vogue. With the need to filter out the carcinogens gone, the sale of loose leaf tobacco had become a booming industry. This shop was like many others he'd seen. Shelves and shelves of aromatic leaves along with a few other varieties of smokable vegetation. Not that he had worried about cancer even before it had been cured. He had never seen the sense in limiting himself out of fear of what might happen in the future, even before he had realized his immortality.

A bell on the door tinkled softly as he stepped into the shop and inhaled deeply. It was heady and rich and almost overwhelming to the senses. He couldn't imagine spending hours in a place like this, day after day. Although it would certainly give a person a new appreciation for the crisp, clean air outside. The smell of the place hung like a curtain across the threshold.

A girl at the counter hummed softly to herself as she refilled and reorganized containers, restocking the plebian cigarettes for those who were too cheap to pay a premium for the loose leaves. Her hair was dark, almost but not quite black, and fell loose to her waist. She glanced over her shoulder at him, and he thought he caught a flash of brilliant emerald-green eyes.

The humming stopped at once, and she turned. "Can I help you?"

He stared at her face for a long moment. Her eyes were so striking. "Do I know you?"

She looked away, back at the stock, shuffling some of the cartons. "I don't think so."

"You don't?"

He stepped around a display to get a better view of her face. Her skin glowed with an olive complexion. Still, there was something familiar about her profile. Not exactly the same, of course. How could it be? But definitely similar. And her eyes . . .

"What's your name?"

She hesitated, her fingers hovering over the cartons. "Renata."

"Renata," he said, studying her still. She was lovely. Maybe it was just the richness of her skin that set off her eyes and made them look that way. But her age was right. There couldn't be more than a year or two between them, if at all. And he was going to be in town for some time. It might be worth cultivating a friend. "That's a pretty name."

"Thank you."

"My name is Jeremiah," he said, leaning against the counter. "I'm in town on business."

"Oh?"

He could feel her interest, reluctant though it was. And her eyes were too close to Eve's to ignore. He couldn't afford to let her slip away. Not yet.

"I know this is terribly forward, but would you like to have dinner with me tonight?" When she looked back at him in surprise, he gave her one of his most charming smiles. "It's just that I don't know the city very well. But you must, surely."

She didn't quite frown, but her forehead wrinkled for a moment. "I'd be happy to suggest a restaurant for you, but I'm not sure if dinner is such a good idea."

"I know what you're thinking," he said, smiling apologetically. "That I'm only interested in you because you're so beautiful. That the kind of man who would ask you to dinner so quickly isn't the kind of man you'd like to get to know. I assure you that it isn't anything of the sort."

She raised an eyebrow. "And how do you know that's what I'm thinking?"

He shrugged. "I'm sure men come in here and hit on you all the time."

"Maybe," she admitted. "Well, if that isn't the reason, then what is?"

He studied her face again, her eyes, her nose, the line of her jaw. There was no way to be certain really. But he thought he would feel her, if he were in her presence. Know her mind if they were in the same room. "You remind me of someone."

"Do I?"

He smiled. "Let me take you to dinner. I promise I'll be a perfect gentleman. What harm could it be, really?"

Her smile didn't quite reach her eyes. "There's a restaurant around the block. An Italian place called *Mangiamo*. I'll meet you there."

"Seven o'clock, then." He tried not to let his disappointment show. Not that she wasn't lovely. Not that she wasn't worth his time, regardless. But he was sure Eve would refuse him when he did find her, finally, in this new life they were living. "A pleasure to meet you, Renata."

The bell on the door chimed again as he showed himself out.

At least he wouldn't be eating alone.

He arrived early to secure a table and was pleasantly surprised by the ambiance of the restaurant. It was something above a pizzeria and something below fine dining, though he didn't feel terribly out of place in his business suit, and there were several other people scattered around the dining room dressed similarly. Human servers gave it even more appeal, but then Montreal was known for the strides it had taken to preserve its history. He made sure that he was given a table with a view of the door, and sipped from his water glass.

Renata entered the restaurant at precisely seven o'clock and he stood to catch her attention. She was dressed in a simple black dress, nothing fancy, which nevertheless could be made to fit any situation from a wedding to a trip to the grocery store. More than likely, the only one she had; the shop she worked in didn't appear to be all that impressive. The fixtures had all been well used, and the cash register was positively antique when most people paid with a tap of their e-vice.

He smiled and let his charm and confidence filter into her mind. Just a touch, nothing forceful or shocking. He wanted her comfortable and willing, but not a drone.

"You look even more lovely than you did this afternoon." He seated her and then took his own chair. Across from her, of course. All the better to meet her eyes if she would ever look up.

"Thank you." She fiddled with her place setting. "Did you have any trouble finding the restaurant?"

"Not at all." He nodded to the menu. "I assume you've eaten here before. Is there anything in particular you'd suggest?"

She dimpled when she smiled, giving him a glimpse of what she must have been like as young girl, just slightly mischievous, but never malicious. "I love the golden veal, but I'm afraid I'm not often able to order it. It's battered and fried and served in an amazing wine sauce with mushrooms."

The waiter arrived and Adam handed him his menu. "Two orders of the golden veal, please, and a bottle of whatever wine the house recommends to go with it." There was no point letting the night go to waste. Maybe he wouldn't have to sleep alone, either.

"Very good, sir," the waiter said, collecting the menus and leaving them alone again.

Renata frowned slightly. "They're bound to bring the most expensive bottle on the menu."

"As long as it pairs well with the meal, I don't see why they shouldn't." He shrugged and sat back in his chair. "Even their most expensive wine is going to be well within my budget, regardless—I got a fantastic exchange rate at the airport." A simple thing, really, to find someone going in the direction he'd come from, and cut the bank out of it altogether. And he had been more than fair, even if he had nudged the man into doing it against his better judgment.

"Aren't you from here?" she asked.

He shook his head. "The United Kingdom, actually."

"But you don't have any accent."

"No," he smiled at her confusion. More proof that she wasn't Eve, if he had needed it. "I guess you could say I have a knack for languages." The wine arrived, and the waiter poured them each a glass before disappearing.

"Along with a knack for getting people to do what you want?" she asked, picking up her glass and taking a sip of the drink.

"I do have a measure of charm, yes." His smile broadened into a grin. "Are you regretting coming to dinner with me?"

She shook her head. "Not yet."

"I'm glad." And he was, though he wished again that he had found what he was looking for. But then, he didn't think Eve would have been so easy with his company. They would have been arguing by now, at the very least.

She set down her glass and leaned forward. "Can I ask you something?"

He reached for the wine bottle and topped off her glass. "Anything you like."

"Who is it that I remind you of?"

"Hm." He sat back again and looked into her eyes. So green. So similar. "That's a bit more complicated an answer than I'd like to divulge on an empty stomach."

She smiled and flipped the napkin of the breadbasket open, nudging it closer to him. "Then eat something."

Maybe it wasn't such a bad thing that he hadn't found Eve, he decided as he let her encourage him to try the bread. This Renata was quite delightful on her own.

Their food arrived and her eyes lit at the entrée. It was clearly a treat to her and she took such pleasure in so simple a thing. It would be a shame to spoil it. He kept the conversation light and her glass full of wine as they ate. The food was everything she'd promised, and he enjoyed it the more for her company.

"Will you have dinner with me again?" he asked, watching her savor a bite of a cake layered with chocolate mousse.

She swallowed and dropped her eyes, fussing with her napkin. "I don't know, Jeremiah."

"Didn't you enjoy yourself?" He knew that she had and didn't understand her reluctance now. "How can I convince you?"

She smiled, and for a moment he thought he saw some kind of sadness in her expression. "How long does your business keep you here?"

"A few weeks, perhaps a month and a half." The waiter arrived with the checkpad, and he paid it quickly, leaving a generous tip. He had no reason to be stingy. His money wouldn't run out.

"And if I agree to have dinner with you again, what then?"

"Then I'll ask you to lunch the following day, I'm sure." He grinned. "Or you can, of course, refuse me. But why not take advantage of the opportunity?"

"What's the harm?" she asked, her lips twitching.

"Precisely."

She shook her head and stood. "I should go. Thank you for dinner. It was wonderful."

"Can I at least give you a ride home?" He rose immediately, putting as much power behind the words as he could without startling her.

"A ride?" she repeated, looking back at him, her forehead creased. "No, no thank you. I'd rather walk. It's a beautiful night."

It was rare that a woman could resist his persuasion, though not unheard of. It didn't stop him from being somewhat irritated by it, as he watched her leave. So familiar and so strange.

He'd have to find out more.

CHAPTER FOUR
164 AD

§

Evaline was a happy girl, all her life. Bright and eager to learn. Was it wrong that he loved her, like the daughter he had never had with Eve? It troubled him, when he found himself returning to the House of Lions, and letting the thunder rumble just loud enough to wake her. She always came running, laughing, joyful. At ten, at twelve, at fourteen and sixteen. At eighteen, even when she had been promised, and at twenty, now, when she was two years married.

It was past midnight, but the moon was bright and full, the sky clear but for the clouds he summoned to make the lightning and bring the thunder that would wake her. He saw her sit up in her bed, and come to the window, and he even saw her smile as she recognized him, silhouetted against the field.

She twisted her hair into a knot and wrapped a palla around her shoulders against the chill. And then she ran to him. "*Tonitrus?*" she whispered into the dark as she came near.

He had returned to the shadows, that if her husband woke, he wouldn't see him. Wouldn't have cause to think his wife left his bed to meet a lover. So that he would not have to explain himself to a Lion who would not understand. He couldn't even explain it to himself, what brought him here. Except that here was someone he was not forbidden to know, not forbidden to see. A family that did not think him disloyal, that respected and loved him still, because of his flaws and weaknesses. Because of what he had done for them and for Eve.

"Little Evaline," he called back.

She turned toward his voice and smiled, moonlight reflecting off her teeth and the whites of her eyes. Her skin had not yet turned brown from the sun after a long winter, though winter here was hardly what it could be in the Northlands.

"Not so little anymore, my lord." She curtsied with grave courtesy.

He laughed. "I'm not your lord, Evaline, and you'll always be little to me. Just a babe for the whole length of your life." He took his cloak from his shoulders and spread it over the grass and dirt for her to sit on, before sitting down beside it. "How fares your family?"

She took her seat and pulled her knees to her chest in a pose so reminiscent of Eve, he had to look away. "We are well. Blessed by the weather you bring us here. We've heard there's been drought in the north, but it has not reached us. Will you not come during the day and spend time with us? Tell us our history?"

"Have you forgotten so quickly?" But he smiled.

She always begged for him to tell her the stories of her family, of Eve. He had even told her the story of his life with Tora. Perhaps that was another reason why he always returned. She wanted to know. She thirsted for the knowledge he brought with him of herself, of her history. He could not speak of Eve to Ra, or Athena, or any of the other gods without causing strain. But Evaline the Lion could not hear enough.

"When you have children, I will come again to visit, and tell your daughters and sons the stories of their ancestors."

"Then you'll have to return to us soon enough." Her hand went to her stomach, and he studied her in the moonlight more closely. It was not as easy to see her pregnancy as it was to see Eve's. He had not noticed it until he looked. "If it is a girl, we're going to name her Eve. My husband has agreed."

Eve. A little baby Eve. If it were twenty, or twenty-five years from now, it might be Eve herself reborn. Was it that simple? Could she be summoned just by the intent to name?

"He is a good man, your husband. A strong leader for your family." He glanced back toward the house and was reassured that no light came from it. It was dark and still and silent. "But he doesn't believe. You must do so for him. Believe, remember."

"How could I not believe?" she asked, laughing. "You are here, now, and always coming back. You never fail to answer my prayers."

He sighed. "I wish you would not pray to me, Evaline. I'm unworthy of it. Pray to your God, and His angels. Gabriel loves God's people, your people."

"Don't you?"

He reached out to ruffle her hair as he had when she was a little girl. It had long ago fallen out of the knot, and it fell fine and shining down her back, soft as silk. "Do you think I would come so often if I did not? Eve's family will always have my love, for all they have done and all they will do. But you are not my people, Evaline. You are God's chosen people. I am just a lesser god who cannot stop himself from interfering."

"I wonder why." It wasn't quite a question. She rested her head on her knees and looked out into the night, her tone thoughtful. "You told me once that Michael said you had no right to love her, but how could such a thing be wrong? Do you think God knew you would come? Knew you would love her and protect her?"

"I do not know the True God's mind. I have never known him."

But her words were echoes of the angel's and he listened to the question ring in his ears. *Did you never wonder why you were drawn here?* He wasn't sure if Gabriel had meant Nazareth, then, or the world. But the world, as opposed to what? Where else would he have gone, if he had not come here with his father?

"Sometimes I pray to Him though. If my father knew, I think he would disown me. It is the blackest kind of blasphemy to lend my power in such a way, to another god who would seek to have us thrown out of this world."

She sighed next to him. "Sometimes I think you gods are not so different from us. The Emperor is only as strong as his army, as the generals who give him their support, as the Praetorian guards who protect him from harm. If the generals and the guards decide to support another, then the Emperor no longer has an empire and becomes just a man like the rest of us, waiting for death to find him."

He chuckled and kissed her forehead. "Do not say it where the gods can hear you. They would be deeply affronted, and it does not do to anger them. But I have kept you up for too long, little Evaline. Had I known you were with child, I would not have woken you." He stood and offered her his hand, pulling her to her feet.

She stood on her tip toes to kiss his cheek, as she had done for years. "Promise you'll always wake me?"

He nodded. "Go back to your husband and your bed."

She smiled. He watched her run barefoot back to the house, her palla streaming behind her. When she disappeared inside, he bent down to pick up his cloak and fastened it around his neck again. He reached for Eve. It was well into morning in the east, and she was busy with something that he could not quite see.

He wished that he could tell her about this granddaughter of hers. This Evaline who reminded him so much of her. He wished that he could have these conversations with Eve instead of Evaline, that he could tell her how her family thrived. But he couldn't.

He couldn't.

He found himself a tree, lower down the mountains, tall and sturdy enough to support his weight, and fell asleep to the sound of wind rustling the leaves with Gabriel's promise in his mind. Someday, he reminded himself, Odin's command be damned, Eve would know him for what he was by the angel's own admission, and she would love him again, and he would worship her until his last breath.

§

"Odin-son." He was prodded awake by a stick and Loki's faintly nasal call.

Thor rubbed his face and remembered where he was. Too near the House of Lions for Loki's presence to be anything but alarming.

He dropped to the ground and snatched the stick from the other god's hands, snapping it in half and tossing the pieces away. "What do you want, Trickster?"

"Is that any way to greet your fellow Aesir, Thor?" Loki feigned hurt, his eyes wide with the lie. "And after all the trouble I went to tracking you."

"You'll never be Aesir, Loki, no matter how many of our women you bed." But he grabbed the god by the arm and pulled him away from the house, away from the Lions. He wouldn't bring his trouble to their door. But he could not go too far, or leave the lands Zeus had granted him, and the right to the use of his own power. "What do you want?"

Loki jerked free and glared, all pretended emotion but hate vanishing from his features. "I come from your father. Sif has begged her release on the grounds of your disinterest and betrayal, and Odin has granted it."

Thor stopped too and stared dumbly at the trees, at the sky. "Her release?"

"Yes, you oaf. She's divorced you." Loki grinned. "More for me, hmm? Or it would be if I hadn't already been enjoying your share. I suppose I'll have to turn my attentions elsewhere. Perhaps to that daughter of Elohim's?"

He twitched, and *Mjölnir* came to his palm. It was a relief to have something to wrap his hand around in his anger. "I thought I made things very clear to you, Loki. You are not to interfere with her."

Loki's smile was a leer. "And have I not kept my word? I did not touch your precious Eve or whisper to her. Nothing sexual at all. But you can hardly forbid me from watching as I will, and without your so regular reports, the Allfather grows ever so curious. And of course, he fears you might be tempted to disobey, now that you're free of your wife."

Sif had finally done it. Divorced him. Freed him. But for what reason? Just to tempt him? To see him punished even further for the disobedience she was so sure would follow? He shook his head with disgust and hung *Mjölnir* back on his belt. Loki did not have the freedom to haunt Eve, no matter how much he might have liked to. Not while the other gods protected her.

"If you remain here, I'll bring the lightning down on your head so hard you'll never leave again. Your message has been given along with your threats. Return to Asgard."

Loki sneered again. "We're in Olympian lands, brother. You have no power here."

Thor let the sky turn black. Lightning flashed and thunder cracked overhead. "Zeus wants me for his son-in-law, Loki. Do you think he would not give me a little piece of his world?"

Loki's eyes filled with fear. Just for a moment, before it was hidden by hate and anger. Thor let lightning strike the ground an arm's length from him, just to drive his point home, and smiled an awful smile as he thought of how much of a relief it would be to have done with the Trickster forever with another bolt.

But Loki did not test him further. He was not Aesir, or even Vanir. He did not have the courage of warriors, or feel compelled to rise to a challenge when he could not win it. Before Thor could summon another bolt of lightning to the ground at his feet, Loki fled.

CHAPTER FIVE
Present

❧

Eve wasn't exactly surprised when she received the phone call from her mother a few months later with the news that Mia was pregnant. Not exactly, because in the competition Mia had imagined between them, it made perfect sense that she would want a baby now that Eve had one. Mia wouldn't want to be left behind, reproductively. Nor would she allow their mother's interest to be taken from her by Alexandre. By becoming pregnant, Mia placed herself right back into the center of everyone's attention.

"But doesn't it seem odd to you that Adam would go along with this? I can't imagine she has the maturity to raise a baby, and what I knew of him was never very paternal."

Garrit didn't lift his eyes from the paper he was reading, even as he ripped apart a croissant. "It's just one more reason I'm happy they don't live in France."

She frowned. His disinterest could be understood, even if it was highly irritating to her at that moment. "That's almost cruel, Garrit. I wouldn't wish indifferent parents on any child."

He sighed and looked up at her then. "You know that isn't what I

35

meant."

"Then what did you mean?"

He raised an eyebrow and she grimaced. These games were so much easier to play when her husband didn't know she could read minds. As it was, any misunderstanding was always seen as willful. And for the most part, he wasn't wrong.

"I'm only saying that if we were nearer, at least the baby would have family that cared for it," she said.

"Somehow I don't think I would make a very loving surrogate for any of Adam's *progéniture.*"

"Garrit!"

He shrugged. "*Pardonne-moi,* Abby. I don't care for the man, and I don't look forward to his using the excuse of family to impose himself on us. Any children she has are his, and I wouldn't be surprised if the whole thing was his idea to begin with."

"I'll admit that my brother is self-serving, but I have a hard time believing he'd put himself out with a child just to force us into the same room with him." And then there was the other matter. The one she hadn't told Garrit about. Adam's new and complete avoidance of her. He hadn't so much as whispered a thought in her direction since Christmas. "Are you incapable of believing even for a minute that maybe he really does love Mia?"

"I'm incapable of believing even for a minute that the man is capable of love of any kind, Abby. For your sister or otherwise."

She frowned again, thinking of the agony in his thoughts. "People change."

He folded his paper and stared at her levelly. "Unfortunately, I'm not in a position to risk giving him the benefit of the doubt. If he has changed, I'm happy for you both, but I can't trust it and neither should you."

"Do you even know what you're protecting me from? Why it's so important to keep us apart?"

"Because the fact that he's manipulative and cruel isn't enough?"

She shook her head. It was probably for the best that her family didn't know the details of how they would all die anyway, by Michael's hand or the child's. And it wasn't as if she really understood them herself. The longer she lived, the more she realized how limited the power of the Fruit really was. There were things in this world man wasn't meant to understand.

"I'm married. Adam is married. If he couldn't violate that covenant at Creation, I really don't see how he could start now."

"Changed or not, in love with Mia or not, this was always about you."

She looked away. He had no idea how right he was and she had no intention of enlightening him. Silence was a much better alternative to explanation at the moment, and it had the added advantage of allowing him to interpret it in any way he desired. But she couldn't forget Adam's heartbreak as he had fled at Christmas. He wouldn't have left if he hadn't changed. He wouldn't have cared about Mia's feelings at all.

Garrit cleared his throat. "I'll plan a vacation for the weeks surrounding her due date. We'll go see them, if that's what you want."

"Without a DeLeon contingent?" She glanced back at his face, frankly surprised he was offering her the option at all.

He smiled. "Not unless Alex counts as a contingent."

"Let me think about it. And talk to Mum and Mia." And Adam. Though, perhaps he would be grateful for Garrit's presence. If Garrit could be trusted to offer support instead of sneering.

"Don't look at me like that, Abby. When have I not behaved myself in company?"

She sighed. "I just don't want to cause Mia any extra stress. She knows you don't like her husband."

"If you want to go, we'll go. Just let me know when you've made up your mind."

"I will."

Alex started to cry, and she moved to get up, but Garrit stopped her with a hand on her arm. "Finish your breakfast. It's my turn."

She watched him go. Having a husband interested in taking part in childcare was definitely a blessing in the modern world. Ryam had always loved his children, but his interest in them as babies was severely limited by the disturbance to his otherwise ordered household. The nursery had been at the opposite end of the manor, where they couldn't hear the babies crying at night. But then, Ryam had insisted on a wet nurse as well, ignoring her preference to care for the children herself.

Unsurprising, really, considering everything else he'd done without her consent and against her wishes. To be fair, though, she had honestly believed she was keeping her share of secrets then.

She drank her tea and frowned at the mystery. It was unlikely she'd ever find the answers she wanted, outside of bizarrely vivid and nonsensical dreams. Odd that she would dream of Thorgrim after all these years. Odder still that she couldn't quite shake the feeling that there was some connection to him she was missing.

Thorgrim had not only known everything there was to know about her history, he had outlived her. If she had learned anything in this lifetime, it was that the men who loved her would do whatever they felt was best for her future, regardless of her wishes. Couldn't Thorgrim have told his son her story? And Owen passed it on to his own children, age after age, until his descendants found the House of Lions, with the same preserved truth.

It was a long time to remember, but not impossible. Reu's sons proved that every generation. If it could happen here, there was no reason why it couldn't have happened there and then.

Thorgrim had been a good man.

She shook her head and cleared her breakfast dishes away. Ruminating over past husbands was neither appropriate nor helpful at this point. Ryam's secrets were too well kept, and Thorgrim . . .

Thorgrim, she imagined, would always be the husband by which she measured every other, unfair though it was. She tried desperately to take each life as it came to her, to take each man as he was, without comparison to those that came before, but the more lives she lived the harder it was becoming. She always served her purpose. Married, produced children, passing on her wisdom and genetics to the next generation. And as the world acknowledged and embraced the rights of women once more, she found love more often, too. But she had yet to meet a man capable of the love Thorgrim had shown her. Not even Garrit. Not even Ryam or Reu.

Perhaps in her next life, she would return to the North lands.

Enough. There were more important things to see to, now, than wishing for something long dead and buried. And Garrit made her happy, gave her a joy she rarely found. She couldn't blame him for his mistrust of Adam. He hadn't felt what she'd felt, the agony of Adam's thoughts and feelings as he left them those months ago.

Eve slipped into the library and curled up in her favorite armchair. If she was going to reach Adam, it might as well be sooner rather than later. While he still would have a moment to himself without Mia demanding he wait on her hand and foot. She closed her eyes and made herself as comfortable as possible, breathing deeply to focus her mind.

Adam?

Startled dismay reached her and she began to withdraw. She didn't want to cause him any problems. This was bound to be difficult for him as it was.

No, please. I just wasn't expecting to hear from you. Foolish of me, perhaps. Anne called you?

Yes.

A congratulatory message could have been as effectively conveyed over the phone, you know. I'm sure Mia is waiting for you to call.

She sighed. *It would be awkward to discuss through Mia the feelings you left me with at our last encounter.*

Ah.

I just wanted to know if you'd be bothered if we came for the birth.

She distinctly heard a mental snort. *I suppose that depends on how many Lions your husband insists on bringing along to protect you from the menace of being in the same room as my person.*

Just our son.

Shocking. But he abandoned the sarcasm quickly. *Mia loves attention, Eve. Especially yours. If you didn't come, she'd be offended.*

This isn't just about her, Adam.

There was a flurry of emotion not unlike snow on a television signal. Too much and too quickly for her to follow any of it. But when he spoke, his mental tone was steady and almost snide. *If your husband allows it and that's what you want, then come.*

You're certain?

I don't need you to coddle me, Eve. Do what you wish.

And then he was gone from her mind.

She wasn't sure if she should be offended, or even more concerned as she mulled over that absence. When Garrit arrived with Alex, she didn't have time to reflect any further on the conversation. Later, she decided. And she would call Mia, too.

Not that she mistrusted Adam's assessment of her sister. But Mia would be pleased if she asked. Her sister always liked to think she was in charge. She tried not to scowl, but she couldn't help but wonder: how on earth did Mia get along with Adam?

CHAPTER SIX
Future

🔖

After walking around the block half a dozen times, Adam couldn't resist returning to the small shop the next day. There was something about her, something he hadn't felt in a long time. Not since Eve. He couldn't continue his search until he understood. Adam pushed open the door and the chime of the bell gave him away.

"I'll be right with you," Renata called over her shoulder. She balanced on a ladder fearlessly, juggling packages of overstock.

He said nothing, leaning against the counter and watching her as she finished and then dropped gracefully from the ladder. She turned, a polite smile fixed on her face which faltered at the sight of him. "Oh."

"Did you think I wouldn't come looking for you after you ran out on me last night?" But he smiled to take the accusation from his words.

Her face had paled noticeably and she moved behind the counter, almost as though looking for something to put between them. "I don't know. A man like you, I'm sure there are plenty of women in the city who would be willing to show you around to their favorite restaurants. It seemed selfish to keep you to myself."

He laughed. This was exactly why he sought her company.

"Considerate as well as lovely. Do you have any faults?"

The smile faltered again and she looked away. "I hope you'll never know them."

"I hope that I might. Somehow I think they'll be just as charming as your attributes." He hated when she turned from him that way. Her face was so animated. "You're not disappointed to see me are you?"

Her smile didn't return. "No."

There was something haunting her, he decided, and her expression was almost sad. "But you're not happy to see me, either?"

She sighed and turned her back on him altogether, straightening shelves already kept perfectly organized. "I shouldn't be happy to see you."

"Why not?"

"It's complicated."

"I'm sure I have both the time and the patience to understand." Honestly her sudden caginess baffled him. He could feel her interest. What had he done to make her cautious of him? She had laughed at all of his jokes last night. He was certain she'd enjoyed herself. He'd made sure of it. Or was she engaged? But she wore no ring, no mark at all of having committed herself elsewhere. "Please, Renata."

"It will only hurt more later, if I let you have your way."

He was certain then, at that moment, she felt it too. The same thing that had brought him back here to find her. Like a rubber band stretched between them, drawing them together for some purpose. "I won't hurt you."

She glanced back over her shoulder, and he saw the sad little smile tug at her lips. "I believe you."

"Then there's no reason why we can't have dinner again." He smiled in what he hoped was an encouraging way. "Besides, I never did get to tell you who you reminded me of. I thought you wanted to know."

"Is that supposed to be some sort of bribe? If I have dinner with you, you'll confess all your secrets?"

"Not all, certainly, but a few, perhaps. If you ask the right questions."

She laughed and then turned, studying his face. "You're not going to leave until I agree, are you?"

He met her gaze levelly and tried to sound thoughtful. "I haven't decided quite yet. I don't want to come on too strong, you know."

"No, of course not. The last thing you want is for me to think you're some kind of stalker." She shook her head, her eyes rising to the ceiling in an expression close to exasperation. "Seven o'clock then. What kind of food would you like?"

He grinned. "Somehow I don't think we've plumbed the depths of *Mangiamo's* menu, yet. There must be more to them than their golden veal."

"You don't want to try somewhere else?"

"Why ruin a good thing?" he shrugged. And it helped that she was comfortable there. As reluctant as she was to allow him this second date, he didn't want to give her any excuse not to show up.

"If that's what you want, I won't object. I can't say no to good Italian food when it isn't going to cost me anything." She shook her head again. "My parents aren't going to be happy about this."

He raised both eyebrows. "Would it help if I picked you up? I'm sure if they met me they wouldn't mind." He'd make sure of it. It would hardly take more than a thought—

"No, no. I'll meet you at the restaurant. Don't worry about it."

"Are you sure? I'd be more than happy—"

She laughed. "No, it's fine. I'll figure something out."

"Seven o'clock then. I'll be looking forward to it."

She nodded. "Now that you've secured me for dinner, will you let me get back to work?"

He smiled and stepped back from the counter. "Certainly." And when she made a shooing motion, waving him away, he left with a laugh.

§

"You never did say what you were here for," Renata said, swirling her wine in her glass. She rested her chin in her hand, propped up by her elbow on the edge of the table.

The wine was beginning to have an effect on her, and Adam smiled. He hadn't expected her to become so relaxed. "Sure I did. I told you I was here on business."

She raised an eyebrow and sipped her wine. "So specific."

He laughed, topping off her glass again. It was their second bottle of the night. Dinner had been as excellent as it was the night before, and he had encouraged her to order whatever she liked, the more expensive the better. Judging by the fact that she was wearing the same simple dress that she had worn the previous evening, he wasn't wrong about her finances, and with a little bit of persuasion, she had been tempted to try something new after he had announced he would be ordering the most expensive item on the menu and a very pricey bottle of wine to go with it.

"You ask me all the hard questions, Renata."

"This time you have a full stomach, so that can't be your excuse. What's so difficult about telling me what you do for a living?"

He smiled, shaking his head. It was too entertaining to tease her. "My business is not my living. At least not in this case."

He leaned back in his seat, wondering if he should tell her the truth or not. She was bound to think it odd, and there were so many things he couldn't explain. Was this how Eve had felt, every time she met someone new? It was like teetering on the edge of a knife. How much could he share before his balance was tipped one way or the other? But somehow he felt he could trust her, at least with this much.

Her brow furrowed and he could feel her curiosity. "Are you going to make me guess?"

"Do you have one?"

"A guess? No. Although it must be something that doesn't require you to spend your days in an office, since you seem to have all the time in the world to pester me at the shop."

"My business here does not keep me in an office, no. In fact, spending the day in an office would be counter-productive to my goals."

"And what are your goals?" she asked, leaning forward. "Or are you going to refuse to tell me that too?"

He laughed and tossed his napkin onto the table. "I was under the impression that you were the one refusing me."

"Deflection." She made a noise in the back of her throat and sat up, sipping the wine again. "I've had more than my fill of that particular conversational device for this lifetime and the next, thank you very much."

He stopped, watching her closely for a moment. Something about the way she said it made him think it wasn't just colloquialism. But it couldn't be. He'd have known it long before now, and she never would've agreed to come to dinner with him the first time, never mind the second. Would she?

"It's late," she said. "I should probably get home. My parents will be waiting for me."

"It's not that late." He reached for her hand but she pulled it away to take another drink just at that moment. "And if you stay a bit longer I promise to give you at least one direct answer."

Her eyes narrowed, but she smiled. "You just want to serve me more wine."

He shrugged, looking into her eyes again, though she wouldn't meet his. Those green eyes, so like Eve's. "I can't say the thought didn't occur to me. But I won't ply you if you don't want me to."

"It isn't about what I want, Jeremiah. You're a man who expects to get things his way, and somehow always manages it. Am I right?"

"You're not wrong." Except for one thing. The reason he was in this country to begin with. He made up his mind then, for better or worse.

"I'm looking for someone."

"What?" she asked, blinking.

He laughed. The wine had caused her cheeks to flush, and he was beginning to hear its influence in her voice. "You asked me why I'm here. What my business is. I'm looking for someone."

She drank the last of the wine and set the glass down carefully, her gaze averted. "Who?"

"A woman. She's . . ." He wasn't sure how to describe her. His sister? His friend? His family? None of the terms seemed to fit. He shrugged. "An old acquaintance of mine."

"What does she look like?"

He smiled slightly. "Another hard question."

She lifted an eyebrow, her expression oddly serious. "If you know her, how is it hard to describe her?"

"It's been a long time since I saw her last. But she has green eyes, like yours. Very much like yours."

"Ah." She sighed. "I remind you of the woman you're looking for, don't I? This old friend of yours."

He nodded. "But she never would have let herself get drunk at dinner with me, I don't think. Unless she was trying to purposely mislead me."

She was studying the bottle of wine now, as though considering another glass. "Why would she want to mislead you?"

He took the bottle from her hand and their fingers brushed. It was like fire and lightning, racing through him but she pulled her hand away at once, hiding it in her lap. He stared at her, but she didn't meet his eyes.

"I think she's afraid of what would happen if I found her," he said slowly, a pressure growing against his heart. He refilled her glass.

But Eve wouldn't have had to ask any of these questions. And he'd never known her to be deceitful. She'd never lied to him, never hidden. It would have been beneath her to do so. And God help him, but this woman was everything he hadn't realized he wanted. Everything he had wanted from Eve that she'd refused to give him. And it would be so easy. So much easier than it could ever be with Eve.

"I want to see you again, Renata."

She closed her eyes and looked away, silent for a long moment. "If you're in love with this other woman, I'm not sure there's any point."

He shook his head, sure of himself now, more sure than he had been even about Mia, when they had first met in Paris and he had realized at once she was exactly what he was looking for. "If I'm in love with anyone, it's you."

She swallowed hard and looked back at his face; her own was twisted with grief. "I have to go to the restroom."

He watched her stand up, unsteady on her feet, and wondered if he should offer to walk her there, but she seemed to manage.

It was fifteen minutes before he realized she wasn't coming back.

CHAPTER SEVEN
165 AD

§

Thor stayed a few more days near the House of Lions, to be sure that Loki didn't return to bother Evaline or her husband. The last thing he wished was to bring this descendant of Eve his troubles with the Trickster, but at least here he could enforce his own rules and use his power to protect them without concern for the wrath of Zeus or Odin.

He went north to see to Owen's people, so far removed now from the son of Eve that none remembered who his father was any longer. Still, he made sure they had rain and sun as needed, and renewed the proper signs and sacrifices to ensure Freyr did not overlook them. He did not dare return to Asgard though, or speak to Freyr personally. Doing so would only cause Sif to take notice, and he had no desire to test her. And then there was Odin, and the banishment that had yet to be lifted. For the best, perhaps. He had no wish to look upon his father, knowing what he did now. All the betrayal, all the faithlessness. On earth, he need not be reminded of it.

As long as Eve stayed in the Far East, and Adam in the west, he felt it safe enough not to haunt her steps, and it made his heart ache to look on her and know that whatever Gabriel had said, the time when she would know him could not be soon. Maybe that was why Sif had divorced him at last. To make it all the more bittersweet, all the more trying. Even unmarried he could not have Eve. He felt Sif mocking him from Asgard, and he traveled south again. Away. Always away.

There was no moon so the stars shone more brightly. With the depth of shadows in the dark, it was some time before he realized that he was being followed, lost as he was in his own misery, and the riddles that dogged him. He stopped and waited.

"Were you ever going to come to me?"

Athena. Of course. And no doubt Sif had made sure word had reached her. Wasn't it enough that she tortured him, without making Athena suffer as well?

He turned to see her standing along the road, shining in the starlight, brilliant as the moon in spite of its absence. "It doesn't change things between us, Athena, and I did not want to give you false hope."

"You've been gone for so long."

"Would seeing me more frequently have made it easier?"

She sighed. "You would know better than I, wouldn't you?"

"As well as you, at least." He stared at the ground, though he couldn't see much of it. "I'm sorry."

"I hoped you'd at least need some kind of comfort. That you'd at least turn to me for that." She was standing in front of him now. Her white stola gleaming, and her pale skin like cream.

He shook his head. "It would've been cruel of me." But he raised his eyes to hers and caressed her cheek. "And this has been going on for so long. This thing with Sif. I resigned myself to the pain of it long ago. I'm well, Athena, truly."

She pressed his hand to her cheek and held it there, her eyes drifting half closed. "Sometimes I wish you weren't so honorable, Thor." Then she pulled his hand away and looked up at him again. "Come stay with us. Father won't object. You should not have to be alone, wandering the earth like some beggar. Mount Olympus is no Asgard, but let it be your home until you can return."

It was a generous offer, and it touched him, but he knew he would not be comfortable there. Zeus's daughters would give him no peace and Sif's jealousy and spite would be enflamed, even if she wasn't his wife any longer. Even if she had never loved him to begin with.

Athena smiled sadly, as if following his thoughts. "Then at least go to Ra. He worries for you, Thor. You're like a son to him."

He nodded. A journey to Egypt would not be without its own benefits. He'd hardly spoken with Ra since his exile, and before that, it had been the coming Council meeting which kept them apart. In truth, he had meant to return there, long ago. If anyone would know the answers to the angel's riddles, it must be him.

"If it will ease both your minds, I'll beg a bed from him. But I don't mind sleeping under the open sky. I hardly need worry about the weather." That made her smother a laugh and he was glad, though he didn't smile. "The things that pain me a bed won't help, one way or the other. I wait for Odin's forgiveness."

"And Eve's love?" He knew she tried to hide her jealousy, but there was still a hint of it in her tone. A longing.

He looked away. "I try not to think of what I cannot have. It cuts too deeply even to dream of."

"Yes." She sighed again. "I understand."

"Do you regret helping me? Saving her?" He wasn't sure why he asked, but he felt that he needed to know.

Athena turned his face back to hers. "I regret only that there is nothing I can do to help you now, Thor. I wish I could give you peace. I wish you could find peace in me."

He leaned down to kiss her forehead. "You are too generous."

She grimaced. "If only it served me better."

"Are you sure you will not consider my brother, Baldur?"

She laughed and pushed him away, but it faded quickly and her expression became solemn. "Perhaps if your brother Baldur had stood at your side instead of letting Odin cast you out, he would have had a better chance."

He smiled then, for her loyalty. "Thank you, Athena."

She waved him off. "Go to Ra. If not for your sake, then for his. And come back to the grove after you've reassured him you are well, if you wish to share a meal with a friend."

"Aye." He offered her a bow, to make her smile more than anything else, and then did as he was told.

§

Ra was scowling deeply by the time Thor finished his story about what Gabriel had told him so long ago, and what Frigg had said before he had left Asgard. It had been keeping him up at night, and of all the gods, Ra knew the most about the True God and his angels.

"Could my mother, Jörd, have come here to this world?" he asked finally. "And why has she not shown herself?"

Ra shook his head, looking at him through narrowed eyes. His expression was unreadable. "You say that Gabriel called you by your mother's name? A mother you don't even remember?"

He nodded. "Frigg seems to believe I have a sister. But Odin has no daughters. She could only mean a half-sister, born of my mother, though I was led to believe that my mother was not just gone, but no longer living. That all we had left of her was the world-tree."

"Yes. The tree with the golden apples." Ra frowned, and turned to stare out the window. "Athena mentioned it."

"If anyone would know if my mother was here, it would be you. Surely she would have made her vows, and you hold all our oaths."

"Blood calls to blood, Thor. My not knowing does not mean she isn't here, only that I haven't seen or heard of her. From what you say, if she came, it was a long time ago. Perhaps before the Covenant. Perhaps before even Bhagavan. If the angels know her, it is likely, though I don't understand their interest in you."

He rubbed at his face and tried not to be disappointed. Ra's words reminded him of Evaline, and the questions she had asked. Her baby would be long born by now. She was probably wondering why he had not returned for the birth. But it wouldn't have been safe. Not with Loki knowing to look for him there.

"You're distracted, Thor. You've spent too much time alone these last years. Just because Odin does not wish to see you does not mean you must forsake all company."

Thor forced himself to smile. "I haven't been wholly alone. I've been spending time with the House of Lions. Odin did not think to take that much from me, at least."

"Odin's punishment was excessive," Ra said, his eyes sad. "I wish it had gone differently for you."

He shrugged. "I would have left them anyway, even if Odin hadn't driven me away. How could I live among them knowing what my father had done? Knowing how I had been used? No. I would not have remained for long."

Ra raised one eyebrow. "Perhaps not, but it is a different thing to leave than it is to be denied by your father in such a way."

"He granted Sif her freedom. I don't know if Athena told you. I no longer have a wife."

"If only it were so simple for you." Ra poured him a cup of wine. "But I'm afraid that even with Sif's divorce, you are still married. Or will you pretend that you are not suffering from that decree of Odin's as well?"

He took the cup and said nothing. Ra did not need him to make the admission, and he did not want to consider it. Dwelling upon Eve only made him more miserable.

"If you desire to stay, Thor, a place can be made for you. Even if it is only a spare room with a bed for the nights you are sick of sleeping in trees. You need not even tell us when you come or go."

"Athena worries."

"As do I."

He drank down the wine and set the cup aside. "I'm well able to care for myself, Ra. It is not the first time I've spent my days wandering the earth, nor do I suspect it will be the last. And perhaps it is fitting. Perhaps I am more my mother's son than I had realized before now."

"How so?"

He looked up at the old god, surprised he had to ask. "In the oldest language known to the Aesir, Jörd means earth. Where my father prized wisdom, my mother preferred the world itself. Worlds, I suppose, and understanding those magics which connect them."

Ra's face paled, and then he turned away, walking to the window and staring out at the Nile. "There are only two stories of trees that bear golden fruit, Thor. Only two that I have ever known in all my travels. Have you heard them before?"

He shook his head, then realized Ra was not looking. "I have not." But he wasn't sure he had followed the conversational leap the older god had taken.

"It is said that Hera keeps such a tree in her garden, guarded by a dragon. But she did not bring it with her to this world. I believe she found it growing wild sometime after your people arrived. The only life in an otherwise dead place. Surrounded by ashes, she told me once. She had Zeus and Poseidon uproot it for her, and replanted it with the other fruit bearing trees she had collected. The source of the golden apples that Aphrodite sometimes uses to tempt those poor, unsuspecting women who aren't interested in their suitors—you heard of Atalanta, I'm certain." Ra turned back to him then, at last, and his face was grave. His age carved deeply in his skin. Thor shifted uncomfortably under his gaze. "But there is an earlier story, perhaps you heard it from Eve and did not realize the significance, for Elohim's chosen people write that the Tree of Knowledge also bore golden fruit, and it was for eating this fruit that Adam and Eve were punished with exile from Eden."

"Eve said that Adam burned the Garden after he had been cast from it. Because the angels refused him entrance to that which he felt belonged to him."

"Burned it to ash and cinders?" Ra asked, his tone mild, musing.

"You believe the trees are the same. That the one which Hera keeps is this Tree of Knowledge from Adam's Garden?" He wondered what Eve would think of this. What Adam would do, if he knew that the Olympian goddess had taken the tree he had coveted. If he ever remembered it.

"It seems a reasonable conclusion." Ra was studying him again, closely, but Thor was not certain why. "Don't you think they're related? Two such trees, existing independently of one another, seems an incredible coincidence, otherwise. An even greater coincidence for there to be three, unrelated."

"Perhaps so. Though if it is Elohim's tree, from the Garden, I'm surprised the angels have allowed the Olympians to keep it."

Ra looked as though he was trying not to smile. "Yes. It is odd, isn't it? Michael certainly watches over this world jealously. I don't believe anything of God's escapes his notice."

Thor thought of Eve. Of the hostility the angel had shown him, unprovoked. "No. I don't believe it does."

CHAPTER EIGHT
Present

§

"Abby. Garrit." Adam nodded politely and took the luggage from her hand. "It's kind of you to come."

She balanced Alex on her hip and frowned, trying to catch her brother's eye, but he turned away. "How is Mia?"

"She's doing just fine. A little bit anxious and terrified but nothing that isn't normal, from what I remember." Adam guided them through the house, keeping his back to her even while he spoke. "I'll take your things up to the bedroom for you. Mia is in the living room with your mother, Abby, if you'd like to join them."

The house was beautiful. All hardwoods and incredible workmanship. She followed the molding with her eyes and would've walked into a banister if Garrit hadn't grabbed her. "This is amazing."

"Thank you." Adam nodded to Garrit. "If you'll follow me, I'll show you to your guestroom. Abby, the living room is the next door on your right."

She glanced anxiously at her husband, but he had fixed his expression into a polite mask and was already following Adam up the stairs. For people who couldn't stand one another, they sure spent a lot of time in secret conference behind her back. She shook her head and shifting Alex slightly, walked on to the living room.

"Oh, Abby." Mia was reclining in an easy chair, her feet up, and her mother was sitting nearby on the sofa. Both had their eyes glued to the soap opera on the television. *Afterlife.*

Eve sat down next to her mother and let Alex squirm onto the cushion next to her. He had a hand wedged into his mouth as he took in his new surroundings. It always took him some time to warm up to new places, and it had been a long time since he'd seen either his grandmother or his aunt.

"Where's Dad?"

"Oh, he's somewhere." Mia shrugged.

"In the library," her mother added. Then she smiled at Alex. "How big you've grown!"

Alex hid his face against her side, and Eve laughed. *It's all right.* "Say hello to your Grandmother Watson, Alex."

He peeked out, his hand still in his mouth, and his eyes wide. "*Bonjo'.*"

"Oh!" Her mother smiled again, her attention finally diverted from the television. "How long has he been talking?"

"Not long. And not much yet, but we've been practicing hello and goodbye."

"He's barely a year old!"

"Almost thirteen months, now."

"We see so little of you, Abby. Why can't you move back to England? Poor Alex will never get to see his cousins, and he'll never understand them if you raise him to speak French."

She sighed. It was one of the unavoidable topics that always seemed to come up in any conversation. "France is home for us, Mum. And Garrit is busy. He can't always get away for a trip so easily."

"Well that's no reason why you can't come visit by yourself!"

"Alex was much too young to be carted all around the continent. I'm sure you'll see more of us in the future." She wasn't sure if it was an empty reassurance or not. A lot depended on how this visit went, and what happened with Adam. Garrit would never be easy letting her visit alone. "You're always welcome to come see us, too."

Mia sighed loudly. "Mum, I need you to fix my pillow. And I can't hear my show! Can't you two wait until it's over before you start in on these things?"

"What things?" Garrit asked, stopping to greet his mother-in-law with a kiss on the cheek. "Anne, *tu es ravissante*. How are you?"

"Oh, fine, fine. I was just telling Abby how we missed seeing you at Christmas." She helped Mia with the pillows.

Garrit picked up Alex and sat down next to Eve. "You're more than welcome to visit any time you wish, Anne. I'd be happy to send you tickets."

"It's just not the same as having my daughter home, Garrit. I'm sure you understand."

"Unfortunately, we've had our hands full with Alex this year, but I'm sure things will start evening out soon. I'm so sorry I keep Abby from you."

"I'm sure Abby wouldn't be kept if she didn't want to be," Adam said from the doorway. She frowned at him, but he seemed to ignore it. "I was under the impression that once you left for university, you were rarely spotted at home again."

"In the way of all poor students, I'm afraid it was cheaper to stay on the continent than go back and forth all the time."

"And why wouldn't you? France is quite lovely."

"Very." But she had no idea what he was getting at. Or why. And she could feel Garrit's growing irritation beside her. "How was your holiday?"

"It was very nice. But it would have been so much nicer to have everyone home," Anne said.

Eve sighed. If this was how the whole visit was going to go, she might insist they get a hotel room somewhere. And thank God they were staying with Mia and not her parents.

Adam laughed. Then cleared his throat, stopping as suddenly as he had started. "Sorry."

She glared at him.

It's just entertaining to know that I'm your preferred irritant, that's all. This time two years ago, you wouldn't have dreamed of sitting in the same room with me. Now you're grateful to be sleeping under my roof.

There's still plenty of time for me to change my mind.

He smirked, but he didn't look in her direction, his eyes on Mia with all apparent attention to what she was saying. *I don't doubt that you will.*

"Garrit, do you mind keeping Alex? I want to go find my father."

"Of course." He kissed her cheek. "If you need anything, just shout."

"I think I'll be fine."

His eyes shifted from her face to Adam. "Even so."

She nodded and stood up, excusing herself to follow the trail of her father's mind and escape her brother's thoughts.

§

When Adam joined her in the library a short time later, Eve was surprised Garrit wasn't fast on his heels.

Can't you take a hint?

He smiled and sat down across from her. *I'm sorry, I was under the impression you were trying to escape your mother.*

I don't know why I even came.

If you hadn't, you would've been subjected to the same criticisms, only more vociferous. Why do you care? These Watsons aren't your family. You've made that clear.

She frowned and glanced at her father, who sat snoring in a chair with a book open in his lap and half a glass of port at his elbow. *They raised me. They loved me. Just because they're not DeLeons doesn't mean I don't consider them to be family. And if I didn't, do you really think they'd be able to drive me this crazy?*

He chuckled. *Anne is certainly problematic.*

Mia, too. She sighed. *But it would be cruel to abandon them, regardless.*

Abandon them to me, you mean. That's what you're really worried about, isn't it? What I'll do to them if you absent yourself completely.

She looked back at him, startled. *No.*

No? He stared at her. *Is that trust, Eve? Maybe just a hint of it?*

No. I just think you care about Mia.

His forehead furrowed and he looked away. *Not enough.*

Enough to leave.

I'm not a monster, Eve. And hurting your sister will hardly help me later.

She shook her head, but said nothing. It troubled her that he was thinking to the future. To a future that may involve her. It was an impossible thing. All of this.

He didn't come alone, you know, he said. She could tell he was irritated, now. Whether from her unspoken thoughts, or because he had admitted more than he had meant to, she didn't know.

Who?

Your husband. Didn't you wonder why he agreed to this so easily? Here, in my own home, where he has no control? Where your safety isn't guaranteed by DeLeon lands?

She scowled. *Since I have yet to discover what exactly DeLeon lands offer for protection that the rest of the earth doesn't, I didn't really think about it.*

He smirked. *Ah, yes. How could I forget that they prefer to keep you in ignorance.*

The secrets he keeps aren't his to tell. Nor, I suspect, are they yours.

I don't understand why you don't just read their minds. You're more than capable. Or maybe you aren't. Frankly, I can't imagine how you've lived all these years, remembering everything, without the slightest clue. It all seems so obvious.

What are you talking about?

Thunder rumbled, and his eyes left hers. He stared past her with an expression of growing disgust. *Nothing. I'm not talking about anything.*

She looked over her shoulder, but there was nothing more than the window. The sky had grown dark, and lightning flashed in the distance, followed by more thunder. "It's a little bit cold for thunderstorms, isn't it?"

Adam snorted. "Somehow I don't think the weather has anything to do with it."

Lightning flashed again, and thunder crashed loudly enough that her father sat up in his chair. "Oh. Abby. When did you arrive?"

"A bit ago." She crossed the room to hug her father. "I didn't want to wake you."

"I was just resting my eyes, that's all." He kissed her cheek. "Where's my grandson?"

"Garrit has him, with Mum and Mia."

He grunted. "Braver man than I, then. Still, I suppose I should go say hello and reassure your mother I'm still alive."

"One of these afternoons you'll wake up to find you have another grandchild, John."

Her father smiled and gripped Adam's shoulder as he passed him on the way to the door. "Yes, well, the sooner the better for you, the way the women have been carrying on. It's a relief to have you join us, Abby. Other than Ethan, there hasn't been a shred of reason in this house."

Adam grimaced. "Maybe I'll be able to convince the doctor to induce labor the next time Mia makes me call him in a panic at two in the morning."

"It'll pass, Ethan. And you'll forget all about it when you have your baby in your arms. Too busy screaming at it to stop crying all night long to care about how miserable a pregnancy it was." Her father chuckled at himself and left.

She shook her head, waiting until the door had shut behind him. "It really isn't that bad, you know."

"Easy for you to say, you were made for it." Adam leaned back in his chair, stretching his legs out in front of him. "It will certainly be a relief not to worry that Mia is going to burst while I'm out getting groceries."

"You're better suited to be a father than anyone else on this earth, Adam."

He laughed. "I think that's the last thing I ever expected to hear you say."

"You know what I mean."

"Do I? I always thought you found me lacking."

"I was referring to your innate talents. Your personality has nothing to do with that."

"Ah." He smiled. "And here I thought maybe I had made some progress."

Adam. You know it isn't that simple.

Why not?

There are rules.

God has been gone a long time, Eve. Those rules haven't applied in millennia.

The angels are still here.

When was the last time you saw one? Spoke with one? Heard of one?

She frowned and turned her face away. Michael's reminder wasn't something she wanted to talk about with Adam of all people. She didn't even want to remember it had happened. And there hadn't been any sign of him since, thank all that was holy.

Even If the angels are here, I think they're the least of our worries. He leaned forward. *I'm in love with you, Eve.*

I'm sorry.

You wouldn't even be having this conversation with me if there wasn't something in you that wanted me too.

She shook her head. *I don't. I'm happily married. I love Garrit. And you love Mia.*

Not like this.

She swallowed, looking away from him. Maybe this was the reason she had dreamed of Thorgrim. But she didn't want to sympathize. She didn't want to grant him understanding. Whatever it was he felt, it didn't matter. It was too dangerous. They couldn't be together. Not without ruining everything. And she'd already lost the man she loved most.

"Who was Thorgrim?"

She stiffened, just hearing his name bringing his face to her mind, as she had seen him in her last life, while she had been hallucinating. "No one."

"No!" Adam's fury erupted out of nowhere, and he was on his feet suddenly, grabbing her by the shoulders. "Look at me." He shook her. "Who was he? Look at me, Eve!"

"No one!" But he was staring into her eyes, using the contact to rip into her mind. Thorgrim's face hung between them, her life with him playing behind her eyes uncalled. Thorgrim working on the boats for the village. Thorgrim, kissing her by the rocks. Thorgrim holding her while she confessed her history. Thorgrim feeding her strawberries he'd found, God knows where. Thorgrim making love to her, devouring her with his eyes, the heat of him seeping into her soul. Thorgrim glowing with pride as he held their son.

"No. No, No, No!" He let her go so forcefully the chair slid back almost a foot. "You arrogant bastard! You had no *right*! She was mine!"

She closed her eyes, her head pounding. His shouting made no sense to her, and his anger was overwhelming.

Lightning flashed so bright even her closed eyes were stunned, and then a thunderclap shook the windows. Her headache eased and Garrit pulled her into his arms, murmuring reassurance. She heard Alex crying distantly, and Adam still shouting. Still raging. Against Thorgrim?

"He's dead, Adam. It was three thousand years ago!"

"You!" Adam stabbed a finger at Garrit. "You invited him into your home. Do you have any idea who he is? Who he was? What he's doing? What he's already done!"

"Ethan! What happened?"

He spun and stared at his wife, and Eve felt the fury drain out of him in that moment. "Nothing. I'm sorry." He crossed to her and buried his face in Mia's hair. "I'm sorry."

Garrit pulled her to her feet. "*Ça va?*"

"I'm fine. I don't know what happened. One minute it was fine. Everything was fine. I was telling him what a good father he would be, and the next . . ." She shook her head, staring at Adam and Mia. She was running her fingers through his hair and he was kissing her as though they were alone in the room. Eve looked away, back to Garrit. "He just started shouting at the window."

"Raving like a madman, more like." Garrit frowned. "Who were you talking about? Who is dead?"

She shook her head again. Wishing the thought had never occurred to her. Wishing she'd never laid eyes on Lars Owen to remind her. "Just a man I used to know. One of my husbands, ages ago."

Garrit's hands tightened. "*Quoi?*"

"You're hurting me, Garrit. Let go." She pulled free and stared up at his face. He looked gray. "What's the matter?"

He stared over her head and she turned to look. Adam held Mia, her back to them, and his face twisted still, but she saw them exchange a look. Garrit and Adam. A look of understanding and determination. And then Mia pulled him from the room.

CHAPTER NINE
Future

§

Adam waited at the shop bright and early the next morning. She fumbled with the keys, her eyes hidden behind dark glasses. He didn't think she noticed him at first, leaning against his car. She dropped the keys, and mumbled what might have been the most obscure curse he'd ever heard before she retrieved them and finally managed to get the door open.

He chuckled and she turned, dropping the keys a second time. "You again!"

"I didn't mean to startle you." He picked up the keys and handed them back to her.

She pushed the glasses up into her hair and stared at him for a long moment. As if something had pained her. He could well imagine she was suffering from the wine, especially if she didn't drink often.

He softened his voice and smiled. "Can I speak with you?"

"Somehow I don't think saying no will stop you." She held the door open and he walked in.

The smell of the place on a wine-soured stomach would be revolting, but he wasn't sure if there was anything he could to do help her with that. Eve might have known. It was the sort of thing she wouldn't have considered offensive to the rules she lived by. Renata flipped on lights and moved around the store without more than a swallow to indicate any kind of distress.

He'd spent the night mulling over her response to him at the restaurant, but he still didn't know what to make of it. Why did women have to be so infernally confounding? They always had been. And he had never understood Eve, though he didn't remember the details of their earliest days.

"Well?" she asked, coming to a stop behind the register and counting out the money into the till. It was bizarre to watch. How many cash customers could they really have? "Are you going to talk, or just lurk in the doorway all morning?"

"You disappeared on me again." It wasn't what he'd meant to start with, and he shook his head, crossing the room so he wouldn't have to shout. "Did you expect me to just ignore that?"

She stopped counting and looked up at him. "You told me you might love me. After two dates. When you're only here for a month. How was I supposed to respond?"

"I thought women were supposed to be sensitive."

"I thought men were supposed to be emotionally stunted." She pressed her lips together into a thin line, studying his face. "I'm sorry. I guess I just . . . panicked."

He laughed. "First you're upset because you think that I'm interested in another woman, then when I tell you I'm interested in you, you run. Was there any possible way for me to win?"

She almost smiled. "No, I don't think so." But it faded away too soon. "Not at all, really."

"What now, then?"

She shook her head and went back to counting the money out, her lips moving soundlessly.

"Maybe you could admit that you're interested in me, too," he suggested.

Her hands froze and she bit her lip. She moved slowly then, putting away the money and closing the drawer. "Even if I was, there's no point. You're only here for a month and a half at the most. There's no future for us, Jeremiah."

"You're so sure of that." It was infuriating, this not knowing. Having these pointless conversations which got them nowhere. But she couldn't be Eve. He didn't want her to be Eve. It was simpler this way. "But my not living here doesn't have to stand in the way. It's really quite easy for me to travel."

"Maybe for you, but not for me. I can't afford to go gallivanting off and fly around the world for a man I've only just met. And even if I could, my parents need me here."

Her parents. That was something he couldn't ever understand. That bond of familial loyalty to the people that had born her. He was her parent as much as anyone. Maybe more so. He'd certainly had enough children over the generations to account for it, even if he hadn't been First Made. The mold from which everyone else had sprung. But born and reborn as he was, with new parents in every generation, he felt no special love for them, no obligation once he had become an adult. He had his own money, his own life to live.

"You're an adult, Renata. You're free to make your own choices. But if you stay here, make sure it's for you, too. Not just them."

She stared at him as if he'd said something astounding, then shook her head. "I don't see how you can be so convinced after a handful of hours that I'm someone you could love."

Always the hard questions. The things he couldn't explain. But he was sure. Certain. And he knew she felt it too. There was an ache underlying all of this, as if she were trying to convince herself even while she spoke to him.

"What's the harm of spending the time we have together? These aren't decisions you have to make now. And if at the end of a month you still feel the same way, you'll never have to see me again. But why not just try?"

She looked away. "I can't afford to fall in love with you. You're not the kind of man who would be happy settling for the things I want."

"You don't know that. You've barely had the chance to get to know me at all."

"I know you well enough to know that you're rich."

He laughed at the way she said it, as if it were some kind of slur. "Is it a crime to live comfortably? Do you really prefer to scrape by, counting every Loonie? Is that such a good life?"

"It isn't a bad one!"

"Renata, please. Be reasonable." He didn't want to know why she was being so difficult about it, but the worry was nagging at him all the same. Clawing about in the back of his mind. Were these the specious arguments of his sister? Of his Eve? Excuses to avoid seeing him again? Made to force him to leave her alone? "I just want to know you. To enjoy your company. Can I have that much, while I'm here?"

"It isn't going to be enough," she said, shaking her head again. "You know it won't be."

"I'll worry about that when the time comes. It won't be your concern, I promise you."

"Won't it?"

He sighed, reaching out to touch her cheek. The heat, the fire that raced through him was less of a shock this second time, though he still marveled at the sensation. "I'll make sure of it."

She closed her eyes and turned her face away. "I don't see how."

"Just trust me. Please. Look at me."

Her eyes opened, and he caught them with his own. It wasn't that he wanted to take away her choice, or her will. Just to reassure her. To convince her that he could do as he said. Could make it all go away for her, if it ever came to that. The suggestion that it was impossible that he would hurt her.

She blinked several times and then pulled his hand away from her face. "It would be so much easier," she said softly, "if you weren't so used to getting your own way."

He smiled. "Does that mean you'll have lunch with me, after all?"

She sighed and dropped her eyes to the countertop between them. "I can't. I have to work."

"Then I'll bring you something. What would you like? Just tell me where to go and get it. Anything."

She looked at him, frowning slightly, and he thought she would refuse.

"There's a little deli south of here that makes an incredible roast beef sandwich. My father used to bring one home to share with me and my mother as a treat sometimes when I was a little girl."

"I'll bring you one."

She smiled. "You won't regret it. It's the best sandwich I've ever had in my life."

He left the shop with her directions some time later and walked the two blocks south. He had worried for a moment, when she seemed to hesitate, that she was sending him out for a sandwich that didn't exist just to get rid of him, but the deli waited for him just where she had said it would be, and it was doing a brisk early lunch business when he arrived. It made a startling contrast to Renata's shop, in which he had yet to see a customer other than himself. He waited in line, and ordered precisely what she had told him to.

The sandwich-maker smiled with appreciation and put it together while he watched. Adam almost balked at the price, but if they were as good as she seemed to think they were, it would be worth it. It would be worth it even if they weren't, as long as she enjoyed hers.

It was a ten minute walk back to the shop, and he stepped confidently through the door, only to find himself facing a thick, balding man. What little hair was left on his face and head—primarily his eyebrows, though there were tufts left above his ears—was all gray, and he looked at Adam with narrowed eyes. "Can I help you?"

He stopped short, his stomach sinking. "Where's Renata?"

The man shrugged, his eyes narrowing further. "We're having a sale on the cherry flavored chew this week."

"No, thank you." He pressed his lips together. When would he learn not to let her leave his sight? But how long could she really hide? He stepped up to the counter and set down the sandwich he had brought for her. "If Renata comes back, this is for her."

"If she'd really wanted it, she would've waited." The man sniffed.

There was no sign of her in the shop. He thought he would have felt her if she were hiding. If she were actually present. All that he felt was the old man, and his mistrust. He left and sat in the car, waiting and watching the door, hoping that perhaps if he wasn't there she would come back.

The old man locked up the store at dusk and left. Adam watched him walk away, considering for a moment following him, but he doubted it would get him anywhere. And even if it brought him to her, it would only aggravate things.

He spent a sleepless night in his hotel, and all he could think of was how right she had been. The sandwich had been excellent. But he would have traded a thousand of them for a night with her.

§

Adam haunted the shop for days after that, but every time he went in, it was the same man at the counter, with bushy graying eyebrows and suspicious eyes. The man's scrutiny had begun to make him self-conscious, which wasn't at all a feeling he was used to and something he resented to the extreme. By the second trip into the shop he felt compelled to buy something in order to justify his presence, and by the end of the week he thought he'd given the place more business than it had seen in months.

Eve, he thought. It had to be Eve, or why else would she run off this way? Unless it was just that she worried about falling in love with him when she thought he would be leaving. But he didn't have to go. He had no reason to go on, to keep looking, when what he sought was right here. Either way, it was here. Either way he had found it, if she was Eve or not. And he was determined to find her again.

"You know Renata?" he finally asked the man while he purchased yet another bunch of tobacco he didn't need. He was running out of places to store it in his hotel room.

The man grunted, his eyes narrowing. "What about her?"

"I was just hoping to see her. Can you tell me when she'll be working again?" He offered an ingratiating smile and as much persuasion as he could, but the man's mind was hard as a rock; an unmovable boulder against his attempts.

"I can, but I won't," the man said, spitting into a bowl he kept at the register for the purpose. He seemed to enjoy chewing the very leaves he sold, taking pinches right from the inventory. Either he was some kind of cheat, or he was the owner, but worrying about it got him no closer to finding Renata.

Adam pinched the bridge of his nose, trying to forestall a headache. "Is there any way that I can contact her? Could you give her a message for me?"

The man chewed slowly, watching him with narrowed eyes. "Depends on what the message is."

"Will you tell her I'm not going anywhere? I'm going to stay." He took out a card from his jacket pocket and scribbled the hotel and room number where he was staying. "Give her this. Tell her I want to see her. Whenever she's ready. The lobby is very public, there's a bar that's frequently full. She can have the concierge ring me and I'll come down and meet her there, if she'd like."

The man grunted again, pocketing the card. Adam wasn't sure if that was an agreement or not, but it didn't matter. He'd come back again tomorrow. And the day after and the day after that. As many times as it took. She couldn't stay gone forever. This was her job.

He left the shop with his package, pushing it off on his driver. "Smoke it, sell it, give it away, I don't care." Then he waved the man off, determined to walk off his frustration at another fruitless day.

The thing of it was, he wasn't sure which way he wanted it to be. Did he want it to be Eve? Or didn't he?

CHAPTER TEN
168 AD

§

He returned to Evaline, as he had promised he would, and stood on the edge of a field of ripening wheat. It was a clear day, and he saw her husband driving the goats. If he summoned lightning now, it would be the goatherds who came first, not Evaline, and he had no desire to speak to her husband. Not yet.

He settled into a nearby tree to wait. Evaline was used to his arrival at dusk, and she would be sure she was the one to come looking if he called her with thunder then. A bird cried above him, warning others of his presence, and the other creatures quieted, scurrying to hide or freezing where they stood. Thor kept still and waited for them to become accustomed to him. But there was another sound that didn't fit among the trees. Human. A sniffling, like a child weeping at the edge of the wood. He dropped back to the earth and followed it.

A woman with dark hair sat on the bank of a creek, and though she had not yet turned, he felt certain it was Evaline. The water turned red, and he swore, lurching out of the shadows and grabbing her by the arm to stop her.

Blood was everywhere. Spilling bright from the veins in her arms.

He wrapped his hand over the largest cut, applying pressure to slow the bleeding. But there was already so much.

"*Tonitrus?*" she whispered, staring at him with wide eyes in a white face.

"Little Evaline." He sighed. She held a dagger in her other hand. "Why would you do this?"

She was crying again, harder now. And he worried that she would make herself pass out between the sobs and the blood she had lost. "He said you wouldn't come back again unless I sacrificed. That you were angry with me. He said you would only answer to my blood."

"Oh Evaline . . ." He could feel the pulse of her heart in the rush of her blood against his hand. He didn't dare to fool with it further. Once he had drawn lightning into his palm to cauterize a man's arm when he had lost it in a sword fight, but if he tried that now, she might lose the limb. He wished he had Idunn's healing touch, or even Eve's memory for herbs. If he could get her back to the house, they were sure to have some kind of healer. "Who told you this?"

"He said he was a god. He said he was your uncle. That you had sent him. He called himself Lopter. When I said I didn't believe him, he turned into a monster. He said he would eat little Eve if I didn't do as he told me."

Loki, then. He bit back a curse and focused on keeping the pressure on her arm. With his other hand, he fumbled for the hem of his cloak, and then tore strips from the bottom with his teeth. The pressure against his hand seemed to ebb, and he began to wrap it with the strips of woolen cloth, so that he could carry her back to the house. There was a chuckle, he thought, from deeper in the wood. Loki, staying to admire his handiwork?

"I have never asked for blood, Evaline. Not from my people, and certainly not from you. Nor would I ever harm your child, or let harm befall her."

But what could he tell her to do if Loki returned? Zeus did not guard this land, and the True God did not seem to bestir himself. He grimaced. Charms of protection would have to be wrought. He would need help to do it right. Now that Loki had seen him helping her, there was no way the Trickster would leave them alone.

"Let me take you home."

He lifted her into his arms, supporting her head against his shoulder when it lolled. Her eyes closed and he let the lightning carry them, flaring white and hot, crawling over both their forms and swallowing them whole. Faster to deliver her, and less likely to jog her arm and start the bleeding again. They reappeared in her bedroom and he laid her down on the mattress, calling for a servant or a healer, and someone to find her husband.

Athena?

Thor. You're upset?

I have need of you, and your sister Artemis. And Apollo, if he will come. He showed her Evaline, in the bed, and gave her his knowledge of how it had come to pass. *Please, Athena. I dare not ask my own people, for fear my father will forbid me from this too.*

She was silent for a moment, and he felt her distraction. *Better not to ask my sister or brother, but Ra will send Isis to you. She will be able to do the work of both without risking it revealed to your Trickster.*

And you?

I come.

A woman came into the room and stopped short at the sight of him, crossing herself and mumbling a prayer. His eyes blazed white, and he forced himself to calm. "She's lost blood. Heat water for me, please."

She disappeared again just as quickly, and he checked Evaline's arm. The bandage was wet, but with Isis coming he was less concerned. She would be healed.

He moved to the window, looking for the goddesses, anxious for their arrival. Loki stood outside the house, cloaked and grinning. Thor growled, the sky blackening but before the lightning charged, Loki flickered and disappeared.

Light filled the room, blinding in its intensity, and then Isis was there. A welcome distraction from his anger and frustration, which already rattled the house. Thunder boomed and rolled across the sky, impotent and useless.

"Quiet, Thunderer, is what this girl needs," Isis said. She tsked, her fingers moving delicately over Evaline's skin, tracing the bleeding scratches. The wounds healed almost at once, and she unwrapped his crude bandage, sighing at what she found. "Self-inflicted?"

"She was tricked," he said.

Isis nodded acceptance and wrapped her hands around the deep cut on Evaline's arm, speaking so quickly and so softly that he could not hear what she said. Light filled the room again, softer now, but just as powerful, turning Evaline's skin translucent.

"What is this? Who are you? What's happened to my wife?" a man's voice demanded.

Thor grabbed him by the arm and hauled him back out of the room so as not to disturb Isis. "Do you know me?" he asked.

The man, Gaius, hesitated, then nodded. "Thor of the North. *Tonitrus.*"

Evaline had kept her word. He relaxed slightly. "I found her in the wood. There was an accident." He did not want this man to think she had hurt herself purposely. Nor did he want to explain Loki. The Trickster would not be troubling these people again, regardless. "Isis heals her at my request, but she will need her rest."

The man's eyes narrowed. "How did you know to find her?"

"I am a god, Gaius."

Though he did not want to think what would have happened if he hadn't arrived then. Or had Loki's manipulation been timed for his benefit? How long had Loki been waiting to do this, watching the House of Lions. He grimaced as he considered that Sif might have been with him. It didn't matter. Once the charms were cast, she would not be able to harm these people either. Nor would Odin forbid him from protecting them. Banishment served him in this, if nothing else.

"Do you still doubt me?" Thor asked.

Evaline's husband glanced at the doorway. White light streamed through it, brighter than sunlight. An owl swooped through an open window, and melted into Athena. Gaius swallowed audibly, staring at the goddess with dawning comprehension.

"My Lady Minerva!" He dropped to his knees.

Thor sighed. "Me, he questions, but you he knows on sight."

Athena smiled without humor. "And well he should. He comes from my lands." She waved the man to his feet. "Your family is thrice blessed, Gaius. Thor does much to aid you."

Gaius stood, but kept his head bowed. "We're honored by your presence. Can we offer you wine? Bread?"

Athena shook her head. "Call your people in from the fields. We have work to do to protect your household now that your wife is healed. Do not disturb us." The man bowed and went to do as he was bid.

Thor returned to the bedroom. Evaline was awake, watching Isis with something close to fear. Her expression cleared the moment she looked upon him, and he crossed to her side, taking her hand.

"Little Evaline. You've nothing to fear now."

"Please, will you stay? For dinner? To tell us our history?" To keep the other away, her eyes said, to protect my daughter.

He stroked her hair from her face, and glanced at Isis. She withdrew to wait with Athena. Evaline looked so small, so fragile. He forced his jaw to relax, his tension to ease. It would not do to show her his own pain, now. She needed his strength.

"I've work to do this night to keep your family safe," he said gently. "Make a bed for me and I'll share the meal with you in the morning. But you must make me a promise Evaline."

"Anything," she said. Her fingers tightened around his hand.

"You cannot leave your lands. Keep yourself and your children within the boundaries that have been marked. And never offer your blood in sacrifice again to any god, no matter what you've been told."

She turned her face away and closed her eyes. "Forgive me."

"No, Evaline." He knelt beside her and wiped the tears from her cheeks. "I brought this trouble to you. Lopter—Loki, he only came here to hurt me. But I promise you, this land will be made safe. No immortal meaning harm will be allowed to pass through its borders. I should have done it long ago."

Gaius has brought his people inside. We may begin.

He kissed her forehead. "Rest, little Evaline. I will be here all night. Bringing thunder and lightning for Isis to work her magic." He let her go then, and though he knew she wished he would stay, he left the room. Gaius would offer her better comfort, besides.

I have already called for him, Athena said.

Thank you. He rolled his shoulders, fighting the weight of his own guilt. Now was not the time for recrimination. It would only interfere with the work that must be done. "Thank you."

"Let this thing be done quickly," Isis said. "Before the Trickster returns to do more injury."

He led the way through the fields and the trees to the edge of the land belonging to the House of Lions. The edge of the lands Zeus had ceded to him. It had grown dark, and Athena sent her owls to fly and watch for Loki and Sif. They walked the border together, and with lightning and the magic Isis wove through it, drove the symbols and runes of protection deep into the earth as they went. They carved the marks into the trees and stones as well, to warn those who passed this way. This land was claimed. This land was protected. This land was saved.

It took them all night, but when Isis left them, he knew Loki would not be able to reach these people again, and he had kept the pledge he had made to the House of Lions over a thousand years ago. The pledge he had renewed each time he returned. And the next time Eve returned here, she would be safer than she had ever been before. Safe from Adam, safe from Sif and Loki, safe even from the angels if they ever sought to harm her.

Athena returned with him to the house where Evaline lived, and he collapsed onto the bed that had been made for him, too tired even to object when Athena rolled him over and crawled beneath the blanket beside him.

"My price for removing your boots," she murmured, curling up against his side.

He heard nothing more until morning, when the birds and the sun brought him half-awake. Athena lay beside him still, her skin soft and warm, and the spice of olive and lightning in her hair. His arm tightened around her waist, drawing her nearer, fitting her into the curve of his body. It had been so long . . .

Evaline's voice rose sharply through the window, chiding a slave, and he jerked back, nearly falling out of the bed. Athena. Not Athena, of all women. To use her that way—to even think of it, at all—was unforgivable.

He stumbled out of the room, for he had promised Evaline he would join the family for their morning meal, and he had never been gladder to take up his duty.

§

When he returned to the room to sleep off the remainder of his fatigue, Athena was gone. But he missed her warmth in the bed and the sound of her heartbeat, and his body did not forget how perfectly she had fit against him. How desperately he had wanted her closer, skin to skin and hardened need sinking deep inside her welcoming heat.

Thor lay awake, staring at the ceiling. Clearly, he had been too long alone if he could be tempted so easily by a warm, soft body in his bed. And it was very good, he thought, before sleep finally claimed him again, that Evaline was married.

CHAPTER ELEVEN
Present

§

"Are you certain you're well, Abby?"

She opened her eyes. Garrit was propped up on one elbow in the bed, watching her. She sighed and sat up, giving up on the pretense of sleep, and pulling her knees to her chest. "Adam didn't do anything to me, if that's what you're worried about."

He rubbed her back, and she could feel his eyes on her still. "I'm worried about *you*. You've been distant and distracted all night."

She glanced over her shoulder at him. The room was dark except for the light coming from the street. How long had she been lying in bed pretending to sleep and thinking about Thorgrim, and Lars, and Adam's curses for a man long dead. And how long had Garrit been lying beside her waiting for her to talk. Hoping she would. She had been too wrapped up in memories to notice.

She laid a hand on his chest, over his heart. She could feel the steadiness of its beat. "I'm sorry."

"What's bothering you?"

"Everything and nothing. Past lives, a future of avoidance." She shrugged.

He sat up and brushed her hair from her shoulders, kissing the bare skin there and pulling her against him. His body was warm and comforting. She loved the heat of him when he touched her. The dry warmth of his skin against hers. When she was honest with herself she thought it might have something to do with those first days, and the way Adam's skin had burned against hers in the Garden. It was as if he had set a flame on her heart, though at the time his touch had been more discomfiting than anything else.

"*Dis-moi tout*," Garrit said.

It was getting increasingly difficult for her to focus, with his lips against her skin that way, and his palm flat against the curve of her waist, his fingers not quite digging into her body, but gripping her with just the right amount of pressure. "I'm not sure there's anything to tell."

He sighed and kissed her behind her ear. "If there's nothing to tell, Abby, why is it keeping you up? What happened today? Did he resurrect the memory of some abusive husband?"

His breath against her ear made her shiver. "No."

"Then what?"

She hesitated, but he was kissing her again. The length of her neck back down to her shoulder, while his hand inched up along her ribs. "That man, Lars. I think he's one of my many-times-great-grandchildren, three thousand years after the fact."

"Oh?"

She twisted to face him, placing her hands on either side of his face. "Would you like me to show you?"

"Can you do that?"

She shrugged. "I don't see why not. It isn't any different from what Adam can do, to get people to do what he wants them to."

He arched an eyebrow. "*Vraiment?*"

Eve flushed. "That isn't what I meant, and you can hardly believe I'd meddle with your free will, Garrit."

His lips curved just slightly. "*Fais-moi voir.*"

She closed her eyes and found the image of Thorgrim as she had known him, gently setting it in his thoughts. "Do you see that?"

"Yes." His voice was rough.

She removed herself from his mind and opened her eyes again. "They look very much alike."

"He was your husband?"

"A very long time ago." She frowned and wondered if she could put a date to it. "It was maybe nine or ten lives before Christ. Before even Rome was founded."

He pulled away from her and swung his legs over the edge of the bed. "*Bien sûr.*"

"What do you mean, of course?" She hadn't meant to upset him. It was always a mistake to talk about her pasts. Always. Why did she insist on repeating that blunder time and again? "Garrit? You're not mad at me are you? I assumed René must have known, and that was why the family trusted him."

"*Non.*" He stopped and rubbed his face. Just sitting there. "*Non,*" he said again more gently. "I am not mad at you, Abby. I just wish things were a little bit less complicated."

She sighed. "I'm sorry."

He shook his head and lay back in the bed again. Whatever decision he had made about getting up abandoned. "This isn't in any way your fault. You have nothing at all to apologize for. Nothing at all."

She curled up against his side, resting her head against his chest and listening to his heartbeat. His skin was even warmer now. As if his frustration and anger had been turned directly into body heat. "It was easier when I was just Abby, for you. If I could forget, and just be Abby, without all the memory of Eve, it would be easier for you."

"*Peut-être.*" He held her against him and kissed the top of her head. "But even when you were just Abby, you were still Eve. You would not be the same person without all those memories."

"No. Probably not." One day, she would ask Adam what it was like, living life after life without remembering. If it was easier or better. "I think I would miss knowing my family."

"We would have missed knowing you."

She frowned. "You wouldn't have known what you were missing."

He stroked her hair. "What was his name?"

"Who?"

"The man you showed me."

She hesitated, only because she didn't want to encourage him. Or let him realize that she remembered that life as though it had happened yesterday. Bad enough he already had to live in Ryam's shadow. "Thorgrim."

He laughed, but she didn't know why. "Fitting."

"I guess." She didn't want to admit she remembered her own name, too.

"He's the man your brother was shouting about?"

She propped herself up and frowned at him. He was staring at the ceiling, but he looked at her when she moved. "You're very curious."

"And you are not your usual forthcoming self."

"Some things are better left in the past."

He caressed her cheek. "Then let me help you to forget."

She was glad that Alex was sleeping in the nursery, and they had the room to themselves.

§

Mia went into labor the following day, and they went as a family to the hospital to wait. Alex didn't care for the waiting room, with the biting scent of antiseptic and sterile walls, and fussed until Eve settled him in her lap and read to him. It was probably half her own fault. If she hadn't been uncomfortable in hospitals already, after her last life in the mental institute, Michael's visit after Alex's birth had ensured she'd never feel safe in one again. Especially not with Adam so near.

He sat across the room, since Mia had kicked him out of the

delivery room in favor of her mother, and together with her father and Garrit, the three men sat staring at the ceiling and the floor, anywhere but at each other, in silence.

Mostly silence anyway.

I'm sorry about yesterday, Adam said.

She tripped over the sentence she was reading, though she probably shouldn't have been surprised that he would try to talk to her now. Alex didn't notice, and neither did Garrit. *I'm not sure I want an explanation.*

Oh, I'm sure you'd love it. But I couldn't explain if I wanted to. Not now.

I don't think now is appropriate anyway. Mia is in the process of giving birth to your child, Adam. She continued reading aloud, though Alex was starting to droop. Hopefully he would fall asleep and nap through a good portion of the wait.

Yes. And she loves me so much she doesn't want me to be part of it.

She tried not to frown. *Don't be ridiculous. She's probably kicked you out for fear you'll find her forever repulsive if you witness the mess of it.*

She saw him smile out of the corner of her eye. *That sounds like Mia.*

She can be impossibly shallow sometimes.

There was a mental snort. *Not impossibly, just foolishly.*

She finished reading the book and set it aside. Alex had fallen asleep in her lap. All the better to keep him from picking up on her own anxiety. Not that she was sure what bothered her more—memories of women screaming and weeping, tortured as much by their visitors as they were the doctors, or the thought of Michael returning to make good on his threats. At least Adam was a distraction.

You make her happy, she assured him, though she hadn't ever thought he'd need reassurance of that kind. He must know. Unless he wasn't using his power at all. She wasn't sure she wanted to know, either way. She already liked him more than she wanted to admit, and if he had learned restraint . . .

I try.

I know.

You really think parenting is easy?

She smiled. *It is when you can read your baby's mind. You'll be able to skip all the guesswork and always know why he's crying and what he needs. I don't know how the rest of them fumble through it.*

Garrit seems to do just fine with Alex.

You'll be fine, Adam. You'll be a good father. It isn't as if you haven't ever done it before. You've had families, children, in the past.

Mmm. She followed his thoughts as he considered that. Moments of fatherhood flitting through his mind from centuries ago. Crying children being whisked out of his sight by servants and slaves and nannies. *I don't think any of that counts in my favor. I was never an attentive parent, it seems. I left the childrearing to my wives.*

She sighed. *You weren't the only man to do so.*

He smirked, then looked back at the ceiling. *I suppose if I ask your husband for parenting tips, he'll give me dirty looks and be snide.*

Who knows. Maybe you can bond over your kids. Not that she was going to hold her breath, but Garrit had seemed a bit less tense today. Or at least less tense about Adam. She told herself it was a good thing.

No, I don't suppose he hates me anymore.

Why do you say that?

He shook his head almost imperceptibly. *Now probably isn't the time.*

She stared at him, but he ignored her, standing up and walking out of the waiting room to go check on Mia. Maybe if Michael had gone to visit Adam instead, he'd be less . . . whatever it was he was being.

"Anything I should know?" Garrit asked quietly.

"What?"

He raised an eyebrow. "You don't usually have such an animated expression when you're thinking, or am I wrong and you weren't talking to him?"

"Oh." But he wasn't nearly as annoyed as she thought he'd be, and she wasn't sure how she felt about that either. "He's just nervous about being a father. He wanted to know if he could ask you for some parenting tips or if you'd glare at him."

He grimaced. "I suppose, all things considered, that's a fair question. What did you tell him?"

She kissed his cheek. "I told him I was holding out hope that maybe you'd bond over your children."

"You would." He smiled. "One of the many reasons I love you."

"Yes, yes. And one of the many reasons I vex you, too. Go talk to him, would you? For Mia, if not for him."

He frowned, glancing toward the door. "*Puisque tu insistes.* But if punches are thrown, it's on your head."

"Garrit!"

He flashed a grin, kissed the top of Alex's head, and then followed Adam out of the room.

§

When they didn't come back within the hour, she began to wonder if it had been a mistake to suggest it. Alex was still asleep, and she couldn't exactly leave him with her father, who could never be relied on to pay close attention. Not in a hospital, and not under the circumstances. She tapped her foot and checked her watch. If there was an actual fist fight, she would have heard something. Someone would've called the police. And she would've felt something, too, she suspected. Not that she kept tabs on Garrit, but that kind of violence spoke for itself with plenty of volume, emotionally and psychologically. And she was all too familiar with the flavor.

Eve bit her lip and forced her thoughts to remain firmly in the present. She would not remember the mental institute. Not now. This was a happy occasion. Mia was having a baby, and she was going to be an aunt. Alex was going to have a cousin. And she was married to

Garrit. Very happily married.

Still, it was irritating to be left hanging. Couldn't they have come back to talk? It wasn't as though fatherhood was a secret society. She debated the ethics of attempting to listen in, just to make sure things weren't getting out of hand, but she still felt guilty about having eavesdropped on Adam's explanation to Mia last Christmas, and Garrit had too many secrets for her to listen without uncovering something she probably shouldn't. That was a breach of trust that would be unacceptable.

She sighed. She'd been spending too much time with Adam. He wouldn't have thought twice of eavesdropping on her. And as irritating to her as it was, it wouldn't help anything to behave similarly.

Then she heard them, outside the door to the waiting room. The frustration in Garrit's tone brought her to her feet, but then she realized that he wasn't talking to Adam at all. And he was speaking in French.

"What, was he afraid to come himself?"

"It would be imprudent of him to come here, now. You know the laws, Garrit. They have been made clear to you and Ethan both," a woman replied.

Eve tried to see who it was, if it was anyone she knew, but the woman was behind the shadow of the door. She could see Garrit though, and Adam with his arms crossed, looking far too satisfied with himself.

"You tell him we're done. I won't have him interfering any further. The fact that he kept this from us is ridiculous."

"Be cautious where you place your trust, Lion, or your jealousy will undo all you have fought for." The woman sounded angry, or offended, perhaps.

"I'll place my trust with my wife. If she isn't concerned, I certainly don't need his services. If he wants to argue with Brienne he's more than welcome, but I don't want any more of his help."

Eve glanced back at Alex, covered with her jacket and still asleep curled up in the chair next to hers. She wasn't going far. Just to the hall. She didn't like the way Adam was smirking.

"You take a foolish risk, trusting *that*, over one sworn to protection, held to it by law. He's done nothing to betray you, and everything to assist."

Eve pushed open the door. The woman was beautiful. More beautiful than any woman had a right to be, all dark hair and alabaster skin, with sharp, gray eyes. But there was something in her face that made Eve shiver. Too perfect. Like an angel's face.

"What's going on?"

Garrit swore and looked away, pinching the bridge of his nose. "It's nothing, Abby."

Adam laughed. "You really think that's going to help?"

She ignored her brother and frowned at the woman. "Are you a friend of the family?"

"*Non,*" Garrit said firmly. "She is not."

"I'm a friend of friend," she said. Then sighed and looked back at Garrit. "I will deliver your message, but I urge you to reconsider. Nor can I promise that your desire will be heeded."

Garrit nodded stiffly to the woman and took Eve by the arm, guiding her back into the waiting room and leaving the woman behind in the hall. "Forgive me, Abby. If it makes you feel any better, I'm starting to feel a bit more charitably toward your brother."

She glanced over her shoulder to see the woman watching her, and Adam murmuring something she couldn't hear. For some reason she wasn't sure it helped her feelings at all, though it should have. "Who is she?"

"She's someone who has no business offering opinions, or getting involved." He shook his head and pulled her down into a seat next to him. "This is all getting a little bit ridiculous."

"I don't understand." Ridiculous was an understatement. If this was another secret she was going to have to take on faith, there were going to be some unkind words spoken of the living and the dead. "What's going on? Can you even tell me her name or is that a secret too?"

"Minerva. Her name is Minerva." He sighed and dropped his head to his hands. "I guess she knows Ethan somehow, which is frankly unnerving."

She leaned over to get a glimpse out the door, but Garrit was in her way now, and she couldn't see Adam anymore. "Are you really not going to tell me anything? Who were you talking about? Whose help?"

"Please, Abby. If I could tell you more, I would."

"She said you were jealous."

He lifted his head to look at her. "Let's just say that I'm unwilling to help further the agenda of a man who is in love with my wife."

Adam walked back into the waiting room and sat down by her father. She watched him and wondered. If it wasn't Adam he was talking about, then who?

CHAPTER TWELVE
Future

She fingered the business card, staring at the main entrance of the hotel, complete with a maroon uniformed doorman, and an antique revolving door. Through the doors, she told herself, and into the bar. A nice public place, where she could ask the bartender to call up for her.

Because he wasn't going to go away. She should have known he wouldn't, but she had hoped that if she kept herself out of sight, he'd find someone else to amuse himself with. He should have found someone else, by all rights. He should have forgotten her when she refused to play his game, and gone in search of someone who would. He liked being in control, getting his way. He liked women who gave the appearance of resistance, hoping to be charmed all along.

She'd just been hoping he wouldn't see through her. But no matter how many nice meals or fancy bottles of wine, he must have realized he wasn't going to have her.

She straightened, taking a deep breath to steady her nerves, and stepped forward. The doorman smiled pleasantly, touching the brim of his hat in respectful acknowledgment as she passed, and then she was inside.

The bar was just as he had promised, and at this time of the day, moderately full with businessmen taking advantage of Happy Hour. Cologne and smoke and clean male musk, and something else, something familiar and out of place, like thunderstorms and sunsets on the beach. She scanned the room, but of course it was foolish even to look. Lars Owen was long dead by now, just like Thorgrim before him, and the odds of even her family finding her now were so impossible, it wasn't worth considering. A few men in suits smiled at her, their eyes making promises of too-friendly conversations, but she ducked their gazes and slipped onto an empty stool at the bar, away from the crowd.

The bartender tossed a towel over his shoulder and placed his hands on the bartop. "What can I get for you?"

"I'm actually supposed to be meeting someone, but I think he's forgotten me. Would it be too much to ask you to call up and let him know I'm waiting?"

"Anyone who's forgotten you isn't worth reminding," he said, smiling. "But sure. What's the room number?"

She set the business card on the bar, spinning it toward him. "I didn't give him too much encouragement, so it's possible he just thought I wasn't coming."

The bartender laughed, taking the card. "Fair enough."

She folded in the corners of a napkin while she waited, then folded them again, and again.

The bartender didn't take long, returning the card to her. "He'll be down in a minute. Sounded like he couldn't believe his luck. Something to drink while you wait?"

"No, thank you. Not yet." She frowned at the napkin. "Maybe just an empty shot glass?"

His eyebrows rose, but he didn't argue. The shot glass appeared a moment later, and she flipped the napkin upside down over it, pulling the corners back down around the glass, like flower petals. Anything to keep her mind off what she was doing.

It had been stupid, really. All of it. But she'd wanted—well, it didn't matter. The past was dead and buried, and looking back wasn't going to make this life any easier.

She set the flower she'd made on the bar, and used it for a coaster beneath the shot glass. Just the slightest effort, and she could feel his anticipation, his anxiety that by the time he reached her, she would be gone. Maybe it was all as simple as wanting what he didn't think he could have. Nothing but ego and arrogance. She didn't want it to be.

She didn't really believe it was.

And then he was there, behind her. Her hands shook as she fidgeted with the napkin, giving herself another moment. Another steadying breath.

"Renata?"

She turned, avoiding his eyes. His tie hung loose around his neck, as if he'd pulled out the knot and forgotten what he was doing. She caught the silk, the same storm gray as his eyes, and tugged it from his collar.

"I was hoping you'd come," he said, catching her hand. Even so small a touch sent a shiver down her spine. "But I wasn't sure you'd get my message."

She smiled, pulling her hand free and twisting the silk between her fingers. "My father secretly likes you. Or at least he likes your money. I think he always hoped I'd be thrown into the path of some rich man, though he'd never admit it."

"If he won't admit it, then how do you know?"

"Oh." She shrugged. "He's like any father, really. Just wants to know I'll be taken care of."

"And no matter what you say, he'll never believe you can take care of yourself, will he?"

"Not without a husband, at least. He's traditional that way. Very old world."

"Are you?"

She shook her head, blinking against the pressure behind her eyes and staring at the tie, knotted now. It would be so much easier if all this wasn't so natural between them. If he pushed her, or behaved rudely. If he would only be furious with her, instead of laughing at her escapes.

"He had a funny way of showing he liked me," he said, and she could hear his smile, rueful and self-deprecating. "But he isn't wrong, Renata." His voice softened, and he tipped her chin up, so gently. "I would care for you, if you would only let me."

Her breath caught at the warmth in his eyes, colored with anguish and hope. She dropped her gaze, smoothed his collar instead. Because looking at him, seeing it was so much temptation, and she couldn't. She couldn't ever give in, not to this, no matter how much she wanted to give him the chance—to know the man he'd become.

"I can't," she managed, though the words came out hoarse.

"Of course you can," he said, catching her hand again, holding it against his heart. The warmth of his body seeped into her palm, and she couldn't bring herself to pull away. "It's easy. I know you hate my money, but I can make it work for you. I can move here. I could buy a flat right now. Anywhere you want, anything you want, I can give it to you. I don't have to leave here, if you want to stay. I'll stay too."

"It's not that simple." She swallowed. Her throat was tight. That he was willing to give up whatever life he'd built for himself to start over at her side—but for a rich man, it wasn't really a sacrifice, was it? He wouldn't lose anything by relocating. He'd still have all the same freedoms. But even so. Part of her couldn't help but think, want to believe . . .

It didn't matter. It didn't matter what she wanted to believe, or what was true, or what was just another manipulation. It didn't matter if he was a good man or a bad one. The answer was still the same. Would always have to be the same.

"I don't want you."

He dropped her hand as though he'd been burned. "If this is about your parents—"

"Adam."

His jaw snapped shut, and she met his eyes then, opened herself up so he could feel her the way she could feel him, recognize her for what she was. She had hoped that if she only hid, it would be enough. That he'd go on looking, to the next girl, and the next, but somehow, even not knowing, even not realizing, he had still fixed himself on her, and the only argument she had left was the truth.

"I'm so sorry," she said. "I'm so sorry it had to be this way. But we can't. Whatever you feel for me, whatever I feel for you, it doesn't matter. It can't matter."

"Eve." He let out a breath, shook his head as if to clear it. "I had almost hoped. But I didn't want it to be you."

"I never thought—" She had to stop, breathe, steady the quaver in her voice. This was so much harder than she thought it would be, seeing all that pain in his eyes, feeling it between them. "What was the harm, you said." She could have laughed if her stomach hadn't been so twisted. "Fool that I am, I believed you."

He pressed his lips together, studying her face. "You won't see me again, will you?"

She didn't answer. Couldn't force the words from her lips. To see him again, to be with him, even as friends. God, she wanted it. She wanted to have someone in her life who could know her for who she was. Just one person, forever, who she didn't have to lie to! She turned away, so he wouldn't see her longing, or the tears burning behind her eyes. It wasn't fair to give him even that much encouragement. She signaled the bartender for a drink, using the order for an excuse. He frowned at her, his gaze flickering in wordless question. She forced herself to smile, dissolving his concern with a gentle nudge of reassurance.

"It doesn't have to be this way, Eve." Adam stepped closer, his voice low, and touched her arm. "It doesn't have to be all or nothing. It's not forbidden to love."

"You say that now." She fumbled for her e-vice to pay.

"Charge it to my room, please," he said, stopping her from offering it. She blinked up at him, and he shrugged. "It isn't forbidden for me to buy you a drink, either, Evey. To be your friend."

"You don't want friendship."

"If that's the only way I can be in your life, the only way we can have one another. Don't shut me out. Don't give this up. Just—just sit with me."

"I shouldn't." Every minute she spent with him, every word they exchanged was only going to make him hope, make it hurt that much more when she had to leave. It had been one thing when they were both married, but like this? When they had started as a romance?

God help them both, but she had enjoyed herself, flirting with him, teasing him. But it would never be enough. If she stayed, let him be part of her life in any way, how long until he convinced himself that taking more, insisting on more, was what he deserved—what they both deserved?

"Please, Evey."

The bartender set her drink on the counter and she made no move to touch it, just stared at the liquid. Anything to keep from seeing the emotion in his eyes, from thinking of the warmth that blossomed inside her with his touch. How could it feel so right, so natural?

Adam picked it up, his other hand fitting around hers. "I won't ask you to stay for more than this drink," he promised.

When he tugged her toward a booth, she let herself go with him. Just a drink. To say goodbye. He deserved that much, and so did she. She slid across the bench, and he set down her drink, then sat beside her.

"You know, Mia told me once that you said love should be easy. That a person knew when they had found the one they were meant for."

"There's nothing easy about this, Adam. And it never will be. Not for us."

"This? No. This isn't easy." She felt him studying her in the dim light and forced herself not to meet his eyes. "But when you were just

Renata, and I was just Jeremiah, it was the easiest thing I had ever done. Surely that means something. Something important."

She played intently with the drink, twisting the stem of the glass between her fingers. "Not more important than the world. What you want has always been impossible."

"What I want is your love, Eve. How is that so impossible? How is that so wrong?"

"Love." *Is that truly what you feel for me? There were times I wondered if you were capable of such a thing.*

I wondered too, until I found you. "You feel it. I know that you do."

She didn't respond, but picked up her drink and swallowed it in one long draught. It was time for her to leave. Time to say goodbye and walk away and not look back.

"I searched the world for you, Eve. I'm not going to let this stop me now."

She laughed, the sound bitter even to her own ears. "And you wonder why I resist. Don't you see, Adam? No matter what the risks, you'll find a reason, convince yourself it's for the best, that you're not doing anything wrong." Worse, maybe he would even convince her. She couldn't take that risk. Not now, not ever.

"If it came to that, they would stop us. The angels, the g—on behalf of God. But you can't tell me you haven't ever even wondered what it meant that we were capable of this. You can't tell me you haven't asked yourself how you could love me at all, if God hadn't meant for it to happen."

Love. Was that why this was so hard? Because she wanted to love him? She closed her eyes. Now wasn't the time to examine that feeling, to admit that it might be something more than just the chance to live another life as Eve. She pushed it away, stamped it down, buried it before he caught even the barest flicker from her emotions.

"How long will you stay after you realize I won't be persuaded?" she asked softly.

"I'll stay as long as you want me here."

She opened her eyes and met his, cool and distant and steady. She had to be steady now. "And if I ask you to go?"

"You don't want me to go," he said. "Whatever else there is between us, that's clear."

He never had understood. Not really. "Sometimes, Adam, it isn't about what we want."

His jaw tightened, and he looked away, stared at the empty seat across from them.

And then he got up.

When he walked away, it took every ounce of her strength not to call him back.

CHAPTER THIRTEEN
247 AD

§

With such protection in place, it wasn't necessary for him to return to the House of Lions with frequency, but he did anyway, for Evaline's sake, witnessing the birth of her son Lucius, and a second daughter, who Gaius allowed her to name Tora, for the life Eve had lived as Thor's wife. Evaline made sure there was always a bed for him to sleep in, and wine and mead for him to drink.

After Gaius died, and the lands passed to Evaline's son, Thor made sure to stop and see her every full moon. And before her own death, when he saw she did not have much longer left in this world, he stayed at her bedside for weeks, so that when she woke he could ease her suffering by telling her the stories she so loved, and when she was pained, he could give her dreams of times long past to distract her.

Her children and grandchildren always kept a bed for him, but he found that returning after Evaline's death made his heart ache as much as watching Eve, and but for the times when he felt they were on the verge of forgetting who they were and what their history was, he did not return with the frequency required to form any family bonds with the House of Lions. They had his protection, and he ensured they had rain and sun for their crops, and an understanding of who they were, and who Eve was, but that was all.

"You take her death too much to heart, Thor. She was mortal. You knew the time would come. It is a wonder she lived as long as she did."

He was in the grove, sitting on the ground and leaning against the bench which had somehow not yet crumbled to dust. Athena sat above him, and he felt her concern but could not bring himself to break the melancholy which had descended upon him and hovered for the last three decades.

"She was like a daughter to me, Athena. The only piece of Eve that I could touch." And now it was one more piece of Eve he had lost. He shook his head and stared at the olive trees without really seeing them. This was why gods did not live among men. Why they lived on their mountains or in their cities in the heavens. Why they consorted among themselves for the most part, and did not form close relationships with mortals.

"You will forever want what you cannot have, won't you Thor?" She said it with a sigh, resigned and even understanding. She slid to the ground beside him, and slipped her arm through his, resting her head against his shoulder. "I wonder how Ra did it, when he worked so closely with the Pharaohs. It must have pained him when they died. Do you suppose he sees it as a blessing or a curse that he's starting to be forgotten?"

"I think Ra is old and tired and conserves his strength. But none of us will be remembered for much longer if the True God has his way. What does Zeus plan to do about the Christians?"

Athena's laugh was bitter. "My father does not concern himself with them at all. How much harm can they do, he says. Look at how few the Jews are after so long, and how many our people are, he says. He convinces himself that this prophet Jesus will be forgotten before the cult grows any stronger. I've warned him that they have already written holy books, adding them to the Torah, but he thinks I worry too much, and reminds me that few people read." She made a noise of disparagement, deep in her throat. "Does he not realize that it only takes one who can read to tell the story to the rest who cannot?"

He grunted. "It will be trouble for all of us if he's wrong."

"But less trouble than your Eve, and Adam her twin. There will always be people to worship us, Thor, but only if there is a world for them to live within."

"She would never allow her brother to touch her."

"How can you be so certain?"

He sighed, rubbing his face and then climbed to his feet. "I was her husband, Athena. I know her."

"It was a long time ago. Perhaps she's changed."

"No." He paced to the little spring and let his hands fill with water, drinking it as an excuse to keep his back to her. He didn't want her to know how much her words upset him. How much it reminded him of Odin's mistrust. So strong still that a hundred years later he was not permitted to return home. "This isn't a question of changing. Eve cares about the world, and the people in it. She would not risk them. And the penalty for her is death if she did. She knows this. Even if she did not care, the personal risk is too great. She would gain nothing and lose everything."

"She told you this?"

"She told me everything, Athena. Everything that mattered." He took another drink, then straightened and turned to face her again. "She trusted me with all her secrets, though I did not trust her with mine."

Athena was sitting on the bench once more, stroking the little snake around her wrist with a finger. "What do you suppose she thinks of the Christian cult?"

He sat back down beside her and shrugged. "It's one of the many questions I'd like to ask. I cannot imagine it was easy for her to see her son martyred, though I do not know if she realized he was more than a man. I don't think she recognizes immortality the way we can, and certainly she attributes the acts of the other gods to Elohim's angels, so why not the miracles performed by Jesus as well? Just tricks, the lot of it."

"Only a fool would not suspect something after he rose from the dead, especially after his ascension."

"Perhaps she did. I didn't stay long enough to bear witness, for fear that Sif would follow me. But she told me she never knew her God. That he had died with her creation. I don't think she would believe that Jesus was anything more than a tool of the angels, and she had a healthy fear for them." He grimaced. "I can begin to understand better why, after having met Michael. That creature has very little love for anything but the True God, and His law."

"But you said that Gabriel was kind, that your impression of him was much more positive."

"But how much of that was because he had been raised by Eve?" He shook his head. "I do not know what to make of the True God, or his angels. Or this cult. We'll just have to wait and hope that your father is right that they will grow no larger."

Athena sighed. "I suppose I cannot talk you into joining us for dinner tonight?"

"How much of your family is home?"

She made a face. "Hermes and Ares will not be there, if that is what you fear. But Aphrodite and Dionysus will. They've been asking about you. I promise not to abandon you, Thor. Nor will I let them refill your cup unendingly."

Drink might do him good, at that. But he had been determined to avoid Aphrodite for the better part of the last century, since Sif had divorced him. Without the protection of his marriage, he had no hope of not offending her when he refused her advances. And no hope of not hurting Athena if he didn't, though a woman in his bed would be a welcome relief. He'd been aching for one since that morning, long ago, when Athena had been nestled so invitingly.

"Please, Thor."

"Perhaps another time." He stood before she could tempt him any further. "I would not be very good company to anyone, I think, and I know Zeus hates when his feasting is not perfectly festive."

Knowing it as an excuse, still she had the grace to let him go. Next time, he would have to accept, if only to avoid causing Zeus offense. The god had allowed him great liberty within Olympian lands since his exile from Asgard and Thor couldn't afford to appear ungrateful. He couldn't afford to alienate himself any further than he already had.

A god without people, a god without a home. A vagabond, an intruder. Sometimes he was even a thief. Taking apples, poaching game. He was everything Michael had said. And Frigg, the only mother he had ever known, and not even until he had already been more man than boy, told him this was how he was supposed to be. That wandering the earth was where he was meant to go. Odin was meant to exile him, and he was meant to ache. To feel this loss, this pain. To be alone. He was supposed to hurt.

It didn't make him feel any better to think about what Frigg had told him. Turning it over in his mind just frustrated him. He wasn't any closer to the answers or any kind of truth. It was just another way of wandering, and he grew tired of it. Tired of wanting what he couldn't have. Tired of agonizing over the fact that Eve would suffer in the same way if he didn't obey his father's command. Tired of walking without a set course. Tired of balancing between all the other gods, between offense and inoffense. Tired of denying himself. Tired of living alone, and not understanding the reasons. Tired of all of it.

He slept in the trees that night. Somewhere in northern Gaul. Not quite on the edge of the Roman reach, but far enough away from the House of Lions that he wouldn't be tempted to look for a bed there, and certainly distant enough from Mount Olympus that those gods would have to go out of their way to find him.

It rained, though he didn't remember consciously suggesting it. The water soaked through his cloak and his clothes to his skin, clammy and cold, but he wasn't made uncomfortable. In the dream he was in Syria, walking along a river. A man was baptizing people with water in the name of a god who would come. The water ran clean and clear and when he followed it on, Odin stood with Heimdall at a bridge. His father reached for him, clasped his hand, and welcomed him home. The river turned to stone as they crossed it, and he stared at the foundation of a hall larger than had ever been built in Asgard. He knew it was his own. The closer he drew to it, the more clear it became. Stones piled upon one another, and he felt the rock against his palms as if he had hewed them. When he reached it, it was complete, and he wandered the corridors until he lost count of the rooms inside. Finally, he reached his own chambers, *Mjölnir* waiting at his bedside, and a woman framed in the fading light of the window, her hair the rainbow of black oil. She heard him and began to turn—

A raven pecked him awake, but it was not Odin's bird. He shooed it away and frowned. The woman had been so familiar, even without seeing her face. If the bird had only left him alone for another moment . . .

He shook his head to clear it, and dropped from the tree to go in search of a meadow, where he could clear the sky and lie in the sun to dry. The grasses were green, and scratched him less than the wool of his cloak and shirt. Ra had offered him linen, but as often as he slept against rough bark, it would not have lasted him more than a month before turning into rags, and he preferred the longer lasting woolen fabrics. He set a trap, hoping for rabbit to make into a meal, and then he stripped off his wet clothes and laid them out. The way the grasses were bent, it was clear the deer had spent their night here, making a ready bed for him. He found a soft place to curl up, with enough shade for comfort, and went back to sleep.

He dreamed of a god without a home, without a family, without a world of her own. A god who wandered the void, a vagabond and lonely, just like Thor wandered the earth. And he dreamed of Eve, loving and warm, welcoming him home to their small hut in the village. The last peace he had ever known.

He thought he was still dreaming when he woke to a hand on his shoulder, and looked into Eve's eyes and dimpled smile. She held his cloak, long dry, blushing at the nakedness she tried not to see.

He thought he was still dreaming when he caught her hand and pulled her down into the grass with him. It was only when he kissed her, and she responded with surprise, and then need, that he realized he was not.

With a muttered oath, he grabbed his cloak and his clothes and his boots, kissed her one more time, and fled.

CHAPTER FOURTEEN
Present

Benjamin Adam Hastings was born after ten long hours of labor by his mother. Ten hours and an eventual c-section which left Mia exhausted and pale. Eve held her new nephew and looked up at her brother. "Benjamin Adam? Really?"

"Why not?" He shrugged, but his eyes didn't leave the baby in her arms, and even in the afterglow of his newfound paternal instinct, she could still feel his wish that she was the mother of his child now, and not Mia.

You know that isn't possible.

He raised his eyes to her face. *We'll see.*

She sighed and kissed the baby's forehead before handing him back to his mother. "He's a beautiful baby boy, Mia." She kissed her sister too, and excused herself from the room. She already had enough nightmares without Adam broadcasting his dreams for a future that couldn't exist.

Garrit offered her a cup of hot tea when she found him in the waiting room, sitting with Alex who had long ago woken, played, eaten, and fallen back to sleep again. "How is she?"

"She'll be fine."

They were alone in the room, having been abandoned by her parents the moment the baby was available to be viewed. "How's your brother?"

She sipped her tea. "I think he'll be fine, too. Did you actually get a chance to talk to him about fatherhood, or were you too distracted by whatever that situation was in the hall?"

"We talked. For whatever help it was. Not that it matters. If he has half the talent you do, it will be simple enough."

"Garrit, this can't go on."

He looked away. "*Qu'est ce que tu veux que je te dise?*" he asked softly. *What do you want me to say?*

She studied his face. The way his forehead creased and his lips thinned. His eyes stayed fixed on his coffee cup, but from the way his jaw flexed, she was sure he knew she was watching him. "Maybe Ryam had his reasons for keeping these secrets, Garrit, but do they still apply? This family isn't just his. It isn't just Reu's line, it's mine too."

He raked his fingers through his hair, leaning forward to rest his elbows on his knees. "It isn't that simple, Abby."

"Why can't it be that simple?"

"It's not just Ryam's reasons, or Ryam's rules. If it were just him, I would tell you everything I know. I honestly don't think he knew what all of this would mean, later, or he never would've agreed to it." He snorted. "I would never have agreed to it, but nobody asked me."

She frowned. The obligation of the oath carried through blood for generations was ridiculous. More so when the renewal was made by children who didn't know the meaning of the words they spoke. But Reu had made his decisions, and Ryam his, and there was nothing she could do about any of what had happened centuries ago.

"I'm not doing this to our children, Garrit. I'm not making them take any vows."

"Certainly not these, no." He swirled the tea in his cup. "But there are things they're going to learn, regardless, and things they'll have to keep to themselves. Secrets they'll have to keep. And when do we trust them with the truth of who they are and where they come from? Who their mother is?"

"Are you changing the subject on purpose?"

He laughed darkly. "My answers can't change, Abby. What I can tell you won't change."

"But you can tell Adam. And Lars Owen. And Juliette. And this Minerva woman who you dislike so much." Maybe that was what bothered her most. Everyone seemed to know what was going on. All these people she had never known, would never meet again, seemed to have this intimate knowledge of her life and the DeLeon plan for it, but they wouldn't tell her.

And Adam. It irked her that he could throw it in her face. That even he knew. Of course, that much of it made some kind of sense, since it all revolved around him, and keeping them apart. And she still wasn't sure if they even knew why.

"I didn't tell any of them anything."

His vehemence startled her out of her thoughts and she blinked. "Then how do they know? René?"

"Oh, my father told my mother, of course. She's known the basics since I was born. The details probably didn't come until after you showed up. The others had nothing to do with us, though. Your brother knew a great deal before I ever spoke to him, and not just what he picked from my mother's mind."

Since this was more than he'd admitted about anything, she took a moment to digest it. "Then I'm right about Lars."

The paper cup in Garrit's hand crumpled, his tone emotionless. "I couldn't say."

"How else could he know?"

He shook his head and said nothing.

She frowned again, because his irritation was putting her on edge. "Every time he comes up, you get weird, Garrit."

"Perhaps you should stop bringing him up." He stood and dropped the cup in the trash. Then he kissed her forehead. She could feel his contrition in the gesture, though he didn't offer an apology. "I should go see our newest nephew before Mia decides I don't care for her children."

"Yes." She watched him go, feeling relief and frustration simultaneously. There was something about that man he wasn't telling her. But what she couldn't figure out was how it had anything to do with Ryam.

And if it was Ryam and the family vow that kept her husband from talking, what was keeping Adam from telling her everything? The more this went on, the more tempting it was to find the answers through her brother rather than her family. And if he let her, it wasn't really a breach of trust, was it?

I'm surprised at you, Eve. I thought you had morals.

I'm not prying am I? Thinking about it is not the same as acting on the thought.

Adam chuckled softly in the back of her mind. *Is it really prying when he wishes he could tell you? Wouldn't it be a kindness to lighten his burden? Isn't there some saying about sharing troubles, or secrets, or something?*

Unlike some people, I respect the privacy of the mind.

I have plenty of respect. But you can't tell me you aren't tempted. Everything would be so much easier for both of you without all these secrets.

Then tell me.

I'm not really interested in risking my memory or this new lease on life to save your marriage to a man who hates me, Eve.

But if I took it?

He sighed dramatically. *If you took it, I'd be an unfortunate victim of your abandoned principles.*

She frowned. There was something in his tone that bothered her. Like he couldn't wait to see what her response would be. Like he was entertained by the idea. And some sort of odd feelings of retribution. *What do you stand to gain, Adam?*

Everything, Evey.

The way he said it made her shiver. It wasn't menace, exactly. At least not directed at her. It was close though. And paired with a determination that frightened her. Adam had lost none of his arrogance. He still genuinely believed she was meant for him, that they were meant for each other.

Is it just that I refuse you? Is that why you're so determined?

You feel it too, Eve. I know you do. Your heart races every time we touch.

I love my husband.

He sneered. *You love your past with far more passion than your present. That Thorgrim. I saw it, in your mind. In your memories. Your heart still aches for him three thousand years later.*

She wished she could steal the thoughts back from him. Wished that she could wipe even Thorgrim's name from his mind. That he would never even whisper it again. *You have no idea what you're talking about.*

I know better than you think.

She shook her head, even though he couldn't see it. *I'm not even sure you're capable of love, Adam.*

Just the implication that what he felt for her could touch what she had shared with Thorgrim made her feel sick. Thorgrim had been selfless in every way. All he'd ever wanted was her happiness, and he would've moved mountains to provide her the means.

Selfless? If he had been truly selfless he would never have married you! Never have given you the opportunity to love him!

You don't even know him!

He laughed. *But your family does.*

And then his presence disappeared. She couldn't even feel him in the hospital anymore. It was like he had been knocked out.

What did that even mean? It made no sense whatsoever. It wasn't possible that her family had ever known Thorgrim. It would've been months of travel to cross from the Nordic regions through Germany and into DeLeon lands. And it was rare for people to travel more than a day in any direction during the course of their whole lives, then.

She reached for Adam, because she could feel him again, but his mind was shut to her with an absoluteness that stung.

"*Maman?*"

She looked down at her son, he had his arms open and she picked him up to hold in her lap. Alex, at least, was innocent. With no secrets and nothing to drive them apart. As a DeLeon though, he would never have the option to live the rest of his life that way. His future would always be full of those same secrets and truths. Finding a woman who could accept his family with all its mythology would be a challenge for him. Garrit had been lucky, in that respect, to have found her. Someone who already believed. Already knew the truth. Already perpetuated the myth.

Or perhaps not. If it hadn't been her. If it had been any other woman, he wouldn't have had to keep the secrets he did now. He would have been able to tell her everything, as René had told Juliette. And even if Garrit chose not to force his son into the same vow, she had a feeling Alexandre, too, would someday know all of the secrets that were denied her.

"My boy." She kissed the top of his head. "I wish I could give you an easier future."

He squirmed in her arms, reaching for the floor, for the bag with his toys. Of course he didn't understand her words. He was still too young for that. She set him down and he pulled his favorite toy from the bag. The family had found it entertaining to give him a plush lion, and Alex hadn't been parted from it since. He carried it awkwardly as he made a circuit around the room, chair to chair, and she stood up to follow when he began to climb on them with the stuffed animal still in his arms.

Something tickled the back of her mind, and she looked over her shoulder. She was alone in the room, but the feeling that someone was watching her was almost overwhelming. Michael? But no. He wouldn't bother hiding. He'd already proven that. It was just being in the hospital that had her on edge, that was all.

She sighed, and then caught Alex before he fell, and tried to put it all out of her mind.

CHAPTER FIFTEEN
Future

Adam sat in the car outside the shop for hours. He could feel her now, though he wasn't sure why he hadn't before. He could feel her inside, and the agony of her heart, and he wanted nothing more than to go to her, but even being here was too close.

Without conscious decision, he got out of the car and walked to the shop. The bell chimed as he entered. Eve looked up, her lips parted, her expression eager, and when she recognized him, he saw and felt her relief, followed swiftly by guilt.

He stopped a few feet from the counter, wishing he could stop her from feeling that way. She shouldn't have to feel guilty for loving him. She shouldn't have to feel guilty for being happy to see him. But he stood there, at a loss for words now that he was before her.

She stepped around the counter, but seemed to hesitate to close the gap, until she made a strangled noise and reached for him. He took her in his arms, her face hidden against his chest and held her tightly, memorizing the feel of her body against his, murmuring soft reassurances as she tried desperately to keep from sobbing. It was as if a dam had broken, and everything she had controlled so carefully the day before was spilling out. Everything he had hoped she felt, dreamed she might be willing to offer. He hadn't been sure until that moment, not completely, but her feelings burned bright now, branded him, and if it was not love yet, he knew then it could be. If she let it. If he stayed.

All the more reason to go.

"Shh," he said softly, kissing the top of her head. "I'm here."

She shook her head. "I wanted you to come."

He smiled, and closed his eyes. The better to feel her warmth. "I wasn't sure I should."

"I was so afraid you would." She pulled back to look up at his face. "I can't be strong again, Adam. I can't tell you to go. Not a second time."

"You won't have to." He stroked her hair back from her face, and looked into her eyes. "I'm packed. Everything is in the car outside, waiting for me. I'm only here to say goodbye."

"But you don't want to go."

He couldn't stop himself from kissing her forehead. Then her eyelids, and the tip of her nose, and he pressed his forehead against hers, and held her face in his hands, his eyes closed against his own grief. So much pain. He hadn't realized how much it would hurt, but he should have known. He should have known.

"It isn't about what I want. Not this time."

Then she was kissing him, her lips soft against his, then desperate, and he had to pull away before his meager resolve left him. She covered her mouth with her hands, as if she had realized her mistake. "I'm sorry. I'm so sorry."

"You don't have to be sorry, Eve. Not for this." He brushed the tears from her cheek and pulled her back into his arms, tucking her head beneath his chin, breathing in the scent of her, all sunshine and summer, and willing himself to remember this always. "Never for this. Promise me."

I never meant for this, she said.

"I know." He held her all the more tightly. "I should go."

She shook her head and didn't release him. "There has to be a way. There has to be some way that we can do this, Adam."

"No, Evey. This is the best way. The only way." *So that I can love you. Because without the world, we can't even have that.*

She let him disentangle himself from her body and peel her fingers from his shirt with gentle pressure. He stepped back when she had finally let him go, and smiled his most charming smile, putting as much confidence in his tone as he could.

"I'll be right here," and he touched the place over her heart. "I promise."

And then he turned and left. One foot in front of the other, one step following the last, until he was back in the car again outside. With two doors between them, he finally let himself look back.

She stood in the window of the shop. One hand raised against the glass as she watched him. *I love you because you walked away,* she said, soft and miserable.

I know.

The car pulled away into traffic, just as thunder began to roll overhead. He closed his eyes and pinched the bridge of his nose. Better late than never, he supposed, though it would have been nice if the god had arrived a bit sooner. Before he had fallen in love so utterly with Eve.

He directed the driver to pull over in the park district and got out. The thunder had followed him, as he knew it would, and he walked to a bench in the shade of immense oak trees and overlooking a well kept pond. Thor arrived without his usual display of lightning, and sat down beside him without a word.

"What kept you?" Adam asked.

Thor's eyes glowed white, but he stared at the water. "I was here from the moment you set foot in the city."

Useless of him. They were all useless anymore, these gods without people. Vagabonds, now, without their countries. "You should have stopped me."

"I owed her the choice. Free will was not only valued by your God, Adam."

"Yet you have stood in the way of mine for more than a century." He felt disgusted and angry. Thor could have stopped him. Could have prevented all of this. But this time, this once, he let some moral high ground stand in his way. This time, when it was the most important.

Thor growled. "You were given the choice as well. You took power and money in exchange for Eve. That you regret that choice is not my concern or my responsibility."

He sneered. As if any wealth were an even exchange. He had been cheated. Cheated twice because he couldn't have her anyway, as Thor had known. He hated this god. Hated how well he knew her. "For someone who claims to love her, it seems all you do is let her suffer. She wouldn't have to, now, if you had acted as you were bound to do."

"You dare blame me for your own selfishness?" The god's eyes flashed, the glow intensifying, and thunder cracked overhead louder than before. "You knew it was impossible before you set out on this crusade. You knew that she would never have you. Never risk the world! And yet you still hunted for her, still sought her. For what? For a stolen kiss and a river of tears? So that she would share the misery you've lived with? No, Adam. This blame lies on your shoulders alone. This cruelty is your particular brand, borne of twisted emotion masquerading as love."

Thor stood then, and Adam felt his fury barely contained. And something else. Something deeper which kept him from action but which Adam couldn't name. Lightning flashed, and the god was gone without another word.

Adam shook his head and stood up, though Thor's last words still seemed to hang in the air around him. Like weights around his neck. Eve had asked him if he was capable of love, and now he wondered if his answer had been more hope than truth. Did Thor go to Eve now, to comfort her in some mortal guise? If he did, was that not also selfishness? Did they suffer the same flaw? A fault which kept them from the woman they loved eternally?

He went back to his car and drove on to the airport. If he didn't leave the country, he would only return to her, and each time it would be more difficult to go. Each time would be another knife in her heart that he didn't want to be responsible for.

He spent the rest of the day in a fog, waiting for thunder and lightning to signal some new punishment for the state he had left Eve in. It wouldn't have been the first time such a punishment had been exacted. But what was he supposed to do now? How was he to fill the eighty years that stared at him gaping and empty with the knowledge that he could not spend them with Eve?

Eve.

On the jet, he closed his eyes and searched for her presence, clear and bright to him now in the masses of the city. How had he missed it before? She was still in the shop, and he could feel her struggling not to weep. He could feel her losing that struggle, too, and sliding down the wall, her knees to her chest, her face hidden in her arms, and crying.

I'm sorry, he whispered to her.

God was cruel to make us this way, she said.

He sighed. He could not remember much of God, and he wished that he could now, to comfort her with some proof. But those had been memories he'd sought to find in her. Memories he couldn't ask her for now. Not when she suffered so. *I love you.*

Just go, Adam. Just go.

He did as she asked, only then feeling the speed of the jet and the pressure as it rose into the air. Was there nothing he could do to give her comfort?

§

He knew better than to believe it was chance that brought the girl to the bar he chose to drown his sorrows. A girl with green eyes, though they lacked Eve's depth, and dark hair. He stared at her over the rim of his glass, and she smiled prettily, blushing when she noticed. He wondered which god found him so pitiable to send this woman, and how faithless was he that he wanted to take her to bed with him. Would they send a similar man to Eve? Someone who resembled him just enough that she could pretend, if she chose to, that it was him she was loving?

He downed the last of his drink and tried to ignore the image that had sprung into his mind of Eve making love to someone else. He'd had enough of that when she was married to Garrit. Watching her touch him, watching her look at him with adoration. It had been torture. Nor had it made it any easier to know that it could have been worse. One glimpse was all he had ever needed of her life with Thor.

A glass of whiskey slid down the smooth wood into his hand, and he dropped several large bills onto the bar, tapping the counter with an implicit "keep them coming" gesture. Cash did still have its uses, after all. But he hadn't had nearly enough to drink on the plane, and he was determined to get himself so plastered that he wouldn't care that the woman he took to bed with him wasn't Eve.

The money disappeared from the counter and a bottle replaced it with a dull thunk. The bartender had bright red hair, and narrow green eyes. Adam glared at him when he smirked. "You'll like that one," the man said. "Hardest I've got, and well worth the money spent."

Irish, by the sound of him, or else pretending to be to capitalize on his tips. If he was pretending, he did a damn good job of it. Adam lifted the glass, swirling it once, then drank it down. The burn was pleasant, smooth and clean. "Better than the swill they served me on the plane."

The barman grinned and jerked his head to the right. "The woman there said you were a man of distinguished taste and loaded with funds enough to afford it."

Adam glanced over his shoulder. Of course it would be her. The woman met his eyes and smiled, and the resemblance to Eve vanished in the curve of her mouth and a flash of gold in her eyes. Now he was sure it was some trick of the gods, and all the more reason not to get involved with any of it.

He poured another glass and slugged it back. The gods could keep their look-a-likes. He wasn't going to accept substitutes, or if he did, he wanted them to remind him as little of what he'd lost as possible, and even with the smirk and the sundrop eyes, it was too close. "Tell her thanks, but I'm not interested in any consolation prizes. She's better off going home with you."

The barman laughed. "I tell her that often enough. Sometimes she even listens, but you—" He shrugged. "You're exactly what she's been waiting for."

Adam shook his head. "She'll get sick of waiting and crawl back in bed with you, I'm sure."

"She surely will." He grinned and refilled the glass. "But not 'til she's finished in yours."

A hand covered his, manicured nails and soft skin. Even her fingers were shaped like Eve's. He swallowed the whiskey and kept his eyes on the bottle. "You don't even realize you're a pawn, do you? We're all just amusement for some higher power, hoping to see how twisted he can make us before we break."

"We're not all so cruel, Adam," she said.

He looked up at his name, his stomach lurching at the sound of it.

Her dark hair rippled into gold and sunlight, her eyes changing from green to the amber of honey. He looked back at the bottle that had been placed before him, still mostly full, and counted the other empty glasses. Only three. Not enough for him to have imagined this, then.

"Some of us just want to offer what comfort we can give. And perhaps something more. Satisfaction for the pain you've suffered by godly hands."

He blinked at the golden glow that seemed to blur his vision. She was certainly beautiful, and now that she no longer held Eve's form, nothing at all like her. "I was under the impression that your people didn't care for me that much."

"Perhaps I dislike my brethren even more."

"Do I know your name, goddess?"

She smiled and leaned closer, her hand stroking his arm and her breath tickling against his ear. She smelled like honey, too. Or maybe like mead. Whatever it was, he wanted it, though part of him knew it was because she meant him to.

"You can call me Sif," she said.

CHAPTER SIXTEEN
318 AD

He spent decades in hiding. Decades during which he did not even let himself see her, for fear that she might glimpse him and remember that one day, in a meadow, in the middle of nowhere, when she had found him half naked in the grass and he had kissed her. And he worried what Odin would say, what Odin would do to punish him. How many more years must he spend wandering the earth, cast out of Asgard, scorned by his own father? His people? He did not miss Loki, nor Sif, but he missed his brothers, his sons, his daughter. He missed drinking with his family, laughing in Odin's great hall. He missed having a home.

As far as Eve was concerned, he watched over her only by listening to the hum of her thoughts in the din of humanity. He became adept at sitting in the back of her mind, where she didn't notice him, didn't feel him, but he could feel her, follow her, know what she was doing, know that she was safe. He soothed her fears, gentled her dreams. And when she was upset or hurt or angry, he caused her to remember him, to remember his love for her as Thorgrim, and filled her heart with peace. He refused to consider this disobedience to Odin's command.

After all, she did not know he was there.

He fulfilled his duty to the Council by following Adam instead. It wasn't exactly a surprise to him that Eve's brother was among the barbarians causing so much trouble to the Romans. It made it easy for Thor to blend in. Easy for him to move among them. These tribes weren't so different from the Northmen; some of them even looked to Asgard and Odin. They had the warrior's spirit, the warrior's strength.

"Can't stand the cold even here," Adam told him one night, around the fire. The language he spoke was rough compared with the Latin Thor had been using for the last several centuries. "I wouldn't go further north."

"It's not so bad on the coasts. And the gods are good to us." Thor stared at the flames, prodding the kindling with a stick.

Adam snorted. "Gods are good for nothing, no matter where you are. These Romans are always making their sacrifices, always talking about their gods, and what does it get them?"

Thor grinned. It was feral, and he hoped his eyes didn't flash with lightning. "It's gotten them plenty. From Africa to Asia to Britannia. They own more of the world than you'll ever dream of."

"What do you know of the Romans, Northman?" Adam threw a heavy branch onto the fire, causing a spray of sparks to erupt into the dark. "Go join their army if you love them so much. Pay their taxes. Let them tell you how to dress, how to act, how to live. Let them offer you up to die in one of their stupid wars while they sit comfortably in their homes, or out enjoying their circuses."

Thor couldn't quite keep the disgust from his expression. "Romans, Goths. You're all the same. Lucky you have gods at all. Ungrateful no matter what they do for you."

Adam spit in distaste. "I'll keep my faith in my sword and my spear and the things I can touch and feel. I don't need gods to help me win my battles, and any of the others will tell you that's the truth."

"Those are dangerous things to say, Athanareiks. You do not know when the gods are listening." Nor could he recognize one sitting across from him in the firelight. Thor let the thunder come, and the rain. Lightning struck so near, Adam couldn't fail to feel its power. And when the man flinched, throwing himself backward with real fear in his face, Thor did not move, did not blink, and let his eyes glow. "They might take offense."

Adam cursed and stared at him, his expression moving closer to terror. His face was white. "What are you?"

Thor grinned at his shock. The lightning seemed to unnerve him especially, so he called it again, letting it wash the whole camp, leaching the land of color. "If you think yourself a god, Athanareiks, think again. Or at least keep your blasphemy to yourself."

He left him at the fire and disappeared into the night. The next morning, he heard Adam searching for him from the trees, but he didn't return to the camp. He'd had enough of him. Someone would no doubt chastise him for revealing himself even in that small way to Adam, but the man would forget between this life and the next, and he had earned the lesson in humility.

He sank into Eve's mind to calm himself, listening to her sing from half a continent away, as she washed her clothes. She was so unlike her brother.

§

He didn't go south, having been warned of the civil wars by Athena, though that's where Eve was. But word reached him outside of Roman lands that Constantine had converted to Christianity, and won the war against Maxentius with the aid of the True God. He had even made a pact to protect the Christians from persecution.

The news made him grow cold, though the night was warm. Rome held too much of the world, and where the Emperor led, many of his people would follow. Too many people.

Is it true, Athena? Constantine joins the cult?

Her anger was incredible, crackling like lightning in his thoughts. *After everything I did for him. After all the battles I turned in his favor, he repays us with this betrayal. Yes, it's true. Father is angry, but has forbidden me to strike him down for fear of making him another martyr.*

An understandable concern. But what else could be done to stem the tide? *The peace he won cannot last long, perhaps he will yet be destroyed by Licinius in the east.* The wars had torn the empire apart repeatedly, and to hope for more was not something he took pride in, but he did not see how else to dispose of Constantine.

Constantine still sacrifices to Apollo, and my brother will not hear of abandoning him. Artemis has sworn to starve any army we incite against him. These wars do not just divide the Empire, Thor, but my family as well.

He wondered if it was Michael's doing. He imagined the Archangel's face, twisted with amusement at the trouble he had caused. *Be the voice of reason, Athena. If Rome falls to the Christians, there will be little hope for the rest of us. The Olympians must stand together, act together.*

She sighed in despair. *We have never worked unanimously toward any goal, Thor. Always we had our favorites, a city, a warrior, a king or a queen. Always we played them against one another, to relieve our boredom. But this—this is the beginning of our end, if it continues.*

Would my presence help? It was an offer he did not make lightly, and he doubted it would be enough. Fragmented as things sounded, an interloper may not be appreciated.

If only you were my husband, Thor, then your arrival would not be seen as interference. No. It is better that you stay where you are. We shall settle this among ourselves, one way or another.

Come to me if you need a friend, Athena. It is the least I can do.

She plucked the knowledge of where he was, what he had been doing, from his mind and he heard her laugh in his thoughts. *Your father cannot say you did not work for his benefit during your exile. The power of Adam within his fold, even for one generation will bring him new vigor.*

I did not do it for my father. The man's arrogance offends me.

He felt her smile. *The arrogance of immortality, known or not. You can hardly venerate his sister as a goddess, and object to his thinking himself a god.*

Surely you don't defend him.

I am a goddess of war, Thor. Part of me cannot help but appreciate his purpose, even if I do not approve of his actions. But he is the least of my concerns now. I must return to my father.

Good luck, Athena.

I fear we shall need it.

That night, he returned to the House of Lions. There was a bed with clean linens and a small oaken barrel of mead waiting for him. He stared at the bed for a long moment, but all he could think of was the night he had spent with Athena in this same room. He took the mead and went to the stables.

A sleepy shepherd didn't notice him as he passed, creeping into the loft and making a bed in the hay. He nudged the boy awake with a roll of thunder once he was comfortably settled, for if he missed the hulking silhouette of a god, there would be no hope for the sheep and goats if a wolf came looking for a meal, and winter was coming. They would need their livestock.

He pulled the bung on the mead, and poured it into the hollowed horn he carried as a makeshift mug. It served him better than pottery, so easily shattered. When had the Lions begun fermenting mead? He didn't remember it being offered on his last visit. It was a good mead, too. Not too strong and not too sweet. Perhaps Athena had delivered it, thinking of him.

He drank half of the small barrel before corking it and lay back in the hay. He reached for Eve, and felt her sleeping, though even in her dreams she was worried about the wars. What it would do to the people around her. And she worried that one of the Emperors was her brother. Having never met them personally, she did not know for certain, but she was terrified that he was near to her, that he was the reason for all the death and destruction.

He heard himself humming the song she had once sung to their son, Owen, and gently pulled the memory of their life together toward the surface of her dreams, leaving the choice of which to her subconscious. He saw himself sitting in their hut, in front of the hearth, and he heard her singing softly to the baby in her arms, as she danced him to sleep. He saw the smile on his face as he watched her, and their eyes met. He rose and took the baby from her, laying him in the basket she had woven and tucking the blankets around him for warmth. And then he took her in his arms, and sang softly in her ear while they danced together in the little hut to the crackling of the fire and chirp of the insects outside.

It was before he had been made chieftain. Before her father's death. And she had been so soft in his arms, so warm. He had built the hut for her as a wedding gift, more practical than her ivory bangle, and when they had become the leaders of their village, she had refused to move from it into the chieftain's house, saying it was warmer than her father's had ever been.

While she dreamed he reassured her. Adam was in the north, with the Goths. He had no use for the civilized warfare of these frail emperors. Emperors who died, and grew sick, and struggled to control the loyalty of their people. If it were Adam, he reminded her, there would not be a civil war, for his co-emperors would never have crossed him. Never have been allowed to question him. And he did not remember himself. Did not remember her. She was safe, he promised.

He left her mind before his dream-self kissed her, so he would not be tempted to find her come morning.

CHAPTER SEVENTEEN
Present

They spent the week with Mia and Adam, and Eve engaged in the obligatory doting over her nephew and her sister. Garrit however, had become distracted. He smiled and laughed with everyone else, but more often than not he was staring out the window, or slipping off somewhere out of the way.

Safe in the house, she left Alex with his grandfather and went looking for her husband. It was the night before their departure, and he still hadn't packed. It wasn't like him to wait until the last moment. And if she sent him off to get ready, perhaps she could have a moment alone with Adam and get some of the answers denied her for the last two years.

Voices rose from the other end of the hall, and Eve followed them to the library. The door was mostly closed. As though someone had meant for it to be shut, but had been too hurried to be sure it had.

"You must just love all of this," Garrit was saying.

"You would too, if you'd had the experiences with him and his brethren I did." Adam, gloating. Of course. Eve stopped with her hand on the door to listen. "Arrogant upstarts and usurpers is all they are.

Hanging around looking for scraps. It's long past time for them to go, and it's people like you who allow them to maintain a presence. So yes, I do love it. And who can blame me?"

"We trusted him—them—with everything."

Adam laughed. "I won't say they don't have their uses." His voice hardened. "But their time is over. What more proof do you need that I'm not a threat to you or yours? Or at the very least, less a threat than the one that's been under your roof."

Garrit sighed and she felt his frustration, his exhaustion. "I don't know."

"When you find out, be sure to let me know." Footsteps shifted toward her and Eve backed away from the door. Too slow. Adam pulled it open before she'd gone more than two steps. He smirked. *Eavesdropping? Really?*

She flushed. *As if you don't do it constantly.*

He laughed out loud, and she saw Garrit over his shoulder. "I hope you heard something you liked, sister of mine. Or at least something useful." And then he brushed past her, whistling.

"Abby." Garrit rubbed his face. "Are you packed?"

"I am. You aren't." She walked into the library and pulled the door shut behind her, making sure it latched. "What was all this about?"

He shook his head. "I'm still trying to figure that out, myself."

"Has Adam done something?"

"*Non.*" Garrit stood up and smiled, taking her hands. "I'd better go pack." He kissed her forehead. "Don't worry, Abby. It will all sort itself out."

She watched him go and turned back to the window. It was raining again. It was always raining. Winter rains were the worst. Why didn't it ever snow anymore?

Because the gods are cranky, that's why, Adam said.

Eavesdropping? Really?

He chuckled in the back of her mind. *It's my house. If I can't eavesdrop here, where can I?*

She sat down, pinching the bridge of her nose. Her head ached. *This is all so impossible.*

Adam was silent for a moment, and she felt the discomfort around her temples ease with the touch of his mind, bleeding the pain away. *Not impossible, Eve. Just a bit more complicated than it should be. But I can't imagine anything has ever been simple for you.*

Why are you being so nice to me?

He sighed. *I promised myself when you arrived that I wouldn't talk to you, wouldn't reach for you, wouldn't allow myself to be alone in the room with you. I was going to be coldly polite, and nothing more. But this is something I can't fight, Eve.*

You're married, Adam. You have a son. You made your choices.

I hadn't intended on falling in love with you, Eve.

She shook her head. *Don't say that. Don't tell me that you love me. I've made my choices too. And even if I hadn't, I would never choose you.*

She felt his wince, and a lash of pain before he buried it. *Never is a long time for you and me, Eve.* The kindness had left his mental tone. He was angry now. Hurt. *Don't make me any promises you can't keep.*

I'm sorry. She hated hurting him. Didn't like to cause him pain. Especially now, when he had clearly changed so much. She should have been encouraging him, helping him, and instead she was just driving him away, back into the bitterness she remembered from their earliest days. But there was nothing else she could do. Not while Michael watched her so closely. *This is the way it has to be. The way it is. We both know that.*

He didn't respond.

She closed her eyes and curled up in the chair. She didn't understand why God had made them this way. Why God had made *him* this way. It seemed a cruel thing to allow him to love her at all, if she could never love him back. She wished again for the first time in a long time that she had known God, that he hadn't died at her creation. That someone could give her answers to the questions that chased her from life to life.

When she looked out the window again, the rain had turned into snow. She hoped the weather wouldn't delay their departure. It would be best for everyone if she and Garrit got back home.

She went to find Alex, and then to spend what time was left with her family.

On the train the next morning she dreamt of the Garden. Of those first days, when Adam had tried to coerce her into being his wife. Of the moment when his coercion had nearly become rape, and when that failed, violence. She dreamed of the first night she had spent outside of the cave, hidden from Adam within Reu's arms. How had she not known then how Reu cared for her? How he loved her? She had been too innocent even to recognize her own feelings, she supposed. And those first days, before the fruit, the only person's thoughts she could hear were Adam's.

She dreamed of the days after the Garden had burned, when they had wandered across new lands, following the great river north with the lions to help hunt, and later the dogs. It seemed to her, when she woke, that she was still wandering somehow. France was the closest thing to a home she had, but she had spent so little time with her DeLeon family. It was a wonder they remembered her at all. And she had always taken for granted that they would.

The train rocked and she checked on Alex, nudging his mind into a deeper sleep. Garrit kissed the top of her head and left them to go find something to eat.

"*Excusez-moi, madame.*" A man sat down across from her, he looked old and worn away. But she could see in his eyes that his mind was still keen. He was lean, and brown like the desert, and he smiled at her like a doting grandfather.

Something stirred in the back of her mind, a memory she couldn't quite place. She smiled back to keep from frowning. By his accent, he clearly wasn't French. "Hello."

"Ah!" His eyes lit. "I am grateful. My English is much better than my French. I used to be quite fluent in Latin, but I fear I lost my touch."

But it seemed even English was not his first language. He spoke it liquidly, but with the intonation of someone unused to it. She thought perhaps it was a Hindi accent, but she hadn't spent nearly as much time in that part of the world as she had in the west. Or perhaps it was Arabic.

"Where are you from?"

"A complicated question," he said. "With many answers. But I believe it is safe for me to say that I am not from here."

She laughed. There was something about this man. She couldn't quite take any kind of offense. And she was curious in spite of herself. He seemed so familiar, if only she could remember . . . "Then, you've traveled a lot?"

"I have traveled in the past," he agreed, smiling again. "From Egypt to France to India and China and back again."

"What brings you to France now?" Something about the question amused him, but she wasn't sure why. When she tried to find out, to read it from the surface of his mind, it was blank but for the emotion.

"I've come as a favor to a friend. He is worried about his family and hoped I would check in on them." His eyes shifted to Alex, asleep beside her. She thought he seemed curious. "Family is not what it used to be anymore. Things have changed so much."

"You must be very close to your friend."

"He's like a son to me, yes. I would do anything to help him or those he loves."

She smiled. "Then perhaps the most important parts of family are still preserved. Caring for one another, protecting one another. Love."

"Love." The man leaned back in his seat and closed his eyes. He looked much older then, the lines around his mouth and eyes deeply pronounced, as though carved in stone. "Love is not always so simple a thing. Without it, a family is broken, but it is not enough by itself to create family, to protect it, to maintain it."

She thought of Adam and his love for Mia. The love that wasn't enough. She frowned and looked out the window. "And sometimes love divides us more than it draws us together."

"You sound as though you speak from experience."

She shook her head. "A friend of mine. He loves his wife, but he loves another more. Do you believe in soul mates, *monsieur?* Two people, fated to be together?"

He leaned forward, studying her face. "I have seen the power of love. The strength of it. There are times when it is an unstoppable force. As real and as purposeful as gravity, or magnetism. I have seen men sacrifice everything for love, betray their own fathers, betray their own wives. But I have not found any proof that any man was made for any singular woman since Adam and Eve."

"Adam and Eve." Her stomach twisted.

She fussed with the blanket that covered Alex as an excuse to look away. The myth was so pervasive. What was that saying about Frenchmen? Fifty thousand can't be wrong? But they had been, hadn't they? And how could Michael, God's archangel, be wrong? Why would he threaten her, inspire a fear bone deep, soul deep? But if the angels had a role in the Church, why would they propagate such a lie? Why would they endorse a bible full of false truths?

"Do you believe that? The literal creation?"

The man chuckled. "I believe in a greater God who made this world, yes. But as to the book of Genesis, there are many things left unexplained. Untold."

Hearing the truth wasn't as reassuring as she had hoped. She sighed. "Yes."

He laughed again, and offered her his hand. "My name is Horus Amon."

"Abigail. My son is Alex." When she shook his hand, she tried to see his mind again, but it was still blank. So odd. The only other person she'd encountered with such a mind had been Thorgrim, and that had been a long time ago. "You're not at all Scandinavian, are you?"

"Not at all." He seemed amused again, his eyes were almost knowing. As if he had seen so much for so long that there was little that could surprise or shock him. As if he knew exactly what she was thinking before she thought it. "But I traveled there, once. They are a very fine people."

"I haven't been that far north in a long time." She stopped herself before she said she had family there. She had family everywhere. This man might have been her family, for all she knew.

Garrit arrived, then, with pretzels and water, and a pair of sandwiches wrapped in cellophane. "They didn't have any cereal left, but I thought perhaps the banana would serve Alex." He noticed Horus and fell silent. A muscle along his jaw twitched, and he handed her one of the sandwiches. "I thought you would prefer the turkey."

"Thank you." She took the food from him. "Allow me to introduce my husband, Garrit, Mr. Amon."

Horus smiled. "I was just speaking with your wife. She is very kind, a very lovely woman."

"I think so, too." Garrit did not shake his hand, but nodded. It seemed to Eve that he was almost wary. "Have we met before, *Monsieur* Amon?"

"Please, you may call me Horus." He seemed to be studying Garrit, measuring him. "I think you would be a difficult man to forget, sir. Not unlike your wife."

Garrit was looking at him the same way, the food forgotten in his lap as soon as he was seated. "What brings you to France, *monsieur?*"

"I come on behalf of a friend, to see his family. He worries for them, but does not think they would appreciate his presence."

Something in Garrit's face changed, and Eve felt a wave of anger that made her flinch. "Is something wrong?"

He shook his head, and when he spoke there was no hint of distress to his tone. He even smiled politely. "May I ask the name of your friend?"

"Of course." Horus said, smiling again. And Eve thought somehow he knew Garrit's outrage. Had read it even more easily than she. "He is called Lars Owen. I don't suppose either one of you could help direct me to the House of Lions?"

CHAPTER EIGHTEEN
Future

Adam sat up and rubbed his face. The golden hue which had colored his vision was finally gone, and he had the vague feeling that he hadn't been himself.

"Disconcerting, isn't it?" a voice said.

He shook his head. More interference. He wasn't sure he was in the mood for a lecture from a thunder god. Not with the hangover already throbbing behind his eyes. "What are you doing here?"

"Making sure you are freed from her influence. Not that I'd bother if Eve weren't at risk." Thor sat in an armchair in the corner of the room, *Mjölnir* across his knees. "I won't ask what you hoped to accomplish by this; it is Sif's reasons that concern me. What did she offer you?"

He smirked. "Isn't that just another way of asking what I hoped to accomplish?"

The god's eyes flashed white and he stood, filling the room. Adam felt the crackle of static in the air around him and a roaring in his ears. Thor grabbed him one handed by the throat, his face inches away. "I have killed my own to keep her safe, Adam. If you want to test your immortality, try my patience further and we'll see what lightning and steel can do to shorten this life for you."

He choked and coughed, collapsing back on the bed when Thor released him. Adam rubbed his neck. "I don't believe you'd kill her too, even if I thought you could."

Thunder rumbled outside, and the windows rattled from the power thickening the air. "After what you've made her life? I've never seen her weep, never felt her in so much agony as this. It would be a relief to her, to die now. To forget you. To move on."

"To you?" He made himself laugh, though it hurt to do so and caused him to cough even more painfully. "She'd never have you, if she knew what you were."

"And yet, you, her twin, are happy to associate with us. Happy to trade her for your own gain." Thor's hands were fists, and Adam could see him quivering, his anger throwing sparks, and disgust curling his lip. "Do you think she would have you if she knew your deceit? Whether you claim to love her or not?"

"She won't have me." He glared at the god. "At all."

Thor closed his eyes and turned away, one hand still wrapped around the war-hammer. "And to spite her, you turn to Sif. Like a child, angry that he cannot have his toy. What did she offer? What did she want?"

Sif. Sif had promised him this. Revenge against Thor, first and foremost, and pleasure, too. She'd certainly come through.

He smiled. "It infuriates you, doesn't it?"

Thor shook his head. "You really have no idea, do you?"

"I have every idea. Sif promised me you would suffer. And here you are, just as she said you would be."

"You're a fool, Adam." He said it wearily, and his shoulders seemed to bow under an unseen weight. "For six months she's picked through your mind, kept you under her power, paraded you around on her arm. For six months she used you, and you don't even realize how."

His stomach lurched. For the first time he looked at the clock on his wall, and the date it displayed. He only remembered one night. One glorious golden night during which she had made good on her promise that he would forget his sorrow for a time.

Thor turned then, to look back at him, the white gone from his eyes, his expression bleak. "She made sure Eve saw it all."

§

Adam leaned heavily against the tiled wall of the shower, letting the noise drown out the sound of his cursing. When the water became too hot, he turned it frigid until his teeth chattered so hard he couldn't continue swearing and he blasted himself with the heat again, burning his skin until he wanted to scream.

Eve. Evey, I'm so sorry.

But there was no response. As there had been none all day. If she refused to hear him, or she was prevented from doing so, he didn't know, and he started cursing again that he hadn't thought to ask her for a contact number. Why would he ever have need of it? Didn't they have a connection that was far more useful? Couldn't he reach her, always, without ever encountering a busy signal? Without needing to rely on the modern communication technology that pervaded everything.

Of course he hadn't thought anything would stop him. Any*one* would stop him. He hadn't thought he would lose six months of his life to a goddess with a vendetta against Eve. He hadn't considered that anyone would strike at her this way.

No. This was Thor's fault, all of it. If the god hadn't involved himself, hadn't gotten in the way time and again, hadn't stalked her for three thousand years, none of this would have happened. Another reason, as if he had needed one, to hate that god and all his brethren. They had no place in this world. No right! Creation had been meant for him! For Eve!

And where were the angels? Where was Michael to strike them down? To smite them for daring to violate God's children? Where was the Archangel when there was a true threat? Useless. Missing. Gone. Just like God, the angels abandoned them. Except to hang over their heads as a threat. Except for terrifying Eve into believing they would destroy the world because of their love.

Because of his love.

Eve, please. Please hear me.

Thor would call him selfish for trying to reach her. He was probably the reason he couldn't hear her, couldn't feel her. Let her hate you, Thor had told him. Let her live her life without wanting what she can't have. But Adam hadn't meant to hurt her this way. He hadn't meant to make her so miserable. To make her suffer even further because of his love. He couldn't let her think he had done this purposely.

And how could he explain himself, if he did reach her? His silence had been paid for. His silence was enforced. He sagged under the beat of the water on his shoulders, scalding him again. They wouldn't let him speak to her. They wouldn't let him explain himself, even if she would listen.

He slammed his fist into the tile. He could do nothing. Nothing.

The water turned cold. He didn't know how long he'd been in the shower, trying to scrub six months of imagined soil from his skin. No amount of soap would clean his soul of Sif's touch or scour the lies from his mind. That she had stolen the memories from him infuriated him the most. Did she not realize how much he had already lost? How little he would appreciate this added assault? If he could kill her, he would. If he could find a way. Michael, maybe, and his flaming sword.

Damn Michael! There had to be a way to find him. A way to call him from wherever he secreted himself on the earth or beyond it. There had to be a way to reach him, or how else did God's miracles ever occur? The other pantheons would never do anything that would turn followers away from them. Never answer a prayer not addressed to them. Michael had to walk the earth still.

And that sword was the only way he had a chance of destroying Sif. He just hoped Thor wouldn't beat him to it.

He turned off the water and grabbed his towel. He felt slightly better now that he had a goal, even if it was petty. He tried not to think about the fact that the desire to get back at a god was what had placed him in this situation to begin with. Gods. Had he been so wrong then, to consider himself one, when so many surrounded him? If he had kept his memory, and not lost the Garden, would he be as one of them? Elevated to their level of power? Would they treat him as an equal instead of a pestilence?

He would go back to Montreal first. Find Eve. Apologize in person, since they refused to let him reach her from a distance. And that would be on Thor's head, if it upset her further. When would the god learn not to interfere? But perhaps Eve was the place to begin, regardless. She had the memories he didn't. The knowledge of those first days. And the fear of Michael in her heart. Maybe if she called the angels, they would answer.

Scrubbing his hair dry, he sat down on his bed. *Eve?*

I told you to leave her alone, Adam.

He twitched, recognizing Thor's tone immediately. *I thought you owed her choice? Let her refuse me herself, if she wishes.*

Is her silence not enough?

How can I know it's hers, and not yours? And then he could feel her, cold and hurt. Exhausted, but not undone. *Eve?*

Her mental sigh was tired. *Six months you've ignored me, and now you call my name?*

I wasn't myself, Eve. It was the closest to the truth that he could offer her while he felt Thor's presence in the back of her mind. Soothing and calm. How could she not feel his touch?

I think you were more yourself than you realize. You did the same with Mia, after I refused you. It doesn't matter, Adam. It was all a mistake.

I wish I could explain—

Spare me that, please.

I need to see you, Eve.

She was silent, but he could feel her still, thoughtful and confused. Then determined. *I can't control where your business takes you. If it's here, and with me, so be it. But I won't change my mind, Adam, if it's my love that you seek, or a baby of my womb.*

I would never ask it of you.

So you say. And then she was gone from his mind as if she had never been there.

§

He made the arrangements necessary for the following morning. He would be at her side soon enough, and she wouldn't be able to avoid him. Not even if Thor interfered. He ground his teeth. How did Thor sit in her mind that way without calling attention to himself? How did she not realize he was there?

Thor had always seemed brutish to him. Quick tempered and easy to provoke. That he could maintain that level of contact with such subtlety made Adam uneasy. If Thor could do it to Eve, did he also do it to him? Monitor his thoughts? No. No, he would know. Adam would recognize the stench of that god anywhere, after all he had done to him.

He had to believe it, or else drive himself mad.

He shook his head and began to pack. Perhaps if he found Michael he could do more than destroy Sif. Perhaps with the angels he could drive these gods away at last. Or at least into submission.

The thought made him smile. To have them in his power would be ideal. There would be nothing that he couldn't do, nothing that he couldn't have. Eve wouldn't like it, he supposed. She never wanted to rule. But the gods kept themselves from her knowledge. What she did not know could hardly upset her. Besides, she would like less knowing that one sat in watch over her, over her very thoughts, following her from life to life. An invasion of privacy. An invasion of her mind.

Yes, she would like that much, much less. If he could just get her to realize it.

CHAPTER NINETEEN
520 AD
§

The Christians spilled over the empire like a tidal wave. Flooding everything, washing everything in their new faith, in white light and clean spirits and second comings. The words of the so-called prophet were twisted to appeal to the masses. Messages of love turned to hate, turned to persecution and condemnation of sects with differing interpretations. It became the state religion, and enforced by the state. Rome had fallen in the west, sacked by Adam's son Alaric. And it was dying in the east, though it did not know it yet. Those who still sacrificed to the Olympians did so privately, hidden and secret, and the once powerful pantheon suffered. Not just for the lack of worshippers. It was more, and so much less than that.

Athena had found him at the House of Lions. Woken him from a mead induced sleep deeper than he'd had in months. He rubbed his face and sat up at the edge of the bed, blinking at her where she stood, somehow capturing moonlight even with the shutters shut and fastened. They had a chapel here, and a priest, but still they kept his bed and his mead and didn't question the truths he told them. They put on the clothes of the Christian faith, as Eve had always worn the religion of the people around her, but they had their own beliefs. Their own God.

"Athena?" He was sure, somehow, that it was a dream. He hadn't seen much of her since Theodosius had made the empire Christian and the Olympians had begun fighting amongst themselves in earnest.

She dropped to her knees and hid her face against his thigh.

And wept.

He sighed and stroked her hair. Not a dream. And she was crying. How many times had he listened to Eve cry this way, and been unable to comfort her? And here was Athena, weeping in his lap. Needing this from him. Needing him.

She lifted her face, looked up at him, leaned up to kiss him. He held her face in his hands, felt the softness of her skin. Was he dreaming? He'd had too much mead. Too much to drink. Because he was kissing her back. Hard and deep and full. She tasted like wine, and she smelled like trees in bloom, earthy and rich, and he wanted more.

She pressed him back, pushed him down against the feather filled mattress. She pulled his shirt up. Her hands were cold. Her skin was cold. It had been so long since he'd had a woman. Since a woman had touched him this way. With want. With need. But Athena, it couldn't be Athena.

He groaned.

"Please, Thor," she whispered against his lips, then against his ear. So close he could feel her breath. "I just need a friend."

And he had promised to be one.

She was still so cold, lying naked next to him. He rubbed at her arms and her back and pulled the blanket up over her shoulder. He kissed the side of her head, above her temple. She slid her arm across his chest and then rolled away, curling up into a ball.

"My uncles are leaving," she said.

He propped himself up on an elbow and leaned over her, his other hand on her waist. It fit just below her ribcage. Her skin, even there, was cool to the touch. He pulled her back against his body, wrapping his arm around her, to warm her. "Your father, too?"

She sighed and turned her face away. "He hasn't decided. No one else has decided. They found another plane with a new world. My family has been broken by this, Thor. Ripped apart by the loss of Rome and our people."

"They've given up."

"You knew this would happen. That the Christians would overtake us. That we would lose everything."

He stroked her hair, kissed her temple, her jaw. "I guessed. And I am sorry to be right."

She rolled over and stared into his eyes. "When your people are caught by this web, will you stay?"

Yes. He would stay forever. As long as Eve was here. As long as Eve was here, this was his home, his place, where he was meant to be. Where he had to be. "I don't know, Athena. I don't know what Odin will do. What he'll want us to do."

She smiled. "Part of that is a lie, Odin-son."

"The part of it that should be." He kissed her forehead. And then her lips, red and still swollen. He studied her face, looking for any sign of discomfort, of pain, of distress. He had tried to be gentle. Tried not to hurt her, physically. But she was a warrior, and he wasn't sure she would admit if he'd caused her any pain. "I won't leave, Athena. Unless I have no other choice."

"Her. You won't leave her."

He kissed her again. So that he didn't have to answer. Because it wasn't something that should be said while he was lying in bed next to her, her bare skin pressed against his. Athena was wise, a patroness of reason, but he wouldn't press his luck. Wouldn't say the things he knew would hurt her.

She sighed and hid her face against his chest. "I should never have come here, like this. Never have asked this of you."

"Mm." He lay back. She wasn't nearly as cold anymore, and he liked the warmth of her body beside him. He tucked the blanket around her. He hadn't lit a fire in the hearth when he went to bed, and hadn't thought to light one after Athena had arrived, when he had been half asleep and half drunk. No wonder she had been chilled. "I don't think there's anything rational about regret."

"I just couldn't—" She stopped. He could feel her eyelashes brushing against his skin. "I didn't want to leave without knowing this."

The pressure against his chest was more than just the weight of her body. He swallowed and forced himself to breathe. To continue to breathe, but the room was suffocating. "You're going to go?"

"Would you ask me to stay?"

He was having trouble keeping air in his lungs. It went out of him as though he'd been kicked in the stomach. He knew what she wanted him to say. But she must know it wasn't something he could give.

"Not for me." She had to know. "For yourself, if it was what you wanted. If this world was what you wanted."

These weren't things that should be said at a moment like this. He wished he could sit up, turn his back to her and dress. That they were having this conversation in the grove, and not here. Not now. Not after he'd taken her virginity.

"But not for me, Athena."

She said nothing. The air felt thicker, heavier. She didn't move, but he almost wished she would. To prove she wasn't hurt. He was a beast to have let this happen. To have taken her this way, even if she had thought it was what she wanted. He drew breath as if to speak, but didn't know what else to say. He didn't want her to go. He didn't want her to leave. But it would be cruel to ask her to stay. Cruel to admit it, when he couldn't give her more. There was only one thing left, and it felt empty. Trite.

"I'm sorry," he told her.

She rolled away from him, onto her side, curling back into a ball. "I know."

He moved with her, wrapping her in his arms, and kissed her shoulder blade, where it began to curve toward her spine.

There was nothing more to say. So he held her and hid his face in her hair and hoped that his body said everything he couldn't.

§

When she asked him to come with her to Egypt, he didn't feel as though he could refuse. Ra looked old and tired, but when he saw Athena he rose from his seat, his eyes lighting. "My dear, what an unexpected pleasure."

His eyes shifted over her shoulder to Thor, and he shook his head just slightly. No, it wasn't what it appeared. This was not a trip of glad tidings. Athena kissed Ra's cheek and walked him back to his throne. She poured wine for all three of them.

"You've heard the news of my uncles?"

Thor accepted his cup and crossed to the window, leaning against the stone and staring out at the Nile. He wasn't sure why she wanted him here, so he simply listened as she spoke.

"I think my father will go. Perhaps not immediately, but eventually. They've offered you a place, Ra, if you wish it."

Ra grunted, and Thor felt his eyes on him again. "That is very kind of them. Have I you to thank for this thoughtfulness, Athena?"

"There's nothing left for you here, my friend. You have been forgotten, and it only grows worse. The auguries point to another prophet for the True God." That was news Athena had not shared with him, and Thor turned, his attention caught completely. "As if we had not been beaten enough. There will be nothing left of your people when he is done. There are so few left even now."

144

Ra raised his hand to her shoulder. Athena had knelt beside his chair, her eyes wide, beseeching. "As long as there is one, Athena, I will not abandon him. And when there are none, I will still care for the children and grandchildren of those who looked to me. It is what they have asked for and what I have promised. Being forgotten does not absolve me of responsibility toward my flock."

She raised her eyes to Thor, and he realized why she had wanted him there. But she could not have believed he would help her in this? Maybe it wasn't to convince Ra, but to witness her effort.

"My uncles have great need of your wisdom and your counsel. You would be invigorated by their attention. By their power."

"What would they need my counsel for when they have such a niece as you?" Ra asked. Athena bit her lip, and dropped her eyes. "Have you not decided to go? What would your father do without you?"

"Perhaps Athena welcomes the freedom of no longer having to hold her father's hand," Thor suggested.

Ra raised an eyebrow, looking up at him. "And what would you do without her loyal friendship, Thor? Without her help and kindness?"

He pressed his lips into a thin line. Perhaps the reason she had required his presence had nothing to do with Ra at all, and everything to do with forcing words from his mouth that she otherwise would not hear.

"Thankfully it looks as though I will still have you, my friend, even if Athena leaves our company."

Athena looked as though she had sipped something bitter from her wine glass, and Ra laughed. "Fairly spoken, Thor."

"Yes, he has quite the knack for escaping direct answers, doesn't he?" Athena stood and turned her back to him.

"Athena, you cannot think we would not miss you?" Ra sounded almost contrite. "But this choice is one you must make for yourself. Just as Thor and I must do the same."

"It seems so much easier for you," she said.

Thor shrugged. "Our people still worship us. The Christians have not reached them yet, and until they do my responsibilities are clear."

"And for my part," Ra said, "I am too old to go on to a new world, too attached to this world and the feckless people in it. And I confess to a great curiosity for what the angels will serve us next. I believe I would enjoy having a conversation with the True God if he ever chose to walk among us."

Athena studied Ra's face. She said nothing aloud, but Thor thought something passed between them. Ra appeared to incline his head just slightly, and Athena looked away again. "Perhaps I should stay, if only to be sure you are kept in wine."

Ra smiled, and Thor felt a relief more intense than anything but the love he had for Eve. If he had not thought it would hurt her, he would have taken her back to his bed and showed her how happy he was that she would stay. And she would now, he was sure of it. She would not abandon Ra. She would not abandon either of them.

"When my father allows me to return to Asgard, and I have built my hall, you will both be welcome there."

"I would be very interested in seeing your Asgard, Thor, and this tree of your mother's. But in the meantime, you and Athena are both welcome in my home for as long as it remains standing."

Athena's forehead creased into troubled lines. "As long as it remains standing may not be as long as we wish."

"Then perhaps we will impose on the House of Lions," Ra said. "Isis tells me their lands are beautiful."

Thor grimaced. "As long as they remember."

"You will remember for them, Thor. As you have done, and will continue to do." Ra raised his glass. "To better days and long memories."

Thor raised his glass, his eyes on Athena. And then he drank deep.

CHAPTER TWENTY
Present

§

Garrit swore colorfully in French, speaking so quickly Eve caught only half of it. She placed her hand on his knee. A muted plea for him to remember himself. And Alex, who could wake up any moment. The last thing she wanted was for her son to hear his father cursing so violently. He stood up, walking a few rows away.

"I'm so sorry," she said to Horus. She didn't understand why Garrit was so upset, and while he had stopped swearing, she could still feel him simmering with anger.

The brown man was leaning back in his seat again, watching her husband and seemingly trying not to smile. "No, no. No need to apologize."

"I knew I remembered you," Garrit said. It was somewhere between a whisper and a growl. "I knew it."

"Garrit." She grabbed him by the arm and forced him into a seat. "*Qu'est-ce que t'as?*" *What is your problem?* But he only shook his head in response and glared at Horus.

"I apologize for causing your husband such distress, *madame*. I suppose I won't be needing directions to the House of Lions after all."

Garrit swore again. "As if you didn't know."

She frowned at him until he looked away, then she glanced at Horus. "How do you know Lars?"

"We worked together." Garrit snorted, but Horus ignored it. "As I said, he is a son to me. And he cares very much for your family. They have been a home to him, away from home."

"Yes, I'm sure it's been a very fruitful relationship for him," Garrit said. "What does he want, then? Are you here to beg me to reconsider?"

"On the contrary, *monsieur*. I'm here to offer my services instead." He smiled that knowing smile again. "You can hardly be threatened by a man as old as I am."

Eve said nothing, staring at Horus. None of this made any sense to her. Did this mean that Lars Owen had been the man who was in love with her? She had barely spoken with him. Barely even met him. And Horus had said Lars considered them family.

"I'd be even less threatened by Minerva, if I was to be given a choice in the matter." Garrit said. "Not that it matters. Things are well in hand."

Horus raised an eyebrow. "Perhaps we could discuss this with your aunt and father. You risk too much, Garrit, by becoming complacent."

Alex stirred, then sat up, rubbing his eyes. Garrit took the banana he had set aside and peeled it, slicing it into pieces for their son. Eve wasn't fooled. His anger and frustration had blossomed again, fed by Horus's soft spoken suggestion. Alex crammed a piece of the banana into his mouth, his eyes wide as he stared at the stranger.

She had to know. Even if it upset Garrit further. "Lars is my family?"

Horus's gaze shifted to her. His smile thinned, but the affection didn't leave his features. "I'm afraid the answer to that question is not a simple one, and now is neither the time nor the place to have the conversation that would follow."

She nodded and removed the cellophane from the sandwich Garrit had brought her. It was probably the most direct answer she was going to get. And it made perfect sense. To explain the relationship to the House of Lions would be nearly impossible. Technically, she supposed Owen, her son Owen from whom she guessed Lars was descended, would be half brother to the sons she had born Ryam. That would make Garrit a very distant cousin by blood. She grimaced at the mess it all made in her mind. She had been born too many times to make sense of the relationships she had left behind in each life, never mind reconciling them to each other.

"I suppose there isn't any way to talk you out of coming?" Garrit said, finally.

"Would you give up, if you were him?" Horus asked.

Garrit's expression became grim. He didn't answer aloud, but Eve heard his mind whisper, *never.*

Horus nodded as if he heard it too, then rested his head against the back of his seat and closed his eyes. She watched him sleep, and the only person who spoke the rest of the trip was Alex. Even worse, it was the toddler who made the most sense.

§

Juliette took Alex from her arms the minute they stepped through the door. *"Mon garçon!* How did you enjoy your trip?" She kissed both the baby's cheeks, then Eve's and Garrit's, and swept away again, carrying Alex off with her.

Horus came to stand beside Eve, smiling politely. She frowned, not sure what to do with the man, and still not sure why he had come.

"My mother-in-law, Juliette," she offered by way of introduction. For lack of anything better. "She takes her grandmothering very seriously."

Horus smiled. "I'm sure she does it very well. Your son is very lucky to have so much family to love him."

"This is my father, René." Garrit said, interrupting them. "I'm afraid my aunt will not be here until the weekend. In the meantime, perhaps we could speak in my study?"

"Of course." Horus nodded politely to Eve, and excused himself.

She watched him walk away with Garrit and René until Juliette came back out with Alex on her hip. "Do not worry yourself, overmuch, Abby. They are your sons. They only do what they do to protect you."

"It almost makes me wish I had born more daughters." She shook her head. "If you don't mind keeping Alex, I think I'd like to take a walk. Stretch my legs after the trip."

Juliette laughed. "Go. I have missed my grandson, it's no bother."

It had been a long time since she had walked the land. Ryam had allowed her a significant amount of freedom until just before the birth of their first child, and she had gone riding almost every day. When he asked her not to, to stay close to the manor unless he was with her, she had not made much of a fuss about it. But she had missed riding. Had missed packing herself a lunch and picnicking in a convenient tree, with a view of the manor and the fields and the mountains.

Garrit kept horses still, beautiful animals with lineages as complex as his own, but he rarely had time to go riding anymore. Juliette did, however. Every morning, often with René. She smiled to herself. Juliette was the kind of woman you couldn't help but admire. Everything she did, she did well, and the things she didn't do were very few.

She skirted one of the fields and took a dirt path, only realizing where she was going when she glanced up and saw the trees. The poor trees which had received more than their fair share of lightning strikes these past years. They were lucky there hadn't been a fire. Even luckier the manor hadn't been struck as repeatedly.

One tree in particular looked pathetically sorry. It was split down the middle and scarred with burn marks in so many places she wasn't sure how it had survived. She touched its trunk and felt the life within it still, saw the little bits of new growth from the previous summer. It was an old tree, and it ached.

She rested her forehead against the rough, pocked bark, and closed her eyes, opening herself to the forest, to the land around her, sifting through the presences that were familiar. The dogs in their kennels, the horses in the stable, the sheep that were still kept to graze as well as for wool and mutton. She remembered a time when there had been lions here. And babies raised playing with cubs. But the others had never been easy around the great cats, and Eve had been forced to send them away, fearing for what would happen to the pride after her death. But her sons and grandsons, Reu's sons and grandsons, had not given up the name. They were still marked by the claws of the lions they had played with as children.

The presence of the people burned even more brightly than the animals. She felt Garrit's agitation, René's determined calm, Juliette's complete trust in her husband and son, and Alex's pleasure to be among familiar people and things.

And then she felt someone else, behind her. She didn't turn, though, not wanting to startle them. Whoever it was. She frowned at the feelings she couldn't name that came from them. Him, she decided. It was a man. A man trying to force himself not to feel.

"I know you're there," she said softly. "But I don't know why you're hiding."

There was a muttered curse in a language she thought might have been Icelandic, but it was different somehow, too. She had a feeling she knew who it would be before the hand touched her shoulder. She turned.

Lars dropped his hand at once, but she rubbed the spot where he had touched her and frowned up at him. "What are you doing out here?"

He studied her face in a way that made her cheeks flush hot, and brought memories back to her mind. The way Thorgrim had looked at her. It was as though she was water and he had crossed a desert to find her. Lars lifted his hand again, and it brushed her hair. A leaf. He showed it to her and then let it fall to the ground. But she couldn't take her eyes from him. He was so immense. Broad shouldered and perfectly muscled. She couldn't imagine what he did for a living to maintain that physique.

He cleared his throat. "Forgive me. I often walk these woods. René was kind enough to allow me that freedom, when it belonged to him. I thought this might be my last opportunity to do so for some time."

"Why?" He looked so much like Thorgrim. It made her throat close. And the way he looked at her didn't help anything.

Then he smiled, and she pressed her hand against her chest, because even though his hair was the wrong color, the familiarity of the expression, even after all these years, caused her a physical pain. Like something had stabbed her in the heart. *Oh, Adam. Is this what it feels like every time you look at me?* She didn't want to hear his answer, but she felt him there in her mind, looking through her eyes. It was dizzying, and she stumbled back against the tree.

Lars's hands, huge and warm, caught her around the waist. "Are you all right?"

She felt Adam's withdrawal. It left behind a sorrow that made her head ache along with her heart. She steadied herself. One hand against the tree, the other gripping Lars's arm. Until she realized he was still holding her, looking at her with concern, and she pulled her hand away and dropped her eyes.

"I'm fine. Just a headache, suddenly."

"You should get back to the house," Lars said. And even his voice was Thorgrim's. "Your husband would never let you hear the end of it if you passed out in the woods."

It wasn't helping her dizziness to listen to him. The memories of her past overlapping her present. He had Thorgrim's eyes too. The resemblance was uncanny when he stood this close to her. Now that she knew what it was. What to look for. She couldn't not see Thorgrim, and she found herself reaching for him, pressing her palm against his cheek.

He closed his eyes, and she felt his jaw clench, and then his fingers closed around her wrist as if he meant to pull her hand away. But he didn't, and his eyes opened again, and stared into hers like mirrors. Mirrors for the agony even the sight of him caused. And the way her heart raced with his touch. She wondered if his did too.

"You're my family," she heard herself say. "One of Owen's. One of mine."

"Yes." His voice was rough. Thick with emotion. And when he spoke again it was almost a whisper. "I'm yours."

She couldn't look away. And his other hand, the one still on her waist, moved to the small of her back. His grip on her wrist had softened, his hand covering hers, and he pulled it from his face, holding it against his chest. She imagined she could feel his heartbeat then. Hard and fast.

And then her whole body exploded in blinding pain. She heard herself screaming, and the echo of Adam's agony from so far away, and everything went dark.

CHAPTER TWENTY-ONE
Future

Adam pushed open the door and stopped, staring at Eve. Drinking her in. His body knew he'd been away from her for six months, even if his mind didn't, and his arms ached for her. His hands twitched to hold her, to stroke her hair, to frame her face and feel the fire that he knew would be there when he touched her skin.

There was someone else in the shop. A tall woman with dark hair and a face so beautiful it almost hurt to look at. He cursed under his breath. He should have realized that Thor wouldn't let him have this moment. Wouldn't let him be alone with her if he could stop it. But he didn't know if it was to protect their secrets, or Eve's heart.

Athena raised her eyes to his and didn't smile. *You should not have come.*

Then Eve turned and he didn't care about the goddess, or her thoughts. Except that he wondered how Eve didn't recognize her from that day so long ago. He shook his head and offered her a smile. Nothing charming. Nothing artful. There was too much pain in her eyes, in her face, for him to behave in any other way but honestly.

"Can I help you with something?" she asked. As if he were any other customer or maybe some stranger she didn't know.

He tried not to let it hurt. "I hope so."

She stared at him for a long moment and then turned away again, picking up a box and carrying it behind the counter. The movements lacked her usual grace, and the box thumped heavily on the floor.

"What do you want, Adam? Why are you here? After everything?"

"I wanted to apologize." When he said it out loud, it sounded small and weak. "I didn't mean to hurt you."

You hurt her more by coming. Why won't you let her live?

He didn't look at the goddess. *This is none of your affair. If Thor has something to say to me, let him do it himself.*

"You owe me nothing, Adam." Eve said, her back to him still. "Live your life. Do what you want to do. I'm glad you moved on."

It was a lie, but he could tell she wanted to believe it. She wanted to think it was the truth. "I thought that I could. I thought I could walk away from you." The words came to him without conscious thought, but he knew he meant them. She glanced over her shoulder and he thought her expression had softened. "I can't."

You made us promises, Adam. We don't forget. Thor's personal feelings aside, we have an agreement.

"I told you." Eve said. "My answer is still the same. I won't risk the world."

He ignored Athena, concentrating instead on Eve. She had to understand. This wasn't about the godchild. "I'm not asking you to. I won't ask it of you."

"But you're here." She spun and faced him. "You're here, anyway. Don't you see that it's the same?"

Athena's laugh in his mind was derogatory. Mocking. *Hera was right about her; she is discerning.*

Leave, Athena. "No." He stepped toward Eve, even as he felt Athena move away. The bell chimed as she left the store. Of course she wasn't gone. Not really. Just as Thor's physical absence didn't mean he wasn't listening. Watching. Waiting. "It isn't the same."

He had come around the counter now, and she had backed up against the shelves behind it. Trapped between the shelves, the wall, the countertop and him. But there was no fear in her face, as there once might have been and her eyes never left his.

"And yet . . ." She raised her hand to his chest and it lit a fire in his heart.

Sif's golden touch had been nothing to this. He thought maybe he could understand Thor's obsession, to have something so pale in comparison. He cupped her cheek.

"This isn't why I came, Evey. But I can't pretend it doesn't exist."

"You've apologized. I've accepted. If that's all, then you can go."

He shook his head. "I wanted to ask you something. For something. I need to know what you know, Eve."

She stared at him, waiting, her hand still against his chest, over his heart, warm and comforting. "About what?"

He raised his other hand to her face, framing it. It had been a long time since he had been given reason to invade a mind. A long time since he'd rummaged through memories for the things he sought. He didn't want to hurt her, and he knew that it would. It was never a pleasant experience, no matter how delicate the touch and he hoped she wouldn't make him try.

"I need to find Michael."

She pulled his hands from her face and frowned. There was a flash of fear in her eyes, quickly repressed. "Michael? For what?"

"I need to speak with him. I need to know the truth."

"The truth." She laughed, bitter and broken. "I've told you the truth. He won't give you what you want, Adam. He can't give you permission for this. It's God's law. He'd just as soon kill you as anything else."

"Do you know how to find him?"

"This is why you came?" She dropped her eyes, and her hands fell to her sides. "You're always looking for something, aren't you? You're never satisfied with what you've been given. There's always something more. Something you have to have. Something you have to know. Truth. Wisdom. Power. Understanding. The Fruit, the Garden. When will you learn, Adam?"

"It isn't what you think, Eve. This isn't about any of that. I need to speak to him, that's all."

He hated the hurt in her eyes when she looked up at him. She shook her head. "I'm sorry. I don't know how to find him." She frowned again, and her eyes lost focus. "Maybe my family knows, but I don't think they would tell me. One of the many things Ryam made them swear to keep to themselves, perhaps."

He saw it in her mind's eye. The image of the man by the smoking tree, and he grimaced. Of course she would bring Thor into this, without even realizing it. He was never far from her thoughts, from her life.

"You're sure you don't know? He didn't leave you some way to reach him, to contact him?"

"No." She shook her head again. "No. They made it clear they wouldn't help me any further than they had. Honestly, I prayed that I'd never see them again, after we left the Garden." Her face paled and she shivered. "I never understood how you didn't fear them."

He smiled faintly. "Arrogance, I would imagine."

"Don't you know?"

"It was a long time ago." He shrugged and then stepped back. "I guess I'll have to start somewhere else then. I just thought perhaps you'd know something I didn't."

She was looking at him oddly, her forehead creased. "I don't understand, Adam. You knew them better than any of us. Reu told me you walked with God. You were his favorite. You knew the angels before the rest of us were even thought of."

"Yes." He pulled himself away from her. He didn't like the way she was looking at him. As if he should have known. He *should've* known. But there was nothing he could do about that. Not without hurting her. He turned away. "Until you. You're their favorite now."

"I don't think the angels care about humanity one way or the other. Any of us. Maybe especially not us. Michael isn't exactly reasonable. I don't know what you think you can accomplish by going to them."

No. The angels didn't care. But the gods did. They lined up to protect her three deep. Except for Sif. And who else? He wished he knew.

He turned back and grabbed her by the arm, pulling her against him and looking into her eyes. Was Thor there? Inside her now? Listening to every word? She jerked back almost at once, but he didn't let go, instead allowing himself to dream. Imagining how hot her skin would be against his, how sweet and soft her lips would be.

She gasped, her lips parting and her eyes widening, and he held her and let her feel it with him. The dream. The desire. The lust. Her eyes closed and she turned her face from his, as if by looking away she could stop it, but she no longer struggled to free herself and her body softened against his.

"I would give you everything of myself, Eve. Pour myself into you, heart and soul until you were filled to overflowing, glowing with love and life, whether Michael forbid it or not. And I would still face him, still search him out to stand before him even if it meant my head."

There was a hiss deep in the back of his mind, or maybe it was hers? He couldn't tell anymore because he was kissing her and she was kissing him back with a wantonness that shook him. All it would take was a nudge. The slightest of pushes. He felt her hit the wall, and was dimly aware of the contents of a box tipping and falling over them in a shower of cartons and cigarettes. He raised his hand to her face, trailing his fingers along her jaw and into her hair as her lips parted. But there was a dampness where there shouldn't have been. She shuddered, sobbed against his mouth.

He pulled away. "Don't cry, Eve, please."

She shrank from him, and her legs collapsed a heartbeat before he could catch her. The box above rained more cigarettes into her hair as she sank to the floor against the wall. He crouched before her, but she wouldn't look at him.

"You have to go."

"I can't leave you like this."

She took a shuddering breath and then another. "Like this is the only way you can leave me."

"Eve—" but he didn't even know what he meant to say. He had hoped that if he kissed her, if she responded, it would bring Michael down on them both, but there was no sign. No sign but the hiss that had turned into a growl, and the rumble of thunder in the distance that he knew meant Thor, not the angel he sought.

"Leave!"

It was snarl and sob and it startled him into stepping back, even while she cried harder.

Adam! Thor's voice was a roar.

Quickly, please. I don't know if I can keep him out of the store. Athena had appeared and was pulling him away by the arm, her grip firm and fast. Eve didn't even notice. *You should not have tempted him this way, Adam. Not so soon after Sif's betrayal. He'll want to kill you, and he so rarely listens to reason when it comes to his wife.* He wasn't sure whether it was Eve she meant, or Sif, but she sighed. *I should never have left.*

And then he caught sight of a man through the glass, his features blurred though it did not stop his eyes from piercing through to Adam's soul. At last, at last! But Athena didn't slow, even when they were out of the shop and the man watched with narrowed eyes as she towed him past.

"No!" he struggled in her grasp, but she was a goddess and a warrior besides and he had no hope of breaking free if she would not let him. "Let go, Athena, please! It's him! Michael! I must speak to him, I must—"

The Chorus roared in his head, even more loudly than Thor's fury.

Before he fell into the darkness, he prayed that the angel had spared Eve.

CHAPTER TWENTY-TWO
665 AD
§

"Brother!"

They had been dozing in the meadow, watching the goats in exchange for their beds, but Athena sat up at once, frowning toward the shout of their uninvited guest, still hidden from view.

When Thor had arrived with the other two gods, the House of Lions had been quite accommodating. It had been prudent to leave the African coast with the rise of the second prophet, though Thor hated leaving Eve behind when her brother was so near. As far as he could tell, Adam had fathered this new prophet, and then abandoned him. Eve was in Antioch. She had mothered a bishop.

"I thought we had protected these lands," Athena said.

"It's only Baldur," Thor assured her, chasing off a goat which had become interested in her blanket. "Probably because Loki could not come. My brother rarely leaves Asgard."

He didn't call out. Baldur would find them easily enough on his own, and he had no wish to hurry this. It had been more than five hundred years since he had been exiled. His return would wait a few more hours.

"What does he want?" Athena asked.

He scratched his jaw. He'd grown in a beard when he had begun goat-herding. She had found it absurd at first, but agreed that if he was to continue haunting Eve's steps, a periodic change in his appearance might be called for. "I expect he comes on behalf of my father. Probably because I've been traveling with you."

Her lips twisted, rueful. "Then your father will be as disappointed as I have been."

Athena had been upset by her father's decision to leave along with her uncles and Thor had not wished to deny her what comfort he could give. Once they had begun sleeping together, it had been difficult to find a reason to stop, as often as they were in company. Ra had been quietly amused by the development, though he said nothing. Thor saw it in his eyes, and something else. A longing, quiet and rueful, but unmistakable all the same. The old god was directing plans for irrigation of the fields from the mountain stream, and re-engineering the indoor plumbing for the manor, leaving them to their own devices.

"Are you truly disappointed by me?"

She sighed and lay back on the blanket, looking up at the sky. "I did not truly expect anything more. I only wished for it."

He picked pieces of grass from her hair. "Will you come to Asgard? Brave Sif's wrath?"

"Sif does not frighten me, Thor. If you wish for me to come, for whatever reason, I will. For a time, at least. Assuming your father will allow it."

He did not have to tell her Odin would be pleased. He did not have to tell her that bringing her with him would reinforce the false truth of their relationship, convincing Odin that he was no longer under Eve's spell. But his feelings had not altered, and he still sat in the back of her mind, listening, watching, waiting. Loving her.

Athena gave an exasperated sigh. "You think so loudly, it is a wonder Baldur does not hear."

AMALIA DILLIN

"The Aesir do not have the same strength, on the whole. There are exceptions, of course. Odin can make his thoughts known when he wishes to, and Frigg and Loki also. But reading minds has never been within their power. That was my gift alone."

"Odd." Her brow furrowed and she studied his face. "I always knew you were unique among your people, Thor, but I did not realize how extensive the differences. I think Ra is right, and you are your mother's son more than your father's."

"Brother?" Baldur called again.

Thor rolled his eyes. He could hear him now, branches snapping beneath his booted feet as he climbed. And as much as he would have preferred to continue the conversation with Athena, Thor had no wish for Baldur to overhear him.

"Here, brother! Among the goats."

It was only a moment later before Baldur appeared, fighting his way through the scraggly brush and rocks. When he saw Thor, he smiled broadly. "My brother, I bring good news!"

Thor grimaced, warding off a goat when it tried to sniff at Athena's hair. "My father welcomes me with open arms? Does he have need of me for the information I've collected these centuries? Perhaps just my strength, to put to some uprising. Or does he welcome me, but still mistrust my judgment? If he thinks I will follow his commands blindly again, it will not be long before he regrets my homecoming."

Athena sat up, placing a hand on his arm. Thor knew that he sounded bitter, but he could not help it. The wound had been deep, and it still stung. He would never trust his father again, could not even trust his own memories of joy while Sif had been his wife. All of it a lie.

"Do not mind your brother, Baldur; he misses his home, that is all." Athena smiled. "You are welcome, here."

His brother's smile faded, and Thor saw sympathy in his eyes. He rose and extended a hand to him, forcing his scowl away. It was not Baldur he was angry with, after all. It had not been Baldur who had questioned him, doubted him, accused him of not having control of

162

his own mind. Baldur had not used him for millennia upon millennia, wearing the fabric of his honor into a threadbare cloak.

Baldur clasped hands with him and grinned. "It will be good to have you home again, Thor. You are to be welcomed with a feast greater than any we have had in your absence. You were sorely missed by our father."

Thor grunted, but did not argue. Of course Odin had missed him. Loki made a poor lap dog, and Frigg would never have allowed Baldur's abuse. "And will my father allow me to invite my guests?"

Baldur bowed to Athena. "Odin extends a personal invitation to your companions. He invites them to stay within his own hall, to be fed at his own hearth. He is especially interested in meeting you, Athena. Your reputation precedes you, and he is much impressed by the stories told of your wisdom and power."

Athena smiled politely, but Thor did not miss the way her eyes narrowed. She was not deceived by Odin's flattery, even delivered with Baldur's sincerity. "I would, of course, be happy to meet your father, Baldur, and I am honored by his generous offer of hospitality."

"Then we shall go on at once!"

"Not quite, Brother. I must discharge my duty to these people, first. Return to our father and tell him we will arrive tomorrow. I feel certain that Ra will choose to accompany us as well."

Baldur nodded gravely. "Of course." But Thor could tell that he wondered why he had lowered himself to goat-herding in the mountains. He was simply too polite to ask. "Until then."

Athena waited until he had disappeared back into the brush, and then the trees down the mountain before she frowned and turned to him. "Why did you not invite him home with us?"

Thor shook his head. "I would prefer not to explain who these people are until after I have received my father's forgiveness. In truth, I'd prefer not to explain them at all."

She pursed her lips, but said nothing more.

§

Though he looked for her, Sif was not present at the feast and nor was Loki. Thor could only imagine this was his father's way of smoothing his homecoming, and being sure Athena was not chased off. Odin was painfully pleased to meet her, almost exuberant in his greeting and welcome.

She cast him a startled look as Odin took her by the arm and led her away to find refreshments. *What do I say?*

He smiled. *I do not think you could offend him if you tried, Athena. Not today.*

And then Odin began asking her questions, and she could spare no further attention for him. Thor took advantage of his father's distraction to step out of the hall with Ra, walking with him to the world-tree. The tree of his mother.

"Ahh . . ." Ra's eyes lit when he saw it. "It is as I thought."

Thor seated him on the stone bench beneath it and went to the tree, placing his hand against the rough bark of its trunk and feeling in himself the peace of being home for the first time in centuries. "It came with us through five other planes. Five cycles, as we call it, though I hope the fifth was the last. I would hate to see this world laid to waste in Ragnarok."

Ra nodded, but he had eyes only for the tree and its golden fruit. "I do not think the True God would allow it. He seems to have a plan for this world that we are not privy to. Certainly he is amassing a great wealth of power through his Christians."

"And Islam as well, now. It is only a matter of time for us, too, though I do not know if my father realizes it yet." Thor dropped his hand from the tree, sitting down beside Ra on the bench. "And so, you meet what is left of my mother."

Ra smiled. "Do you believe her to be dead, then?"

"I don't know." He shrugged and looked back at the tree. "I

dreamed about her once. That she wandered the planes the way I did the world. But if she is alive, why has she not come to me? Does she not wish to know her son? Have I displeased her in some way?"

"Perhaps it is not yet time. Perhaps you are not meant to know her, or perhaps she watches over you, even now, as you do for Eve, and you do not know it. The gods work in mysterious ways, Thor. But we must keep faith, or how can we expect our people to trust?"

"When I was a boy, I used to pray to her. I used to believe she was there, somewhere. Watching. And then I grew up, and Odin married Frigg. Father suggested it was ungrateful of me to look to a woman I had never known instead of the mother he provided for all of us in Frigg."

"But Frigg herself has told you to remember your mother."

"And I have wandered and wondered and searched and waited for something to be revealed. But this is what I have. This tree is all I have."

"Not all, surely. You have been given many gifts. From whom, if not the spirit of your mother? Certainly your love for Eve was not Odin's to give or Odin's wish."

"My love for Eve is an eternity of heartbreak. You were right that I would have done better to love Athena. I wish every moment she is in my arms that I could give her that. That my heart could forsake Eve."

"Athena has always known the limitations of your relationship with her. She did not enter into this lightly."

"Does it make it right?"

"It does not make it wrong."

Thor grunted, staring at the tree, golden fruits winking in the moonlight. Athena deserved better. Much more than he could give her. "Right or wrong, it isn't enough. But I have needed her friendship, Ra. And yours."

"We will have need of each other yet, if the world continues to turn back to its God and away from us. Perhaps I will move into the East. Buddha would not turn me away, and his followers are still strong.

Perhaps with my help they will remain so. And it is warmer there, for my old bones."

"You will not return to Egypt?" Thor frowned, helping Ra back to his feet. If they absented themselves much longer, someone would notice. "Your temple still stands. Your home awaits."

"We shall see." Ra straightened, turning away from the tree with reluctance. His expression was thoughtful. "The way the new faiths have spread, I worry that my presence may do more harm than good. That if my people feel my Grace, and turn to me, it will bring persecution. I would not wish that for them on my account."

"I would like to believe that is what Zeus was thinking when he made his choice to go."

Ra laughed. "You would give Zeus and his brothers more credit than they deserve. And look! Athena has found us." He took her by the hand and kissed her cheek. "The tree is just like your step-mother's, Athena. But older."

She frowned slightly, and slipped her arm through Thor's. "A fascinating coincidence."

"Is it not?" Ra chuckled to himself. "I think I shall go see your father, Thor. Odin and I have much to discuss."

Athena watched him go and shook her head. "Your father is well into his cups. I do not think Ra will get much sense from him. He calls for you, Thor. The guest of honor should not slip away."

He pulled her against him and kissed her forehead. "My father has lived without me for five centuries. He cannot have missed me so deeply that he will not live without me for such a small moment now. I owe you my thanks, Athena."

She sighed. He wasn't sure if it was contented, or unhappy, but she lifted her face and pulled his head down to kiss him.

And then the door to the hall opened with a swell of laughter and noise, and Odin bellowed his name. Thor growled at the interruption, but Athena only laughed and pulled him by the hand back into the banquet.

CHAPTER TWENTY-THREE
Present

Darkness, and pain, and voices speaking with such intensity it would have been more of a relief if they had been shouting at one another. Every time Eve drifted toward consciousness the pain rose up and forced her back into the blackness. Sometimes she thought she was in a hospital, could hear the whir and beeping of monitors, and her mother's voice and Mia, and she wondered where Garrit was that he would let her be taken there. But then she was at home too, listening to Garrit argue in whispers with a voice that she didn't even want to identify in her sleep, and Juliette reminding them to leave the room if they were going to fight, in a way that made Eve think it was a constant background noise.

She dreamed of Reu and Ryam, and Adam suffering. She dreamed of Thorgrim and Lars. She dreamed of a stolen kiss in a meadow and a man whose eyes blazed white as he squeezed the life from a man's body in her defense. She dreamed of a man who sat across a fire and made promises of fortune and wealth and power, glowing with lightning. In her dreams they blended together, and then Adam's pain overwhelmed her and washed it all away.

She woke up in her bedroom. Her head throbbing and a shooting pain in her legs, and one of her arms. She groaned, and raised the arm that didn't hurt to her face, shielding her eyes from the light. A hand touched her, and the shooting pains became a dull ache. More phantom than anything else, though it did nothing for her head, or the echoes of fractured memories in her mind.

She opened her eyes and saw it was Horus's hand on her arm. Garrit was asleep beside her on the bed, as if he had been watching her while she slept, and Lars stood by the window, his expression completely blank. She could feel the effort it took him to keep it that way, and the relief coming from him in waves made her wince.

"What happened?" she asked. It was almost a croak, her throat was so dry. Lars crossed to the side of the bed and poured a glass of water. Horus helped her to sit up, and she sipped from it while Lars held it to her lips. It was like silk to her parched mouth, but he didn't let her drink more than a few sips. "How long was I out?"

Horus's gaze flickered to Garrit, and her husband sighed and dropped into a deeper sleep. "Four days," he finally admitted. "How are you feeling?"

She kept her eyes from Lars, relieved to be able to answer Horus, and put off thinking about what had nearly happened in the woods. "I don't know. I ache all over."

Horus nodded as if he had expected it. "It's good that Lars found you."

"Yes." She glanced at Garrit. Even in sleep his brow was furrowed with concern. She wanted to ask what had happened, but she had a feeling she already knew and they wouldn't have the answer. She didn't want Lars to tell her, because she could remember dimly the feeling of his arms as he caught her before she fell to the ground and the blackness took her. And Adam's pain echoing in her mind. She had screamed with him.

Something had happened to her brother. But if she was awake, that meant that he was too. At least it hadn't been the angel, then, though after Adam's profession of love, she wouldn't have been surprised if Michael had found him.

"You should be fine, now," Horus said. "Though you seem to have some bruising." His cool fingers touched a ragged line of angry purple on her arm. The one that ached.

She stared at it in confusion. Was the headache a bruise on her head then? Where Adam's skull had been cracked? Her ribs were aching too, now that she was sitting up. Just how many bones had her brother broken? And how?

"Thank you," she mumbled. And she glanced at Lars then, in spite of herself, remembering the wedding when Adam had been knocked unconscious and she had gone into the dark with him. It must have been Lars then, that she had heard speaking. Lars who had knocked Adam out and left before she had seen him. His eyes were tortured. Because of her pain? It was hardly a conversation she could have with Garrit sleeping beside her.

"I'll have the kitchen make you some soup," Horus said, leaving them alone in the room.

With the absence of his touch, light as it had been, the pain came back. She felt tears rise in her eyes as she fought the agony of each breath she took. Had Adam broken his ribs, or just cracked them? By all that was good and holy, it hurt. How could his pain hurt her this badly? How had it never happened before now? But she knew the answer to that, too. They hadn't been this close to one another since the Garden, and she'd felt his pain then as her own, too. The kick to his ribs throbbing in her own side. Since then, she'd never reached for him, never opened her mind to him so widely. Too widely, it seemed.

Lars pulled an armchair to the side of the bed, sitting on the edge of it and leaning forward. She strangled a sob, and he frowned, reaching out to wipe away the tears that spilled down her cheek toward her ears. The pain dulled again with his touch, and he sighed when she clutched at his hand.

She held on so tightly she worried she might be hurting him, but she couldn't bring herself to let go or loosen her hold, in case he pulled away and the pain washed over her again. "It hurts."

"I know." He engulfed her hand in both of his. "I'm sorry. We tried giving you medication, but it didn't seem to help the pain. Horus suggested something to numb your mind, but we couldn't be sure it wouldn't do more harm than good."

It was a struggle to follow his words with her hand in his. The pain was muted, but his touch was as distracting now as it had been in the woods. "Horus is a doctor?"

Lars shrugged. "I think he would be called a homeopathic herbalist these days."

"Oh." Why did Lars affect her this way? She was married. She loved Garrit. She loved her family. But Lars was family too. Thorgrim's descendant. That was all it was. Just a fascination with the similarity. That was all. "I wasn't in the hospital at all, was I?"

"No." Lars frowned. "We didn't think it would be prudent. Physically, there's nothing wrong with you. And there was no way to explain the bruising to a doctor. You understand what's happened?"

She sighed. She didn't understand anything anymore. "I don't know. I think so. Do you?"

"In theory. Though it isn't exactly something that family lore explains. It's nothing you told us about."

"Family lore." She looked at his face, and saw the concern in his expression. The anxiety he had been trying to hide. "What did Thorgrim tell Owen? What did Owen pass on?"

"Enough." Lars seemed to stare at their hands where they rested on top of the blanket. "Enough to know the truth. To share a vow of protection with this family."

Garrit shifted, and Lars pulled his hands from hers before his eyes opened. He saw her awake and relief washed over her again. But not enough to block the pain that swelled, and Eve couldn't quite suppress the cry of shock as it rocked through her bones.

"Are you all right, Abby?" He sat up. "What's wrong?"

She grabbed Garrit's hand, but it didn't help the pain. Why was it Lars's touch that made it dull, and not Garrit's? Horus entered the room then, with a bowl of soup on a tray. He set it down and crossed to her at once, taking her free hand. It was like a balm, and she could breathe again.

"What the hell did my brother do to himself?" It came out with more anger than she'd meant, but the pain had been jarring.

Garrit held her hand tightly, his face grim. "Your father said he was hit by a bus. Mia is a wreck, as you can imagine, with a newborn to take care of and Adam in the hospital. Your mother is with her."

She stared at him. Just stared. She didn't know what to say. "A bus?"

"The doctors say it's a miracle he lived."

Lars snorted. He had retreated to the window again, and Horus had taken the seat by the bed. Still holding her hand and keeping the pain at bay. She was grateful for that, though she didn't know how he did it. Pressure points? Eastern medicine? She wasn't sure she cared as long as it helped.

"I don't understand. How did it even happen?"

"No one is really sure." Garrit searched her face. "When he carried you in, I thought you were dead, Abby."

She freed her hand from his to stroke his face. Her husband. The man she loved. "You know I can't die like that."

He shook his head. "We don't know anything about this thing that happens between the two of you. For every broken bone he has, you share a bruise, Abby, and pain. You would scream and cry in your sleep. You didn't even know where you were half the time. You kept asking why I let you be taken to the hospital." And she could see it had hurt him that she hadn't realized she was home, that even ill, she might have thought he would allow something like that to happen. She didn't tell him she had been in Adam's head. It wouldn't have made him feel any better.

"Delirium does strange things," Horus interrupted. "The mind plays tricks. Even so, perhaps you can tell me what to give you for the pain, now, Abby? Would anti-psychotics help? Or perhaps some kind of sedative?"

"Anti-psychotics make me awful," she said, glad she wouldn't have to explain how she had been back and forth from Adam's mind to her own. "I get lost in the past. Lose track of what life I'm living. I don't hear anyone else, but I can't find myself either."

Garrit's face had turned gray. "How—?"

She didn't answer, didn't meet his eyes. That had been too horrible a life to share with anyone, locked away, being fed drugs that made it all worse. And electro-shock therapy which caused her to retreat even further into her memories and previous lives.

Slitting her wrists hadn't helped, though she had tried it out of desperation. Maybe a bullet between the eyes? But she had never been given the opportunity to test it, and she doubted it would have done the job either. She had learned a long time ago that no one else could kill her. Hurt her immensely, yes, but never kill her. Shots always went wide. Wounds always missed vital organs. It didn't mean she couldn't be driven unconscious by a beating that left her bleeding on the floor, though.

She didn't remember a time when she had been more thankful to die.

A shake of Lars's head caught her attention. His face was blank again, but she could feel the anger that didn't show. He glared out the window and said nothing.

"Sedatives leave me open to everything and everyone," she told Horus, forcing the memories away. "I lose control of what I hear. Everything overwhelms me."

"Hm." Horus nodded to the tray. "Garrit, why don't you give her the soup. Perhaps a full stomach will do her good. Slowly, now."

The soup was good. Not too rich. But it hurt to hold the bowl and feed herself, and she was tired by the time she was done. She felt Garrit worrying, and she sighed. "I'll heal quickly now, Garrit. Don't worry."

"I could kill your brother," he said.

She smiled faintly. "I think that would hurt even more."

"Will you be okay if I leave you to go check on Alex? He's been asking for you, but I didn't want him to be frightened by all this. When you feel up to it, I'll bring him in."

Alex. She could feel his distress now that Garrit had mentioned it. But even her own son had been drowned out by Adam's pain. The pain she shared. She felt a flash of guilt that she hadn't thought of him, but even the idea of having him squirming about on the bed made her bones ache.

Garrit kissed her forehead. "When you're up to it, Abby. Not before. *Maman* is more than capable of keeping him occupied. Just concentrate on feeling better."

She nodded, and he left, and Lars took Horus's place at the side of the bed. She tried to tell herself she hadn't missed his touch, and turned her face away so that she wouldn't have to meet his eyes. Somehow she knew that when she pretended to sleep, he wasn't fooled.

CHAPTER TWENTY-FOUR
Future

Adam groaned, then remembered. His head felt as if it had split open. And Eve had been too close. The Chorus. Had he brought the Chorus down on her too?

"Eve?"

"If you ever make her cry that way again, Adam, I am going to murder you. At once."

A woman sighed. "Be reasonable, Thor."

Athena, then. At least someone would keep calm. He sat up, though it made the pounding in his head worse. He supposed he should be grateful they'd thought to dump him in the grass and not in the pond. The park. He remembered this park, and that bench, with the maple trees. "Where's Michael? I saw him."

"You play a dangerous game, Adam. We do not take the threat of a godchild lightly, nor do We appreciate being made to work with these infidels to secure you."

He turned toward the voice. Michael stared at him, unblinking, and Adam swallowed hard. He remembered his face, and it stirred the pain of that day—ash and soot and flame, waving a torch in the air. He shook himself. He didn't have the time, now, for the distraction of memory.

"I have no intention of destroying the world while Eve lives, Archangel."

"Then shoving your tongue down her throat was just for your amusement?" Thor's grip on his war-hammer made his knuckles white. "You're lucky it was the angel that took your consciousness, if it had been up to me I'd have broken half your face while I was at it."

Michael sneered. "You have no right to interfere with the Son of God, Norseman, no matter his business. We have been lenient for far too long."

"You were happy to have me do your job for the last six hundred years, and now you threaten me? Where were you when Adam found Eve the first time, intent on making her his?"

"She was safe in the bosom of Reu's family, as she will always be. Your protection was redundant. Reu's vow is still kept." Michael said.

"No longer. Eve forbade them from binding her sons with the oath after Alexandre's birth. But I've forgotten. You failed to thwart him then, too, when he played on her emotions. You have done nothing to help her!"

"God's Daughter was given our aid when it was most necessary. She knows her place and keeps it, unlike you and all your kind. Trespassers and thieves. When God rises, you will be cast out with all the others."

"Are you so certain, Michael, that you know your God's mind?" Thor asked. It was a growl and a purr, but it was the present tense that startled Adam.

"What?"

They both turned to look at him. Thor's eyes glowed white hot with his rage, and Athena kept a hand on his arm to stop him from whatever violence tempted him. Michael simply glared, looking at him as if he were an ant beneath his sandaled foot.

Adam didn't care. He would risk whatever punishment the angel chose to deal him. To know the truth—even if he failed in every other way, was worth the pain. "God lives?"

The angel's lip curled. "No thanks to you."

"But God lives?"

"Of course he *lives*, you fool." Thor said. "A god of that power is not simply made to go away. Do you know nothing of your own world?"

He ignored Thor and kept his eyes on the angel. "All this time, you had us believe He was dead. Eve labors even now under the pretense! She suffers for nothing!"

"God does not answer to you or to Eve, and nor do We." He felt himself laid bare before the angel, every moment with Eve played without his consent before his eyes. "Tell Us once and for all your intention. Swear to Us that you do not seek her womb, that you have no intention of using the child for your own ends, and do not stand against God, your Father, now."

It was difficult to make his lips shape the words he wanted to speak. The questions he had to ask before Michael disregarded him once more. "The sword. Give me the use of your sword."

Michael hissed and his wings flared, filling the room with white. "You dare!"

"Where is it?" He had only just noticed its absence from the angel's side. There was no light, no flame. No weapon of any kind. "Why don't you have it?"

The angel raised his chin, arrogant and righteous. "Destroyed. By God's own hand."

"No!" Everything had been for nothing then. The pain to Eve. Her suffering. For nothing! He shoved the angel aside and stumbled away from the thrice-damned gods. He had to get to Eve. He had to apologize. He had to do something. Anything to make it right.

Thor's hand was a vise on his arm and he was dragged back. "You have a vow to make, Adam. To your God and His angels."

Athena sighed. "His word is meaningless, Thor. It doesn't matter who he swears to."

"We'll see."

Struggling as he had been against the god, when he was released suddenly he fell to the ground. He was going to have grass stains if he wasn't careful. Or worse. Adam stood and brushed himself off, eye to eye with Michael. "And if I refuse to swear any vow?"

Thor snorted. "It would be the most honest thing you've ever done."

Michael's gaze ripped into him again. Demanding and impossible to avoid. "What are your intentions, Adam? Merely to call Us? To capture Our attention?"

"I intend to return to Eve."

And do what with her? What more misery can you inflict? She is not a toy for you to play with, Son of God. She is a woman. God's own Daughter. Most precious of His creations.

He swallowed and returned the angel's gaze calmly. *I have loved her for the better part of a century.*

Then it is as God has said. Michael's face twisted with disgust. "Make your vow, Adam."

He shifted his eyes to Thor, over Michael's shoulder, even as he felt the angel search his soul and listen for any lie to his words. "I do not seek a child of her womb, or the power of the godchild you all fear, and certainly I have no intention of standing against Elohim, whatever His will. But I will not swear not to love her, and I will make no promises regarding my intentions toward any other gods upon this earth."

"The vow is made." Michael grimaced and turned away. "He speaks truly."

"That's it? You'll let him walk free again?"

"It is not God's wish to have him caged like an animal, Norseman. His pledge is all that We require." But his eyes flashed and the white wings twitched at his back. "We will brook no further interference from you in the affairs of men. God's plan will be made clear in time."

"God's plan?" Adam asked.

Do not think We will turn a blind eye. Even without the sword, We will have what is Ours when the time comes. Any child of Eve's belongs to God, and by your oath, you have forsaken all claim. Michael sneered again, his perfect face twisted with hate. "When you see us again in this life, Adam, you will not like what We have to say."

"Why?" He didn't like the sound of it already, and what he'd promised . . . he hadn't realized what it meant. What the angel had meant by it—but surely they didn't think Eve would ever risk the world, regardless. "When?"

But Michael ignored him, and left without another word. Athena watched him go thoughtfully, before turning the same gaze upon Adam. "What did you want with the sword?"

He shook his head, thinking of Eve and the tears she had shed so that he could fail to accomplish anything. He didn't deserve her forgiveness this time. Not at all.

When Thor finally let him go, he didn't return to the shop. He didn't think that she'd want to see him, and he wasn't sure he could stand to face her after what he'd done. He went home instead, back to Britain, though this time he avoided the bar. If he lived the rest of his life a monk, it would be better than he deserved for everything he had put her through. Without the sword, there was nothing he could do.

He sat in the dark of his house late that night, a bottle near at hand to drown himself in whenever he started to surface again, turning over the angel's words in his mind. God lived. God lived and He had a plan for him. For Eve too? For both of them? And was Thor truly forbidden to interfere any further? He wasn't sure what that meant, or how much authority was behind it. He had never seen an angel bestir itself to act against the gods, though there had seemed to be no love lost between Thor and Michael.

He smirked. It was almost refreshing to know the angel despised that god as much as he did. Reassuring to know he wasn't alone in his desire to be rid of him. But if Thor spent as much time in Eve's head as Adam suspected, what affect would his withdrawal have on her? If Thor gave her any kind of peace, Adam wouldn't let it be denied her. Nor would Thor permit her to be hurt, regardless of the angel's command. Elohim was not Thor's god, and Adam doubted seriously that he would obey.

He guzzled another portion of the bottle and felt himself sink deeper into the fog of the drink on his mind. Did he even have the strength to reach her now, if he wanted to? He rested his head against the back of the couch and closed his eyes. Surely she would want to know that God lived. Under the influence of so much alcohol, he was almost certain that this piece of information was key. That God's presence meant something more than he had yet discerned. Maybe it would be enough to make her rethink her decision.

Evey?

He got the distinct impression of a dreamscape. Something about lions. He sighed. Always lions. At least she wasn't married to one anymore. Small favors.

Eve, love. I know you're upset with me, but this is important, I promise you.

The dream faded and he felt her consciousness rise, though she seemed distinctly annoyed. *S'two in the morning. Go to bed, Adam.*

He glanced out the window, only then noticing he wasn't sitting in the dark anymore. It was morning, and he'd lost the entire night. *Evey, God lives.*

There was a silence so absolute he wondered if she'd stopped breathing. *How do you know?*

Michael.

Michael? But you said you didn't know how to find him—And then the pain lashed through him, from her heart, from her spirit. *You used me.*

Evey, I'm sorry. I had to see him. There wasn't any other way.

Is that all I am to you? A tool to get what you want?

No, Eve!

I can't do this Adam. I can't. I can't. Her presence disappeared.

He sighed and drank down the rest of the bottle, thanking God for not making him immune to the effects of alcohol. There was entirely too much heartbreak for him to survive without it.

Sometimes he wished Eve had never taught him how to love properly. He wished he'd never seen her with Garrit. Never realized what he had missed. Never understood how much more life could be when you had someone to share it with. He wished he had never known her to love her, to hurt her this way. That she had never had cause to love him back.

He had struggled for so long to be a person she could love. For what? To be mocked by the gods? To be threatened by the angels?

But without the sword . . .

Without the sword, there was no control. No threat left, but weak anger. That he could endure without trouble or concern. Without the sword, there was nothing that Michael could do to stop him.

Perhaps not nothing. The Chorus still drove him into unconsciousness. But there was nothing permanent about the act.

But why would God destroy the sword? The one weapon the angels could use against them. The one thing that they could hold over their heads to keep them apart. To keep them afraid. With the sword gone, there was nothing to stop him but his own conscience. Especially with Thor forbidden to interfere. Was his conscience really something God had that much faith in? After everything he had done and been, it seemed a thin thing to protect the world. A very thin thing.

Ah, but God did not have to count on him alone. And Eve knew her duty, knew her role, knew suffering and sacrifice. What a weight to bury her in. He wondered, not for the first time, why God had forced so much responsibility on her unwilling shoulders. Poor Eve. Poor, lovely, sorrowful Eve.

But the saddest part was that he couldn't even comfort her. Couldn't hold her while she cried. Couldn't care for her without increasing her burden. Without making it all so much worse. And now she didn't even have Thor in the back of her mind, sitting like a balm.

The last thing he remembered thinking before the alcohol and exhaustion claimed him was that God was cruel.

God was cruel to Eve.

CHAPTER TWENTY-FIVE
827 AD

With Athena's help, Ra's knowledge of engineering, and the assistance of the other Aesir, Thor built his hall. It was not the five hundred forty rooms he had dreamed of, but it boasted more than he would ever need. Athena named it Bilskirnir, from the old tongue, for the state of his temper if it ever fell, and they moved their things from Odin's hall before it was finished. Within it, he did not worry that Sif would hear them, or that they would be spied upon by Loki. It was a place untainted by all that had come before, and for the first time in a long time, he felt at home in Asgard.

Ra left once he had seen the first mountainous stone set, to travel east and visit with the gods there. The Norsemen who looked to Odin and the Aesir grew in number and in strength. They spread out, explored, wandered, and raided. They were feared on land and at sea. It was a golden age, in spite of the Christians, and the Aesir grew arrogant.

Thor saw the look in Athena's eyes when Freyr and Baldur laughed over the threat of the Christians. He knew she saw the fall of the Aesir in all their brash words, just as she had watched her own people fall.

But Odin would not listen to the warning Thor gave him, or take lesson from the story of the Olympians.

There were not many of her people left. Most had gone on to the new world Zeus and his brothers had secured. Aside from Athena, those who stayed did not leave Mount Olympus. When she went home, she seemed to return to him more upset than when she had left, but he knew she was not happy in Asgard either. And even with Bilskirnir, Thor found himself missing his days wandering the earth. He missed goat-herding for the House of Lions. He missed being closer to Eve. He missed being able to avoid Sif and Loki for decades at a time.

While Athena was away in the east, he spent most of his time in Eve's head, or else drinking with Baldur. It amounted to the same thing, truly. Distraction and avoidance of the troubles he knew would find the Aesir eventually. But he had tired long ago of arguing, and even Baldur, so well known for his discernment, did not listen.

Athena returned to him more subdued than usual this time. She was distracted through their dinner with the others, and seemed to be measuring each of the Aesir and finding them wanting somehow. When they returned to his hall, she did not sleep, but stood at the window, leaning on her elbows against the sill, the white material of her gown nearly transparent in the moonlight. He watched her for a long time, unable to find sleep himself with the tension that radiated from her body, and rose to stand behind her.

She didn't acknowledge him, her eyes closed and her face tipped up to the sky. He slid the fabric of her gown aside and kissed her pale shoulder. She sighed and turned her face toward his touch, her cheek against her shoulder, though she still did not open her eyes.

"Is Ra unwell?" he asked, for he knew she had gone to see him, and his health was most frequently her concern. "Has the East finally been infiltrated by the Christians, or the Muslims?"

"Not yet." She turned her face back to the night, and opened her eyes. "But they worry. Bhagavan and Buddha. And Ra wants to help them. To at least do for them what we could not do for ourselves. That some of us may be sustained."

He kissed her throat, and ran the back of his finger along the column of her neck. He could feel the tension there, in her neck and shoulders. It didn't help that she was so cold, standing at the window. He found the knots of stress in the muscles and smoothed them, pulling lightning into his hands to warm them, as well as her. His power never burned her, never marred her skin or caused her discomfort. She loved the kiss of the static, especially along her spine, and she relaxed under his hands, the tension draining from her body as he worked.

But not from her mind.

"Something else, Athena?" he asked. "What bothers you so much that you think of it even now?"

She turned, looking up at him, her eyes filled with sadness. When he leaned down to kiss her, she stopped him with a hand against his bare chest, pushing him back. "I have agreed to something that you will not like, Thor. But I do not see how else it is to be done, and I have thought long and hard of the consequences. There is no other way. No other right way. And I pray that you'll forgive me. Forgive us."

"Us?" His hands dropped from her body, the concern in her face beginning to alarm him in a way her silence had not. "Who else? What is it, that you've chosen not to consult me?"

"Ra and I." She dropped her gaze from his face, seeming to stare at some point in the middle of his chest. "We've begun the call for a Council." She swallowed and wrapped her arms around her body. Hugging herself, as if she had no one else to hold. "We hope to have a vote in favor of returning Adam his memory."

He stared at her, his heart twisting. No wonder she had been distant, encouraging him to stay in Asgard when she went to see Ra. No wonder she had been unhappy. For all this time? How long had it been going on? How long had they been planning to put Eve in a danger she hadn't known since Creation?

"Do you even intend to warn her? Were you going to wait to tell me until it had been decided, and the deed done?"

"No, Thor." She was looking up at him again, meeting his eyes. Her hands found his face, trapped it, forcing him to look at her. "We want your help. We need your help. You know him better than anyone. Know them both. We need that knowledge. And this was your idea. You suggested it in Council. That we should bribe him to work for us instead of against."

He pulled her hands away and stepped back. "You know better than anyone that I did not mean it. That it was only to paralyze them. You worry about the threat of the Christians to the East, but you would unleash that madman on the world? You who told me Adam and Eve were the larger threat?"

"You said she would never accept him. Never let him touch her. If that's true, you've nothing to worry about. She'll be safe, whether he accepts our terms or not. The world will be safe. And perhaps it will be enough to slow the tide if we can turn God's own son against Him."

He shook his head. And then again, turning from her. That Athena, who claimed to love him, would do this. With Ra. Conspire together. Against everything he had protected for more than fifteen hundred years. He reached for Eve, and was startled to find Adam near her. Too near to her. They were both in Rome. And he had been what? Trying to seduce Athena from her melancholy, while she and Ra put Eve in the path of harm?

"Thor, please. We need your help. Your cooperation. You cannot turn your back on the rest of the world. Bhagavan and Buddha helped you to spare her life. You owe them this. And if you help, you're sure to find a way to protect her more than she already is."

"I have to go," he said.

"Thor—"

But he did not hear the rest, drowned in the crackle of lightning and the rumble of thunder in his ears. He had arrived in Rome before she had even completed her sentence, the white light dissolving into stone and tenements.

He stumbled into an alley and leaned heavily against one of the buildings, concentrating on his breathing. Focusing on keeping the skies calm, that he would not be found so easily. The feeling of betrayal made his steps heavy, and his stomach twist into knots of grief.

How long had she been sleeping with him, sleeping in his bed and planning all of this with Ra? How long had she let him make love to her, unwitting of her intentions? The two of them had always conspired together, loyal to one another above all. He'd known it from his first days upon this earth.

He never should have let her into his bed. Never should've allowed her into his hall. He wished that she had left with Zeus and her uncles, if this was how she would repay him for his kindness, for his affection. He wished he had never touched her.

In the dark, he went looking for Eve.

It was morning before he found her, and in his exhaustion he almost overlooked her in the crush of people who lined the road. A procession. A parade for something to do with the pope. Keeping his eyes on her, he cast his mind out for Adam, worried that in all this mess he would not be able to locate him. Adam had always been harder for him to find. Eve always glowed bright and hot and beautiful. Adam was more diffuse, a flickering presence that came and went. But not today. Today he burned.

The pitch of the crowd changed, the excitement rising, and he pushed forward through the mob in order to remain near to Eve. Adam was getting closer, and he did not wish to lose sight of her now.

The pope appeared around the corner, carried in a litter, the curtains drawn back. Thor froze at the sight, and the realization that struck him. He turned back to Eve just in time to see her expression twist into dismay. Her skin took on a greenish cast. She turned away from the parade and the pope, and tried to force herself back through the crowd that pressed around her, eager for a glimpse of the man who would ascend to Saint Peter's seat. Her lips were moving, but he couldn't hear what she was saying, and the people did not part for her.

She tripped and fell, and Thor had the sudden fear that she would be trampled by the swarm around her. He threw a large man out of his path and grabbed her by the arm, pulling her with him into the shadow of the alley and safety from Adam's sight as he passed them by in his litter, waving to his people.

Thor felt as though they had both stopped breathing, and it was only after Adam, Pope Valentine, had passed that he exhaled, and she sagged against him.

She glanced up, and then looked at him again, frowning slightly. "Thank you."

He nodded, releasing her arm when he realized he was still holding it. He didn't trust himself to speak. All he wanted to do was draw her closer, lower his head and bring his mouth to hers.

She turned back at the throng, starting to disperse. Some followed the procession, others made their way to their homes.

He cleared his throat. "He has no business leading the Church."

"It was only a matter of time before its corruption was proven," she said softly. "This city was in safer hands when its people worshipped Jupiter. If you have any choice, leave, and do it quickly." She pulled her hood over her head, hiding her face. It took all his will not to stop her when she stepped back out into the street.

Thor felt her determination to follow her own advice, and it was not a moment before she was lost again in the crowds. He wished her well and safely away. Adam as a Pope was something he had never dreamed. Then again, perhaps it would serve the gods. Adam could not help but sow strife around him. Perhaps they would not need to return his memory to him. Perhaps this would be enough. If the Church fell, it might be enough to save the East.

But there would still be the threat of Islam. At least as long as the rival sects fought between themselves, they did not expand. If the Church fell, there would be nothing to stop the spread of the second faith. Had that been the True God's intent?

He cursed.

Athena was right. Adam was their best hope of preserving the East. Thor could protect Eve from Adam after that man's memory was returned to him. If he had to carry her to the House of Lions himself, she would be made safe. And if he helped, if he offered Athena his assistance freely, he could make sure the threat to her was not ignored.

Swear to me you will protect her from him, Athena.

Surprise colored her mind, and then gratitude. *My word. Sworn on the Covenant. Sworn on my love for you.*

He closed his eyes and prayed that Eve would forgive him. *Then you'll have my aid.*

CHAPTER TWENTY-SIX
Present

Lars appeared to be dozing, leaning back in his chair, his hand wrapped loosely around her fingers. Garrit was absent. Judging by the sun, she thought he was probably eating dinner with his parents, and part of her was grateful he wasn't hanging over her, worrying, now that she was healing. She told herself that her relief had absolutely nothing to do with the fact that when Garrit left the room, it was Lars who held her hand to keep the pain away.

She felt the bruising around her ribs with her free hand. Touching the places that hurt and trying to decide if the pain had lessened. It was impossible to tell. She hissed when she pressed too hard against a particularly sore spot, and Lars's fingers twitched, but he didn't open his eyes.

What had possessed Adam? How had he even managed to get hit by a bus in the first place? She supposed she should be grateful it wasn't a train. Still. It made no sense.

Or did it?

Was it her fault? Had she distracted him at just the wrong moment and caused the accident? He had been upset, she knew that, though she hadn't known anything more. She hadn't been aware of his surroundings, just his anguish.

She closed her eyes and even though it hurt, she began to reach for his mind. *Adam?*

Lars's hand closed around her fingers, almost painfully. She opened her eyes to find him staring at her. "Don't," he said.

"Don't what?" He couldn't have known what she was doing. Could he? Or was she so insufficiently healed, so affected by the ordeal that he had heard her?

"All the pain you feel is from him, Abby. Calling to him is the last thing you need."

She looked away, annoyed that she hadn't considered that. "How do you know?"

"I know." There was a hardness in his voice. An absoluteness. It wasn't a statement that should be argued. "Horus is limited in what he can do for you. As am I. No one wants to see you in any further pain."

"Are you some kind of homeopathic herbalist too?" It was less a question and more a jibe, and she felt her cheeks burn. It was as though she were incapable of an appropriate response to this man. This man who somehow took her pain away. She should be grateful to him, and he was her family, besides. "I'm sorry. I didn't mean to be rude."

He stroked her hair from her face, tucking a strand back into place behind her ear. "You're in pain. And you're blaming yourself twice over. I would be more surprised if I didn't get the sharp edge of your tongue."

It was so bizarre to be treated this way by her offspring. As though she were the child. She didn't know what to make of it. He seemed strained and worn, and even hurt as she was, it felt as though she should be doing the caretaking. "How do you know what I'm thinking?"

"You're rather loud right now." He leaned forward, nodding to their hands. "Horus thinks it's because of the trauma. He believes your mind suffered more than anything else. It's still struggling to get back to an equilibrium. One more reason not to reach for your brother."

"Can Garrit hear me too?"

"No." His hand tightened again. "Just us. Because we're drawing off the pain. It's an old Eastern technique. Similar to Reiki, or acupuncture."

She sighed with relief, grimacing as the heavy exhalation caused her ribs to ache. And then she wondered how much Lars could hear, and felt her face flush again. "Oh."

"You're not yourself, Abby. Don't worry."

"You heard it all." Her stomach sank. Garrit was her husband. She couldn't betray him this way.

Something flickered in his eyes and he stared at their hands again. "Believe me, I'm aware of your vows. I would not ask you to break them." He lifted her hand and pressed it to his lips.

Her heart raced, and she knew that she should pull her hand away. But she couldn't. She couldn't bring herself to do it. And the pain that would come if she did provided the most convenient excuse.

"Stop," she said. That was the best she could do. A meek whimper that she didn't mean, and she hated herself for her weakness.

"Forgive me," he said. And he stopped, his face dark with regret as his blue eyes searched hers. "If you knew—" He fell silent and shook his head. "I'm sorry. This is difficult for me."

"I don't understand how." She wanted to look away, but his pain was impossible not to see. And it was Thorgrim's face. Thorgrim's eyes. Seeing him hurt was almost worse than the physical discomfort she was in. "I mean, I don't understand why. We've had so little contact."

"More than you realize." But he pressed his lips together, keeping himself from going on.

She wished she could follow the words he didn't say, but there was nothing there but the emotion. Want and determination. "Just how involved have you been?"

"I consider these people to be my family. The only family I have left now. When they needed me, I came. From the moment Adam set foot on these lands, I was here. To protect them as much as you."

"Private security." Was she delirious again? She could have imagined him, brought him to life and projected his presence to her family. She could have lost her mind again, and not even realized it.

"You're awake. This is real."

"I wish you couldn't hear me."

He smiled Thorgrim's smile. "I can understand why."

"You just remind me so much of him—" her voice broke, and she took a ragged breath. "It's hard to remember that you aren't him. That I'm living a different life. That I'm married to another man."

"I know." He held her hand in both of his again. "I could tell, even at your wedding rehearsal. And if it weren't for your brother, I wouldn't have returned."

She wondered if he realized he was lying. He meant it so sincerely. He wanted to believe it so badly. Just like she wanted to believe that she was only holding his hand to keep the pain away. Just like she wanted to believe that nothing had happened in the woods.

"Nothing did happen," he said.

"Only because of Adam." Was that why? Was that the reason? It seemed almost impossible, but also exactly the wrong kind of truth. She swore. "He did it on purpose."

His face darkened and his gaze shifted toward the window. Thunder rumbled outside. He seemed to be concentrating on his breathing, but his nostrils flared, and she felt his anger.

Horus came into the room, and without a word Lars stood and the brown man slipped into his place. His hands were cool and dry. Together, they watched Lars walk to the window. He stood stiffly, everything about his posture radiating his frustration, his disgust, his fury. Rain splashed against the glass, and Eve felt her sight blur with memory. It was too similar to those days in the ward with the ghost of Thorgrim she'd brought to life. How he had hated seeing her so helpless. It was too much, and the memories began swimming up. The room darkened to dirty gray walls and ugly tile, and the window behind Lars grew bars.

"Lars," Horus called. She could hear the alarm in his voice, but it was distant.

Did you really think I'd let you have her? That I would stand by and do nothing to stop you?

It was Adam's voice. And with it came the pain. Until she fell back into the dark, rolled up in it. It was a relief to feel nothing at all.

§

"He did this to himself, knowing that she would suffer. To cause her to suffer." It was Horus she heard, speaking calmly. For some reason she thought they had been fighting again, but she couldn't remember hearing anything else. "Perhaps it would be prudent to reconsider your position, Garrit."

She didn't open her eyes yet. It was too great an effort just to focus on the voices. Why were they always fighting over her bed? Couldn't they see she was trying to sleep? Trying to rest? She liked the dark. She had always liked the dark. Since her creation, it had been a comfort to her. Blackness and silence. It was the first time she had thought of the void in thousands of years.

A hand brushed over her forehead. She didn't know whose. For that matter, who really was this Horus? Lars at least was family. He belonged well enough. But Horus Amon made no sense to her. Who was he that he seemed to know how best to treat her? That Garrit listened to him and he spoke with authority? Garrit didn't even listen to her!

There was a chuckle. Thorgrim's laugh. "She must be feeling better."

"How can you tell?" Garrit's voice was low, but she could feel his envy. He wished he could feel her the way the other two could. Know her as well as they did. Spending so much time with Lars was making him feel inadequate, insecure, and it drove him crazy. How had his father done it all these years? Formed a relationship with him? A friendship?

"She's becoming much more coherent. Watch your thoughts, Garrit. Conscious or not, she's reading you like a book." And then Thorgrim whispered in her ear. "Come back to us."

But she couldn't go back to Thorgrim. Thorgrim was dead and gone. Just like all the others. Every life a new husband. Every life another death. It was almost worse when she loved them. The ones she hadn't loved, who hadn't loved her, they hadn't been as difficult to lose. They had been easier to mourn. Thorgrim had been different though.

No. Not Thorgrim. Lars. Thorgrim's descendent. Thorgrim's descendent who loved her? And she felt something. Something she shouldn't. She was married. She had a son. Isn't that what she had told Adam? How could he have done this to her? Couldn't he have done something less painful? Knocked himself in the head, instead of getting smashed by a bus? What were they all worried about anyway? It wasn't as though she could die. Nothing could hurt her that badly. Certainly not Adam.

Or was Adam the exception to the rule?

"Wouldn't we all like to know," Lars mumbled. She barely heard him.

She wished he would stop listening to her thoughts. Wished that she could steady her mind enough to prevent it. Bad enough that Adam eavesdropped. Adam. She had to talk to Adam.

"Not until you're well, Eve. It will only hurt you more, now."

Eve. He called her Eve. Lars did. Thorgrim never had. She had always been his Tora. They had been named for the same god. Thor, the god of thunder. A hot-headed drunk and immensely strong. Later there had been something about a hammer. But that had been long after she had lived and died and returned to the south. Generations after she had been made to worship those gods.

"What a god is, and what his people believe him to be, are not often the same things," Lars said. "You should know that better than most."

No. She didn't know. She had never known God at all.

She opened her eyes. Lars sat beside her. Garrit and Horus were no longer in the room. She hadn't heard them leave.

He smiled, but there was something sad about it. "Welcome back."

She stretched gingerly against sore muscles and the bruises all over her body. She wasn't as stiff this time. And she didn't think she was as sore, though that might have been due to Lars's hand on hers. She didn't want him to release her, but she should have. "Am I back?"

"Stay out of your brother's head, and you should be." He let go of her hand then, watching her with narrowed eyes. "How do you feel?"

There was no shock of pain, though she had braced for it. Just a dull ache from her head to her heels. She fingered the bruises on her ribs. They hurt much less. "Better."

Lars nodded and stood up, walking to the door. But he paused before he opened it, his hand on the knob, and glanced back at her. "By the way. Thor only drank so much because he was heartbroken."

She blinked. "I thought Thor was married."

"Sometimes, no matter how hard you try, it just doesn't work out the way you hope it will."

He left before she could respond and she heard him call for Garrit. While she waited for her husband, she wondered if Lars was talking about himself, or the god.

CHAPTER TWENTY-SEVEN
Future

Adam kept finding himself back at the airport. Over and over and over again, he would arrive there, and over and over and over again he would deny himself the ticket he wanted to purchase, substituting something else, somewhere else. He started buying land, for no real discernible reason, all over the world. Every time he found himself at the airport with the intention of going back to North America to see her, he went somewhere else and purchased property.

Maybe it was the challenge of getting people to sell things they didn't want to let go of. Maybe it was just the distraction. Maybe it was the fact that he could never have what he wanted. He would never be rid of the gods, and he would never be rid of the angels, and he would never be rid of this longing for Eve that he couldn't satisfy, and he would never have the world the way he had dreamed—any hope he might have still nursed stripped away with his promise to Michael. Never have it, except for what he could buy.

So he bought more land, on every continent including significant portions of Antarctica, for no other reason than just to have it. The population was exploding and it would only be a matter of time before humanity found a way to adapt itself to that wasteland, or adapt the wasteland to itself. Hadn't they walked on Mars, after all? And what were snow and ice and cold on Earth to Mars?

He thought about leaving Earth altogether. It would be an easy thing to manipulate any test, any board of directors, any system into sending him away. But he couldn't bring himself to go that far. He couldn't bring himself to leave her behind. Leave the range of her thoughts, or leave the world he had been born to, that had been made for him. It was one thing to avoid her, but to not have the option to see her or find her was unthinkable, intolerable.

When the manor in France known as DeLeon Castle was put up for sale, his interest in real estate made it impossible for him not to notice. The idea that it could ever be sold had never occurred to him, and he had to look twice at the listing before he realized exactly what he was seeing.

Those damned Lions. Couldn't he have one life where they didn't foul things up for him somehow? And where was Thor to prevent this kind of foolishness? This was exactly the kind of thing he was supposed to be responsible for. Watching over that family and keeping them from ruining themselves, or Eve. He swore and called the agent handling the sale.

"This is Mr. Carraig, calling for information on the DeLeon property." Adam assumed that the man would know him. He was the largest private land owner in the world by now, twice over. That kind of thing didn't go unnoticed in the circles who handled sales of old and prestigious properties.

"*Monsieur* Carraig, a pleasure! Are you interested in making an offer?"

"Ten million above your highest. I don't care how much it is, and if they counter, ten million above that."

The agent nearly choked. "Of course, *monsieur*. Would you like to arrange a viewing of the estate?"

"No." He didn't care about seeing it. He'd seen too much of it in his past life. Though he was curious if the family would stop him from crossing onto their lands now that they were selling it. Fools. How was Eve supposed to find them if they sold her home? What could have possessed them? "Yes. Yes, I would like to see the estate, and I'd also like to meet with the family, if that can be arranged. As soon as possible."

"*Oui, bien sûr.* I'm sure the family would be happy to meet with you. They are quite attached to the estate, you know. I'm afraid the sale does have some provisos. The land must be kept intact, and undeveloped. It is an historic landmark."

"Do I strike you as the kind of buyer who cares all that much for development? Whatever the stipulations are, I'm happy to agree. Draw up the papers and arrange the meeting for tomorrow."

"*Monsieur,* I will speak with them, but I cannot promise a meeting for tomorrow. Perhaps next week—"

"Tomorrow, Mr. Laurent. Tell them it is on behalf of their Lady."

"Of course, *monsieur,* I will do as you ask."

It was clear by his tone that he didn't have the faintest idea of the meaning, but Adam didn't care. As long as he passed on the message, he was certain that the DeLeons would find the time to meet with him on his terms.

"Excellent. I'll be in touch with your office tomorrow then. If you would be so kind as to drop me a note with the time of the meeting after you've spoken with your clients."

"*Oui.* I look forward to doing business together."

No doubt. He was about to put several millions of dollars into his pocket in commission. "Thank you."

He disconnected and sighed, rubbing his forehead. Eve wasn't going to be happy about this, if she didn't already know. Maybe he would wait to tell her until after he had taken care of it and ensured it remained in her possession. Though how on earth he was going to accomplish it he didn't know.

There was no real way to ensure that any material wealth or goods were passed on to their future selves. The laws and legal systems didn't allow for that sort of thing. He had researched it extensively. The best he had managed to come up with was a lock box with a Swiss institution, where as Ethan he had given strict instructions that the box be awarded to the man who presented them with the key, and no other, to be held indefinitely by them until such a time as the key was presented, and that had required a team of lawyers to make foolproof in his will.

Somehow he didn't think he would be able to fit the DeLeon estate in a box. The DeLeon family, to his understanding, was supposed to be her foolproof lock box. She kept everything with them. He'd seen the vault.

Well. He would find a way. And it would be a perfect gift for Eve. He smiled sadly. Her birthday was coming up, and he had always sent her something during the last five years they'd been apart. Flowers at the least. This year he wouldn't disappoint her.

"You said you speak on behalf of our Lady, *Monsieur* Carraig. Is she here?"

Eve's eldest great-grandson was a boy he remembered as precocious, but charming. He had been named Ryam, for his grandfather. The DeLeons did love their family names. Looking at the middle-aged man he had grown into, his face lined with a seriousness that the child he'd known had always lacked, Adam was quite certain that Eve would have heart failure. Even he had looked twice, Ryam's face and eyes bringing back flashes of memory of Reu in the Garden. Unfortunately, the only thing he remembered clearly was a sense of his own righteous indignation, which wasn't helpful in the slightest.

"*Monsieur* DeLeon, it is kind of you to meet with me on such short notice. I'm sorry to say that your Lady is not with me, but she has granted me all authority in this matter. You do realize what you're doing don't you? Selling this estate? Her home?"

Ryam collapsed into a chair, all poise and grace draining from him. "I had hoped she wouldn't have to know."

Adam shook his head, leaning against the edge of the desk. He had usurped the real estate agent's office for this meeting, not wishing to tempt fate by crossing into DeLeon lands quite yet. The last thing he needed was trouble from Thor complicating things further. "Somehow I think that it would be impossible for her not to notice when she came home to find her family gone, and the place turned into a museum. What possessed you to make this kind of decision?"

"If it were up to me alone, *monsieur*, we would not be selling. Unfortunately, my father chose to bequeath his legacy in equal measure to all his children. My other two brothers do not share my feelings. I tried to talk them into selling it to the family, or to me, but coming up with the kind of money they were looking for was impossible."

By all rights, they ought never to have run out of funds. Unless someone hadn't passed on the secrets of Asgardian gold, and someone else had melted down the source, money never should have been a problem for the House of Lions. Adam watched the man wriggle in the chair as he stood over him, his hair seeming to gray visibly with stress, and thought of how miserable Eve was going to be because Alexandre's son hadn't done as he was told, as tradition dictated, and passed the estate in one piece to his oldest son, with all its secrets intact. Garrit hadn't even believed in Eve before he met her, but he never would've sold his family's land, and these boys didn't have his excuse of long dissociation. They had seen Eve, felt her, touched her. She had held them in her lap as babes.

"This is going to break her heart."

Ryam's face became ashen. "But you have made an offer. Surely this means you do so on her behalf, in her name. It will be hers."

He felt something then, in the back of his mind. The lightest of touches, but he would recognize it always. She so rarely reached for him. *Eve?*

Adam.

He was taken aback by the distress in her mind, the ache in her soul. *What's wrong?*

Bad dreams. There was a flash of flame and smoke, and crying people. *I didn't mean to disturb you.*

You're never a disturbance. I was just thinking of you anyway. I'm sitting with your great-grandson. These men of yours favor their ancestor prodigiously you know. Alex didn't so much, but Ryam is the spitting image of his founding father.

But why? He felt her confusion, even a touch of anxiety. *Why would you meet with them?*

They're selling DeLeon Castle, Eve. I came to try to stop them, or at the very least ensure I was the one who bought it. I'm sorry.

A maelstrom of emotion ripped through her, and he flinched, turning away from Ryam. All of it sorrowful. All of it shock and misery. He thought she might be trying not to cry, and he wished that he were there with her. Comforting her. *Adam, they can't!*

I'm sorry, love. I'm sorry.

There must be something . . . But despair settled and he followed her thoughts. She had no wealth, no power. She had nothing to offer them, nothing to provide. She couldn't even afford a flight to speak with them herself. If only she could, perhaps she could make them see sense—*Adam. Will you lend me some money?*

He smiled, knowing at once what she asked of him. *Your tickets will be waiting for you at the nearest airport. I'll make the arrangements at once.*

"*Monsieur* Carraig?"

He cleared his throat and turned back to face Ryam. "Forgive me. This isn't as simple as that, Mr. DeLeon. Her wealth, unfortunately, is all yours. Everything she owns devolves to you, her family, each time she dies. You see the difficulty? She has no resources of her own that are not in the hands of your family already. If you sell this estate, it leaves your family, and she has no way to keep track of you to pass it on. No way to ensure it returns to you intact." To say nothing of the protections Thor had afforded it, all of which were bound to the lands themselves, but if they had melted down the gold, the likelihood they understood the rest of what they would lose was unlikely.

"I don't understand." Ahh, yes. There it was. The first mote of suspicion. Ryam studied him through narrowed eyes. "What exactly is your relationship with our Lady? How do you come to know her?"

Adam ignored the question. It would be made clear to them in time, or it wouldn't. Either way if Ryam were stupid enough not to figure it out on his own, he had no business knowing at all. "I have made arrangements for your Lady's arrival. She will no doubt want a better explanation from you and your brothers. Will you meet with her in two days? Give her at least this satisfaction?"

Ryam shifted uncomfortably, his mouth pressed into the same thin line that Garrit had often affected in his irritation. His eyes shifted to the window behind him, but there was no thunder, no rain, no flash of lightning. Still, the man looked rather sick. "I can't deny her, can I?"

"Not without betraying everything your family stands for, Ryam."

He nodded. "Two days, then. I'll speak with my brothers." Ryam stood, and without a farewell, left the office.

Adam watched him go, and hoped that by the time they met again, with Eve, he had a different story to tell. One in which they declined to sell.

CHAPTER TWENTY-EIGHT
1018 AD

§

Thor sat in the shadowed corner of the tavern, cloaked and hooded, and watched Eve laugh and tease a patron as she refilled the other man's mug. It was a special kind of torture to inflict upon himself. After every meeting spent with Ra and Athena, every expedition to talk another god into agreeing to their cause, every time he did anything that took them a step closer to returning Adam his memory, he found Eve.

Athena had long ago stopped trying to talk him out of these trips, and Ra had never begun to try. This life of hers was more convenient than the others. He had become a regular customer easily. Sometimes she even spoke to him, and it made his pulse quicken, and his guilt flare. So he drank and made sure to tip her well.

"I did wonder why London had become so overcast."

Thor did not look at the man who sat down beside him. Did not have to raise his eyes to see the leer on Loki's face. He knocked back what was left of his beer and slammed the mug to the tabletop to signal for more. "Any native will tell you it has always been so."

"Proof only that you've been meddling in the minds of men." Loki shrugged, leaning back in his seat and kicking his feet up on the table. "You're so mind-numbingly predictable, Thor. And Odin was so sure that you had changed. That Athena had broken the woman's spell over you."

"It drives you mad that Athena won't even look at you, doesn't it?" Part of him wanted to see Loki try his luck with her. Athena hadn't shared Thor's own bed in nearly two centuries, but he knew she would not take another lover. And if Loki tried to force her, she was more than capable of handling him. He would be a bloody pulp by the time she was through.

Loki chuckled, dropping his feet and lowering his voice. "Have you bedded her recently?" He made a noise which was unmistakable. Lust and appreciation and arrogance rolled together obscenely as he stared at Eve. "Is she not full of spirit? All these millennia, marrying and remarrying. She must be an exceptional whore."

Thor ground his teeth, determined to say nothing that would encourage Loki. Nothing to give away how infuriated he was by such a statement. Such a slur.

Eve refilled Thor's mug and smiled warmly, though he did not let her take too great of an interest in him. Every time she tried to look at his face, he distracted her with something else. Even if it was only the call of another patron who needed his glass filled. He couldn't let her recognize him.

Loki grabbed her around the waist and pulled her into his lap, murmuring something in her ear that Thor couldn't hear. Eve's smile was fixed to her face, incongruous with the look of disgust in her eyes, and she pushed him firmly away, tsking at him. Thor's hands became fists, and *Mjölnir* weighed heavily on his hip.

Loki let Eve go, and laughed. "Mead, woman!" he called after her.

She glanced over her shoulder, her expression darkening for just a moment before she noticed Thor watching, and it cleared again. The smile she offered him was vaguely reassuring. As though she recognized some malevolence in his eyes, or some offense at her treatment.

He grunted and looked away. She probably felt it. His fury. His frustration. His disgust. She had always been adept at reading his emotions. He imagined she had only honed her skills over the years. Become more finely tuned to the people around her.

"But I'd forgotten. You're still bound by Odin, aren't you? Forbidden to touch her." Loki sighed. "A shame, really. Perhaps I'll just have to do it for you."

Thor was on his feet before he even registered his own intent, and Loki was pinned against the wall by the hand at his throat, his toes reaching for the floor. He could feel the other god's pulse against his fingers, and tightened his hand until it slowed and Loki's face began to turn purple.

He leaned in close, and heard himself growl. "I believe I made it clear to you Loki, that I would not suffer any interference in her life. You will not touch her."

Loki clawed at Thor's hand and arm, his nails gouging and leaving trails of blood. Thor ignored it. But then another hand touched his shoulder. A touch he couldn't ignore. Would never wish to. All conversation in the tavern had ceased and the silence thundered. Or perhaps it was the thunder which thundered. He did not care which when he looked into her eyes. Those green eyes that had no match. The eyes he dreamed of. The woman he dreamed of.

"Please," she said. "Let him go."

He couldn't look away from her. The hardness in her eyes was what surprised him most, though. She had always been so warm, so loving, but in this there was no tolerance. No understanding. Her grip on his arm tightened, and he felt heat spreading from the point of contact. Heat, and a compulsion to do what she asked that had nothing to do with his love for her. Maybe she hadn't trusted him with all her secrets, after all. Or maybe she had not known her own strength then. Her own power. Did she even realize she was using it now?

"I will not have men killed in my tavern," she said. Her voice was low, but firm. It brooked no argument, and if he had been a man, he doubted very much that he would have the faculties to do anything but obey. "Release him."

He didn't want to let Loki go. He didn't want to let this moment pass. Still, he relaxed the hold he had on the other god's neck. "As you wish."

Loki dropped, and Thor kicked him away.

She stared at him for a moment longer. Her hand on his arm. Her eyes narrowed just slightly, and her head tilted to the side. He gently pushed her hand away, and turned from her, using the bond they shared to repress the memories she sought. The ones that stirred in recognition. He painted over the image of his own face in her mind, changing the color of his eyes, and turning his hair black instead of red-gold.

And then he left the tavern altogether, to stand outside in the rain that had come with his anger. He closed his eyes and turned his face to the sky. He tried to tell himself, for a moment, that he would not have killed Loki. But it was too large of a lie, and too appealing of a truth. If Eve had not intervened, Loki would have been dead.

He looked back into the front room through the window. Eve was helping Loki up from the ground. The god had somehow obtained a split lip, and she dabbed at the blood with a towel. Her back was to Thor, and Loki stared over her shoulder at him and grinned.

Lightning flashed and thunder cracked overhead, loud enough to cause mugs to rattle. He would kill him next time. There was no question in his mind. If he touched her without her consent, harmed her in any way, Loki would not survive the encounter which would follow.

§

As he watched Loki attempt to insinuate himself into Eve's life over the next weeks, Thor meditated on the power Eve had shown. Meditated, and wondered. Had Odin been right? Had she held him to her will all these years, not realizing that he would not die?

He pulled his hood down farther over his eyes when Eve approached him and refilled his mug. Her forehead furrowed as she glanced up at him, but then she smiled and he felt his heart race. "I've never seen a man drink as much as you do and still be able to walk himself out the door."

"No doubt." Perhaps he had been drinking overmuch, but it was difficult for him to watch these other men grope her. It was difficult for him to watch Loki worm his way into her good graces. Though each time she rebuffed the Trickster, he felt a little more hope. If she could fend off Loki, surely her brother would be no threat to her.

Thor's hope that Adam's reign as pope would cause enough unrest to slow Athena and Ra's plans had been crippled before he had even voiced it. Adam had not lasted two months before he had revealed himself to be so corrupted by such power that the archangel Michael himself had thrown him from Saint Peter's chair. He had been lucky to escape from the angel with his life.

Eve frowned again. Setting the pitcher on the table before him. "Have we—"

Another patron bellowed for more drink, pounding his fist against the table top. She sighed and picked up the pitcher, glancing back over her shoulder at Thor as she walked away.

He slouched in his seat and tried to pretend he wasn't watching her as he pulled his hood down. From his position against the corner of the room, he had a clear view of the rest of the tavern. Men filled the tables in the front of the room, not bothering to seat themselves at the bar against the far wall when Eve would refill their glasses no matter where they sat. Behind the bar was the door to the store room and the kitchen. The cook had long gone home. No one came this late looking for food.

Loki was among the group which had just called for Eve, and he grabbed her backside as she leaned to fill a glass. She spilled beer on the table, and slapped his hand away. The men laughed, and thunder rolled outside. Thor felt his eyes burn, the color draining from the room. But not yet. He had to wait.

A man entered the tavern from the rain and removed his hat. Eve smiled at him in recognition. "I'll have your wine in just a moment."

"My thanks, Lilah." He nodded and took a seat with two other men. Regulars all three. Thor was still trying to decide if the man was married or not, and if he wasn't, whether he was trying to work up the nerve to ask Eve for her hand.

Eve slipped around the bar into the store room to find the wine, nearly disappearing from sight. Loki pushed back his chair, excusing himself to piss, and followed her. Thor's knuckles ached from the fists his hands had made, but still he did not move. He had to wait. Wait until she asked. And if he saw what she was capable of to protect herself, so much the better. It was information he needed when her brother's memory was returned.

It was dark in the room, but he could make out the shadow of the two of them, and the white of Eve's skirt. It looked as though Loki was backing her against the wall. Eve slipped beneath his arm with the wine she had been after, but he grabbed her by the arm and pulled her back roughly. Thor heard a hiccupped exclamation, and then a crash, and . . .

Help!

Before he could make it across the room, four other men had risen as if sleepwalking. Loki was grabbed from behind and thrown off her.

The Trickster landed at Thor's feet.

He smiled wolfishly and grabbed Loki by his shirt, dragging him out of the tavern. Dirt and filth covered the street and the rain beat down on the cobbled stones, lightning crackling. Thor tossed him into the biggest puddle he could find.

Loki scrambled to his feet in the mud as Thor stalked toward him. "You can't hurt me, Odin-son. You're bound by the Covenant."

Thor grinned and grabbed him by the throat. *Mjölnir* hummed in the back of his mind. Eve would not spare him this time. He was not within her tavern. And Loki had earned this.

"You broke the Covenant when you interfered with God's daughter, Loki. Or don't you remember? We agreed she would not be touched. And I would watch her."

Loki struggled against his grip, and Thor felt him begin to shape-shift, but he pulled him closer to his face, staring into the Trickster's eyes and clamping his mind around the power before it could be done.

Loki hissed, and his eyes widened with panic. "Only Odin can strip our power!"

"Is that so?" Thor tightened his grip until Loki's eyes bulged and the god's throat popped, then crunched. "No more lies, Trickster. No more interference. No more games."

Loki choked something, but Thor had done enough damage he could not speak. Never again would he whisper lewd suggestions in Eve's ear. *You'll be punished.*

"It will be worth it," Thor agreed.

He braced Loki's body with his other hand, and tore the god's head from his shoulders.

The body dropped and a bolt of lightning incinerated it. Loki's eyes stared at him in shocked surprise, and then closed. What was left of the god's essence slipped out of the world, back to the gates of Hel.

Thor threw his head into the gutter. It was where the Trickster had always belonged.

He inhaled deeply and let the rain wash the blood from his hands and from the street. Let it cleanse him and calm him. And then he went back into the tavern. Eve stared at him, the pitcher in her hands, as he took his seat at the table in the corner. The other men had returned to their chairs, laughing amongst themselves as if nothing had happened. Thor suspected they would not remember that anything had.

She filled his cup and waited. He tapped his fingers on the handle of the mug, willing her to turn, to leave. But she didn't, and when he lifted his gaze, her expression was inscrutable.

He raised the mug and swallowed a large mouthful of ale.

"Don't let me see you kill another man again," she said.

Thor looked into her eyes, and wondered how much she had seen. What would she let herself believe? But he would have killed Loki a hundred times over to protect her. He would have killed any god who tried to hurt her.

"As you wish," he said.

She topped off his mug with what remained in the pitcher, and walked away.

CHAPTER TWENTY-NINE
Present

☙

Eve was able to join the others for dinner that night, a fact that was celebrated with a fine sparkling white wine and a meal of her favorite fish. She never got tired of eating fish. Maybe because there had been so little of it to eat in her first life, when they had lived off the land, hunting what the lions did. Fish hadn't come into her diet until a later life, and then of course there had been Thorgrim, much, much later.

But as hard as she tried not to look, her gaze kept going to Lars. He had been seated at the foot of the table, between Juliette and René, who both seemed unreservedly pleased to see him. Horus asked her for the salad, seated across from her, and she shook her head, tearing her eyes away, and smiling at him as she passed it. Garrit sat at the head of the table, and Alex in his high-chair positioned at the corner between them. He was happily playing with his food, and the Belgian Shepherd Garrit had gifted her with as a wedding present lay beside the baby's seat, snatching up pieces of dinner that inevitably landed on the ground.

"How long will you be with us, Horus?" she asked. It was the first opportunity she'd had to speak with him since the train, really, that hadn't revolved around how much pain she was feeling.

He shrugged, the movement surprisingly graceful for an older man. "That will depend upon your husband and Lars, I think. As long as I'm needed, certainly. And it is a great pleasure to visit these lands again, see this house."

"Have you been here before?" The way he talked made her think he held some kind of nostalgia for it.

"Oh, yes," he said. And there was that amusement again. Never far from him, when they spoke, it seemed. "But it was a very long time ago. Sometimes it seems another lifetime. I used to be something of an architect, you see, in my youth. I helped with some of the renovations."

Garrit coughed. It almost sounded like a strangled laugh, and she glanced at him, but he only shook his head and sipped his water.

"Architecture seems a long way from homeopathic remedies." Everyone seemed to be paying attention to the amount of wine in her glass and food on her plate. She wasn't sure if they were more worried about her overeating or not eating enough, but it annoyed her either way.

"Quite, yes." Horus said. "I took an interest in herbal remedies while I was in China and learned as much as I could. I have a great appetite for knowledge." He smiled that grandfather's smile. "Not unlike yourself, I think? Do you not also collect herbal and traditional remedies?"

She wondered where he had learned that, and glanced at Garrit. But had Garrit even known? She didn't remember mentioning it to him. Her education in this life had been in history.

"I have, in the past." Considering that medicine had descended into drilling holes into the heads of patients, or else engaging in exorcism, the knowledge had proven more than useful. "It seemed prudent at the time. But I never did learn the technique you and Lars used to help alleviate the pain."

"It's very uncommon." Horus said. "Very few are able to master it."

Juliette leaned over. "Abby, you have barely eaten. *Monsieur* Amon, you must not keep her from her food!"

Horus bowed his head. "You are right, of course, *madame*. Forgive me." But his eyes sparkled, and Eve thought that he enjoyed humoring Juliette.

What had she missed while she had been sleeping? She caught Alex's bowl before he could throw that to the dog as well, removing it from his tray. But even Alex seemed to have become used to the two men. He smiled now at Horus across from him, and Horus made faces back until he laughed.

Garrit seemed to be the only person who wasn't entirely thrilled with his guests. He kept frowning in Lars's direction, which of course caused her to look to see what the man had done, and didn't help her at all to focus on not thinking about Thorgrim. The strangest part was that Lars seemed to be doing nothing more than eating, and chuckling at René and Juliette's banter. Eve never even caught him looking at her, something which she wasn't sure she was pleased or disappointed about. Pleased, she decided with determination. She was married. She had a son. She could not feel this way about another man. She had never felt this way about another man. Not ever, in any of her very long lives.

She grimaced, and glanced in his direction. When he met her eyes, she felt herself flush, and dropped her gaze to her plate, pushing some of the food around it.

"Don't eat too much, Abby," Horus said softly. "Your stomach will not thank you for it after living nearly a week on just the broth we spooned down your throat. Had you been anyone else . . ."

She forced herself to smile. "Had I been anyone else, I would not have suffered a trauma from my brother's choice to throw himself in front of a bus."

The humor left the man's face then. He looked very old when he wasn't smiling. "You can't trust him."

Odd how many people knew Adam. It clearly hadn't been a well kept secret. "I know my brother, Horus. I know what he wants. I trust that he'll do everything in his power to achieve it."

Garrit touched her arm. *"T'as l'air fatiguée."*

Yes. She felt tired. Drained. And she still ached. Especially her head.

"If you'll excuse me," she said to the table at large. She smiled at her husband. "I think I'll go sit in the library in front of the fire."

Garrit raised her hand to his lips and kissed it before letting her go.

She hated that she found herself wishing it had been Lars's touch as she walked away.

Eve stared at the journal in her hands and wondered why it was that in a life where she had married for love, she could not stop thinking about other men.

There was Ryam, of course, who haunted her here. Though it only served to make her feel more strongly about her DeLeon family. Intensifying her frustration. Deepening her love. It would have been more unusual if she hadn't thought of Ryam, looking at his grandchildren. Her grandchildren. Looking at René, who had Ryam's looks. Certainly though, Ryam had never had René's sense of humor. He had always been very serious. As if he carried the world on his shoulders.

She could even understand if she thought of Reu. Garrit was incredibly like him, from his habit of running his fingers through his hair, to the way he looked at her, the way he touched her. And all the DeLeon men had Reu's eyes. But digging up memories of Reu was an effort. She remembered him, remembered her creation and the Garden, but it grew more difficult to bring his face to her mind, and the world was so changed, she could not even imagine how he would have responded to the things she took for granted, now.

Her strongest memories of that life were the terrible parts. Her fear of Adam in the Garden and its burning, the threat of the angels that she had never quite been able to escape. But she remembered clearly the moment when Reu had kissed her and she had known she was meant to be his wife. That much, she did not think she would ever forget.

Thorgrim, though. She sighed and stood up, putting the journal back in its cabinet and moving to the window. The glass was cool, and it felt good against the flush of her cheeks. She forced herself to keep her eyes open, because if she closed them, his face would rise in her mind. Lars's face, too, and she didn't want to see it. Didn't want to witness her own betrayal.

She didn't understand why she kept thinking of Thorgrim. And her memory of that life was astonishingly well preserved. She could revisit each day that they lived together with perfect clarity. In her worst lives, the most difficult ones she had lived, it had been her life with Thorgrim she had returned to, dreamed of, remembered. When she had been hospitalized, it was where she had retreated. She had tricked herself into believing he was present with her, in addition to projecting him to the doctors when she made her escape. She distinctly remembered having conversations with him about the modern world. Telling him stories about the lives they had spent apart. And kissing him.

Oh, kissing him. She trailed her fingers over her lips, and wished she hadn't remembered that part. As delusions and hallucinations went, she had never achieved anything as real as those moments. She had been able to feel the heat of his body against hers, the soft tickle of his breath against her ear, his lips on her neck. The roughness of his hands on her skin.

She had even, in her insanity, in her desperation, believed that she had made love to him in the night. Her face burned even hotter as she remembered it. Remembered begging him. He had refused her at first. Insisted it wasn't right. That he shouldn't. That she wasn't in her right mind. And she remembered finding it endlessly amusing that her own hallucination should point that out to her. How odd that she had been so aware, and yet so completely caught up in the delusion. Of course she had convinced him. How could she not have convinced her own mind, when she wanted it so badly? And she had so many years of memories of lovemaking with Thorgrim to call upon.

She didn't think she would ever be able to repeat the experience. The manipulation of her own mind that had allowed her to honestly believe he had been there, that he was touching her, that she was touching him, and that he was inside her.

But that had been a situation she had no desire to ever find herself in again. She never wanted to be so desperate to escape her life that she was forced to manufacture a hallucination so incredible. So real.

The door opened, and she saw the reflection of Thorgrim standing there in the window. No, she reminded herself forcefully as she turned to look at him, not Thorgrim. Lars. He shut the door behind him without a sound, and stared at her. Stared with eyes that devoured her.

She felt as though she were laid bare before him. As though he had known what she was thinking of, what she had been remembering. As if he had been called to her by the memories.

He stepped toward her. Once. Twice.

He crossed the room, and she realized that she wanted him to, and it was as if the thought gave him confidence, because he raised his hand to her face, stroked her cheek and stared into her eyes. He was so tall. She had almost forgotten how tall he was. The top of her head was barely level with his shoulder.

She covered his hand with her own, holding it against her cheek. It had been so long. She had missed Thorgrim so much. His easy confidence. His absolute adoration for her. Like the warmth of a fire in winter. He had made every other man's love into a mere candle, he had burned so bright and hot.

"This is real," he said softly, looking into her eyes. "Have no doubt about it."

And then he drew her against him, lifted her face to his, and kissed her until she couldn't even remember to breathe, couldn't remember anything outside of his lips, his mouth, his hands . . .

"Oh," she heard herself say, when she could think again enough to talk. His forehead touched hers, allowing the smallest sliver of space between them. "I almost wish you hadn't done that."

He chuckled, and his breath tickled her throat as he kissed her jaw. "Only almost?"

He kissed her again, claiming her completely. Long and deep and hard and real. So real she trembled with need, and something dormant inside her bloomed into life—something she had been missing for so long. Too long.

Her heart broke when he let her go, her mind clearing too quickly from the fog of memory, leaving behind the same bone deep certainty that had come with Reu's kiss.

Because, in this life, she was already married.

CHAPTER THIRTY
Future

Fire and ash and fear, so much fear, bitter on her tongue and souring her stomach. Soot floated from the sky in thick, silver flakes, dusting her hair. The flames hadn't kept to the Garden itself, the dry grassland outside its gates just so much tinder, encouraging it to spread, burning everything in its path. She could feel the heat on her back as she ran.

The sharp ding of the seatbelt sign jerked her out of the dream, and Eve took a breath of the smoke-free air in the cabin, oddly comforted by the tang of deodorizers and humidifiers. Circulation systems had come a long way, stripping out viruses and bacteria that spread disease on long flights, and somehow, it had only made planes smell worse. But the taint pulled her further from the dream—the memory. Another reminder of how long it had been, how much things had changed. How much Adam had changed, no matter how desperately she tried to cling to the past.

"Prepare for landing," a woman's voice chimed, the cadence not quite right, artificial. The seat righted itself into the approved angles, and the table folded itself into the cabin wall. Eve shivered. She'd never quite grown used to that kind of automation. Just like she still hadn't given up on paper books, or writing things by hand.

She would have preferred to travel by the slower, lower-tech airships, truthfully, but Adam must have gone to a lot of trouble to get her booked on one of the super-sonic high-altitude jets. Normally, someone in her tax bracket wouldn't come anywhere near the inside of one, never mind on such short notice. She couldn't fault his generosity, but there was no way she would ever be able to pay him back. Not for this. Not for any of it.

The drop from high-altitude and deceleration pressed her into the cushioning of the seat, and her stomach lurched. What she would have given for a train line across the Atlantic. Something safe and grounded. Compared to wheels, pushed, pulled, on tracks or otherwise, flying was so new. And it had really only been the last two lifetimes that she'd had any experience with it.

Eve closed her eyes, breathing deeply to settle her nerves, and tried to remember. But the flames licking behind her eyelids became the wide, round hearth at the heart of Sparta's megaron, and Paris— Adam—lifting his cup in silent salute from across the fire, his lips curving with promise and his eyes gathering her in, making her whole body flush. She gripped the armrests and pushed the memory away, counting instead, to distract herself. One-locomotive, two-locomotive, three-locomotive . . .

The jet landed with another stomach turning jolt and Eve relaxed into the pressure as it slowed. Almost over. Almost there. And soon enough she'd be with her family. Her real family, the DeLeons. She tried to tell herself that was what she wanted most, what she most looked forward to, but she couldn't stop the twist of her heart when she thought of Adam waiting for her, felt the gentle welcome of his mind against her own. Just the lightest touch, like a butterfly kiss, and a warmth that settled in the pit of her stomach.

Deplaning took another lifetime, and then she was in the terminal, searching eagerly for one dark head among so many. Airports hadn't changed much in the last century, and the French clung to their liberty. Security officers strolled casually throughout the concourse, sprinkled among the passengers and their families, in plain clothes as well as uniformed, but they didn't stop husbands from saying goodbye to their wives, or children from clinging to their fathers until the very last boarding call.

Adam stepped forward, his eyes lighting at the sight of her, and her heart picked up speed. This trip wasn't about him. It wasn't about whatever they felt for one another, she reminded herself sternly. This trip was about her family. That was all. It sounded hollow even in her own thoughts.

The light died with her lack of response, his forehead furrowing instead, and he took the bag from her shoulder. *After all this time, won't you forgive me, Evey?*

She pressed her lips together and looked away, guilt sitting like lead in her stomach. She'd let him believe she was angry about that kiss, and everything that had come before it, for far too long, and the lie tasted all the more bitter when his pain touched her thoughts.

"How was your flight?" he asked gently.

"I slept most of the way." She forced a polite smile, but looking at his face only caused her gaze to drift lower. The memory of his kiss, so long ago, bubbled up to the surface of her thoughts, making her flush. She bit the inside of her cheek, but the pain wasn't enough to distract her. As useless as her memories. "You didn't have to fly me first class, you know."

"Nothing but the best for you, Eve. Always." He smiled back, his eyes searching hers. "Are you all right?"

It had been so much easier when he had been selfish and self-absorbed, too wrapped up in himself and his own needs to notice hers. It had been easier when he had only been her brother-in-law, but the harder she grasped for those feelings from their last life, familial tolerance and safe, sisterly affection, the more they slipped through the cracks of her memory, pushed out by the present. The fit of her hand in his. The bittersweet half-smile when he'd said goodbye. The warmth of his arms, and the scent of his skin, all fresh earth and cinnamon, with just the slightest hint of vanilla. His lips on hers, and the mint of his mouth feeding the spark of desire.

She tore her eyes away from his lips and stared over his head at the signs, looking for the exit. "Shall we?"

Evey? What are you keeping from me?

She shook her head and started walking. *Things that should be kept. It doesn't matter, Adam. It's all behind us.*

He frowned, guiding her deftly with a hand at the small of her back. She tried to ignore the warmth that spread up her spine. Outside, a car waited for them, sleek and black. The driver touched the brim of his hat, opening the door for them, and then shutting it again after they'd slid inside. Eve stared out the window, determined not to look at him. In such a close space, all she wanted to do was curl up against his side, and she didn't dare. Not when he was so concerned, so considerate, so damn worried about her.

Coming here was a mistake. Seeing him. Being anywhere near him. It was one thing to talk to him from half a world away, but this, now . . .

She wanted this too much.

"The meeting is tomorrow," he said, his voice as distant as she felt. "Ryam had some things to discuss with his brothers beforehand, but they're expecting you."

"They should have been expecting me the moment they put the property up for sale." She frowned. It wasn't like her family to be so careless, and if Adam hadn't been paying attention—but he had. There was no use agonizing over what might have happened. "Thank you for doing this. I know things haven't been easy between us these last years, and I had no right to ask it of you. I'm afraid I'll have to ask even more from you still, if they insist on selling."

He covered her hand where it lay between them on the seat, warm and dry and comforting, and she wanted so much to lace her fingers through his. "You have every right to ask it of me. To ask anything. I am sorry, Eve, for using you that way. I never wanted to hurt you."

"You never mean it, but you do." She pulled her hand free and hid it between her thighs in her lap, before he realized how much of an affect he had on her. "And it hurts so much more. If I could just convince myself you didn't love me, then maybe it would be less painful. But it's so hard to lie when I can feel the truth."

You love me, too, Eve.

She closed her eyes. *More the fool, me.* She reached for the fire again, let it lick at the edges of her mind. The crying people. The flare of brilliant white wings and a sword of light. Her eyes snapped open again and she grimaced. She didn't want to think of Michael. The last time she'd gotten too close to Adam, he'd arrived in the flesh to threaten her, her family, her son. No matter how desperately she wanted to remind herself of the danger, she didn't want to think of him. It wouldn't come to that. No matter what, she wouldn't let it.

He studied her face. "What is it that bothers you so much? If it's this business with Michael, I swear I'll never—"

"It isn't. It's nothing. Just dreams of old memories."

"Nightmares, you mean. I can see it in your mind. Whatever it is, it's haunting you."

She sighed. "It's nothing I can't handle, Adam. And for what it's worth—" She pressed her lips together, hesitating, but the guilt that kept welling up between them, the pain, it was more misery than she could stand. She was so tired of the lies. Her whole life was built on one lie after another, and if she couldn't have Adam, couldn't be with him, at least she could be honest. "For what it's worth, I've forgiven you for that. Whatever it was you needed from Michael, I don't see how you could have found him any other way."

"You must be starving," he said, his gaze sliding away. "I have a flat here. I could make you something, or would you prefer to go out? Anything you like."

"You own property in France?" Of course he owned property in France. She should have guessed as much, after everything they'd shared.

"I own property everywhere. But keeping a place here seemed prudent, in case you wanted to come back." He shrugged. "I'm afraid that I'm guilty of wishful thinking."

"And here I am."

"I could wish the circumstances were better. That this could be a happy reunion for you, rather than what's shaping up to be an unhappy chastisement. If they can't be dissuaded, Eve, you won't lose it. I'll find a way, I promise."

She stared out the window again, watching the countryside rush past them. So familiar and so strange at the same time. But it had only been what? Twenty-five years? It felt like so much longer. Lifetimes ago. She never would have imagined she'd be coming back this way, with Adam at her side, acting as her champion, determined to rescue her family's estate.

She snorted. Garrit was probably spinning in his grave.

Adam carried her luggage into the flat, showing her to her room. She stared at his back, following in silence. He was built more like a runner than a wrestler, lean and lithe, but not too tall. If it hadn't been for his grace, just slightly more natural in every motion, he could have been anyone, really. An average Joe, with a much too charming smile, and striking gray eyes. Or maybe not *so* average.

He pushed open the door to the guest room, turning back to her, and Eve jerked her gaze from his body to the bed, then flushed. The bed. This wasn't the first time he'd shown her to a bed. She hugged herself and stepped into the room, careful not to brush against him as she passed.

"If there's anything you need, just let me know. I want you to be comfortable."

"Thank you." She ran her fingertips along the mahogany dresser, the silken finish cool against her too warm skin. The bed was mahogany too, with bookshelves built into the headboard. She picked up a small hardcover, bound with fraying green canvas, and lettered with gold. Norse Mythology. She frowned at the other volumes beside it. More myths from different cultures. Roman, Greek, Egyptian, South-East Asian, South American. Hinduism and Buddhism, the Bible and the Koran. "Some light reading?"

He shrugged. "I like to know my competition."

"Even if you told them the truth, they wouldn't believe you." She put the book back, and tried to ignore the sinking feeling in her stomach. "But I wish you the best of luck."

He laughed. "Evey, I'm not interested in making myself a god. You'd never forgive me if I tried, even if I succeeded, not in a million years."

"Then why?"

"You've never wondered at all? If we exist, if the Bible holds even such a small grain of truth, couldn't these other religions offer something, mean something?"

She shook her head. "God made us, made the world."

"*This* world, Evey."

"You can't be serious? You of all people to doubt God, the angels. All these myths, they're probably just some twisted game of Michael's. Or Lucifer, maybe, to get beneath Michael's skin. And even if it were true, by some—some miracle, I never saw any evidence, any proof. Life after life, and no matter how many sacrifices I made, no matter how many prayers I said, I never saw even the barest glimmer of anything in response."

"You're right, of course." His gaze shifted to the window over her shoulder, then away again. "I suppose I just like the idea of it. That maybe we aren't so alone. If we can't have each other maybe—" he swallowed, and when he spoke again, his voice had thickened. "Maybe there's someone else who might truly be worthy of you."

"Adam." Her heart twisted and she reached for him. Couldn't stop herself from stroking his cheek. "I never wanted a god, Adam. Never wanted anything like that."

He pulled her hand away. "But you deserved it. That kind of love. The same kind of love that you give."

"Stop." She caught a handful of his shirt. "Just stop, please. Love is love, unselfish and beautiful and shining, and I know you, Adam. I know your heart. The things I said before, every cruel thing I said to push you away," she stopped, blinking rapidly against the tears that pricked her eyes. "When you were with Mia, married to her, I looked at you, and I knew you loved her, cared for her. I knew something in you had changed beyond just remembering. After that, I always knew." *I know love, Adam. I know when it's real, when it isn't. I don't fight it because you can't give it back. I fight it because I know you can give me everything. More than I ever dreamed.*

You're too generous, Evey. Too forgiving. But his hand covered hers and held it tight. Then he let her go and stepped back. "You should eat something. It was a long flight, and I know firsthand how appalling the meal options can be."

She let her hand drop, her heart raw and her body cold without his touch. Facing this, all of it, hurt so much. "Maybe just some wine, if you have it."

His eyebrows lifted. "Are you sure?"

"I'm sure." *To take the edge off.*

"It's not exactly a prudent choice."

She wrinkled her nose. "Since when do you let prudence stand in your way?"

He almost smiled. "You'd be surprised." But he didn't argue any further.

Eve followed him out of the room again, retracing their steps down the hall, through the living room. A leather sofa and a matching armchair faced a cozy fireplace. Gas, of course, and enclosed with glass. What was it about the rich that made them want to control even flame? And everything was so neat. Too neat. But on the other side of the room, a set of French doors opened onto a balcony, with a view of the mountains. Her mountains.

"Do you live here?" she asked, tearing herself away from the glimpse of the countryside and catching up with him in the kitchen. It was more of the same. Not a crumb to be seen anywhere, and everything in its place.

"Sometimes." He was rummaging through a drawer, a bottle of wine in his hand. A nice, full bodied red, by the label. He closed that drawer and opened another, then a third before he found the corkscrew, and tossed her a sheepish smile. "This is kind of a vacation spot, I suppose. As much as I vacation anywhere. Half the year I spend in Britain, to appease my parents. Most of the other half I spend here."

"I see." He had to check two different cabinets before he found the wine glasses. Sometimes, indeed. She drank her glass without tasting it, and held it out for more.

"You're going to get yourself drunk, Evey." He refilled the glass anyway. "Are you sure I can't tempt you to eat? I have strawberries . . ."

"Just wine, thank you." But she sipped it this time. She'd never forget her first meal of berries and nuts. The way he smiled when he saw her pleasure as the flavor filled her mouth. "Maybe I should have stayed in a hotel."

He took the glass from her hand, ducking his head to catch her eyes. "I couldn't bear it if you did. All this time apart. We're not forbidden to see one another, Eve. It doesn't have to be this way."

"We keep having this conversation, over and over again, but you know it isn't that simple. When you touch me, when we kiss—" she swallowed, and met his gaze. "I don't want to stop."

"Do you really think I could risk losing you? I know I've made mistakes. I know I'm not perfect at this. I've stayed away, like you've asked. How many more years do I have to spend like this to prove that I won't hurt you? How many years do you have to spend in agony before you allow yourself some small kind of comfort?"

She bit her lip and stared at her wine glass, sitting beyond him on the marble countertop. He lifted her chin, bringing her attention back to his face, and her mouth went dry. The way he was looking at her, the softness in his eyes. He stroked her cheek and her eyes closed. It had been so long since anyone had touched her so gently.

Please.

His lips brushed hers, questioning, and she sighed, her hands finding his chest, sliding to his shoulders. He pulled her closer and covered her mouth with his, lighting everything inside her until she melted into his body. She drank the wine from his lips, her fingers threading through his short hair. His hand at her waist burned through the cotton of her shirt, igniting a spark of tingling need.

He groaned softly, his fingers digging into the softness of her hip, and then he turned his head, breaking the kiss.

She hid her face against his chest, hoping it muffled the edge of hysteria, of desperation and desire. It felt so good to be in his arms again, to be held safe, wrapped in his affection, his love. Too good.

"It isn't you I don't trust, Adam," she murmured, once his heartbeat had slowed beneath her cheek. He smoothed her hair, tucking her head beneath his chin, and she didn't think she could bring herself to pull away, no matter how many dreams of flaming swords and burning ash Michael sent as reminders. "Not this time."

CHAPTER THIRTY-ONE
1412 AD

§

The Northlands had fallen to the Christians, one after another. All but the Sami, in the far north, and the peasants and Samogitians of Lithuania, to the east, had converted. The old ways were outlawed along with the worship of the gods who had nurtured them for so long. There were those among the converted lands who still made sacrifice in private, praying to Freyr to protect their crops, or calling upon Odin to give them strength in battle, but every year, they grew fewer in number. Every year, the gods of Asgard spoke of moving on. And every year, Odin refused to be persuaded, his one-eyed gaze falling upon Thor, and grimmer lines forming around his mouth and eyes. Odin had never forgiven him for Loki's murder, nor was he at all pleased that the Council had sanctioned it. But that was not all that lay between them.

"All these years, and you are still under her spell," Odin had spat, after Thor had told him he would not go on to the new world that Zeus and his brothers had found, regardless of any decision made by the Aesir.

Hermes and Anubis traveled between the two planes, now and

again, bringing news and invitations. The Covenant had forged bonds between pantheons that had not been forgotten, and Zeus had not quite given up on reclaiming his wisest daughter. Most of the Egyptians had left, at Ra's urging, and a good many of the Persians had followed. There was no longer room for any worship but that of Elohim in those lands.

"I have obligations, people who look to me still for help and protection. Eve is part of it, of course, but she is not all that holds me here."

"You would abandon your family, your brothers, your children to remain here?" Odin demanded. "Never to know their fates!"

"Unlike you, Father, I do not feel compelled to keep my children leashed. Thrud and Ullr will no doubt follow their mother, and Magni and Modi have yet to decide what path they will take, but I will not argue with them, one way or the other. My daughter knows she will always have my love, as do my sons, and they will know too, where to find me, if they ever wish to return."

"She does not even know you live, boy!" Odin slammed his fist against the arm of his throne. "You betray everything for nothing more than a child's fantasy, and you expect me to stand by and watch? To allow it!"

Thor met his father's gaze, his own eyes burning. "And why is it, Father, that she does not know I live?"

Odin had thrown him out of his chamber after that, cursing him for insolence, and Thor had known even then, he had made a mistake. If Odin had not been certain whether to remain before, he had reason to do so now. Spite, more than anything, kept the Aesir on this earth. And Odin's stubborn refusal to accept that he had lost his son.

And so Thor waited, and watched Eve from a distance, for Odin had taken to sending Baldur or Freyr to follow him when he walked the earth. Heimdall's observations, it seemed, were no longer enough. But at least he did not send Sif to haunt his steps. From what Thor had heard, she was much too busy finding comfort in Lugh's arms, now that Loki was trapped in Hel. He would not have wished her on any Aesir, nor did he truly wish her on the Celt, Trickster or not, but if either one found pleasure in the match, that was their business. Sif was, after all, no longer his wife, and he was well rid of her.

"Have you been to Avignon?" Heimdall asked him one day, when Thor had gone to join him at his post. The cliff's edge seemed to have crumbled in the last century, but Bifrost still sprung burning from its stones, bending toward the earth in a rainbow of fire and light.

"Not since before the popes settled there." Thor passed him a horn of mead. Heimdall was not often able to attend the feasts in Odin's hall, but Thor and his brothers had always taken turns bringing him some refreshment while he stood watch. Even now, Heimdall did not turn his gaze from the distance, staring out across the world, marking the comings and goings of the Aesir and listening to the prayers of their people.

Heimdall accepted the mead, frowning. "It is not possible to watch the earth and not see your Eve, burning more brightly than even our bridge. Odin prefers I not speak of it. Prefers, I think, to pretend she does not live, but he cannot make me blind to her, nor prevent me from seeing."

"And what have you seen, to speak of that which my father has forbidden?"

"I have seen Avignon," Heimdall said, slanting him a strange glance. "And were I you, and charged with her keeping, I would find her there."

§

France had suffered tremendously in the last centuries—all of the continent had—but Thor had done what he could to ensure the House of Lions had remained untouched, both by plague and war. Athena had helped, and Ra as well. Even Baldur had been lured from Asgard by the promise of good mead and an escape from the cloud of despair which had settled over Odin's house.

The streets of Paris were not much of an improvement. Between the warring Dukes, the Mad King Charles, and the threat of the English, the city knew no peace. But neither was the country safe, Thor realized, for as he traveled, he passed villages burned to ash and abandoned, ravaged by war and marauders, both.

Avignon, in the south, was fortunate. While the pope resided, the city had swelled, protected by its walls and the gold paid in ransom. Plague had struck, and the population thinned, but it was not as devastated as it might have been, and even without Rome's presence, trade made Avignon rich. Benedict, true pope or not, had not been gone so long that the people suffered for his absence. In fact, they thrived.

When Thor arrived, the streets buzzed with news of a coming trial, and Thor could not take three steps without running into another monk or priest, hurrying by in some kind of preparation. Whoever the poor girl was, by the way the city talked, she was already condemned.

"Her poor sister," he heard one woman flutter as she passed him on the street. "Such an innocent to be so exposed. And the stories she told of the devil! As if he were some old friend! Why Pierre did not remarry when he had the chance, I'll never understand. A good wife would have put a stop to any witchcraft beneath his roof, and saved him the disgrace."

"He'll never find a wife now," her companion agreed. "And poor Aimee. Who will want a woman so ruined? And she was such a charming little thing. So delicate and beautiful."

"The only place for her now is the convent," the first woman said. "And the sooner, the better, before the news spreads any further. Perhaps in a year or two, there might be a lord in England willing to take her, the poor dear. It certainly isn't her fault, if she was bewitched."

Thor snorted. There was, of course, a seed of truth to the idea of bewitchment. The Olympians had taken great advantage of the art, certainly, encouraging one or another of their heroes to this or that act. But from all Eve had told him of the Garden, Lucifer was unlikely to be involved in any of it. The Fallen One had gone to ground so thoroughly he had not been seen or heard from for as long as Thor had walked the earth and even Ra was uncertain of his fate. Lucifer had frightened Eve, but only because of his strangeness, and in the end, it was his wisdom which had given her the strength to save her people.

His steps slowed and his chest tightened. *As if he were some old friend.*

He'd known for some time the Church might consider Eve a threat, but he had never imagined she would speak of her pasts so carelessly as to bring herself to their attention. Always, she had been cautious. Always, she had protected herself, preferring not to speak of her history at all, from what he had witnessed, unless she believed the person worthy of her trust and love.

But Heimdall had sent him here for a reason. For Eve.

Might Eve have trusted a sister? Told stories to entertain a child?

He closed his eyes, searching for the bright light of her presence, so familiar to him after so many years. Where? Heimdall could not have been wrong, and Thor trusted him not to lie. At worst, Heimdall would only keep his own counsel—

There. Too dim and flickering, but impossible to confuse for any other. He followed his sense of her, and the nearer he went, the more her anxiety wrapped around his heart, thick and bitter. And then he stood upon the gray stone esplanade, before the immense palace built by the popes. There was no reason Eve should have been inside such a fortress. Even if she were a legate's daughter, or some bastard child of a cardinal, she would have been removed after the siege. And it was not as if there were not enough luxurious apartments within the city walls.

A carriage rolled to a stop before the main entrance, the horses pawing at the stone, nostrils flaring and coats lathered. The man who stepped out was clearly a priest of some kind, a bishop at least, judging by how richly he was dressed. He adjusted his gloves and took the steps two at a time, his expression grim.

But Thor did not wait to see him enter the palace. There was no need, for the man's intent was more than clear in his thoughts.

Thunder rumbled overhead, and Thor reached for the lightning that crackled between the clouds, drawing it down. Liquid light spilled through his veins, and the esplanade with its palace dissolved into mountains and fields as familiar as the touch of Eve's mind. Perhaps he could not reveal himself to her, but that did not mean he could not send her aid, and what was the House of Lions for, if not this?

He only hoped he would not be too late, for the Church had sent inquisitors, and they meant to judge Eve.

Heretic or witch, it hardly mattered now.

"Thor of the North." The man looking down on him from the back of a horse had the same dark eyes and dark hair of his Lion predecessors, with a rather larger portion of caution and reserve. Thor could hardly blame him. There were far too many bandits and marauders roaming about the countryside, even in the mountains, and with lands so near France's border, the Lions faced assault from foreigners as well. But Thor did not have the time to humor his suspicion.

"I come on behalf of your Lady," Thor said. "Who even now requires your protection."

Ryam's eyes narrowed, his horse dancing beneath him, black and glossy. "You come with lightning and thunder and speak of our Lady, but what possible protection might I offer her that you cannot? Thor of the North is said to be a god."

He let his eyes haze white, the green and gold of the fields leaching to gray in his vision. Thunder rumbled again, overhead. "Even gods have limits. Most especially in lands belonging to another. Your Lady is in Avignon."

Ryam tightened his grip on the reins, and his horse snorted. "Surely the angels—"

"Will stand by and watch her burn for heresy and witchcraft!" Lightning flashed, betraying his impatience. "I can take you to Avignon with my own power, but I dare not influence their minds. It must be you, Ryam."

"Marquis DeLeon," he corrected him stiffly. "Lord DeLeon, at the least."

His jaw clenched, but he acknowledged the title with the barest of nods. "Lord DeLeon. Will you retrieve your Lady and uphold your oaths, or must I find her another champion? One who is not too proud to protect her?"

Ryam lifted his chin, his lip curling. "If it is as you say, no Lion would refuse. She cannot be left to the justice of the inquisitors, but nor are they likely to bargain with a Marquis. Even kings must submit to the power of the Church."

"Then appeal to her father," Thor said. "Give him the opportunity to save his daughter's life. Even her honor, if a match might be made with such a noble house. But it must be done quickly, whatever it is. Tonight."

"On my fastest horse, I could not make it to Avignon before nightfall tomorrow."

He bared his teeth. "Fortunate then, that you need not travel by horse alone. Go and ready yourself and a carriage. Lightning will provide the rest."

§

In spite of the risk, Thor couldn't stop himself from following as Ryam climbed the stone steps, Eve's father, the hapless Pierre, beside him. It had taken the Marquis less than an hour to learn all that mattered regarding Eve's latest family, and with even less effort, he had persuaded Pierre, a minor Baron, to assist him.

"I will not say Aimee has no reason to be jealous. Anessa is indecently beautiful," Eve's father was saying. "And I fear this hasty marriage will not help matters. The best Aimee can hope for now is some fool Englishman. Or perhaps an Italian Baron, if her condition is kept quiet."

"Aimee need not know her sister's fate," Ryam said. "She will never see Anessa again."

"My daughter will not wish to be so isolated, Marquis DeLeon," Pierre argued.

Ryam stopped at the top of the stairs, his mouth a grim line. "Your daughter will be mine, Lord Gauldry. And I do not mean to risk a second trial of her soul. If that means isolation in the Alps, then so be it, but I do not think she will find the living difficult." His gaze flicked to Thor. "Assuming my information is not wrong."

Thor ignored the implications, nodding him onward. "The longer we linger, the more likely there will be complications."

"My Lords?" A priest had come out to meet them at the arching entrance, bald and befuddled. "I fear it is too late to call upon the inquisitor with testimonies. He has retired for the evening."

"Lord Gauldry wishes to see his daughter, and as her cousin, I insist upon the right as well," Ryam said, his tone firm. "Surely you will not refuse her such a small comfort?"

"Her cousin?" the priest repeated, frowning up at him. "I'm afraid I have not had the honor."

"The Marquis DeLeon," Pierre supplied. "A connection on my late wife's side. I tried to reason with him, Father, but he would not hear of waiting after coming so far."

"Ah." The priest pursed his lips. "I am indeed honored, Lord DeLeon, but Avignon is a long way from your home, is it not?"

"Not so long a way to come for my betrothed," Ryam replied smoothly. "Though it seems the Church stands between me and what is mine."

"Under the circumstances, the Church would of course support your request for a dissolution of your betrothal, my lord."

"You misunderstand me, Father." Ryam's words were clipped, his jaw tight. "I have no intention of leaving Avignon without my bride."

"Her trial—"

"Is of no concern to me. Lady Gauldry is my intended, and I would have her know she is not without support. I am certain, Father, you are aware of the generosity of such support, when we choose to give it?"

The priest hesitated, his fingers drumming against his robes. "There are many who say the wealth of the DeLeons is exaggerated."

Thor snorted, turning his face away before the priest saw his disgust. He might have provided gold himself, though without a family name to support it, he doubted the priest would have trusted him. If it were only men, instead of priests, he might have risked the use of more effective methods of persuasion, but fooling with the minds of church men was bound to bring too much notice to his presence. As it was, he dared not do more than make himself overlooked. The Covenant still stood, after all, no matter how few the gods were in number. And God help Eve if Michael believed she worked against the church he had built, against her own father, though she could hardly have known it.

"The Pope himself knows otherwise," Ryam said, his voice cool. "And so might you, if you would give me what I wish."

The priest hesitated another moment, then nodded. "This way, Lord DeLeon, Lord Gauldry."

And Ryam had worried that the Church would not bargain with a Marquis. Thor followed them through the gate and into the courtyard, where the priest took up a torch. "Much of the palace is damaged, from the siege. It will be expensive to repair, and while the city refuses the papal claims to the grounds, the Church cannot see it done. But it is a great shame to see it in such ruin . . ."

"Perhaps a private patron can see it restored," Ryam suggested. "And when it is returned to the Church, it will not be in so unforgivable a state."

"I am certain any man so determined would receive the blessings of Our Lord." He led them to another doorway, much less ostentatious, with a stairwell descending into darkness. Thor's eyes narrowed. So they had locked her in some cell where no one might hear her, so afraid of what she might say. Old fools. Were they so insecure in their faith that they feared a girl's stories?

Perhaps he should not blame them. Michael was hardly a fit guardian for the True God's people, and Elohim himself was far too weak to make himself known. The silence must have been deafening to those who sought God's favor, and so gathered power to themselves to fill the emptiness of their souls. Thor shook his head. They would have done better to listen to Eve than to silence her. She might have granted them some sort of grace.

Down the stairwell, the shadows dancing in the torchlight, and at the bottom, a series of cells lined the walls, with only open grating for doors. The priest lifted a square of cloth to his nose, and Thor resisted the urge to fill the dungeon with scorching lightning, if only to burn away the stench of waste and the rot of forgotten corpses.

Eve sat in one of the fetid cells, her knees pulled to her chest and tucked beneath the thin fabric of an unembroidered chemise. Dark hair fell in a thick braid over her shoulder, a tattered ribbon of soft cream traveling through it. It looked as though someone had tried to tear the silk from her tresses, careless of the way her hair had pulled with it, uneven and twisted. She plucked at a frayed edge almost absently, tucking it into place, but it refused to stay.

Thor held himself back, keeping to the gloom where she would not see his face, and shutting his eyes against the burning glow that would give him away. He could not afford to lose his temper. Not now. He forced himself to calm before he allowed himself to look at her again.

"Where is her gown?" Ryam demanded.

"The inquisitor ordered her stripped, that she might better understand her place before God." The priest crossed himself, the pale patch of fabric flapping in his hand, and Thor caught the scent of lavender. He could not stand the stench himself for more than a moment unaided, and he had still left her this way? Any other woman would have risked death so exposed, between the vermin and the cold, damp quarters.

"Father?" Eve rose, coming to the grate. She smiled, seemingly undisturbed by her circumstances. But of course she would not have been bothered by rats, and why should she fear for herself, knowing even death would only bring new life? Not that the inquisitor held her life in his hands. "I did not think they would allow you to come!"

Pierre covered his daughter's hand, wrapped around the iron bars. "My dearest."

"Unlock the door," Ryam said. "And pass me that torch."

Eve frowned, her gaze shifting from her father to Ryam. "I don't understand."

"Let me see your eyes," Ryam said gently, holding the torch so the light fell brightly across her features. Eve's eyes widened, and she pressed her lips together, lifting her face. Her eyes glinted green, like emeralds in the firelight. Ryam blew out a breath, his whole demeanor softening once he'd looked his fill. As if Thor could ever mistake her, but Ryam was not the kind of man to trust what he did not see, touch, smell with his own senses. "My Lady. Forgive me for not coming sooner."

"The Marquis will take you away from here," her father said, stepping back to let the priest fumble with the lock. "Once you reach the safety of his estate, you'll be married."

"Truly, Father, you need not have gone to these lengths. I told you before, you need not fear for me. I am safe, always, in God's Grace."

"As the wife of a Marquis you will be well cared for, your future secure. No one will know you, there. What rumors have flown so far did not carry your name with them."

"Father—"

The priest pulled the door open, and Ryam stepped forward,

offering his hand. "You would live, my Lady, whatever trials you faced, but you would not be safe. We both know that."

Her eyebrows crashed together, her head tilting, just so. "Do we?"

"It would be a shame to have such beauty marred by the scars of flame. Truly, you must possess the splendor of Eve herself."

She stared at him, her eyes narrowing. "I can hardly accept such a compliment."

"Go with him, Anessa. For my sake, if not your own. Do not make me watch you burn."

Eve placed her hand in Ryam's, cautious but steady. She lifted her chin, giving no ground even in surrender. Thor ached to feel her hand in his, to stand by her in Ryam's place. He forced his hands into fists at his sides, keeping himself still. Revealing himself now would only cause her greater grief.

"And what is the name of my husband," she asked, "or am I to call you only Marquis, forevermore?"

Ryam smiled. "I think you will guess it on your own, before long."

"All the same," she said coolly.

"Ryam DeLeon, my Lady." He pressed a kiss to her knuckles. "I've come to bring you home."

CHAPTER THIRTY-TWO
Present

Lars pulled away and Eve stumbled back against the window before he caught her with a steadying arm. She raised her hand to her mouth, to her lips, and stared at him. He kissed like Thorgrim. No. Not like Thorgrim. It was Thorgrim's kiss. How was that even possible?

"Forgive me," he mumbled. "You're married. I had no right."

She felt sick and giddy, and sick for feeling giddy. She was married. To Garrit. She loved Garrit. She didn't know what to say. The absurdity of what had just happened, of what she had just felt, was too complicated for words. How did one demand to know why they kissed like their forefather, dead three thousand years? And why had it felt as though she'd come home, suddenly and completely? She was married! Garrit was her family, her everything.

His expression had grown more serious by the minute as he watched her. "Are you all right?"

"How did you—what did you—?" She was at a loss as to how to finish the sentence and gave up. "I don't understand."

"You seemed so upset." But it was as though after he said it, he realized how inadequate it was. "The things you were thinking. I just couldn't let you go on—" He shook his head. "I didn't want that to be how you remembered him—us. Me."

"Oh." She wrapped her arms around her body, feeling more naked than she ever had before. That he had heard those things. Witnessed those memories. They were things she had never told anyone. Never shared with anyone. "Oh."

"Forgive me," he said again. But she wasn't sure what he was apologizing for. If it was the kiss, or the inadvertent eavesdropping. "I should go."

"Wait." He turned back to her, but he looked as though he wasn't sure if he should have. "That kiss. You. How is it possible?"

He shook his head, opening the door. But then he shut it and turned back again, gripping the door knob as though it were his anchor. The only thing that kept him from crossing the room to her, the only thing that kept him from kissing her again. "I just need to know."

She waited, leaning back against the window frame, her own fingers curled around the wood, holding her in place, even as she stared at his hand, and then at his mouth, his lips, his face, wondering how they had done what they'd done. And she wanted to kiss him again, just to see if it would be the same. If it would be Thorgrim kissing her back.

"If you had to choose, Eve. If you could be with one of them for eternity. Would it be these men? Your DeLeon husbands? Reu, or Ryam, or Garrit?"

Garrit. She was married to Garrit, now, not Thorgrim. She couldn't kiss Lars again. Not even for Thorgrim. What had he asked? Eve. He'd called her Eve. Could she answer that question without it sounding like a betrayal? She pressed her lips together, and looked into his eyes. She could see the need in them. Naked and anguished. She owed him the truth. Whoever he was. Because it was all they could ever share, no matter how much she wanted more.

"No," she whispered. She hoped that she could be forgiven for this. For saying it. For confessing it while she was married to another man.

It seemed disloyal even to think it.

He nodded, and she thought she saw some kind of relief in his face. As if he had dreaded her answer, somehow. "Thank you."

And then he left her, standing there, and she sagged against the windowsill and forced herself not to cry.

§

She hid in the nursery with Alex for the rest of that day and all of the next. Alex was a living reminder of her marriage to Garrit, of which life she was living and which family she owed her loyalty to. But her mind still revisited Lars's kiss, and she could not understand at all how it had happened. How it could have even existed. How he existed. She'd never been this conflicted before, never been tempted by infidelity. And she loved Garrit. She loved her husband, but what she had felt from Lars—it had been so long since she'd known that kind of love. Theseus had been the last, and even that had been so pale in comparison to Thorgrim.

Unfortunately, Juliette considered herself neglectful if she didn't take care of Alex for a few hours each day, and wouldn't hear of anything else. It was the first time that Eve had felt anything but relief to have a few hours to herself. And it was the first time in this life that she'd felt so out of touch with her present. It was as though, without Alex, she might forget what life she was living, and her memories of Thorgrim from the mental institute threatened to swallow her whole.

"Go visit with our guests, if you can think of nothing else you need to do, Abby. But do something. It's good for Alex not to be with you all the hours of the day. You know this." Juliette took Alex from her arms and waved her toward the door. "Garrit would tell you the same."

"Somehow I don't think Garrit would send me off to spend time with Lars."

Juliette laughed. "*Oui,* I am not certain why he is so jealous now.

He used to play with Lars as a boy, always begging to know when he would come to visit next. Garrit thought the world of him."

Eve frowned. "Strange that he never mentioned it."

"*Non,* he would not have thought to." Juliette smiled at Alex. "But your father is such a silly man sometimes. Just like your grandfather." And she kissed the baby's cheek. "Let's hope you've inherited your mother's sense."

It was difficult to imagine Garrit and Lars playing together as boys, but she couldn't believe they were much apart in age. "What about Horus?"

"He didn't spend as much time here. I only ever met him the once, before now, and Garrit was very young then. But he is a very interesting man, isn't he? René was very pleased to see him again."

"I wish I could say the same for Garrit."

"Yes. That son of mine. He seems to have forgotten how much our family has benefitted from their help."

"How exactly?"

Juliette only smiled. "You worry too much about the details, Abby. I'm sure you have more valuable things you could be doing with yourself than listening to me go on."

She forced herself to smile, swallowing her disappointment. "Of course."

§

Eve avoided the library, thinking it was the first place that Lars would look for her, and she worried that if he found her alone again, she would dwell too much on Thorgrim. She didn't want to allow herself the temptation of revisiting that kiss, or falling back into the past which threatened to overwhelm her with Lars's touch.

She went to her bedroom instead, and lay on the bed she and Garrit shared, trying to think of anything other than that moment. She managed to control her conscious thoughts until she dozed off and dreamed about it, and woke up wishing she had gone to the library after all. But she wasn't sure if it was because she might not have slept, or because Lars might have found her and she wouldn't have had to dream of kissing him.

It was an awful thought, and she buried it away. She couldn't let him touch her. Couldn't let him near her. She couldn't live in the past. She loved Garrit.

It doesn't help, does it?

She flinched at the pain that laced Adam's tone. It made her bones ache along with her head. *I wish you wouldn't share that.*

The discomfort dulled, and she felt like she could breathe again. Or at least her ribs had stopped aching in sympathy. *I'm sorry.*

She sighed. *Are you really?*

I didn't realize how much it would pain you, Eve. She could feel it was the truth. He was troubled by how much distress he'd caused her. There was silence for a moment, while she considered it, turning it over in her mind. *To answer your question, yes. That is how it feels. Like a tightness in my chest. Every time I see you in Garrit's arms, feel you make love to him. Every minute of it is torture. And when I'm with you, when it's just the two of us, I want nothing more than to touch you. To hold you.*

She closed her eyes. Hearing him this way brought the emotions with it. His anguish, his agony, his heartbreak. It was harder to listen to because of how well she knew it. *This isn't the same, Adam. I don't love Lars.*

That isn't what it felt like.

She hated him for suggesting it and putting the idea in her head. But it was Thorgrim that she loved. Who she had loved once. Who she missed now. It was Thorgrim who Lars reminded her of so forcefully. That was all. It had to be all.

Ah. Yes. Thorgrim. A dead man from a dead past. What is it about him, Eve?

She thought of the kiss. Of the way Thorgrim, and now Lars, held her as if she was made of blown glass. Breakable, delicate, beautiful. Something they didn't want to let go of, didn't want to risk allowing to slip away. The way his mouth claimed her, when he kissed, without the impression of possession. They had belonged to one another, but he had never owned her. Had always wanted her freedom.

I wish you wouldn't share that, he said as he picked up the images and emotions from her mind. She felt his jealousy, his hurt. *How could you have let him touch you?*

It wasn't that she had let Lars touch her so much as her rejection of Adam. He didn't bother to hide it, and the accusation in his mind stung her. *He's my family.*

Adam scoffed. *What he is, and what you think he is, will never be the same thing. Thorgrim is your past, Eve. Just like these DeLeons are.*

If Lars and Garrit are only ghosts from my past, memories made flesh, then why is it you're so threatened by them, Adam? What is it about Thorgrim that makes you so angry? Adam said nothing, but she felt his irritation. It fed her own. *In the future, I'd appreciate it if you didn't step in front of any buses in an attempt to control my life.*

If I wanted to control you, Eve, I would do it with far more subtlety.

Is that some kind of threat?

The truth. Do you think I would have kept my word not to hurt your family if I had intended to abuse you? Or even made the promise to begin with?

It made her sick to think of what he could do to them. The things he was capable of. *Should I be impressed that you've behaved like a human being? That you chose not to be a monster? That you care about someone other than yourself? For a moment at Christmas, I thought you had changed.* She shook her head, curling up into a ball on the bed. She couldn't tell if she was crying because of the pain that leaked with his anger into her body, or because she realized just how wrong she had been. *You don't know what love is, Adam.*

His anger drained away. Replaced with sadness and sorrow. But he said nothing more. She was left alone, with her own thoughts, and his pain.

§

She stayed that way for some time. Until Garrit came home and found her there. She tried to sit up, then, to wipe the tears from her face and hide the fact that she had been crying, but her ribs ached, and she cried out in pain when she moved.

Garrit's expression darkened. "You spoke to your brother."

She shook her head. "He reached for me."

Garrit called for Horus and sat down next to her, stroking her hair back from her face and staring at the door. "He did it deliberately. All of this. Didn't he?"

She closed her eyes. The footsteps she heard a moment later weren't Horus's. Lars's hand was warm and dry against her forehead, and the pain eased at once. She didn't answer Garrit. Couldn't bring herself to form the sentences, to explain and defend him. She didn't want to defend him. And she didn't want to open her eyes and see Lars watching her. She tried to convince herself that it was Horus's hand on her forehead. Horus who took her pain away.

"You can't keep doing this to yourself, Eve." Lars's voice was soft. "It only makes it more difficult."

She tried not to think what else he meant by it, and crawled into Garrit's lap for comfort. Garrit. Her husband. Her love of this life.

She kept her eyes shut tight.

CHAPTER THIRTY-THREE
Future

§

"Madame!" Ryam stood immediately at the sight of Eve in the doorway, and Adam felt her shock even though he had warned her. This man resembled Reu more than Garrit ever had, and that had been startling enough. Ryam bowed over her hand, kissing the back of it. *"Arrière-grand-mère."*

She frowned, and flicked her fingers, freeing her hand and gesturing for him to seat himself. Adam had felt it prudent that this meeting take place not in the abused Mr. Laurent's office, but in Adam's own home. The better to guarantee privacy. Ryam sat back down in the armchair he had abandoned and cleared his throat, glancing uneasily at Adam.

"You may speak freely in front of Mr. Carraig, Ryam. He's aware of the details or he wouldn't be involved." She spoke in English, Adam assumed, for his benefit. Or the benefit of the role he was playing, in any event.

"Oui, madame." Then he looked at her again and smiled. "Or are you *mademoiselle,* now?"

Look at that smile. Just like Garrit's. There was an ache in her heart again, and it twisted his own. "I am Eve, as I always ever was."

You lived a long and happy life with him, Eve. He wouldn't want you grieving for him now. "I trust, Mr. DeLeon, that you had time to speak to your brothers? I had understood they would be with you today."

"I am afraid my brothers and I did not come to an agreement. René still insists on his portion of the estate becoming liquid. Luc, I think, could be convinced with the right pressure, but he is already being hounded by our brother's creditors and wishes to see those debts paid."

"Creditors?" Eve's forehead creased and she sat so lightly on the sofa that Adam was sure she was ready to leap back to her feet at any moment. "What's going on, Ryam?"

Ryam dropped his eyes to the floor and cleared his throat again. "Gambling, *madame.* We did not realize what had happened until it was far too late, and by then he had leveraged the entirety of his inheritance."

She swore colorfully and stood, turning her back on the man and walking to the window. *All that money, tied to the estate for its taxes and upkeep. All of that money lost because my eldest grandson couldn't choose to leave the estate to his two responsible sons. And Garrit thought it was so clever to booby-trap it that way. Removing temptation, he said. Now this.*

There must be some way to salvage it. Some loophole. Adam did his best to ignore the way Ryam's leg bounced in his agitation. He was clearly upset at having to bring this news to Eve. Adam thought perhaps his brothers had refused to come just to avoid precisely this situation.

"How much is his debt?"

"Jeremiah, you can't—"

He could. He would. "How much, Mr. DeLeon, does your brother owe his creditors?"

Ryam hesitated, glancing between them. Adam silently removed a stylus from his jacket pocket and presented him with the pad to write down the figure. He glanced again at Eve before making the note and passing it back to him. Adam glanced at it and deleted it. The sum was ungodly. No wonder he hadn't wanted to say it out loud.

"Perhaps there's another agreement we could come to?" he suggested.

You can't, Adam. What will he learn if you bail him out? And you don't even care for the DeLeon line!

Would you prefer to lose the estate? To have your family lose the lands you settled and nurtured because of one foolish man?

"What kind of agreement did you have in mind, *Monsieur* Carraig?"

She swore again and turned to stare at them. "You can't be serious."

Perfectly serious. "A loan for the figure named, with which you may buy your brother out and keep the estate shared between yourself and Mr. Luc DeLeon. Or, if your other brother cannot be made to see reason, twice that amount to buy out both of them, with your word as a DeLeon that you'll do everything in your power to prevent something like this happening again in the future."

Ryam's eyes widened and he glanced from Eve to Adam again. "*Monsieur,* it is not that I do not appreciate the offer, but I do not understand why you would make it."

"Out of love for your Lady and respect for her family." He didn't look away from the man's face. "Are we agreed?"

"Adam!"

He glanced at Eve then, biting his tongue on a curse. The way her face paled and her eyes darted to Ryam made him think the slip was accidental. Or else she had grown into a very accomplished liar in the years they had been apart. He was beginning to believe it was the latter. "Pardon?"

But Ryam had leapt to his feet, his eyes narrowed. "I knew it! There was something too familiar about you, too smooth. *Grand-oncle.* You are Ethan, are you not? Her brother, Adam?"

"Ryam, sit down." Eve sighed when he didn't follow her instruction at once. "Sit down!" she repeated. "I don't know what your grandfather told you, or your great-grandfather, or what that wretched journal insists upon, but this is hardly the point."

"But why are you in his company?"

She could look quite intimidating when she wanted to, Adam reflected, and the withering look she bestowed on her descendant made him glad he hadn't earned the same for himself.

"If you must know, he informed me of this disgraceful sale of the family estate and offered to help by arranging my travel so that I could talk some sense into you. Though apparently it's your brother who seems to be lacking it."

"But—"

"My identity aside, Mr. DeLeon, my offer still stands."

He wondered if this was what Eve had intended, by letting his name slip. He could see the play of emotions in Ryam's face, even in his thoughts. Accepting help from him of all people was anathema to a DeLeon, but to not accept meant too large a loss. Adam suspected Ryam wanted less to disappoint Eve than he desired to stand on family principles he had never fully understood.

"You swear this is no trick? No means by which you intend to manipulate us?" Ryam asked.

"You have my word. Eve can tell you I'm not lying, though she worries that by helping you this way none of you boys will learn from your mistakes." He offered a small smile. And it didn't escape Ryam's notice that a man half his age had just called him a child. "But I believe it humbles you too greatly to accept, especially from me, to allow yourself to forget what brought you to this point. I don't believe you'll let it happen again."

Ryam grimaced. *"C'est vrai."*

"Then we have a deal."

He sighed and extended his hand. "God help me, but yes."

Adam clasped hands with him. Neither one of them smiled. Eve shook her head and turned away, back to the window.

You should be proud of them that they kept it intact for this long, Eve. How many hundreds of years? Or has it been thousands?

A long time. And I'm sure it hurts his pride more to accept this loan from you than any other punishment I could have devised, though this is hardly Ryam's fault. René was smart not to come. I would have had his head.

"I'll draw up the paperwork tonight and have it sent to you in the morning."

Ryam nodded. *"Merci, monsieur."* He glanced at Eve, and his expression faltered. *"Madame,* if you wish to stay with us, we would be honored."

"Not this time, I think, Ryam. But perhaps we can arrange something in the future. My name is Renata DeLuca in this life, if you wish to look for me, but I'm afraid I don't have the means to travel from Canada often, if at all."

He crossed to her, catching her hand and bowing over it again. "You have only to call upon us, my Lady."

She kissed his cheek. "You have your great-grandfather's smile, Ryam, and my first husband's eyes. Take care of the family."

"Oui, madame." He cast one last uneasy look at Adam, and then left. Adam hoped he would go to his brother Luc and talk him into buying out René, but in the end it would cost him nothing. Asgardian gold never diminished and it was fitting that Thor's funds would go to this. Though he would have given his right arm to know what had happened to their own treasury.

Eve was still frowning, and he moved to her side, taking her hand as Ryam had done, and raising it to his lips. "How is it that you ever tolerated the title of Lady from your Lions?"

"I can't stand it," she admitted, then smiled. "I had to choose my battles with them, I suppose. I didn't argue with them when they referred to me that way in exchange for not allowing them to spoil Alexandre rotten."

"They only want to honor you."

"You didn't have to do this, Adam. To help them. They've done little to deserve your kindness."

He shook his head. "It isn't for them, Eve. I think they know that too."

She leaned against him, and he wrapped his arms around her. These moments were too short, and none of it would last. Soon she would be back home, and he knew she wouldn't let him come with her, regardless of what liberties she allowed him now. Stolen kisses and intimacies were all he would have for the rest of this lifetime and he meant to take advantage of what time they had.

"We should have dinner."

"We should have wine."

He chuckled and kissed the pulse of her throat. "Can you only tolerate my touch when you're drunk?"

She didn't respond, exactly, but turned in his arms and pulled his head down to hers to kiss him. It would've been so easy to fall into the sweetness of her mouth, to abandon himself to her touch, but the idea of begging her for this all over again didn't appeal to him at all, nor did the tears he knew she would shed, and the pain he knew it would cause. He disentangled himself and set her away.

"Wine, then, for you," he said.

She pulled open the door to the balcony and stepped outside, and he left her to get the wine she seemed so intent on. He wasn't sure what to make of her mood, or the thoughts that kept flitting through her mind. He poured her a glass, and joined her on the balcony. She was leaning against the railing, looking out at the mountains.

"Eve?"

She blushed and he wondered what she was thinking to cause such a reaction. She took the glass from his hand and drank from it, not dropping her eyes from the view. "I always liked the mountains here."

"I would've thought you'd prefer forest and richer, more fertile lands."

"Because of the Garden?"

"It was where you were made. Where you're from."

She shook her head. "The Garden was never mine, Adam. It was full of bitter memories, more than anything, for me. My happiest days were the ones I spent alone with Reu in our cave with the lions."

He grimaced and took the wine from her hand, stealing a sip of it for himself. If she was going to reminisce over Reu, he would need more than wine to get him through the night without his mood becoming foul. "That was a long time ago."

"I've been dreaming about it. The Garden. When it burned. All of it."

"I wonder why?"

She sighed and turned her back to the mountains and the view. "I just want to be here, with you, and leave the past where it belongs." *I want to sleep in your bed tonight, Adam, in your arms. Or is that too much to ask of you?*

It's where I've wanted you for years. Her eyes were sad though, haunted. For all her talk about leaving the past behind, she carried it with her still. He caressed her cheek and kissed her forehead. *I only wish I could keep you.*

§

The pillowcase was damp. Adam's mind registered it only groggily, until he heard Eve sob.

"No, please, no." It was so quiet, half mumbled, but it brought him fully awake. Eve was curled into the smallest ball possible in the bed next to him, tears streaking her cheeks.

"Shh, Evey." He wiped the tears away with his thumb, sitting up. She didn't seem to hear him, because she didn't stir, except for another begging sob from whatever dream she was caught within. He shook her gently by the shoulder. "Eve, love, wake up."

She jerked away from him in the dark and then she gasped, her eyes wide.

"It was just a dream, Eve." He tucked her hair behind her ear and pulled her against him. "Just a dream, whatever it was."

She shuddered and let herself be held. Her tears burned against his chest. "Not just a dream."

"Memory then?"

"I can't." She pulled away, throwing the sheet from her body and drawing her knees to her chest, burying her face in her arms. "Oh, what am I doing? What am I doing?"

He reached for the light. They'd fallen asleep together, the most restful sleep he'd ever had, but to wake up this way was an agony. He rubbed his face, trying to gather his wits enough to follow what was in her mind. *What's wrong, Eve?*

She rocked back and forth on her tailbone, not lifting her face. Her breathing was ragged and broken by sobbing. *I can't Adam. I can't. He'll come. He'll kill us both. He'll kill us both, and I don't want to die. He promised. He promised he'd stop at nothing.*

Who, Evey? He tried to touch her but somehow he couldn't reach, as though a weight held him in place, a pressure. His mind felt thick and sluggish, but there was something familiar about it. Something—the realization was like a blow. She was manipulating him, preventing him from touching her, holding him away. She was that strong? *Eve, you're safe. You're safe here.*

No. No, I'm not safe anywhere. He'll find us, Adam. He'll find us no matter where we go. And the baby. The poor baby. She looked up and her eyes were red and full of tears. *He'll kill us.*

There's no baby, Eve. You're safe. I won't let him hurt you. He was beginning to understand what had upset her. Who she was talking about. It could only be Michael, really. Or God. *You've done nothing wrong, Eve.*

When she released him, he almost fell into her. She hid her face in her arms again, and her whole body shook with her sobs. *But I want to.*

He reached for her again, pulling her against him and stroking her hair. "It doesn't matter, Eve. He can't hurt us anymore. He can't hurt you."

How do you know?

"The sword is destroyed. He doesn't have it anymore. He can't harm you, or any baby." He thought she began to calm, or at least her sobs were quieting. "God destroyed it."

He promised me, Adam. After the Garden. After they caught you. He promised me that if I ever let you touch me, he'd kill me and all my kin. Reu's children. He'd make me watch them die, first. He'd do anything to prevent our child being born. He made me swear never to allow it. And then after Alexandre was born, at the hospital, he came again. He threatened my son, my family.

"Was that your dream?"

Yes.

He cursed God, silently. It wasn't fair to do this to her, to put all this on her shoulders. How long had she lived with this threat on her head? No wonder she had been so upset to see him all those years ago, envisioning her own death with his presence.

It doesn't matter now, Eve. He doesn't have the power anymore. You're safe, I promise you. And even if he comes—when he comes. But he wouldn't tell her that. She didn't need to be afraid anymore. *Even if he comes, I'll protect you. I won't let him do anything to hurt you.*

"I should go," she said.

"In the middle of the night? Eve, it was just a dream." *Stay with me. Come back to sleep. Even if this is the only night we have.*

She looked up at him, and he could tell she wanted to stay. But that impulse was what terrified her most. "This was all a mistake, staying here with you."

"Love isn't a mistake, Evey. This is what we were made for. You especially."

She rubbed her eyes and let herself be coaxed into lying down beside him, her head on his shoulder. He turned the light back off.

"God knew I would love you, one day," she said into the dark.

"Did he?"

She sighed. "There's so much I never knew. Never understood. I wish I had known God, Adam. I wish I could know him now. Understand what he asks of me, what I'm meant to do."

"Maybe this is how we're supposed to know him. Maybe you've known him all along."

I don't understand.

He smoothed her hair where it tickled his face and hoped what he was thinking wasn't just another delusion, another justification for what seemed so wrong to her. It couldn't be another way to convince her to give him just one more night, one more morning, one more day. But how long could he sleep by her side before it was impossible to keep himself from touching her? How long could he have her in his arms without wanting to love her, too? He wouldn't let it be, wouldn't let her stay beyond his own limits. But she had a right to know, and something about it seemed so right. Like a truth that had eluded him for years, for millennia.

She had a right to peace, even if it only lasted a moment.

"Maybe God is love."

CHAPTER THIRTY-FOUR
1414 AD

§

Thor stood looking over the land he had protected and nurtured and watered and sunned and herded goats within. The village had grown just in the two years since Eve had returned to these lands and Ryam was exactly what he had hoped for her and her people. Her family. Even if he was insufferable at times.

Marquis DeLeon, proud of his title and DeLeon Castle.

He supposed it must have seemed like one. Ra had returned periodically to help with repairs. While the rest of the world had slid into dark ages and the Roman advances crumbled away around them, the DeLeons had flourished with the patronage of the old gods they didn't worship. They'd kept the land that Thor had imbued with protection, and even expanded. Powerful in their own right, they had submitted first to the Carolingian kings, then the dynasties that followed, not involving themselves with the wars of either the Frankish state, or the schisms of the Church, just as they had avoided engaging in the old Roman politics.

He was putting it off. As if not meeting with Ryam would prevent it from happening. As if he weren't running out of time. Athena would find Mnemosyne and then they would find Adam, and she would call for him, and he was bound to help.

Thor was the one who would speak to him for the others. Because he had already revealed himself and in theory, Adam would remember him. Because the Norse gods still lived in recent memory, more so than the others. The Norse gods were still worshipped.

He called the thunder as he walked to the edge of the forest, and then the lightning, while he stood at the edge of the field. The tree beside him smoked and he brought rain to put out the fire before it spread. Smoke still rose, but the flame was reduced to ember and Thor waited. Ryam had given him chapter and verse about the risk to his lumber the last time he had come.

Hooves pounded the damp earth, and a man came riding out from the manor. He assumed it was Ryam, wanting the high ground, and the opportunity to be able to look down on him from the back of his horse. He wasn't exactly an arrogant man, but he appreciated having the upper hand. And he understood that he was only a man, and Thor was a god. More importantly, Ryam knew his wife was a goddess. He knew his wife was Eve.

And somehow, he had realized Thor loved her.

Ryam rode to the tree first, circling it, before acknowledging Thor with a stiff nod, and dismounting. Thor had stopped expecting the House of Lions to treat him with any deference, and as long as they kept a bed for him when he needed one, even if it was in the stable with the horses now, he didn't care. As long as Eve was safe, he didn't care.

"You're lucky that one was rotting," Ryam said.

The rain had turned into a mist, and Thor waved the last of it off as the tree stopped smoking. "Luck had little to do with it."

Ryam smiled without humor and removed his gloves. The horse stamped and sighed behind him. "I imagine this is something important."

"Have I bothered you when it wasn't?" Thor asked, taking the horse in hand and stroking its nose, murmuring softly to calm it.

"He doesn't like the thunder. Every time you come, it causes panic in the stables. My grooms complain bitterly about it."

Thor laughed. "Would you prefer I come more frequently so they grow used to it?" But he glanced back at Ryam then, and his smile faded. "Your wife, Anessa, is well?"

He nodded. "We expect our first child before winter. She assures me that the pregnancy will be easy." Ryam glanced from the manor, back to Thor. "She tells me I shouldn't worry."

"You shouldn't." But he realized after he said it that he was lying. His entire reason for coming was to make Ryam worry. To alert him to the threat that was coming for her. "Not about the pregnancy. As long as she has good food and plenty of rest, the baby will be born healthy."

"You know this?"

Thor shook his head. "I don't see the future, Ryam. My powers in that regard are limited. But I've watched her bear children for more than two thousand years." Including his own son. And even knowing she was capable, he had worried too. "She can't be harmed, regardless. Not by the birth."

Ryam slapped his gloves against his thigh. "I appreciate your reassurance."

Thor looked back at the manor. He could feel her there, inside. And when he listened through the link they shared, he heard her humming. The same song she had sung for so many years. "There's a threat coming to her, Ryam. The least I can do is keep you from worrying about the things that can't hurt her."

The man's face stiffened, and his eyes hardened. "Why have you come?"

"Has she told you of her brother?"

"Anessa has no brother. Just that wretched sister, Aimee." Even two years later, long after the threat had passed, Ryam was still bitter. It seemed Aimee had accused her sister of witchcraft after she found herself pregnant by one of the Papal legates. Bewitchment had excused them both of any guilt, placing it all squarely upon Eve.

"Aimee is no more her sister than I am her father. Anessa's only true brother is Adam. Adam to her Eve. Until now, he has been without his memory. But the gods work to return it to him."

"The gods move in mysterious ways, I suppose." Ryam took back the reins of his horse, and it snorted, tossing its head. Picking up the anger of its rider. "Much like Anessa."

"Anessa guards her secrets." Part of him was glad. She could not be that deeply in love with Ryam if she did not even tell him about Adam.

Ryam glared at him. "After what nearly happened because of them, I can hardly blame her for that. Nor do I have any intention of prying out of her anything she does not wish to share freely. She's earned that much from me, and more."

"Do you really think I'd ask it? Do you really think I want her with anyone who would try? Care for her. Protect her. Love her."

"She's safe here, Thor. I have seen to it."

"It is not enough that she's safe here, Ryam. These lands grant their own protection. It's when she walks outside of them that she's at risk. Adam is a cruel man who cares only for himself. He will not hesitate to use her for his advantage. To abuse her."

"What does he look like? When will he come?"

Thor gripped him by the shoulder, using the contact to sear the image of Adam in Ryam's mind. The eyes were the most important, the only feature that wouldn't change. "Your family was made to protect her, Ryam. From him. That was Reu's vow, for himself and his sons. Adam is never to touch her, never to hurt her again."

The muscles along Ryam's jaw twitched and Thor imagined he was grinding his teeth. "Our purpose is limited by what she allows us to do, Thunderer. If she does not return to us, how can we keep her safe?"

Thor shook his head, releasing Ryam. "I wish I had the answer."

"It would be a great help if you did." Ryam stroked the neck of his horse. Thor felt his resignation, followed by determination. A sweeping calm. This was why Ryam was her husband. Why Ryam had been the right choice to care for her. Because he did what had to be done. In the face of uncertainty, he always rose above fear. "I trust you'd prefer I not tell Anessa."

"I'd prefer that she did not live her lives worried and waiting. Afraid. It may not even be this lifetime."

Ryam nodded. "As long as I live, she will at least be given that much peace."

"My thanks, Lord DeLeon."

Ryam looked up at him, and his face was lined by the weight of it all. By the truths he held and must keep. There was so much he could not share with his wife, so much he must shoulder alone. Thor looked away first. Ryam was a Lion. This burden was part of his birth. And he had Eve.

Thor closed his eyes and reached for her, feeling her standing at the window, looking for her husband. Missing her husband.

Ryam had Eve's love.

§

"If it's to be done, now is the time," Thor said. Adam was being held against his will, tied to a tree. He kept struggling against the ropes.

Athena had found him in German lands. "So you've said. And you still stand here. Would you prefer if I spoke to him?"

He shook his head and stepped out from behind the trees.

Adam stopped struggling, and stared. "Who are you? What do you people want from me?"

Thor crouched down in front of him. He looked small tied up that way, but the fury in his eyes was unmistakable. "We hope to be your friends. Or at least not your enemies. We can tell you who you are. Give you back everything you've lost."

"As far as I can tell, what I've lost is my freedom. I want to be let go." And there was that compulsion, that power. Just like Eve, though it lacked her subtlety. "Untie me."

Thor grinned and let his eyes burn. "No."

Adam's eyes widened, his face pale, but Thor wasn't sure if it was because he had refused him, or because his eyes were white with lightning. "Who are you?"

"We've met before. Several times. Before Rome fell, we had a talk beside a fire. In this very forest. Your son was Alaric, the man who led the Goths into Rome and sacked the city. I've always thought that was the straw that broke the camel's back, for the west. Though the forty days you spent as pope did nearly as much damage."

"You're lying."

Thor snorted. "I wish I was. You have no idea how much I wish it were all a lie. That you didn't live. That you didn't exist. But you do, Adam. You live to spite us all."

"That isn't my name."

Thor stood up and walked to the fire, throwing another branch onto it. "Have you read the Bible? The book of Genesis? The creation story, about the first man, and the first woman."

"Adam and Eve." He sounded annoyed. "Everyone knows the story. Is that what you brought me here for? To talk about religion? I don't believe in God. I don't care about any of it."

Thor laughed. He didn't mean to, but he did. Losing his memory had done nothing to erase the man's arrogance. "You told me that before, too."

He turned back to Adam, and reached for the storm overhead, blotting out the stars.

Lightning forked through the sky, drawn directly into his body. The warmth of an old friend, familiar and energizing. It crackled and spider-webbed over his skin, over his clothing, and lit his eyes again with white fire.

Adam screamed, and Thor smiled. That was another reason why he had been chosen to speak on behalf of the gods. Adam was afraid of lightning. Thor didn't know why, but he had noticed it time and again.

"Let me know when you've changed your mind, Adam. We'll be waiting."

Athena cut the ropes that held him to the tree and he stumbled and fell, then climbed back to his feet. He looked from her to Thor and back again. As if he wasn't sure he was really being let free.

Thor pointed in the direction of the road, where his horse and his things were waiting for him. Adam ran.

Athena frowned as she watched him disappear into the trees. "Are you sure this is the best way?"

"It has to be his choice or Mnemosyne will have no hope of returning his memory. Tonight he'll have the dreams that keep haunting him, and realize we were telling him the truth. He'll come back to us for answers and agree to whatever we ask for." He looked up at the sky, stared at the stars winking through the dispersing clouds. Prayed to Eve for forgiveness. "And then he'll betray us, and Michael will be too busy trying to keep him from Eve to start another movement for the True God in the East. There will be no third prophet, Athena. Ask the Norns to read the runes tonight, and they will tell you. By this act, we've changed everything."

Athena touched his arm.

Thor shook his head and walked away.

CHAPTER THIRTY-FIVE
Present

She slept most of the evening, dimly aware of Lars at her bedside, and Garrit coming and going. The conversations she heard, half-conscious, made no sense to her, though they were whispered so urgently that she felt they must be important, somehow.

"You shouldn't stay," Horus was saying. "It's obviously causing her distress."

"She's meant to know me, Ra," Lars said. "Perhaps now is that time."

"If it were, she would not be married. And she would have understood by now. Instead, she's been pained by it."

"Pained by her brother. And if I go, what then? She'll be left open to him, to his mind, to the pain he shares with her." Lars sounded miserable. "Part of me wants to believe that she does this to keep me here."

"And what of her husband? Marriage protects her from Adam as much as anything else. If she breaks that covenant, there will be nothing left to stop him next time. This is not the time, Thor. You've waited so long, what's one more life?"

Lars's fingers tightened around her hand. "You were always against this." His voice was hoarse.

"If God's messenger has spoken, I will not argue. But it is clearly not yet." Horus was silent for a moment. "And perhaps I was wrong about your relationship with her. With this family. With this world."

"I will never belong. No matter how much I wish to."

"Time will tell," Horus said. "I will stay with them for as long as I'm needed. And remain in the country for as long as you wish me nearby. But for her sake, now, it would be best if you left. Whether it's what she wants or not."

She sank back into her dreams then, and Lars's response was swallowed up in memories of fishing with Thorgrim off the shore.

Garrit's voice roused her later, because of the anger and accusation in his tone. "Horus could have done all this. We didn't need you here, too."

"Garrit!" René hissed. "You forget yourself."

"No, René, he's right," Lars said. He sounded calm. Tired. Almost bored. "I'll be gone soon enough. As soon as I'm sure she's well again."

"We're grateful for what you've done," René said. Eve thought he was trying to apologize. "My son forgets how much we owe you."

"I don't see you offering him *Maman* in repayment," Garrit snarled. "You realize that's what he wants, don't you? My wife. And you can't expect me to stand by and let him try to take her without a word of objection."

"Are you really so afraid she'll leave you?" Lars asked, his voice mild.

"I would be a fool to think I deserve her. That I can offer her what you can."

"You do your wife a great disservice, Garrit."

"Do you really think I haven't seen the way you look at her? The way she looks at you? The way that she talks about Thorgrim? Am I supposed to believe that you're not a threat?"

"I'm not half the threat to her or you that Adam is. You've seen what he's willing to do. And while I have been content to wait, Adam has already shown himself to be impatient."

"She doesn't love Adam. She doesn't dream of her life with him. She was never Adam's wife."

"Don't be a damned fool, Garrit," René said.

Lars sighed. Tired again. "She would never turn her back on you. On her vows. On her family. Not for me, not now."

"Then why do you stay? Why show yourself at all, if you have no hope?"

"For the same reason that Adam married Mia, knowing it would infuriate her. It has been a long time since I was allowed the indulgence of an association. And being part of this, part of her family however distantly, is a gift that I find difficult to give up."

She wasn't sure if it was memory or dreams, but the conversation faded, and she was sitting with Thorgrim on the narrow bunk in the hospital. Bunk was a generous term for what she slept on and she found herself missing the straw pallets of earlier lives. He stroked her hair, and she curled up on her side, her head pillowed against his thigh.

"I wish I could take you from here," he said. "I wish I had found you in time to prevent this."

"It isn't the first time I've suffered this way. It happens sometimes, when I forget. When I tell too many stories as a child, and my parents realize how sincerely I believe them. They used to think I was possessed somehow. By the devil, or evil spirits of some kind. Now they call me insane. I think I preferred the exorcisms to the pills though." She rolled onto her back, and looked up at him. Memorizing his face. Comparing it to memories of him in their little village. "At least the exorcisms didn't cause me to hallucinate."

"Does it upset you to see me?"

"Should it?" She reached up to touch his face, tracing her fingers over his lips. If she kissed him, would the delusion hold? Or would it ruin the realness? Force her mind to recognize he wasn't actually there? "I don't mind being crazy if it means I can be with you. Feel you. Touch you. Even if it's all in my head. Maybe it won't be such a bad thing to spend this life living in the past, in my memory, in my dreams."

"What do you dream of, Tora?"

She smiled. "Isn't that obvious? How else do you think you got here?"

"Only when you're unhappy?" he asked, caressing her cheek. She was surprised by the warmth of his fingers, and the way it made her heart race.

"Always, Thorgrim. I always dream of your love. Of your kindness. I wish so much that you were real. That you were really here. That you lived, and we could run away together. To France. To the mountains. I always loved the mountains."

"Not to the Norse lands?"

She grimaced. "The winters there are so bitter."

He chuckled. "I would build you a warm house."

"And wrap me in your arms. In your warmth. In your love. We could stay inside all winter, with a fire and blankets."

"Doesn't that sound better than your French mountains?"

"Perhaps. If it were just the two of us somewhere hidden away. With no one to tell me what I should believe. What god to worship. What prayers to say."

"I would like that for you. That freedom."

"I think I would like it for me, too," she said, hiding her face against his body. He smelled like rain and the moment before a thunderstorm when you know what's coming. The only thing that wasn't quite right was the color of his hair. For some reason, she couldn't remember the right shade of brown, and it just looked strawberry-blonde. Almost red. "But anything is better than here."

He leaned down to kiss her.

And she woke up.

§

It was dark. Garrit slept heavily beside her. Dead to the world. She slipped from the bed and tiptoed out of the room with her robe, closing the door silently behind her. She could feel him outside and thought that maybe he had called her. Maybe that was what had woken her from the dream.

He was standing at the edge of the field. Waiting for her. When he saw her, he smiled. "I wasn't sure you would come."

"I shouldn't have." She wrapped the robe around her more tightly and shook her head. "I shouldn't have done any of this."

"It isn't your fault. I should have left."

Looking at him now, after having dreamed of Thorgrim, made her ache. "You're leaving."

He nodded, and stepped toward her, reaching out to stroke her cheek. "I shouldn't have ever come. I just wanted to know you. Even if it was only for a moment."

She shook her head and stepped back. All of this felt like more of the dream. Of the conversations that made no sense to her. But she couldn't let him touch her. "I keep thinking of Thorgrim. Remembering him. Dreaming of him. And then I see you, and it's like I'm still in the memory. I just want to fall into my past and stay there. Stay with you. But you aren't Thorgrim."

He ducked his head, not meeting her eyes. "Garrit is a good man. If he's jealous, it's only because he knows how great a gift it is to have your love. I can't blame him for feeling as though he's unworthy of it. But he loves you. He'll take care of you if you let him."

"Where will you go?" It was cold. She had goosebumps, standing there. "I thought we were your family."

"Always." He smiled again. "No doubt I'll return. Though with you here, there's less need of it."

She didn't understand that, but she wasn't sure it mattered. "If you ever need anything, come. I owe you at least that."

"You owe me nothing, Eve." He raised his hand as if to touch her, but closed it instead, and his arm dropped back to his side again. "Just stay out of your brother's mind until he's healed. I can't imagine it will be much longer, regardless, but please, promise me that much."

"I'll make every effort." It wasn't exactly a promise, but it was the best she felt she could offer.

"Don't let Garrit trust him. He wants to. I don't know why. Maybe just because he dislikes me so. But don't let him."

"Juliette said you used to play together. That he loved you once."

Lars laughed. "Yes. Once upon a time."

"What happened?"

He met her eyes, and his expression grew serious again. All humor fading. "He realized that we both loved the same woman and he worried I was the better man. I had kept it from him. The whole truth of my feelings. He considered it a betrayal."

"Oh." Love. All those years she spent without it. All those lives she spent with men who didn't care. Who weren't interested in anything but her body when their need drove them to her, and now in this life she was overwhelmed by love. "I'm sorry that you lost your friend."

He shook his head and his smile was forced. "You should get back to bed. You're freezing."

She wasn't, though. She felt warmed from the inside out. "Goodbye."

It seemed totally inadequate. Empty of real meaning. But if she said more, did more, she knew it would be too much. Too painful. Her hold on her present was still tenuous, and it was tempting to get lost in her past for a moment. To let him kiss her, and pretend that it was Thorgrim. It wouldn't be fair to anyone. Especially not her husband.

She turned to walk back to the house. Somehow, she barely noticed the cold anymore, a warmth swelling up inside her from her bare feet into her heart, radiating down her limbs. As if she basked in the glow of a fire. When she reached the house, she glanced back over her shoulder. He stood there still, in the field. Watching her. He raised a hand in farewell. She went inside, but couldn't stop herself from going to the window. To catch one last glimpse of this man who reminded her so forcefully of her past, so familiar and so strange.

But he was already gone.

She crawled back into bed with Garrit, curling up in his arms. He sighed into her hair, falling into a deeper sleep. She lay awake until morning, just so that she wouldn't dream of Thorgrim.

CHAPTER THIRTY-SIX
Future

§

Eve stared at the ceiling for a long time after that, turning Adam's words over and over in her thoughts. In her heart. She listened to his breathing beside her, curled against his side. It didn't seem as though he was sleeping either. But he didn't say anything more, didn't try to argue his point any further, or even reach for her response.

She let out a breath and wished she had a clear view of the stars. As if their patterns held any answers. But she still remembered Reu's story, about the god who had given up his eye for the wisdom to save his son, his people. Sometimes, reaching for power was the right thing. She had made that decision once before, taken the fruit, eaten from it and gifted her descendents with the strength to live freely, to choose their own fates. In the process, though, she had bound Reu and all his sons to her protection, and she had wandered ever after, lost, from one life to the next, without purpose, without understanding.

With Adam, lying beside him, loving him, kissing him, wanting him, she felt whole for the first time in far too long. It wasn't only the way her body fit against his, her head resting perfectly within the hollow of his shoulder, her fingers lacing between his as if they belonged. There was something more, as if his spirit had left an impression upon hers, and his love filled in all the cracks, mending her heart, her soul.

It was the way she had felt with Thorgrim, and Reu before that. Reu, whose love for her had been God's final gift, made perfect between them. She had no explanation for Thorgrim. And as for Adam—

She wasn't sure what to think of what she felt for Adam, what Adam felt for her. She wasn't sure what to think, knowing that what they felt was so close to what she had known of Elohim. And if it were wrong . . .

Love should be easy. She had said it herself. Love should be easy, when it's right, natural. Why would God, living all this time, allow for this possibility at all, if he had not meant for it to come to pass? Or was it all a test of faith, of obedience?

She had broken God's law by tasting the fruit, and saved the world in the choosing. But Adam was right about one thing. Love had never been forbidden. What Elohim had told Adam, all those lifetimes ago, at the dawn of Creation, had not been *never*. Never had come later, from Michael, and the sword which no longer threatened them.

But Elohim? Their God, their Father, had only said, *Not yet.*

§

Dawn came, sunlight creeping fingers through the blinds and bending over the bed. Eve rose, knowing as she crossed to the bathroom, that Adam's gaze followed her. The mattress sighed as Adam's weight shifted, but she didn't look back. If she saw his concern now, she wouldn't have the courage to go on. If she let him argue at all, let him use his not inconsiderable charm, his gentle persuasion, the threadbare cloak of her resolve would shred. And he would argue. He would fight. She had listened to his regret, his fears, all night.

But this choice was hers. As it had been in the beginning, as it had always been, no matter how many times he had tried to take it from her. In the Garden, as Paris in Sparta, when he had first come to her in their last lifetime, before he had married Mia.

She cannot love you, yet, and you are forbidden to force her. Those had been Elohim's words, and she had held them so close, grasped them tight for an eternity. And He had been right, then. The Adam she had known in the Garden, determined to make himself a God, to grind their people beneath his heel and turn them into slaves—she could not have loved him, could never have wanted him.

Eve splashed water on her face, glancing at the mirror over the sink only long enough to be sure he had noticed her. He was still watching, his gaze unguarded, heating her like a physical caress. She pulled the pajama shirt over her head, careful to stand where he could see her back. Her skin prickled, goosebumps rising on her arms, anticipating his touch. She could feel him standing behind her. Just standing there. She slipped out of her shorts, letting them fall from her hips to the floor in a puddle, and then the soft lace beneath. Her only indulgence, that lace, and when she turned to face him, his storm cloud eyes darkened with desire, she flushed.

Adam swallowed, licked his lips, dragged his eyes back to her face much, much too slowly. "You left the door open."

He was flustered, she realized, taking a step toward him. She'd never seen him flustered before. Not while he was married to Mia, certainly not in the Garden. Always, he had been confident, arrogant, smirking, or at his worst, angry. Her fingers found the warm skin under his shirt, traced the lines of muscle hidden beneath the soft cotton. He made a soft noise, half-groan, half-objection, his hands closing around her wrists.

"Evey, I promised you—"

She stopped him with a kiss before he said something she didn't want to hear, nibbling his lower lip. His fingers, vise-like with his determination, slackened, and it was all the opening she needed. A nudge of her thoughts against his, and he released her altogether, lifting his arms so she could pull the shirt over his head. His eyes sharpened, locked on hers with new realization.

Evey, love . . .

Once, he might have been stronger, when she was newly made, before the Fruit. But not now. Not when she had honed her power for millennia upon millennia. He fought, his thoughts fluttering defiance. Instead of stepping back, he reached for her. Instead of turning away, his forehead touched hers, their noses brushing. She framed his face in her hands, held him to her by force of will.

It's my choice, Adam. My right. My love to give.

He closed his eyes, drawing her closer of his own accord. "This isn't why I asked you here. It isn't what I meant to happen."

She lifted her face, pressing her lips to his. The heat of his skin against hers made her ache, and she didn't want to talk. They had waited so long, and she could feel the strain of his body, hard and hot with need. She dropped her hands from his face, trailing them down his chest, his abdomen, his waist.

He let out a shuddering breath, and all his resistance went with it. His mouth claimed hers, demanding entrance, and his fingers dug into the softness of her hips, just short of bruising. He pushed her back until she was pressed against the tile wall, the shock of the cold sending a shiver down her spine, even while the rest of her melted with his heat, seeping deep and settling in the pit of her stomach.

Whatever sin this was, she thought wildly, as his lips left hers to follow her jaw line, whatever punishment came after, she would make it hers, and hers alone.

Then his teeth grazed her earlobe, sparks of fire lighting where the heat had been, until her whole body turned to flame. And there was no more room in her thoughts for words, no more thoughts, at all.

Just love.

§

She lay against his chest, after, and studied his face while he slept. His lips curved in just the slightest smile, his head turned to the right, toward her. One of his hands rested at the small of her back, the other tangled in her hair. As if he feared she might slip away while his eyes were closed. She pressed a kiss to his chest, smiling sadly.

"I love you," she said, too low to wake him, but maybe just loud enough that it would linger in his dreams. Another kiss, at the pulse of his throat, and a gentle nudge against his sleeping mind, and she freed herself carefully from his grasp. She'd stayed too long already.

With any luck, he wouldn't wake until she'd boarded an airship—there were always seats available, and once she traded in her return ticket by jet, she'd have money to spare. But it had to be now, before she lost her will to go and let herself be lulled to sleep by his warmth, and his comfort, and his love, still filling her heart to overflowing.

Eve dressed and packed, and let herself out of the apartment. Because if she stayed, she'd only want to make love to him again. Once had been dangerous enough, for him, for her, for her family and the world . . .

But she wouldn't take it back. Wouldn't give it up for anything, now. And the way Michael had haunted her in the past—the way he had threatened her even before she had known her own heart, her own mind—he should have come already to make good on her punishment. The moment she'd considered it, the moment she'd committed to following through.

She shook her head and started down the street. Two blocks to the nearest cardock, and then another fifteen minutes to reach the airport. She glanced at her watch, and broke into a jog. The next airship would be leaving in just an hour, and she'd lost more time than she'd meant to, looking for something to write on to leave him some kind of note.

Her heart twisted at the thought of how he'd find it, realizing she was gone, knowing he was too late. She had to believe he would understand, had to hope he would let her explain. He had to know she wouldn't have left him if there had been any other way. Michael would come for her—just like he'd come for Adam, after that ill-advised kiss—and when he did, she didn't want Adam involved. She'd tell the archangel she had forced him, used her power to persuade him. And then she would pray that she wasn't carrying his child.

She'd had her implant, of course, but if there was one thing she understood after so many lifetimes, it was the vagaries of mother nature—of God, Himself. She shouldn't have been able to conceive, should have been safe, and with anyone but Adam, she wouldn't have been worried. But if he was right, if they were both right, and this had been God's plan . . .

If it was Elohim's plan, she didn't have to be afraid. Not if he was alive, like Adam had told her. Not if the sword was gone, and Michael no longer held power over the world.

But she didn't want to risk more than she already had, one way or the other. Not until she knew. And just as Adam could not have found Michael without her five years ago, she didn't see how they would've learned the truth without acting as they had, now.

And if Adam was right. If they could be together, without fear. Eve swallowed hard, her throat thick and her eyes stinging. To be able to spend the rest of eternity with Adam, to go forward with the knowledge that she would always be loved, always be free to be herself, to live as Eve.

She was afraid to even think of it, because it would hurt so much more if she was wrong.

CHAPTER THIRTY-SEVEN
1632 AD

§

Ra took Adam in after they returned his memory, nursed him in Egypt when it became clear he could not care for himself. Thor almost pitied him, would have, if it were not for Eve. It was only a matter of time now until his mind healed and once he remembered, understood his own power, his desire for Eve would only grow.

But Thor need not have worried Ryam. The rest of that first life, Adam had done nothing more than sit in a corner, twitching, his eyes flickering and unfocused. Lightning sent him into fits, making him weep like a child. Thor stayed only long enough to be certain he was no threat, then left again, to give Ryam what news there was. It was a thin excuse to catch some glimpse of Eve, even to his own ears, and it did not fool Ryam in the slightest. Those journeys almost always resulted in Thor drinking himself beneath the table with his brothers later, so he would not have to think of any of it.

The second life was a different matter. They had promised Adam wealth and power if he would leave Eve alone, and by some magic Thor had never understood, he had been born a son of the Sultan in the Ottoman Empire. Adam became known as Suleiman the

Magnificent after he took his father's place—Thor had no illusions as to what role poison had played in his father's sudden demise, or by whose hand it had been delivered—and with the strength of the empire behind him, took to the business of conquering the world as if it were his birthright.

Thor was only grateful that Eve had been born in the New World, as the blossoming urge for exploration had spread her bloodline west to the Americas. Half of France was some relation of hers, and a good portion of Spain and Portugal as well. If what Buddha and Ra theorized was to be believed, every by-blow of the explorers among the natives strengthened her ties to those discovered lands, and Thor could only hope she would remain there for some time, oceans apart from her brother.

But of course it wouldn't last. It never did. And Adam's third life brought them much too close to one another.

"I admit it does not surprise me that he would rise up against Rome, one way or another," Ra told him, as they watched the columns of men passing below. Night was falling quickly, and it was clear the Protestant army would not reach the Catholic forces in Lutzen. Thor would not have cared either way, but for the fact that Eve was the queen of Germany and the archduchess consort of Austria, married to the Holy Roman Emperor, Ferdinand II. "But to go from a leader of an Islamic empire in one life, to the king of a Christian nation in the next must be disconcerting."

Adam led the army of course, as King Gustavus Adolphus of Sweden. Also known as King Gustavus the Great, naturally. Thor did not think Adam would ever tire of placing honorifics after his name.

"As he believes in none of it, I doubt he's bothered in the least," Thor said. "But you're right about Rome. I imagine the memory of being thrown off St. Peter's chair by the Archangels haunts him excessively. If he's found it, anyway."

"But more importantly, I wonder, does he march now for Eve?"

Thor's jaw tightened, and he only shook his head. He could not be certain if Adam knew how to find her, truly, but he had done his best to cloak her presence from him with his own. In Adam's last life, it did not seem as though he had understood how to use his power, but for what came to him on instinct. Charm, more than anything, and persuasiveness in argument, but nothing of the manipulation that he was capable of. It was too much to hope he would never re-learn its use, but if he reached out with his thoughts, searching, the bright spot of Eve's Grace should look more to him like the hum of lightning.

"This modern warfare, these pistols and muskets. Sixteen hundred years they've praised Christ and his Peace, and what do they bring upon one another but one war after another, without even any honor in the fighting of it." Ra snorted. "How Achilles would sneer if these men followed him to Hades."

"As they are Christians, all, it seems unlikely he'll ever be forced to endure their company," Thor said, watching Adam ride down the line of his men. "Did you hear him earlier? 'The Lord God is my armor' indeed."

"Mm." Ra's eyes narrowed. "It will require a careful balance, Thor. Enough to goad him on, but not so much that he will think he acts in our interests. He must have heard of the Archduchess's beauty, if nothing else. Perhaps if someone mentioned the color of her eyes?"

He grunted. It was a dangerous game they played, now. But Michael had to be convinced of the threat and for that, they required Adam. "I'm certain I can think of something appropriate."

"Then I will leave it in your hands, my friend." Ra offered him a brittle smile, his expression strained. "But do be cautious. We will only have one opportunity to set him upon the path he must walk."

"You need not worry, Ra. I know my duty."

The old god touched his shoulder, part-sympathy and part-encouragement. "I have never doubted it."

And then Thor stood alone.

§

Adam and his army had lost the advantage of surprise, and the Catholic army had deployed itself in the night. Thor did his part by raising a mist over the battlefield and building storm-dark clouds to block the sun. Thunder rumbled ominously in warning, and he was rewarded by Adam's growing unease. Even through the mist and the sound of soldiers, Thor could hear the sharpening tone of his commands, the thinning of his patience for any delay. This would be the first contact he would have with the gods since they had returned his memory, and Thor was determined that he would not forget it.

Thor waited until the battle had begun, waited for Adam to become separated from his army by smoke and mist and the chaos inherent in such a clash. And when the moment was right, Adam stranded and struck by gunshot, Thor let the lightning take him, standing suspended in its liquid heat as the hilltop dissolved. Another blinding white bolt set Thor directly in his path.

Adam's horse reared, and with only one arm capable of any strength, he could not steady his beast or arrest his fall, but the moment he struck the ground, he was already scrambling back, naked fear in his gray eyes. His left arm hung useless, the bone mangled and visibly shattered, pale ivory cutting through flesh. Blood was spreading thick and dark through the fabric of his coat, spattered and staining his leather waistcoat as well. Thor only regretted it would not kill him.

"You!"

Thor allowed himself a smile. "How reassuring, to be recognized."

Adam sneered. "You have no business here, no right to interfere."

"Don't I?" Thor asked, keeping his voice mild.

"The church, these Christians, they belong to the archangels, not you or any of yours!"

"I'm not here for them." He caught Adam by his gilt lace collar, and bared his teeth. "You dare come for Eve? Do you think we can't take back what we've given? That we will stand by and let you forswear yourself, stealing this world out from under us with the power of her womb?"

Adam opened his mouth, his one good hand wrapped around Thor's wrist. Then he shut it again, his eyes narrowing. "You're afraid."

Thor curled his lip and dropped him back into the dirt. "You know nothing. Just an ant wishing he had even the strength of a man. Why should I fear you?"

He rose to his feet stiffly, favoring his left side, and brushed himself off. "Because Eve and I, we can destroy you. We can turn you out into the void, unmake you into ashes."

"She'd never let a snake like you near enough to touch her, even if you could reach the castle walls."

"Then I guess you don't have anything to worry about, do you? No reason to come here, threatening me, disrupting my war."

"She's married. And so are you."

"For now." Adam grinned slowly. "But that won't last forever. Everyone dies, you know. And my wife, as anyone will tell you, is quite ill. As for Eve's husband, I'm certain he can be disposed of just as easily."

Thor growled, thunder echoing overhead, but Adam didn't so much as twitch, too caught up in his dream of Eve as his wife. Lightning flashed, and then something else—smaller, from the corner of his eye, with a muffled bang. Adam's smile froze, then crumpled along with his body.

The bullet had struck him in the back of his head, and when Thor crouched down beside him to check, it was clear his skull had been cracked, but the bullet had cut a groove along the bone instead of passing straight through. Any other man would have been dead already, but Adam blinked up at him, merely dazed. Blood had already begun to pour from the wound, running into his ear and down his neck, dripping into his collar.

He grasped Thor's arm when he made to rise. "Everyone dies,

Thunder God. But you can be sure I'll outlive you. Eve and I, both."

§

"King Gustavus was declared dead?" Athena repeated, arching an eyebrow. Thor had gone to the olive grove to meet with Ra, and found her waiting at the older god's side. Not that it should have surprised him; they were never apart for long, anymore. "How in the name of Hades did he accomplish that?"

"Stripped another corpse, dressed it in his clothes, disfigured the poor man's face, and waited until one of his men stumbled across him. Then he just implanted the suggestion, even helped his soldier carry the body back, convincing everyone else along the way, though how he managed that much with a shattered arm, a ruined shoulder, and a cracked skull, I don't want to consider. He's gone in search of Eve, now."

"I suppose that answers your question about whether he's rediscovered his talents," Ra said, staring up through the olive trees to the sky. "He'll be all the more dangerous now."

Thor shrugged. "He was already dangerous. Even without his memory. And you saw what he did to his own son, when he lived as Suleiman. At least this way he's spared his wife. He was planning her murder before the second bullet struck him."

"And did you tell him where Eve was?" Athena asked.

"Near enough," Thor grumbled. It went against everything in him to give Adam even as much as he had, but he'd stopped short of admitting exactly who Eve was. Bad enough he was on his way to Austria. "I mean to go to Vienna. Perhaps Ferdinand will take me on as a bodyguard of some kind."

"And if Michael knows you're there, guarding her, he'll have no reason to bestir himself at all. No," Athena said. "I know it isn't what you'd prefer, but you can't hover over her shoulder. Not now. The threat must be real."

Thor snarled, lightning cracking in sympathy. "If you think I'll stand by and let her fall into his hands—"

"I'll go," Ra interrupted, rising from the marble bench. It was gray and pitted, but still standing strong. He smiled, and patted Athena's arm. "You needn't worry, my dear. Michael will never know me. I'm capable of cloaking myself quite well, after all these years, and it is no hardship to me to restrain myself from using my power. I expect it will be quite invigorating to live as if I were a mortal."

He nodded to Thor. "Go home, Thor. Before your father wonders what's become of you. The last thing we need now is another Council called to disrupt our plans. I'll keep her safe for the rest of this life, you have my word."

It was not the first time Ra had made him such a promise, nor, Thor suspected, would it be the last.

CHAPTER THIRTY-EIGHT
Present

§

Eve had made a habit of getting up with the sun. More often before it. She spent only long enough in bed to pretend to rest, dreading when exhaustion overtook her and jerking herself awake, time and again, just before she began to dream. She needed something to keep herself busy while the rest of the house slept. Something to keep her from the past, which had haunted her since Lars left, and the confusion of feelings which had come with his kiss.

"You haven't been sleeping," Garrit said, watching her.

She set the platter of fresh baked croissants in front of him on the table and smiled. "I don't need as much sleep as you do, remember? Besides, are you complaining about home baked goods on your breakfast table?"

"Not at all. They're the best croissants and pastries I've ever had in my life. If you went into business selling them, you'd be famous. Award winning. French chefs would be blown away."

"And horrified to lose their reputation to an Englishwoman." She laughed and put one of the croissants on his plate. "After several millennia of baking, I should hope that I've figured out the trick to a light and flaky crust."

"What else do you do better than anyone else in the world?" He pulled her into his lap and the newspaper crinkled into a wrinkled mess. "You keep so many secrets, Abby."

"There's too much to tell in one lifetime, Garrit. Even if it were all worth sharing." She kissed his cheek and pulled away, standing up again. "Eat your breakfast and don't worry about me. I know what I'm doing."

"Depriving yourself of sleep, it seems. Didn't you get enough of that before Alex began sleeping through the night?"

She shrugged. It was easier not to sleep. Not to dream. Easier to wake up before the cook and bake for her family. For her husband. Easier to stay in the present when she had to remember what Garrit preferred to eat. When she had to think of Garrit.

"Abby." He caught her by the hand, pulling her back to face him. "I'm not the only one worrying about you. *Maman* and *Papa* are too."

She stroked his cheek. "You can reassure them that I'm fine. This happens sometimes, that's all. So many things floating around in my head. It makes it hard to sleep."

"Are you certain that's all?" He was looking at her with worry and love, and it made her feel worse for the things that kept her up at night. "Is there anything I can do?"

"Not unless you can keep me from dreaming." Explaining what bothered her was hardly going to be helpful to anyone. And talking about it was only going to make her more aware. The last thing she needed was help thinking of Thorgrim.

Horus joined them for breakfast then, taking one of the croissants and sitting down. "My compliments to the chef. These breads you make are amazing, Abby. Fit for the gods."

She smiled, grateful for the interruption. *"Merci."*

It had been a week since Lars had gone, but Horus seemed in no hurry to follow. Nor did Garrit seem anxious to see him go. Her husband had relaxed significantly after Lars's departure, and his manners had improved with every day the man stayed gone. Even more reason not to talk about it.

"Perhaps if you went running?" Garrit suggested.

She sighed and went back to the kitchen to pull the popovers from the oven. The cook Garrit had hired watched her with a mix of respect and irritation. Eve couldn't blame him. She hated having him in her kitchen as much as he disliked her presence there. Perhaps more. She'd never been comfortable with having a staff or servants.

She left him some of the popovers. "They're only good when they're warm."

He grunted, mumbling a grudging thanks. She saw him pick one up just as she left, and the door swung shut behind her.

"For what ails her there is no simple fix, Garrit." Horus was saying. "With so much on her mind, and the recent trauma, it's only natural she would have a difficult time sleeping. If she says it's normal, I think we must trust that she knows better than anyone else."

"Talking about me?" She smiled and offered Horus a popover. She still couldn't find it in her to be at all offended by him. Though she did feel a certain amount of irritation toward Garrit for bringing it up with the man. It wasn't anyone's business but her own how much she slept or didn't sleep. "I'm fine, really. I've never needed much sleep unless I was pregnant. And even then, sleep is less important than food."

"I do not doubt you, *madame*." Horus picked one of the popovers and inserted a pad of butter inside to melt. "These smell incredible. Should I ask where you learned to bake like this? No, I can see by your face I shouldn't. Let me just say that I know of people who would give their left arm to be able to make a pastry like yours. Why weren't you exercising this considerable talent before now?"

She laughed. "When I was pregnant with Alex, Garrit wouldn't hear of my lifting a finger to cook or clean. I'm afraid the effects are still lingering."

Garrit snorted. "You had more important things to focus on, like gestating and worrying about your brother. Why should you bother yourself with chores if you don't have to?"

"Because it's fun, that's why. Relaxing even." Maybe she would ask him for a loom someday. Weaving had always done a good job of keeping her mind off things. The simple, repetitive motions of twisting threads over, under, and through, could be mesmerizing. On second thought, maybe weaving wasn't the answer for what ailed her either. It would make her drowsy.

She made herself a cup of coffee quietly, and sat down at the table. Even thinking the word drowsy made her tired. Horus noticed the way she wilted, even if Garrit didn't, and he raised one eyebrow but said nothing. Why did he always look as though he knew what she was thinking? Surely she'd found her center by now and wasn't leaking her thoughts anymore. She had felt much more in control, even exhausted as she was, and the echoes of pain she'd been experiencing from Adam were gone, her bruises healed.

"Cook and bake as much as you like, Abby, but as long as my parents are staying with us, and the family visits so frequently, the cook isn't going anywhere."

She couldn't stop herself from rolling her eyes, and Horus laughed. Then Juliette arrived with Alex and René.

"You must have been up before dawn to do all this, Abby."

Eve sighed internally, resigning herself to a difficult day of being encouraged to nap. She took Alex from Juliette's arms and settled him into his seat. This was probably going to be the most time she'd have to spend with her son today. Garrit and Juliette were exchanging looks that were far too familiar. Conspiratorial. No doubt there would be some fieldtrip for Alex at Juliette's insistence, so that she could stay home and rest without the distraction of checking on her child. She counted the seconds in her head, and tried to find it amusing that the two of them could exchange so much information without the benefit of telepathy.

"I was thinking it would be fun to take Alex to the zoo," Juliette said, before Eve had made it to fifteen.

"Isn't it a bit cold for the zoo?" Eve glanced at Garrit who had invested himself in his newspaper again. As if he weren't listening. "I'd hate for him to catch a chill."

"*Certainement pas*. It's supposed to be quite sunny today. And Alex has all these winter clothes he never uses. I won't let anything happen to him, Abby, you know that."

Alex played with his cereal, and Eve sighed again, watching him, and deftly inserting a spoonful of applesauce into his mouth between bites. "I don't think you'll see much of the animals."

"Not as many as we would with you, *peut-être*, but he is so young it would be a lot to take in. This might be a good introduction." Juliette had an answer for everything. Eve wondered if she even cared that Garrit didn't participate in the persuasion. Maybe she saw it as some kind of challenge. "The two of you hardly get any time alone together these days when you aren't sick in bed, Abby. Go out together. See a film."

Ah. That was new. "Don't you have to work, Garrit?"

He looked up from the paper, searching her face, his expression odd. "It's Saturday, Abby."

"Oh." She should have known that. Losing track of the day of the week wasn't going to help her argument for not needing sleep. "Of course."

They were all looking at her with pity now. And growing concern. Even Horus. She fed Alex mechanically and tried to pretend she didn't notice. Maybe she should have ensured they didn't realize she wasn't sleeping, but she hated using her power that way. Hated it even more with Adam present in her life. He would notice she'd done it, and the last thing she wanted was to give him ideas or make him think she thought it was acceptable. Make him think he could do it to her family.

"I promise you, I'm fine," she said, meeting Garrit's eyes. "I don't see why you worry so much. It isn't as though I'm going to fall sick."

Horus was staring at her. His eyes narrowed slightly. As though he were trying to see more than what was on the surface. She ignored it. Her stomach cramped. Probably from the stress of all of this interrogation.

"*Maman,* I think a trip to the zoo for Alex would be an excellent idea," he said. "He's about finished with his breakfast."

Juliette didn't wait for Eve to agree. She smiled and scooped Alex back up, kissing the baby's cheek and murmuring to him about the animals he would see as she left the room. With a nod from Garrit, René left as well. And then it was only Horus who remained. He hesitated for the briefest of moments, as though there was something he wanted to say, but then he looked at Garrit, shook his head, and excused himself as well.

Garrit waited until the room had emptied, and Eve found herself feeling like a child about to be chastised. It was entirely unacceptable. Didn't he understand that she was doing this for him? For their marriage? For Alex? For her family?

No. Of course not. Because she hadn't told him. But how was she going to explain without making him think she wasn't happy? Lars's words came to her again. Garrit worried he wasn't the better man. That Lars had been who she was meant for. But she hadn't even known him, and it didn't matter, either way. She had married Garrit. Nothing could change that.

"I wish you would tell me what's bothering you," Garrit began softly. "You lie awake for hours at night, staring at the ceiling, trying not to sleep. You've never been this way before, and I'm not sure how to reach you, how to get you to talk to me."

She looked away, brushing the crumbs from the tablecloth into a neat pile. "It's what I have to do."

"Why?"

She shook her head. "The past sneaks up on me, sometimes. Overwhelms me. When things happen the same way, or something reminds me forcefully of another life. And then I dream. Of Creation, of Adam, of my lives as a Greek. Of my life with Ryam. The bad and the good." As much as she hated the secrets he kept from her. The secrets she knew he was keeping, she hated her own secrets more. It was good that Lars had left. That she didn't stare at him and think of Thorgrim.

"Was it Lars?" His voice was flat. As though he were trying to keep it level. Trying not to show how much he cared. But it just seemed strained, somehow. Or maybe that was how he felt. "He reminded you of that other life. Of your other husband."

She closed her eyes. She wasn't sure if it was the memories of Thorgrim from their life together that disturbed her anymore, as much as it was the memories of her hallucinations of him. And the way his presence had brought that whole experience back to mind. An experience she had tried diligently to suppress. To bury. She had no wish to dream of the ward, or the years that had followed.

"He kissed me," she said, finally. Because she didn't want to explain about that life or how difficult it had been. She didn't want to see the horror in his eyes when she recounted it. "I didn't want you to be upset by it. But it resurrected all these things I didn't want to remember, and not sleeping seems to be the only way to avoid thinking of it."

Garrit's face darkened. Blackened. "When?"

There was so much anger, she flinched away. "After that first dinner. When I was well enough to eat. Before my brother chose to give me a second dose of his pain."

His hand had balled into a fist around his napkin. His knuckles white. "Do you love him?"

She stared at him. The question was ludicrous. Even hurtful. But hadn't Adam suggested the same thing? What was it about Lars that scared them so much? "I don't even know him, Garrit. How could I love him?"

"Because he's a weaseling, deceitful, *conspirateur!*" he growled. "As bad as your brother. Perhaps even worse!"

"Garrit. Don't be ridiculous." But she wasn't sure what was

ridiculous about the statement. At least Adam hadn't kissed her or touched her when he knew she was engaged, and then married. She was tired. She didn't want to have this fight. "It doesn't matter. It's over. He's gone."

"He's never gone," Garrit said. He shook his head, and threw his napkin from him, standing up. "And I never should have let him come back here. Never should have let him near you."

She rubbed her face. Her eyes itched. The coffee hadn't been strong enough. Or maybe she hadn't had enough to eat. Or too much to eat, when she had been half starved? She felt sick. Her stomach was cramping. Not her stomach. Her abdomen.

"No," she said softly, recognizing the pain. She counted the days in her head. With all the stress she had assumed—but then the stress could have done it on its own, coupled with her complete lack of sleep. And the fact that she'd been hardly eating. With the trauma of Adam's pain, and her own. "Not again."

Garrit looked at her, then looked again, and swore. "Horus!"

Another cramp made her double over in pain, and she groaned. "I'm sorry, Garrit. I didn't know. I didn't realize."

He was crouched beside her, his hands on her face, on her arm. "What's wrong? *Qu'est-ce qui ne va pas?*"

She felt the tears burning behind her eyes, and couldn't stop them. "I was pregnant."

CHAPTER THIRTY-NINE
Future

When Adam woke, the bed was empty. The pillow beside him no longer held even the impression of her head, and the linens had lost every last molecule of her warmth. "Evey?" There was an emptiness about the flat, and he knew even before he called for her that she wasn't there. Still, he felt compelled to speak, to fill the quiet with something. "Hello?"

He wandered into the kitchen. Coffee would help clear his head. Was it possible that it wasn't a dream? Eve would never have forced him, never have orchestrated something like that. Would she? But his body knew, even while his mind tried to deny it, and he wouldn't have been parading naked around his home if she hadn't stripped him of his clothes earlier that morning.

There was a note under a wine bottle. A scrap of paper, really. He wondered where she had found it, because he didn't think he had any paper anything anymore. Everything was digital, intangible and without substance. He hated it.

The scrap was thick and somewhat damp, and before he read the words—as an excuse not to read the words—he flipped it over.

Packaging from some kind of frozen entrée. Not true paper at all.

But he had no further excuse not to read it and he ran his thumb over the scribbled sentence. It was in French, though he wasn't sure why. *Pardonne-moi, je t'en supplie.*

Did she really think he wouldn't forgive her? That she would have to even ask? Or perhaps it was the fact that she had left him asleep. He wasn't sure why she'd slipped out. There had been a saying— something about closing a barn door after the horses had escaped. It was a bit late for her to run off, with the damage already done. Potentially. He made his coffee and considered the logic. The logic he no doubt would have used to repeat the behavior, over and over and over again until neither one of them could walk.

On second thought, he understood exactly why she had slipped away.

He waited for the coffee to finish heating and sipped it while it was still hot. Too hot. It burned his mouth, but he felt the better for it. There was a lingering muzziness still, from what she had done, as if he weren't entirely in control even now.

Perhaps he wasn't. That would explain the lethargy. The knowledge that he wanted to go after her, but his inability to do so. Every time he tried to think of where she might have gone and how she had gotten there, he felt his mind slip away from the thoughts. He couldn't quite focus, couldn't quite get there.

He supposed he should resent her for that. For this. For whatever it was she had done. But he knew that if she had offered him the opportunity he would have taken it. She had not asked anything of him that he had not wanted to give her. In fact, she had simplified it. He couldn't be angry, couldn't have any regret. He couldn't feel guilty for something he hadn't been responsible for, hadn't been able to stop if he had wanted to. Which he hadn't. Not at all. From the moment he had understood what she was about, what she was doing, there had been no question in his mind of how it would end.

How it would begin?

Eve, love. I wish you hadn't gone.

There was a wash of love, of tenderness. But no words. No words.

§

He waited for the thunder, for the lightning, for the storm. He waited all day for it to come. The rage, the upheaval. He waited for the gods to break down his door, for Michael to swoop down from wherever he hid himself. He waited for the DeLeons to come and demand reparations, or some other nonsense that would make him laugh at their expense. He waited for the promises they had made to be kept. Promises. Threats. It was all the same. And he spent the day sitting, staring out at the mountains, her mountains, with enough wine to drown himself.

But none of it came.

Until that moment it had never occurred to him that if this were to happen, it would be her responsibility. It had never occurred to him to wonder what would happen if it was she, not he, who caused the breach of trust, the bonds to break. And suddenly, he wasn't sure that death wouldn't come looking for her. For all his reassurance that Michael lacked the sword, did that mean he couldn't punish her? Did it mean he wouldn't hunt her down? He'd said he would come for what was his, that any child of Eve's belonged to God . . .

The last of the weight, the drag of Eve's power, left him with the thought, the fear, the terror that came with it. What exactly had he promised, thinking it was impossible, that Eve would never allow even the possibility of it all? He half-sat up with the realization, putting it all together at last. The baby. He moaned, falling back again and raking his fingers through his hair. Eve's baby. He'd sworn away all claim. He'd sworn to give up her child, their child!

Where are you?

Away, Adam. For both our sakes.

Hidden? Safe?

What's the matter? She had caught the edge of his thoughts, of the fears he tried to force away.

He buried them deeply, though if she were insistent, he was sure it wouldn't help. *Come back to me, Eve. Please. So that I know you're well.*

I think I'd better not. Not yet.

And he caught the reasoning from her mind. Not until she knew if she had conceived. Yes, that made sense. That she would wait for that before returning. *What will you do?*

She sighed. *Wait and pray. Then pray again. If God lives, how long can he deny me?*

If God lived, he had denied them both for an eternity already. Left them without guidance, without help. Left them to stumble through the world, through their lives without a whisper, until now. *I wish I knew.*

I love you.

He wished she were there, that he could wrap her in his arms and breathe it in her ear. That he could show her exactly how much he felt for her, how much he lived for her. Before she realized what it all meant, what would come for them both—how he'd betrayed her. Because if the angel came, he'd sworn not to stand in the way.

He felt her laugh, soft and happy. *That's why I had to go. This was risk enough already.*

But why? He still didn't understand, didn't know what had possessed her. *Why would you risk so much? Just for me? Just for this?*

Because you're right, Adam, so right. God is love.

Before he could form a reply she had gone, and there was nothing left to reply to. Of course she would hide herself from him now, while she waited, not realizing the agony it would cause him, thinking of all the threats she couldn't know.

He shook his head and drank more wine to dull the ache of her absence. If he could spend the next weeks too drunk to know the difference between one night and the next, it would be for the best.

There wasn't much else he could do, until she let him. Until she knew.

What did it mean that he found himself praying that she had his child? Hoping that she was pregnant, if only so she could return to him, and they could carry on with nothing standing between them, just for a little while longer? Maybe it would be a little girl, he thought as the alcohol blurred the edges of the truth, pushing away the promises he didn't want to keep. Maybe she would have her mother's eyes, and her mother's laugh, and her mother's love.

What harm could a baby cause? A baby of Eve's blood, Eve's body, with Eve to mother her and love her and want her happiness? How could a baby of Eve's ever hurt this world, when Eve loved it so much she had been prepared to sacrifice everything in her heart to keep it intact?

If God was love, and the baby a god, it could have no greater mother to teach it so.

He woke to pounding on his door, unsure of how long he had slept or how many days he had spent sitting there with his wine and the mountains for company. He rubbed his face, the stubble on his jaw convincing him it hadn't been a multitude of nights, for all he had dreamed they had come and gone. It had been one, maybe two at the most. Perhaps he wouldn't shave then, until he heard from Eve, to help keep track of the days he intended to lose.

Another bang reminded him of why he was awake, and he climbed unsteadily to his feet. He had no business walking anywhere at this point, really. No business attempting anything aside from a coma, but the banging continued and he lurched somehow to the door, releasing the lock and letting it slide open.

The hulking figure on the other side was leaning heavily against the frame. He stumbled in through the door and Adam watched him make his way through the flat toward the kitchen. How long had Thor been drinking? It had to have been even longer than Adam to affect him so severely. Or perhaps it was just a misconception that he had of these gods, that they had greater constitutions than men.

"A bit late, aren't you?" Adam called after him.

Thor helped himself to the contents of the liquor cabinet and came back out of the kitchen with two bottles in each hand, dropping to the couch and staring sullenly at the mountains. "It was what she wanted."

"Yes." He dropped into a seat next to the god and accepted one of the bottles from him, taking a long drink.

There was a grunt, and Thor seemed to notice his appearance. "You're not celebrating."

"No." He shook his head, but the room spun, and he stopped. "She won't even tell me where she is."

"Would you like to know?"

What an awful question. Of course he wanted to know. And part of him was irritated that Thor could find her even when he couldn't. He sighed, took another drink, and wiped his mouth with the back of his hand. "No. Don't tell me. As long as she's safe, that's all that matters."

Thor stared at him, his eyes narrowed. "It's true then."

"What's true?"

The god shook his head. "I never thought it was possible. Though I suppose I should've known. If it were possible, it would be her, wouldn't it?"

Now that he was sitting down again, that pleasant lassitude was spreading through him. He could barely keep his eyes open, never mind puzzle out Thor's words. "You're drunk, Thunderer."

"Aye," Thor said. "And you're in love."

"Aren't you?"

Thor sighed, his head tilting back against the cushion of the sofa. He was so immense he took up half of it. Adam didn't think he'd have fit in the chair comfortably. "Always, Adam. Forever and always."

"I don't know if she'll come back. Not sure that she should, really."

"She will." The god downed a bottle of good triple malt whiskey in one long gulp. "Or at least, you'll be together again. Here, or there, it doesn't matter."

That made him force his eyes open, and he sat up. "How do you know?"

Thor met his gaze then, his expression serious, and far more lucid than he had appeared just moments before. "Congratulations, Adam. You're going to be a father."

CHAPTER FORTY
1920 AD

§

Thor followed Dr. Meek up the wide steps to the hospital, halving his stride to keep from overtaking the smaller man. It had taken a significant amount of cajoling to talk Meek into allowing him to see Eve, and he still refused to discuss her treatments. Seeing her, Thor decided, would be the best first step until he had more information, and the more tight-lipped Dr. Meek became, the more Thor worried.

"Come this way," Meek said, holding open the door. "She has a room to herself. Mr. Newcastle has spared no expense for his wife."

"Of course not," he murmured, half under his breath. "How could he do anything less?"

"Many do," Meek replied. "Quiet divorces resulting in abandonment. Mr. Newcastle comes dutifully to see his wife, regardless of her condition."

Thor kept his opinions of that behavior to himself, but his jaw tightened, and it was an effort to keep himself from growling. He followed Dr. Meek down the hall, past a bank of windows. Rain beat against the glass, and Thor grimaced. The newspaper had predicted sun.

He rolled his shoulders and inhaled deeply through his nose, trying to calm himself, but the sounds of women weeping and beating at the doors made his back stiffen. He didn't allow himself to look into any of the rooms, afraid he would lose his temper. He had to see Eve. He had to focus on Eve, first.

"Dr. Williams has been working quite closely with her, if you'd like to speak with him, but I'm afraid he won't be willing to give you any further information, either."

"I'd like to see her, first, for myself," he said firmly. "To see her condition with my own eyes and offer her the reassurance that I mean to see her taken care of."

Dr. Meek paused by the door, his lips pressed together. "Mr. Sonnungar, I know that you mean well, and it is obvious that you have a great deal of affection for your cousin, but you should know in advance—I doubt very much that she will recognize you. Her mind is—it is a very delicate situation."

Thor stared at the door, wishing he could see through it, or at the very least, rip it from its hinges. "I see."

Meek unlocked the door and entered first, but Thor didn't hesitate to follow, almost treading on his heels.

"Evelyn?" Meek's voice was low and gentle. "You have a visitor, my dear."

His heart constricted at the sight that greeted him. Eve sat in the corner of the room, her arms wrapped around her legs, pulled tight against her chest. She rocked back and forth, her eyes unfocused and she made no sound in response, did not in fact, seem to hear them.

"Eve?" Thor said, stepping forward.

Her head snapped toward them, her lips moving silently as her eyes locked on his face, then widened. She scrambled to her feet, her fingers clawing at the gray cinderblocks behind her.

"Ah." Meek smiled. "Good. You recognize your cousin, my dear? Mr. Sonnungar?"

Thor shook his head just slightly, seeing the confusion in her eyes.

Not yet, he tried to say without words. *Wait until he's left.*

She swallowed. "You see him?"

Meek raised his eyebrows. "But of course, my dear. Mr. Sonnungar and I have been speaking with one another for several weeks. He's expressed a large concern over your care, and I thought it would be best to reassure him." He turned to Thor. "She's been seeing people, you understand. Hallucinations, dreams. But Dr. Williams never mentioned a cousin. They're usually men she claims to have married in previous lives, when we can goad her into talking about them at all. One named Thorgrim in particular."

Thor's throat closed and he had to clear it twice before any sound would come out. Eve was staring at him still, her face white. "Thorgrim, you say?"

"Oh, yes," Meek went on. "She seems particularly affected by him. From what I understand, he's a bit of a Viking. Have you heard the name before?"

"Yes," he managed to say, but his eyes were burning and he closed them before either the doctor or Eve would notice. He turned his face away, taking a long, slow breath.

"Of course Mr. Newcastle wouldn't know," he said, after he'd gathered his wits. "Thorgrim was her fiancé. He was thrown from his horse and died of a broken neck just before the wedding. They were—" He had to stop and clear his throat again. Thunder rumbled outside, and the rain fell with the noise of snare drums against the roof. He opened his eyes and met Eve's. "They were very much in love."

"Really!" Meek's excitement lit his face. "Really! Well. Well, I must say Mr. Sonnungar—Don. I must say, this is quite a breakthrough. We hadn't realized—well, of course we hadn't realized. But a trauma like that, and then her marriage to another man, yes. Yes, certainly that could have caused a break, if she did not ever get over the grief of it. Wonderful!"

Thor grimaced, ignoring the doctor to step closer to Eve. She was shuddering, her eyes filled with tears. He took the blanket from the bed. "Here."

She shrank back, sliding down the wall again.

He crouched and tucked the blanket around her body.

"How?" she breathed. "How are you here?"

He glanced back at the doctor. "Can I have a moment alone with my cousin?"

Dr. Meek's forehead furrowed briefly. "Well, yes. Yes, I think it can be permitted in this instance. Especially if there's anything else—Yes, of course." He walked back to the door. "Knock three times when you'd like to leave, Mr. Sonnungar, and someone will let you out again."

Thor grunted an acknowledgement, turning back to Eve as the door shut and locked behind him. She looked much too thin, with navy circles beneath her eyes. He brushed his fingers against her cheek and she flinched away, her skin chilled to the touch.

"Eve," he whispered. "What have they done to you?"

"Not here," she mumbled, covering her ears. "Can't be here."

"No," he agreed. "I shouldn't be. But I couldn't stand by—" He pulled her hands away, forcing her to look at him. "In order to speak to you, I had to tell them I was your cousin. If they find out I'm not, they won't let me see you. Can you remember that?"

She shook her head. "*Ek skil eigi.*"

He sighed. At least she knew him. Or why else would she be speaking the old tongue? He took her face in his hands, searching her eyes for some kind of recognition even if she said she didn't understand. Understanding was much more than he expected.

"If they ask you, my name is Donar Sonnungar. *Ek heiti* Sonnungar." He ducked his head to keep her eyes locked on his. "*Skilur þú?*"

She wrapped her fingers around his. "Sonnungar?"

"*Já.*" His lips twitched. "For Thor. You remember the gods? Remember, you were named for him too? Because of the storm, the night you were born, and the way you laughed at the thunder. My

Tora."

A strangled sob rose, ragged with agony, and her eyes filled with tears. Even though she trembled, her fingers tightened around his, pressing his hands against her cheeks. "My Thorgrim."

"Always yours," he promised. "I'm going to set you free, Eve. I swear it."

"You can't," she whispered. "It isn't safe."

"Safe?"

"I'll hurt them." Tears slipped down her cheeks. "Like Adam. I'll hurt them."

He wanted to tell her he'd never let her hurt anyone that way. He wanted to tell her she was wrong. But once he freed her, it would be impossible for him to stay. His father would never allow it. Even this was disobedience, if he learned the truth. Punishable by death, if Odin so desired. He wiped her tears away with his thumb and kissed her forehead.

"I'm sorry," he murmured into her hair. It smelled—strange. Familiar in all the wrong ways. "I should have come sooner."

She fell into his arms, her hold so weak. He could feel her ribs, and the ridge of her spine at the small of her back. She should have smelled like sunshine and spring, but what clung to her was acrid, with the tang of venom . . . And then he felt the welts through the thin gown she wore.

She cried out, her back arching beneath his touch, twisting free.

The color leached from the room as lightning struck outside.

"They whipped you." His voice sounded flat even to his own ears. "To the bone."

She leaned against the cinderblocks, and for the first time he saw the blood on the wall where she had pressed her back against it while the wounds healed. More than once, by the smears. The room flashed white again.

"He said it was my fault."

"What was?" he asked.

She turned her face away, her skull making a hollow thunk against the cinderblock. "I couldn't save our son."

Dr. Williams refused to see him, though Dr. Meek had tried to reason with him. "After the information you were able to give us about this Thorgrim, I would think that the benefits would outweigh—well, there's nothing to be done. I'll continue to speak to him on your behalf, Mr. Sonnungar. It's obvious to me that your contributions in this case could be invaluable."

Thor rubbed his face, still staring at the door behind which Eve was locked. He had left her sleeping after she'd cried herself out. There were puncture marks on her arm, ringed with a vile green. He'd seen their kind only once before, a long time ago, on another world. But the scarred skin of her back had shocked him even more, when he'd finally coaxed her into showing him. Her ribs were a mess of black, blue, and green bruises, along with her stomach.

Thor wanted to grab the man by his collar and shake him. "She's being beaten."

"Ah," Meek gave him a sidelong look. "That was quite unfortunate, yes."

"Unfortunate?" He struggled to quiet his tone while thunder rumbled outside. "Do you think that beating her is going to help? That she's going to get better if someone breaks her spine with a switch?"

Dr. Meek made a strangled noise, stepping back, and Thor only realized he had followed when Meek's heels barked against the wall with a click. The smaller man's shoulders were hunched and Meek pushed his glasses up his nose.

"Now, Mr. Sonnungar—Don. That—that had nothing to do with her treatment, of course. I did my best to treat her afterwards, but there's nothing that we can do—that is, it was a domestic dispute, and how a man disciplines his wife—"

"*Disciplines?*" he roared. "When she's cowering in a corner and barely conscious of who she is, you let that fool beat her as punishment? For losing her child! Do you have any idea what that would have done to her already?"

He slammed his fist into the wall. The tiling cracked and dust fell to the floor.

"Mr.—Don. You have to understand, that we can only give her the care she needs for as long as she remains with us," Dr. Meek began, his voice low. He cleared his throat and went on with more confidence. "And while she's here, I believe the frequency of her beatings is much decreased. She is safer here, Mr. Sonnungar. Surely you realize that?"

Thor pressed his forehead against the cool tile of the wall, forcing himself to breathe through his teeth instead of growling. He unclenched his jaw. "Forgive me, Doctor."

"Quite all right, man." Meek's hand fell briefly on his shoulder, but dropped away at once when he glared. "Your distress is, I assure you, understandable. I felt similarly myself, when I learned of what had happened. I can only imagine how difficult it must be for you as her family."

He grunted. "And the abuse of her husband, has that factored into your considerations of her mental state?"

"Of course, Mr. Sonnungar. But the fact remains that a mind must have a—a genetic predisposition toward this fragmentation."

Thor stiffened, turning slowly to face the doctor again. Meek fell back at once. "You haven't sterilized her."

"Well, no. Not as yet, though it would be a kindness to her. Her husband refuses to allow it, determined that she should give him a son. It seems he was concerned about infidelity more than her health. Of course, once she had been admitted, we realized what he'd heard. Just another symptom of her disease . . ."

He let out a breath he didn't know he was holding, closing his eyes. The relief he felt made him almost dizzy, and he grasped the wall in order to keep upright. To sterilize Eve of all people. By all the gods, what was this world coming to? The war that had just ended would only be the beginning.

"Thank you," he said at last. "That is the best news I could hope for."

Meek cleared his throat. "You understand that Mr. Newcastle has only delayed the procedure. Until she gives him his child. After that . . ."

Thor pressed his lips together. There would be no after that. He would have her free before then. He had to have her free before then. That kind of trauma—he did not want to think what it would do to her, when she was already so fragile. And the venom. If a god was involved, it explained much. With the distraction of the war, he had not been watching her as closely as he should have been, only relieved that she was so far away from the front. He had not realized the significance of her silence, and when he had checked on her last, she'd been dreaming of Thorgrim. He should have known. He should have come sooner. Would have, if there had not been such a threat to the House of Lions. Now he wondered if even that had been orchestrated to keep him away.

"How long ago did she miscarry?"

Meek's gaze slid away as he hemmed. "Well, now. That kind of information—"

Thor grabbed him by the lapels of his jacket and jerked him forward until his face was inches away. "You're telling me you think her *husband* has her best interests at heart? That Frank Newcastle, after beating her bloody, has more of a right to make informed decisions about her health than I do, as her cousin, related to her by *blood?*"

Meek scrabbled at his hands, trying to pry his fingers free. "The law—"

"Your oath, doctor," he growled right over his sentence, before the man could infuriate him even further, "is first to do no harm. Sworn to Apollo himself!"

He let Meek go, and the doctor stumbled back into the wall,

breathless, his eyes wide and his brow beaded with sweat.

"What you do to the other women in this ward, I have no right to judge," Thor went on, struggling to control his tone, "but Evelyn is under my protection. Do you understand me?"

Meek swallowed, his Adam's apple bobbing repeatedly. "Of course, Mr. Sonnungar. Yes. Yes, of course."

The rain drummed in Thor's ears, though there were no windows in the hall. He closed his eyes, burning again, and pinched the bridge of his nose. Inhale. Exhale. He could not let his temper get the best of him, not if there were gods involved. But seeing her that way, knowing that Frank Newcastle was responsible for placing her in their hands, for abusing her so completely, and these men, these doctors had done nothing to stop it, made the color leach from his vision. Other men and gods might see red in their anger, but Thor saw lightning white.

"I apologize for my behavior," he said. "But to learn of this the way I did—had I been here, I never would have allowed her husband to mistreat her this way. She never would have been made to endure any of this."

"Oh?" Meek's Adam's apple bobbed again, convulsively. "I had been wondering, of course, why we had never heard of you before now when Mrs. Newcastle has been in our care for so long."

Thor frowned. "I was overseas. In France."

"Of course, of course. In the war. A man like yourself, yes. I should have known."

"If I had known what would happen to Evelyn in my absence—"

"Yes, I see," Dr. Meek said, making a sympathetic noise in his throat. "Quite. Very unfortunate, the timing of all of this."

"Unfortunate." He snorted at what educated men could consider coincidence. So much knowledge, and still they did not see the truth. "Unfortunate does not begin to describe the horrors of that war, nor what this world will face if humanity continues down this path." His hands balled back into fists at his sides. "If you only knew what you were doing—" he clamped his jaw shut. Too much, and the man would think him as crazy as Eve. "We call it the war to end all wars, but I fear that there is greater darkness ahead, Dr. Meek. Seeing what's become of Evelyn, how can I think otherwise? Where are the good men to protect women like her, whose only failing has been too much love for a dead man?"

"We have been doing everything in our power, Mr. Sonnungar, I assure you. Dr. Williams is the best in his field, pioneering new treatments for just such cases as Evelyn's. Your cousin could not be in better hands."

"Better that she not be in any man's hands, if this is how she is treated." He rubbed his forehead. It would have been an easy thing to hand the venom to the right man, encouraging him to explore it as a treatment. Or else the doctor himself? But why? "This cannot be what her father meant for her."

"Her disorder is hardly something he could have planned for, unless there was some history of illness already. Mr. Newcastle could not tell us if her mother ever exhibited any odd behaviors, of course . . ."

Thor shook his head. "No. Her mother was perfectly healthy in every way. A lovely woman." And even if it had been otherwise, he did not dare to speak a word of it. Not when it would only serve as justification to have her sterilized. "Whatever caused this, it has nothing to do with her family history, and everything to do with her husband."

"Mr. Sonnungar, with all due respect—"

"With all due respect, Dr. Meek, I know Evelyn better than any other man alive on this earth. Better than her own father. Maybe with the other women you've worked with you are correct in your theories, but not Evelyn. Not *ever* Evelyn. You cannot use her as one of your case studies, surely you realize that much by now? If she's being beaten, haven't you seen the way her body heals?"

Dr. Meek opened his mouth, then shut it, looking back at the door. His forehead creased, his mouth pressing into a thin line. He removed his glasses, polishing them absently with his handkerchief.

"You discounted it, perhaps," Thor suggested. "Assumed that her injuries had not been quite as severe as they appeared at first."

"I thought the error must have been mine. But when she lost the child, she was so dehydrated, half-starved. I confess that I've never seen anyone in such a weakened state. That she kept that baby as long as she did was something of a miracle."

"And her medication. The doses she requires are no doubt much higher than any of your other patients."

Meek replaced his glasses, staring at Thor now. "How did you know?"

"Evelyn and I have always been close." He held the man's gaze, willing him to believe, to trust. "If you truly wish to help her, Doctor, you cannot depend on Frank Newcastle. He doesn't know her the way I do—the way Thorgrim did. And with the way he treats her, I can't blame her for keeping her secrets."

"Yes," Meek replied. "I begin to see your point." He glanced once more at the door to Eve's room, and then nodded. "Come with me, Mr. Sonnungar. I have copies of all Mrs. Newcastle's charts in my office."

CHAPTER FORTY-ONE
Present

§

Her miscarriages had always been rare. Comparatively few and far between. She could go lives without them. Hundreds, even thousands of years. For the most part, she was more aware of her body than other women. More aware of when she could conceive. More knowledgeable about how to take care of herself and the baby inside her as it grew. More capable of caring for it. She rarely if ever experienced morning sickness. And as long as she was careful, as long as she didn't push herself and her limits, as long as she ate and slept like any other woman, instead of half starved and behaving like an insomniac, her pregnancies had always been without complication. Easy.

But the shock of Adam's self-destructive act and her own recovery had distracted her. Her relapse, and Lars's presence confused her further. And she had not noticed the signs. Had not recognized what her body was trying to tell her. Not until it was too late.

She had miscarried in her last life, too. Again and again, in the hospital. After her husband had sent her away. Because once, she had murmured another man's name in her sleep, and it was only after their marriage that she had realized the kind of man he was. She had

310

watched him beat their dog to death, and when she had tried to stop him, cried and begged him to stop, he had beaten her too. The first of so many, but she had been too afraid of Adam then, and divorce had never been an option she could take. Not without breaking the covenant which protected her. But it drove her husband into madness, thinking she'd carried on some affair, so he locked her away where he could be certain of her fidelity. Listening to so much pain, being treated for a disorder she didn't have, Eve had gone quietly insane.

She had lain on the floor in her own blood after she lost her baby, crying as her whole body shook from the medication they had forced her to take. Lain in her own blood for hours, because she had not the strength to crawl to the bed, the last of her energy wasted by uncontrollable vomiting.

And when Frank had learned about the miscarriage he'd come to see her. He'd been whipping her with the belt. Shouting at her. Accusing her of murdering his child. Something inside her snapped when his stroke landed across her spine, buckle and all. She had screamed then, not with her hollow voice, but with her mind, and Frank had dropped like a rock. Unconscious by her power. Lucky he wasn't dead.

Thorgrim had come to her shortly thereafter. He held her, so gently, so careful, until she collapsed into sleep. And when she had awoken, he was still there, watching her. One of the nurses heard her calling his name, and she had been given more drugs, which made her sicker, still.

The next baby didn't survive either.

"Shh, Eve." Horus said in her ear. "Quiet now. You're not there anymore. You're safe and sound."

She opened her eyes and stared at the old man. For a moment she thought she saw the shadow of wings, but when she blinked they were gone. She shivered and he squeezed her hand.

"I can see now why you didn't wish to sleep, if that's what your dreams have been."

"You saw."

He nodded, his face full of sympathy. "You left us for a moment. Too much stress, I think, and the fatigue, combined with such an unfortunate event."

"Where's Garrit?" She didn't try to sit up, though she was in her room again. She remembered that Garrit had carried her to her bed, and Horus had come to see to her. To do what he could to help. And she had slept for the first time in days, unable to keep her eyes open any longer.

"He went to call his mother. They had already left for the zoo, you see."

The look in Garrit's eyes as the realization and understanding washed over him had been horrifying. He had appeared haunted by the life, the baby, that he would never know. His face white as a sheet as the past tense she had used sunk into his mind.

"Is he angry?"

"Not with you." But Horus's face twisted ruefully, and she thought she saw his regret. "I don't think there's any saving his relationship with Lars now. And Adam certainly hasn't escaped his anger."

"It isn't their fault."

"It isn't yours either. In this life, or the last. You were only defending yourself, Eve. That's what God gave you that power for. To protect yourself. To save yourself and your people. And you've only ever used it for good reason, which is far more than can be said about your brother. Have peace."

She blinked again, staring into his grandfather's face. Peace. It had been a long time since someone had wished her peace outside of a church. "How do you know when it's right?"

He smiled faintly. "You're God's daughter, Eve. He would not want you to stand by and allow yourself to be beaten, to be hurt, to be abused. If he would not allow Adam to treat you thusly, why would he want you to suffer it by any lesser man's hand?"

"Somehow I don't think what Adam did or didn't do had anything to do with what God wanted." She sat up carefully, and Horus slid a pillow behind her back to help. "And I'm not better than any other person on this earth. Neither is he."

He leaned back, watching her with amusement. "Aren't you? Powerful as you are. Immortal as you are."

"But how much harder they work, with less? How much they're capable of doing in such short times. I can cook like a chef, but only because I spent lives upon lives doing it. I'm good with children, but only because I can read their minds, because I've had life after life to perfect the art of parenting. I can weave beautiful things, but if you had seen my attempts in my first lives, compared to the fabric and designs of the other women, you would know that it isn't a natural talent."

"Your modesty is as startling as your brother's arrogance." He studied her face, silent for a moment. "That life was very hard on you. Harder than previous lives of similar situation. And yet, here you are."

She grimaced. "I'd really rather not talk about it."

"Not talking about it hasn't helped you. Dreaming about it keeps you from sleep. Maybe you need to talk about it. To cleanse yourself."

"To you?"

He shrugged. "My purpose now is only to help you, in whatever way I can. To fulfill Lars's vow in his absence."

"Lars." She sighed and looked away. Trying not to think of Thorgrim. "And what exactly was Lars's vow?"

"To protect you and your family," Horus said. "To help your family to protect you from your brother."

"My brother isn't here."

"But he is present, all the same. Feeling your joy and your sorrow. There is a bond there that cannot be ignored. Garrit does not yet realize this, focused as he is on Lars. A dangerous distraction, but maybe for the best. Your husband could never be easy knowing it is only a matter of time."

She frowned. "Only a matter of time?"

"Adam learns even now how best to please you. What to make

himself into so that you are not offended by him, by his love." Horus's eyes were unfocused. He shook his head and looked at her again, after a moment. "I thought once that God's plan for this world could be disrupted. But now I see it is all as He means for it to be. His presence is felt. Nothing we do, nothing we believe will change it now."

It sounded like riddles. And she was frustratingly aware that he wanted her to understand something. But she wasn't sure if he meant it as reassurance or warning. "Who are you?"

He smiled his grandfatherly smile and patted her hand. "A healer. A friend. And an old man caught up in things he should not have believed he had a right to interfere with. But how could I help these people, if I did not work among them? If I did not make myself available? My brothers never understood my need to be present. And to do all this work, to give so much of myself, only to risk its destruction?" He shook his head again and sighed. "It seemed too terrible a waste. I wanted to keep it whole. I failed, as Michael will as well, as we all have, even your Thorgrim. Perhaps if I hadn't cautioned him all those years ago, warned him from interfering as I did, things would have been different now."

"Your brothers—" She narrowed her eyes, blinking against the shadow flaring out from his shoulders. No, not a shadow. Feathers, pure and white, and neatly folded wings. "But you can't be . . . an angel? Archangel? I don't understand, how—what has any of it to do with Thorgrim? With me?" She wished the fruit had been more comprehensive in its gift of knowledge. But she had been wishing for that for eternity to no avail. A ghost she should give up.

"Yes, we all have our ghosts." He frowned as he studied her again, and he reached out to smooth her hair from her forehead. His hand was cool and dry and his touch was gentle. "And there are some things that are better off not remembered. Not known. At least not yet."

She gasped as it all came forward at once, and his hand warmed against her forehead. The hospital floor, cold and gritty against her cheek. The agony of the drugs and the treatments and the sickness and the miscarriages, one after another. The anguish of the others around her, and their suffering. Suffering which drove her deeper into despair. Thorgrim whispering to her of how he planned to free her. Holding her in the dark, in the night, hushing her when she called to him. So that the nurses wouldn't hear. So that the doctors wouldn't force her to take more of the drugs that made her so sick. So sick she wanted to die. Trying to die to escape the horrors her doctor heaped upon her. Letting her blood drain from her body and hoping it would end it all, hoping she could be freed, could escape. That had only resulted in more drugs, more pain.

And then it was gone. Washed over, washed out, wiped away as if it had never happened, and she clung to the present, the memory of Horus's identity, struggled to keep it. "I'm sorry, Eve," she heard him say, as even that last memory slipped from her grasp and exhaustion overtook her, "the balance of power already shifts too easily."

Eve slept in peace for the first time in weeks. She dreamed of the Garden. The angels with the white wings. Michael the protector, Gabriel the messenger, and Raphael the healer, with his grandfather's eyes. And then she dreamed of nothing at all.

CHAPTER FORTY-TWO

Future

Adam jittered the entire flight, going over the conversation he'd had with the god over and over again in his mind. Thor had told him where he could find Eve, though Adam hadn't asked, and he wished he had the god's ability to teleport. To arrive immediately on her doorstep. Thor had snorted and suggested a jet would give him time to sober up. He couldn't deny that he needed it.

If Thor knew she was pregnant, it was only a matter of time before the archangels did, and Adam was determined to be there before Michael thought of arriving. Thor had assured him that he had a significant head start, but the god was drunk, and Athena had arrived not long after to take him away, in the company of another large god with such a striking resemblance Adam thought he must be some relative of Thor's. Maybe a brother.

They were both grim, almost as upset as Thor appeared to be, though whether it was the godchild to come which they feared, or Thor's own distress, thick and dark and twisted, he didn't know. Eve's choice had clearly astonished and wounded the god, but Adam wondered if she would have made the same decision if she had known her Thorgrim lived. Not that it mattered, now. Thor had made his choices, as Eve had, and Adam didn't have time to pity him.

When he did finally arrive in Montreal, and pulled up to the small house on the outskirts of the city, Adam double checked the address. He could feel nothing of Eve inside the place, shaded by two immense maple trees, but he had felt nothing of her for some time, so it didn't mean much. He knocked on the door and waited.

The man with the bushy eyebrows and love of chewing tobacco opened the door, and then grunted. "You."

He smiled, trying to remain polite. "May I speak with Renata?"

"Hmph." The man shut the door again.

If it was a yes or a no, Adam couldn't tell. Just as he was about to knock again, the door opened and Eve was standing before him.

She didn't exactly frown, and he knew on some level she was happy to see him, pleased, but not entirely. "You shouldn't be here."

"I had to come." He stepped forward and touched her face, caressing her cheek. Her eyes closed for just a moment longer than a blink, and then opened again. He kissed her forehead. "I won't let you face him alone."

She shook her head and pulled his hand from her face, stepping forward and closing the door behind her. "This, none of this, is your fault. One way or another. That's part of why I left. Don't you understand? I don't want you to be blamed or punished."

He almost laughed, but it was too awful. "I'm supposed to be protecting *you*, Eve."

"I don't want you to lose your memory again. I don't want you to lose this, who you are, who you've become." She was still holding his hand, and she looked down at their twined fingers. "You've changed so much."

"Let me stay." It wasn't what he had meant to say, but he knew it was right. She could make him leave, if she chose to. Could force him to turn from her and get back on a jet. He would never underestimate her power or strength again. That she hadn't used it before now, when he had caused her so much trouble, so much pain, was perhaps just as astounding to him.

"We can't be together, Adam. Not until we know. And even then—"

"I know."

She looked up at his tone, frowning slightly. "Then why did you come?"

He sighed. "Eve." He took her face in his hands and looked into her eyes. He couldn't explain, but she had to know. If Thor could see it in her, she had to be able to see it in herself. "Evey, you're going to have my baby. Michael is going to come. I don't know when. And I'm not leaving you to face him alone."

"How do you know?" She swallowed, and he could feel her in his mind, feeling the truth of his words. That he believed what he was saying. Her face paled. "How are you so sure? I don't even know yet."

"I just know, Eve. You have to trust me. Or if you don't, at least let me stay. You'll have all the proof you need soon enough."

"Here? You think he'll come here?"

He nodded, letting his hands slip from her face to her shoulders, to her arms. "He told me I'd see him again in this life. That I wouldn't like what he had to say. I think he knew. I think God knew."

"But you didn't force me. I made sure."

"If I hadn't wanted you so badly, hunted for you, tried to become someone that you could love, this never would've happened. It's still my fault, Eve. I knew what I was doing."

She pulled away and shook her head impatiently. "You couldn't have touched me if I hadn't let you. Not now. It doesn't matter." Her hand went to her stomach. "What are we going to do?"

"I'm going to take care of you. Marry you, if you'll let me."

She looked up, her eyes wide. "Marry me? Adam, even if I'm pregnant now, and we have this child, there's no guarantee that we can have anything more than that. This nine months will be a gift, but after that? We'd just be risking the world all over again. Another pregnancy, another godchild, if by some miracle this one doesn't destroy us."

"You don't know that. We don't know what happens next."

"No, we don't know." Sorrow washed over her and she turned away. "There might be nothing left of us, of the world, of Creation."

He said nothing. There was nothing to be said that wouldn't make her feel worse. They had both known the risks. But he pulled her into his arms and held her. His Eve. They had come so far, and the idea that it could end was incomprehensible. God lived. Couldn't God save the world? It wasn't as though this child had been conceived for the purpose of destruction. Michael had made sure of that. There had to be a chance, a way, somehow, that the world would go on. That this baby wouldn't be the end of all things. Or why else would God have ever made it possible? But to have Eve so completely for nine months, and then be forced to give her up, if the world went on, for fear of a second child, or what the next baby might be. For fear that between them, they might birth an entire pantheon of gods . . .

It would be worse than everything else. Harder. They'd only had the smallest taste of what it could be, this love, this union, but to know fully, and then lose her—it would ruin them both. All the more so if Eve lost this child, too. "Maybe you're right." He hated himself for saying it, hated the truth of it all. And hadn't he cursed Thor for the same thing? For seducing her and then leaving her to stumble on alone? "Maybe we shouldn't marry. Maybe the best thing would be for me to stay away altogether. Maybe it won't hurt as much, that way."

She hid her face against his shoulder. *I hate this.*

He kissed the top of her head. "I know."

I want us to be a family. I want to be with you. But why does it all have to be laced with pain?

He sighed. *So we can appreciate fully the good things, maybe. Every moment we have together without grief is a gift, even if knowing it has to end is a misery.*

The misery of an end, looming over them both.

"No," Eve said. "If this is all the time we have, if we have until the baby is born before the world ends, I won't give it up. And if the world survives, I won't give you up now, when I might have no choice but to leave you later."

Are you sure, Evey?

She pulled back to meet his eyes, her hands fists in his shirt. "Why should we, if this is all we can have? If we can have this much, together? We've wasted so much time already, and if this is God's plan or if the world is going to end, I don't want to waste anymore. Not another day that I could spend in your arms, in your bed, in love and living as myself."

The truth was, he wanted it too. Even if it was only a taste. Even if it couldn't last. He dropped his forehead to hers and closed his eyes, breathing her in, with all her strength, and all her determination, and all her love. So, so much love, fierce and impossible to contain.

It was everything he wanted, to be with her, to have her as his own. To be hers. What the cost would be, he didn't know, couldn't even begin to imagine. But if Eve believed it was worth it, he couldn't bring himself to argue.

"For as long as you'll have me, I'm yours," he promised her. But he didn't tell her the rest. After all, there was no knowing what Michael had meant by demanding he give up all claim to the child. There was no knowing at all what would happen after the baby was born, though he could not help but to feel Eve's hope that they might be allowed the luxury of a family. That this had been God's plan, all along.

And it would be better for both of them if she had a reason to hate him when it was over.

§

He bought her a ring. Nothing extravagant, nothing particularly expensive. A simple platinum band for her finger without stones or filigree and the same, only thicker, for himself. They exchanged vows without witnesses. Or without witnesses she was aware of. He felt the weight of Thor's presence as he promised to love and honor her above all others, and knew if he didn't keep his word the god would come.

And then he bought her father's tobacco shop, too, with Asgardian gold, and for five times what it was worth, before he took Eve away. To France first, to her mountains, though they didn't stay longer than it took for Adam to make arrangements for a real honeymoon—a round-the-world airship cruise. Part of him hoped traveling would make it that much harder for Michael to find them, and the rest of him only wondered why the Archangel hadn't come already.

He should have. If not on Adam's heels, at least after the first month. They were in Australia by then, and Eve had begged him to take her into the outback.

"I'm not certain you should risk the snakes and spiders," he said, pulling her into his lap. They were in their suite still, overlooking the ocean. He'd have to remember to ask for a suite on the other side of the ship next time, all they'd seen so far was ocean, glistening blue in the sun, and flat, battleship gray without it. Even if it didn't keep Michael from finding them, it had certainly distracted Eve, and Adam was determined to spoil her. Anything she wanted now—it was the least he could do to make up for what came next. And as husband and wife, they were bound to one another, joined by God, at least for this life. It would make it that much harder for either of them to move on, if everything fell apart.

Eve smiled. "You're not *really* worried about the wildlife?"

He let his hand slip across her stomach. "Shouldn't you be?"

She covered his hand with hers, the smile fading. "I think it's a girl."

"So you believe me?" he asked softly, searching her face. She hadn't let him touch her for weeks, waiting until she was certain. He hadn't pressed her, though he ached for more than just the comfort of sleeping beside her.

"I had to be sure," she said, staring at her own stomach. "But I hate the waiting, Adam. I feel as though I'm always looking over my shoulder. Every flicker of movement in the corner of my eye is Michael, coming for me with his sword."

He stroked her cheek. "Even if he still had it, he'd have to go through me first."

"You say that, but it isn't what I want. This was my choice, and whatever punishment he brings should be mine, too."

Brave, selfless Eve. He kissed her, soft and slow, until she sighed against his lips, her whole body forming to his. "Let's skip the spiders and snakes for today."

She laughed. "You're the one who told me they'd all been made to serve us."

"You, maybe." And then he kissed her again, until she'd forgotten about the outback and all its charms. Until she forgot about Australia altogether. Because now that she was certain, there was no reason not to spend their days making love instead, and that was how he wanted her to remember these days.

With love, above all else.

§

Weeks turned into months, and still they traveled. As long as Eve was comfortable, he had no intention of abandoning their cruise, and every once in a while, they even left the ship to see the sights. But there was so much they didn't know. So much he didn't remember, and Michael still hadn't come.

He lay awake at night with Eve in his arms, and felt the baby as she grew. Her mind was brilliant and happy and full of feeling. A feeling he recognized.

Memories he thought he had lost rose in his mind, nebulous and fleeting. Days spent in the Garden before it had burned, before Eve had been made, or even thought of. He remembered how it had been when he had walked with God and felt His touch within his soul. Ill-defined and immature though it was, this baby was no different. And the more time he spent with Eve and the child inside her, the more he wanted to believe as she did. That there was hope. That even though he had sworn not to use this baby for his own purposes, he might still be her father, her family.

"She feels you reaching for her," Eve said.

He hadn't realized she was awake, but he kissed the side of her head and tucked her more neatly against him. "She's strong for so small a thing."

"But she loves, Adam. Don't you feel it? When she hears your voice, there's a surge of contentment, of adoration. She loves you."

Even as she spoke there was an eagerness in her heart. He could feel the longing she had for this baby, to know her and watch her grow. To love her and teach her to love the world they lived in.

"Adam?" Eve asked. "Are you all right?"

He swallowed against the thickness in his throat and met her eyes. "She only loves me because she doesn't know me yet. Give her time and I'm sure she'll manage a healthy indifference."

"But if we could just make her see," Eve said, frowning slightly. "If we could just show her enough of the world, let her discover its beauty for herself, maybe she'll want to save it, to keep it the way it is."

She was so determined, and it only made his heart ache that much more, because he could promise her nothing. Not even that he would stand with her against whatever Michael might bring against them.

"Evey—"

"We could do it, Adam. We could teach her to love the world, you and me. She doesn't have to be the end of everything. She doesn't have to be a force for destruction and chaos. She could be *good.*"

But if the baby really was that powerful, it would only take one tantrum to undo everything. One fight. One meltdown.

He pressed his lips together and said nothing. Because even in Eve's womb, their daughter already possessed more power than he would ever dream of, and if all that love turned into even one breath of hate, or resentment, or even fear . . .

He didn't want to think what it might do to Eve, never mind the world.

CHAPTER FORTY-THREE
1920 AD

§

The jungle was steaming, and the temple, while it provided shade, wasn't much cooler. Thor pulled at the collar of his shirt and wished that he had taken the time to change before making this trip. He didn't understand how Ra could stand the humidity after living in Egypt for so long. At least it had been dryer there.

"So good of you to come." Ra clasped his hand and smiled. "We have not seen you in much too long."

"I'm afraid this trip isn't for pleasure, my friend." He was too hot to waste time with pleasantries, even with the breeze that blew gently through the temple.

An immense statue of Shiva stared down at him inside the chamber where Ra had led him, and he offered it a polite bow. The stones creaked, and the air around them thickened perceptibly as the rock of the statue ground against itself and the massive head nodded in return. Thor removed his jacket and seriously considered stripping out of his shirt too.

"Oh?" Ra paused in the act of pouring a cup of tea, glancing over his shoulder. "I didn't realize there was much business left for either of us in this world. I did hear about some society in Germany that was reviving the old ways. Your father must have been pleased by that."

Thor grimaced. By all rights, his father should have left, and taken the rest of their people with him. But he was just stubborn enough to stay simply because Thor refused to leave. To ensure he did not go unpunished. "They do not look to gods, only to their own race and their own agendas. They offer us nothing, and in return we give them nothing back."

"Ah. I must have been mistaken then. No matter." Ra flicked his fingers as if giving up the matter to the jungle heat. "Tea?"

"No, thank you. The climate here is too oppressive for hot drink."

Ra laughed. "Indeed. For you, I can well imagine that is so. Athena seems to enjoy it well enough, though." The old man studied him while he sipped from his cup. His eyes were still sharp and brilliant, even as aged as he appeared now. "To what do I owe the honor of your visit?"

"I need a favor." Thor unbuttoned the top buttons of his woolen shirt. Suitable for the cold mental ward where Eve was kept, but not for here. Perhaps he should have gone to France first, before he came to India. But there was no point in applying to the DeLeons if Ra would not help him. She needed a healer first. "It's about Eve."

Ra set down his cup, his eyes lit with what seemed to be amusement. "Yes, of course it is. You've seen her, I take it?"

He hoped that Ra didn't notice the rush of heat to his face. Surely he must already be flushed with the humidity. "She's locked up in a mental institute. By her husband's order."

The old god's eyes narrowed and all humor left his face, leaving it lined and ancient with grief. "Where?"

"The Americas. If she were anyone else, she'd be dead twice over by now. As it is, she loses herself in memories and past lives. Even if I were to remove her, I do not think her mind will heal in this life from the traumas it has sustained. Electro-shock therapy and lithium in such doses that she cannot even lift her head to vomit. And something else,

I'm almost certain. Venom from the world serpent."

"She cannot remain there."

Relief flooded through him. He could see the determination in Ra's face to help. To do what he could. To do everything he could. "I thought to take her to her Lions in France. But I would not burden them with her care. I would not have them see her this way at all. For her as much as for them. She'll need someone to help her, but in France I am too close to my father to see it done myself. I take great risk even now."

Ra nodded. "Of course. Yes. You will have my assistance in this. Have you spoken to your Lions yet?"

He shook his head. "Not since the war."

"I'll go with you. The sooner she can be removed, the better for us all. Though, I'm surprised she allowed it to get this far." Ra had abandoned his tea and moved with an alacrity that belied his age, collecting his things.

"God gave her too great a fear of hubris I think." He picked up his jacket, following Ra out of the chamber. He bowed again to the statue, which nodded back with the scrape of sand and stone. "If she's been poisoned—if Loki has returned from Hel, or even if it is only Sif's work—there is no knowing the damage that has been done. Bad enough she believes herself to be a danger to others in her more lucid moments. She thinks if she uses her power for manipulation, even in her own defense, she will become her brother."

Ra looked grim. "I trust you've assured her she has every right?"

"Not that she'll listen." Would she listen if she knew who he was? What he was? He didn't know, but it wasn't something he could risk. Revealing himself as a god would mean exile from the world at best, and he couldn't leave her behind. Not when she needed him still. "Perhaps she'll accept your word over mine."

Then they were in the jungle again, outside of the temple. Thor looked for the sun. It would be late morning in France, and Eve would still be sleeping in her cot in America. Perhaps he would be able to return to her before dawn. He hated leaving her alone for so long, but at least this time if she tried to bleed herself, Ra would be on hand to heal her.

"I'll follow you to the House of Lions," Ra was saying. "I must take my leave of Bhagavan first."

Thor nodded, and the air thickened with static around him, the green and gold of the jungle and the stones melting away with white light and prickling heat as the lightning took him from India. One last stop, and then she would be free.

§

Thor stood on the edge of the wood, wondering if he should wait for Ra, or go on to the manor. They would already know he was here by the lightning and the smoke rising from the tree beside him. He put out the smoldering wood with the rain and hoped the thunder hadn't upset the horses. Luc DeLeon was not prone to paroxysms of any kind, but Thor didn't particularly want to test him, either. Not when he came to beg a favor from the man.

"Bhagavan sends his regards," Ra said, appearing rather abruptly beside him. "Or at least Brahma does. Shiva probably would prefer we didn't interfere. I was wondering why the world seemed to be going to pieces in the west."

"Brahma is generous." And the only god left with a people who had not turned from him back to Elohim. At least giving Adam back his memory had ensured that much. Thor nodded to the manor, and then set off toward it. The sheep in the pasture ignored him. "And if there was ever an argument for keeping Eve alive in the world, the Great War that just passed should have won it. If any of the other gods were willing to listen."

"I had thought to blame some trickster god for that." Ra said, keeping pace and shooing a particularly brave ewe away from his path.

He had changed, too, for the cooler weather, when he had said his goodbyes to the Hindu god. "But now it makes much more sense. You believe her to be that strong of a force for good in the world? That the repercussions include war?"

"If you had ever known what it was like to make love to her, my friend, you would not have to ask." He felt his face burn with the memory and quickly forced it away.

But when he vaulted over the fence and glanced back at Ra, the old god was watching him with knowing amusement.

"How in the world did you manage to ingratiate yourself with her so completely as to accomplish that?"

Thor clenched his jaw to keep the rumble of thunder at bay and inhaled deeply through his nose. He had to watch his temper so close to his father's lands, or he would risk Baldur coming to investigate. And that would do no one any favors.

"She believed me to be a figment of her imagination, brought to life by the drugs and her own psychosis. But to engage with her on such a level was never my intent." Thor couldn't help but grimace. He never should have let her sway him on that point in the ward. Never should have let her beg him to touch her that way. When the day came that he could reveal himself to her at last, she would not look kindly on him for taking advantage of her belief that he was a delusion. But she had been so warm in his arms, so soft against his body. Her hands slipping out of his grasp to tease him. "She was upset, and I was trying to soothe her. And before I realized what was happening, she had made up her mind. In that regard, she's virtually impossible to argue with."

"I can imagine." Ra's lips twitched in what Thor was sure would have been a smile, if he had not repressed it. "Being who she is, I imagine that was part of God's plan."

He shook his head, rejecting the excuse. He'd had no right to touch her. "I am not one of her people to be so manipulated. I'm a god in my own right." He sighed and rubbed his face. "I should have stopped her. Stopped myself."

Ra touched his shoulder, his grip firm despite his outward frailty. "If what you've told me is true, about her, about her purpose in the world and the love she lends to it, I can't believe your actions were wrong. If she asked it of you, then she needed it. Little wonder, locked away in a place such as that. Those institutions are ghastly."

"Yes." Thor couldn't disagree. There had been more than one night when he had been sorely tempted to tear the place apart, brick by brick, as he lay awake with Eve in his arms, listening to the agony of the others trapped inside. If only he'd been able to reveal himself, it would have been a simple matter to remove her then, but as it was, he had no choice but to work through her doctors. Even returning to her at night had been a risk. "She was lucky her treatment didn't go beyond the attempt to calm her mind, misguided though it was. If they had tried to sterilize her, I don't think I could have let them live."

"Man knows no limits to the torture it inflicts upon itself," Ra murmured.

Luc was watching from the window. The Frenchman gestured to someone out of sight, and the kitchen door opened, his wife, Nicolette waited just inside, wiping her hands on a towel. Luc stood over her shoulder, grim faced.

But Nicolette smiled and held out her hands to Thor, tugging him down to kiss both his cheeks. "It is good to see you, though we were not expecting you again for some time."

He smiled and ducked his head as she pulled him through the door. "*Madame* DeLeon, *monsieur*, I trust you have had no trouble since the war ended."

"None whatsoever," Luc shook his hand and waved him to a seat. "And it was a pleasant surprise to return home and find the lands as I left them. From the news we heard in the army, I feared the worst."

Thor's lips twitched, but he did not smile. He could hardly blame the man for not trusting a promise made to his ancestors by a man who claimed to be a god, even if he'd seen the proof of it with his own eyes. "I do not forget, *Monsieur* DeLeon, what we all owe your family."

"And so gods remind men of the meaning of honor." Luc smiled. "My family will not forget what you have done for us, Thor of the North. But it has been my understanding that your more frequent appearances do not often bring good news." He glanced at Ra, frowning slightly. "And I'm afraid I do not know your companion."

Ra smiled and bowed gracefully. "Horus Amon. Of Egypt. I'm afraid my people overdid it with the falcon heads on my images. Nor do I actually have any power over the sun." His lined face was full of kindness and warmth. "When last I visited your lands, I believe I helped with the plumbing."

Luc nodded acceptance and greeting. Thor appreciated that particular aspect of his character. All the DeLeon men he had known had shared it. They made up their minds quickly, and from that point remained committed to their choice. Eve had the same determination, or else she would have walked herself out of the mental ward some time ago.

"You must forgive my husband," Nicolette said. "He forgets his manners, even if he does not forget his debts. We have not even offered our hospitality and already he pries." She set a small plate of cakes on the table and urged them both to sit. They could hardly refuse. "Coffee or tea?"

Thor smiled. He had spent many an evening with Nicolette during the course of the war, whenever the fighting had moved too close, offering what protection he could. He did not need to concern himself with the movements of the armies so much as the air raids. Much as he preferred not to interfere at all, sometimes the dogfights had drifted too near the DeLeon lands for his peace of mind. It was an easy enough thing to cause the pilots to veer north, and an even easier thing to strike down the wreckage of burning planes before they crashed into DeLeon timber.

"Nothing, thank you."

She fluttered to heat water regardless, and Luc seated himself across the table. "You can understand my concern of course. If there is trouble coming, I would prefer to be prepared for it than caught unaware."

Thor grimaced. There was no easy way to raise the subject, but Luc had always appreciated directness, and Thor rather thought his time in the war had increased his preference for plain speaking.

"I come on behalf of your Lady," he began.

Luc frowned. "But you told us yourself she was safe in America, unbothered by the war."

"Unbothered by the war," Thor agreed. "But not safe, it seems. I'd like to remove her from the care of her husband, and the ward in which she has been placed, but I do not dare to move her until I can be assured she will be cared for."

"Cared for?" Nicolette said, her hand falling to her husband's shoulder. "But surely they would not harm her!"

"Were they just men, I think it would have been unlikely," Thor mumbled, not liking the taste of the words in his mouth. There was only one place where Jormungand's venom might have been found. Hel was not an easy place to return from, but not impossible with the right help. It had to be Loki. And if it was, they were lucky she wasn't dead.

"I don't understand," Nicolette said, her face pale.

"She is not herself," Thor said quietly, meeting Luc's eyes. "Her husband placed her in the care of—in a mental institute, by the excuse of insanity. From what I can tell, the doctors there have taken it upon themselves to see that it is made truth. I did not realize what had happened until it was too late."

"Of course," Luc said. "Of course she is welcome here. Whatever care she requires, we will gladly give it. But I do not understand why you have not brought her to us already. You must have known we would not deny her, or you."

"It is not safe for me to travel in her company so near to my father's lands." He spread his hands on the table, feeling more bound than ever by Odin, though he had sworn to himself he would never serve his father again. "I thought it better that you meet with Horus, first, before he arrived with her so suddenly. Nor do I dare remove her until I know what has been done to her, or it is possible we will have no way of undoing it. I fear a god's influence behind what she suffers."

"Of course," Luc said again. "And if you steal her away, will her enemy follow?"

Thor shook his head. "No immortal intending harm can cross the boundaries of these lands. She would be safe, though I do not know what it will do to her to be here. She seems to be lost in her own mind and the memories of her past lives. Returning her to a place where she has lived may well invite further confusion."

"This house in particular, no doubt." Luc rose, and paced to the window. "Then we will build her a new space, a cottage in the woods. Safely within DeLeon lands, but free of memory. I'll have it done at once."

"And I would join her there, for as long as she requires someone to care for her," Ra said. "I have no small skill when it comes to healing, and from what Thor has said, she will need a great deal of help. More than even your family can provide."

"I can supply you with gold, if you can exchange it for currency," Thor said. "Enough to pay for her cottage and any other needs she might have while in your care."

Luc shook his head. "No. I can see it done with what we have. The army did not pay well, but we have more timber here than any other land in France, now. An embarrassment of riches in the aftermath of that bloodbath. It's only right that the wealth we have should go to her."

Thor nodded, exchanging a glance with Nicolette. Her mouth pressed into a thin line, but a shrug of her shoulder told him she still had the gold he'd brought her during the war to help offset the cost of food and bribe those soldiers who did stumble across the manor into silence. They wouldn't need any more money than that.

"I'll send word as soon as I'm able," he told Luc, rising. "I promise you, I will do everything in my power to help her."

"No one would ever doubt it," Nicolette said, squeezing his hand. "Hurry back with our Lady."

Luc bowed. A gesture not of obedience, but born of courtesy. Thor had long since learned to appreciate the difference. Luc would help them, as was his duty, but he recognized no authority other than that of his Lady, and perhaps the archangels. His family worshipped no gods. For them, like for Eve, God was dead.

With all that had happened since, Thor was beginning to believe the same.

CHAPTER FORTY-FOUR
Present

§

After Horus had gone and Eve was well recovered, Garrit left, not telling her where. He came back two days later, grimly satisfied, and she caught from his mind that he had been to Britain.

"To see Adam," he admitted when she asked. It was late at night, and his return had woken her from a sound and dreamless sleep.

She frowned and studied him more carefully, looking for marks of her brother's meddling. But there were none. "What for?"

He sat on the edge of the bed and leaned down to kiss her forehead. "I told him if he ever did something like this to you again I was going to send Owen after him in earnest, married to Mia or not."

"Oh." She didn't ask if he had seen Lars. Garrit was still touchy about him. Jealous and upset that he had touched her. She couldn't blame him. "What did Adam say?"

"It was the oddest thing. When he realized you had miscarried, his face went gray and he just dropped into a seat. All the anger and arrogance drained from him. He didn't even argue."

"I see." She had no trouble imagining it. Even if he had not cared for her that much, it would have been a difficult thing to be made responsible for. The death of a baby. "You trust him?"

He pressed his lips into a thin line. "I trust that the whole situation put the fear of God into him." He rubbed at his face. "The more important question, Abby, is if *you* trust him?"

She sighed and stared at the ceiling. "I don't think he meant to hurt me. Not like this."

"I don't know how you can be so sure."

"I just am." The last thing Garrit's ego needed was the admission that Adam believed he was in love with her. It hadn't gone over well with Lars, and it would be worse with her brother. "But I don't trust him. Not completely."

Garrit nodded. "Then I guess that's that."

"I guess so."

He laid his hand over her stomach and looked into her eyes. "Will you want to try again?"

She took his hand and pulled him down. Bringing his face to hers and kissing him. "I missed you."

Some of the tension left him, and he caressed her cheek, framing her face with his hands, his weight on his elbows as he hovered over her. "God help me, Abby. I don't know what happened. I knew marrying you would be challenging. That other men would want you, even covet you. I thought I could handle it."

"You are handling it." She kissed him again. "And I'm yours, Garrit. Just because they want me doesn't mean I want them back. I gave myself to you."

"I know." He brushed her hair from her face. "But you gave yourself to other men too. Loved them. Married them. I feel as though I'm competing against an army of ghosts. All those other husbands whispering in my ear. Making me wonder if it's me you're thinking of when you close your eyes, or someone else. Ryam, maybe. Or Thorgrim?"

"Those men are my past, Garrit. There's no use going back to them. Not when I have someone who loves me so well." It wasn't technically a lie. And he needed to hear it. "Maybe if I were miserable. If you beat me, or left me alone for months at a time. If I hadn't married you for love."

His face darkened. She could see the pain in his eyes. "Why did you stay with them?"

She smoothed the creases from his forehead. "Because I was bound to them. Because marriage wasn't always about love and even being married to someone who didn't care about me was often an improvement over what my life would have been unmarried." She shook her head. He had to understand. She had to make him understand. "I didn't even marry Ryam for love. You must realize that. He was a stranger when he proposed to me, when he asked my father for my hand. I didn't even know he was a DeLeon until after it had already been arranged. I don't know how he knew I was Eve."

"But he loved you."

"Not at first." She smiled. "And I didn't really care for him that much either. He was arrogant, always assuming he knew what was best for me. I was grateful that he had saved me, but it was half a year before we began to know one another. Before we even liked one another, never mind loved."

He rested his forehead against hers. "Sometimes, I'm a damned fool."

She laughed. "I don't know. I think you do pretty well, all things considered. Not many men could get over the fact that they're sleeping with their great-great-great-great-great—"

He covered her mouth with his hand. "Don't even think it, Abby. It took me a week to forget it the first time."

She pulled his fingers away and tried not to laugh. And then he kissed her, and things didn't seem nearly as funny anymore, because she didn't want to wait a week before he was willing to make love to her again.

§

Eve?

She was so startled by Adam's voice that she spilled milk all over the counter. The cook muttered behind her and sighed. She mopped up the mess before he could complain further.

Sorry, he said, when he realized what had happened.

It's just milk. She caught an edge of excitement from his tone and took her coffee from the kitchen so that the cook wouldn't keep glowering at her. *What do you want?*

Ben's first word, Eve. He said his first word today.

Is he really that old already? She touched her rounded stomach, and counted the months. Time had gotten away from her. It was rather nice, though, after the stress of everything, to lose track of time because she was happy. Because things were going well. *What did he say?*

He was definitely elated, she thought, listening to the emotion that came before his response. *Daddy.*

She smiled and sipped from her cup. Technically she shouldn't have the caffeine, but neither alcohol nor caffeine in moderation had ever harmed one of her children before. *Congratulations, Adam.*

You're pregnant? He was surprised. Not exactly pleased. But there was relief. As if he had worried he'd hurt her too badly. Men really didn't understand childbirth. *Mia never mentioned it.*

It isn't as though she ever does. She shook her head at her sister's foibles. Even married with a baby, Mia hadn't changed much. The only difference was that she included her child in her self-indulgence. Eve was grateful for even that much, though. What little she'd seen and heard of her nephew left her with the impression that he was spoiled, but well cared for. *It's a girl this time.*

Adam laughed in the back of her mind. It was the first time she had heard him do so when it hadn't been meanly meant, and the sound was refreshing. Joyful. *Thank God for that.*

She smiled again. *That was my thought as well. Don't tell Garrit though. He wants another son.*

I never realized it could be like this, Eve. And even through his happiness, she could feel the underlying ache. The wish that they were doing it together and he could be with her, or at least nearer to her. *You were right, though. I never get tired of listening to his mind. My son. My boy. Feeling his pleasure when he sees me walk into the room. And then he smiles, and laughs. I've never felt any of this before.*

I'm happy for you, Adam. She sat down in the library. Garrit had arranged pillows on the couch there for her, so she could sit comfortably. She had been reading Ryam's journal, finally, front to back, and she was beginning to understand why Garrit had felt as insecure as he had. In the beginning. In the face of Lars. Ryam had made her into a goddess. His perfect wife. A woman to be worshipped as an ideal in all things.

You should be, he said softly. *You are, in every way, ideal. A perfect example of what love should be. What a woman should be. He was right to consider you a goddess.*

She frowned. *Don't start, please.*

I'm only agreeing with your late husband, that's all. And he sighed. *I couldn't leave Ben, now, if I wanted to.*

As it should be. She saw the images in his mind, in his thoughts. Mia holding Ben. Adam staring down at his son in his own arms. Ben with half his fist in his mouth, his eyes wide and bright with delight. Somehow he even managed to smile around his fingers. *He's a beautiful boy.*

If it hadn't been for you, I don't think I ever would have known this.

She didn't know if he meant Mia, or just the happiness of family in general. *You would have found it eventually, Adam. Even without your memory.*

I'm not sure I would have. But his mood shifted. *When are you due?*

Another month. I don't think we'll make it for Christmas.

Because of me?

She sipped from the coffee again and settled more comfortably against the pillows, watching the flicker of the flame in the fireplace. *Garrit won't want to travel with a newborn and a toddler, regardless of where we were going.*

I suppose he'll never trust me.

She hoped it was true. Even happy as Adam was, she could still feel his want for her. *Not with me. Though I hope he'll come around enough to let me send our children to my mother's in the summers when they're older. I think they'd like it. And I'd like them to know their cousin.*

I wouldn't harm your children, Eve. Even if I could get away with it.

I know.

He doesn't?

She shrugged though he couldn't see. He would feel it. *He will. As long as you don't jump in front of anymore buses.*

Not in this lifetime, I think, he agreed with a flash of guilt. *I hated being so helpless. I don't think I had ever been hurt that severely in any of my lives before now. Not since Michael took my memory. Somehow I always escaped any serious harm, until this life.*

I guess we're just lucky that way.

Adam snorted. *Luckier still if we had been made invulnerable.*

"Abby?" Garrit knocked on the door, and she smiled at him. He joined her then, and she nestled against his side, closing her eyes. She could use a nap, now that he was here, and warm, and comfortable.

She felt Adam wince. *Good luck with the baby.* And then he was gone.

She sighed with contentment, and Garrit tucked her head beneath his chin the way he always did when they sat together this way. "I think I'm going to fall asleep on you."

He kissed the top of her head. "Feel free. *Maman* is keeping Alex for the rest of the night. We have nothing to do but feed ourselves and go to bed. I thought you could use the time to yourself."

"I could use the time with you. Have to enjoy it while it lasts. Before the baby comes and we're too busy for proper naps together."

"I'll never be too busy for this, Abby. Not as long as I live."

She smiled. "Does that mean we get a happily ever after?"

He kissed her again, and she felt him settle in more comfortably on the couch. "That was always my intention."

She fell asleep before she could think of anything suitably flippant in response.

CHAPTER FORTY-FIVE
Future

§

He brought Eve home to France in the last month of her pregnancy, renting the small cottage from the DeLeon's where she had lived once before. Not because they were pleased about providing their Lady a home, married to a man they had considered their enemy for generations, but as Adam argued, because they would know then, at least, that no immortal could reach her if they meant her any harm. Himself, included.

Adam stayed at her side, all the same, and within the lands belonging to the House of Lions, he knew without any doubt she had Thor's protection as well, could even catch glimpses of him in the back of her mind on the days she struggled against the awkwardness of her body, and cursed its limitations. And with his presence, she would smile, her day made that much easier and brighter. Adam couldn't even bring himself to resent it. Not when it made her happy, gave her peace.

He watched for the angels, for any sign that it was time, but they still hadn't come, and Eve, he knew had found some strange serenity in their absence, which he couldn't share.

"There's only one explanation that makes sense," she'd told him some time ago. "This was what we were supposed to do, what God meant for us. There's no reason for the angels to come if we're following God's plan."

He hadn't wanted to upset her so close to term, when she was already in enough physical discomfort to make up for any peace of mind she'd managed to keep. At least that was what he told himself, and there was always another excuse like it. Another reason why he couldn't bring himself to ruin what little happiness they had found together. And it was happiness—sometimes even more than that. So close to Nirvana he understood why people worked so hard to experience it, to live in that same state forever. Because when Eve loved, the whole world bloomed around her. She was the reason those old folk tales were filled with beautiful young women who sang with songbirds and spoke with sparrows. And she was his.

She was his, and he couldn't stand the thought of losing her a moment sooner than he must.

"Don't worry, Adam," she told him, more than once. "Everything will be fine, you'll see."

He only wished he could be so certain.

§

It was Gabriel who came on the day, and Adam greeted him on the porch. Eve had gone into labor, but she had refused the help of any doctor or midwife, so he had made the bed with blankets and sheets that would resist the stain of her blood, and watched over her as he was able. He didn't think she could die in childbirth, even when birthing a god, but if she did, he took comfort from the fact that he would go with her. "I had expected Michael long before now," he said.

Gabriel shook his head, and folded his wings to his back before stepping into the cottage. "Michael has his uses, but diplomacy has never been one of them. Eve requires our understanding, not our arrogance."

"What are you going to do?"

"Nothing today." Gabriel's eyes narrowed, looking through him. "You've kept it from her? The vow you made?"

"Do you really think she could have had any joy if I hadn't?" he snapped. "She thinks we can raise the baby ourselves, that there isn't anything to fear from a child, no matter how powerful. We'll teach it to love—to want to preserve Creation."

"And you?"

"It doesn't matter what I believe, does it? Your brother has already extracted my oath. I have no right to her anymore. No right to object to anything God commands, and if I do—" He stopped himself. The last time he hadn't kept his word, he'd had his memory ripped away and lived life after life in that purgatory, making the same mistakes over and over again, without even the wit to learn from them. But this time, he'd be lucky to have a life to live. "If I had known then what I do now . . ."

"You would have seen reason," Gabriel said. "You would have known the risk is too great to leave to hope and chance. Eve is many things, but even her perfection is not perfection enough for this. Elah must be given into God's hands."

"So you've named her." He couldn't keep the bitterness from his words. "It isn't enough that you'll take her, God intends to take everything else from us, too."

"You should rejoice, Adam. You've fulfilled your purpose and the child will live. You have your freedom now. You both do."

"Is that what you call it when you rip out our hearts? Freedom?"

But Eve cried out inside the house, and Gabriel disappeared. Adam swore, running after him. That every other god in every other heaven had the ability to transport himself instantly was infuriating enough. That it extended to the angels too was enough to make him want to behead someone.

Peace, Adam, Gabriel said as he burst into Eve's room and found him inside. *We must have peace, now, or risk everything.*

The angel sat on the edge of the bed, taking Eve's hand in his own and stroking her hair from her forehead with grave tenderness. "God grants me leave to take your pain, Eve. You will not suffer."

Her eyes widened, and she reached for Adam. He sat down on her other side and she took his hand as the angel released her. She sobbed, but it wasn't from the contractions that shook her.

He squeezed her hand. "It's all right, Eve. He's only come to help."

"Angels always gather at the birth of gods and prophets," Gabriel said, smiling. "You have nothing to fear from me, nor does the child. You must tell Elah this is so. She must trust me, now."

"Gabriel isn't Michael," Adam said, when Eve looked to him for reassurance. "He won't harm you. Either of you. Or I wouldn't have let him come."

She let out a strangled laugh. "As if you could have stopped him."

His jaw clenched, and he held her eyes with his. "There are ways to stop even the angels, I promise you."

"Peace," Gabriel reminded him, his eyes sharpening. "I beg of you both. Even without her full power, Elah can unmake Eve with a thought in her desire to leave the womb, and it will not be clean or painless if she does so. She needs your reassurance, not your threats."

Adam gripped Eve's hand that much harder, forcing himself to calm, urging her to do the same, because he could feel the edge of fear in her mind. *This is God's plan, remember? Everything's going to be fine. You're going to be fine. She loves you.*

Elah. Our daughter is named Elah. And he felt her grasping for that comfort, the knowledge that she had been right. They were having a daughter. And that choice she had made so long ago, it had been the right one. Eve let out a breath, the tension leaving her body, and she tipped her head back, closing her eyes.

He smoothed her hair back from her face and leaned down, pressing a kiss to her forehead. *I love you. Remember that.*

The baby's joy was impossible not to feel, and Gabriel, with God's power, made the delivery quick, though whether it was for Eve's sake or the world's, Adam couldn't be certain. Whatever the reason, Eve felt no pain, and the angel brought the baby from between her legs, and swaddled her in white.

Eve held out her arms and Gabriel did not deny her the right to hold her child, her daughter, for the first time.

"She's beautiful," Eve murmured, kissing the small, wrinkled brow. Instead of crying, Elah smiled, little arms reaching for her mother's face, tiny fingers curling around her nose. Eve laughed and looked up at him. "Adam, look at her. She's so perfect."

He forced himself to smile. "Doesn't every parent think so?"

But he took the baby into his arms all the same, his heart swelling with love and sorrow, both. *It's crueler to let us keep her, only to take her later.*

But necessary, Gabriel said, watching in silence at the bedside. *Just as the risk itself is necessary, or this day would never have come.*

"I will leave you," the Archangel said softly, bowing his head.

"Wait." Eve struggled upright, catching his arm as he turned to go.

She drew her hand back quickly, as if she'd been burned, but Gabriel only smiled, taking her hand in both of his, and kneeling beside her.

"How might I serve, Mother?" he asked gently. Adam had never heard an angel speak so kindly. "You need only ask, and if it is within my power to give, you shall have it."

Mother? Adam demanded.

Gabriel's eyes laughed. *Did you never wonder who Jesus might be?*

Adam snorted, and Elah cooed at the sound, reaching for his face. It hardly mattered. Whatever Jesus had preached, Elah changed everything. For better or worse, but when he looked on her, looked into her eyes, so brilliant blue one moment, and the emerald of her mother's the next, he wasn't sure he could bring himself to care about anything else.

"What does this mean?" Eve asked almost shyly. Adam lifted his gaze and found her watching him, felt her hope, her need. "For us?"

It was the last of her fears, he knew, but he couldn't have brought himself to ask the question. No matter what the angel answered, it wouldn't change anything between them. It wouldn't change how broken they would both be when Elah was torn from their arms and Eve learned that Adam had given up all right to stop it.

"Ah," Gabriel said, his smile widening. "God would not teach you to love one another only to have you suffer for eternity apart, if that is your fear. Until and unless Elah is lost, there will be no more children between you. That purpose has been fulfilled at last, through her birth."

Adam wished he could share in her relief. Instead, when the angel turned to leave them again, he gave Elah back to her mother and followed.

"How long?" he asked, when the door to the house had shut behind them both, and he was sure Eve wouldn't hear him.

Gabriel lifted his gaze to the sky, his wings twitching in what seemed very much like a shrug. "Long enough for the child to bond with her mother. Beyond that, I can promise nothing."

He swallowed, his throat suddenly tight. "Long enough to break her heart utterly when the time comes."

"It isn't as though she'll be left to die, Adam," Gabriel said. "Isn't it enough that you'll have one another, after all this time?"

"You know it won't be."

The Archangel sighed. "She could have chosen otherwise. You both could have. The world would have gone on as it has since Creation, and perhaps God would have risen again another way. More likely, though, he would only continue to diminish, and Michael's authority would have become absolute. Either path would have brought its own risks, its own sacrifices. Death and betrayal and pain for both of you. We can only do now what must be done, to preserve the world as best as we are able. But God asks nothing of Eve He did not ask of Himself, when He gave her up into your keeping. At least you might console yourself with the knowledge that Elah will be well loved and cared for. She will suffer no abuse at our hands. Whether the reverse will be true, we can only pray."

"But it's possible that Eve is right. That we could raise Elah to love us all."

"It is too great a risk," Gabriel said, the words hard.

Adam shook his head. "But Eve—"

"It is not Eve we cannot trust, Adam." Gabriel spread his wings, and rose, the downstroke blasting dust enough that Adam had to shield his eyes.

And then he was gone, and Adam hated himself that much more.

Because every sorrow, every grief, every heartbreak that Eve would suffer in the coming days, was because of him.

§

Adam stroked Elah's cheek with the back of his finger, and his daughter laughed, making Eve smile and hold her that much closer. He had never seen anything so beautiful, anything so perfect. Seeing Eve holding his child, their child, made his heart soar. How many times had he dreamed of this moment, while she had held Garrit's children in her arms? How many times had he watched Mia hold his baby and wished she were Eve?

His heart was already breaking, knowing it couldn't last.

"You see?" Eve said. "I told you everything would be fine. And she's so happy, Adam. Can't you feel it?"

He couldn't answer, couldn't force a single word from his lips, too afraid she would hear the pain beneath, the grief.

"And we can be together," she went on. "We don't have to be afraid of another baby, or Michael coming in the night to tear us apart. It's all over, Adam. We're free from all of it."

He wanted to weep. "Evey—" he cleared his throat when his voice broke on her name, and tried again. "It isn't quite . . ." the words caught and jumbled, almost choking him. But she had to know. He had to tell her.

But if he did, what then? What if she didn't love Elah the way she should, knowing what was going to come, protecting part of her heart from the pain of that loss. And what if Elah knew it? What if, because of that hesitation, that reservation which she was sure to sense, Elah didn't love them back, not enough. Not when whatever pain Eve shared with her daughter combined with Adam's own faults and imperfections.

"What's the matter?" Eve asked, frowning up at him. "You look as though you've seen a ghost."

He forced himself to smile and kissed her forehead, then Elah's. "I'm just relieved that you're both safe and sound, that's all. Even as practiced as you are with childbirth, I couldn't shake this fear that you wouldn't . . . that something would go wrong."

She laughed. "I've never had a single husband who believed me when I told him I knew what I was doing. I suppose I shouldn't be surprised you didn't, either."

"I suppose you shouldn't," he said, the lie bitter on his tongue, twisting his stomach into knots and souring it with bile.

He couldn't. He couldn't risk telling her, and he couldn't stand here and pretend nothing was wrong, pretend that everything spread out before them was sunshine and roses and happily ever afters.

Gabriel's words echoed in his thoughts. *It is not Eve we cannot trust . . .*

"I'll go get you some water," he managed to say, and hoped she understood what he didn't. *I love you. I love you. I love you.* "I'm sure you're thirsty."

She laughed again, looking up at him, glowing with beauty and adoration and love. *I love you, too. And now we have forever, Adam. We can have forever.*

But it didn't matter how much he loved her or she loved him, if there was no world left, if they were both destroyed in its unmaking. If forever were only the next few months, or few weeks, or few days. Eve had to bond with Elah. They had to love one another with their whole hearts, and he couldn't . . .

He couldn't stand by and let her, knowing what he did. He couldn't encourage her when he knew what was coming, and how much it would break her heart. He couldn't be part of making it worse. For her. For the world. No matter what he chose, it would bring ruin and destruction. And maybe there was another way. A way to give Eve more time.

Because it wasn't Eve that they didn't trust to raise her.

Adam raked his fingers through his hair, and allowed himself one last look. One last memory of Eve holding their daughter, radiant with peace and love and everything he had always hoped to give her.

And then he left his wife and his daughter behind.

For the world.

For Eve.

For love.

CHAPTER FORTY-SIX
1920 AD
§

Ra may have been old, but he was hardly weak. He had only to shake Dr. Meek's hand, and the poor man was bowing and scraping, eager to do anything he could to help them. The release forms were produced at once, without any hesitation, and Ra signed them as Eve's grandfather. How long the illusion would last, Thor didn't know, but with any luck, Eve would be in France before her husband learned she had been stolen from his keeping. And long before any other god learned exactly who had helped to free her.

"She'll need to take the lithium at the least," Dr. Meek said. "Or I fear her other personalities will surface all the more strongly, and there are a great many. Better still if you brought her back to us at least once a week for the electro-shock therapy Dr. Williams has been testing."

"Of course," Ra said, studying the bottle of pills gravely. "She'll have the best of care, with all the proper medication and treatment. Perhaps if you'll just provide us with a copy of her records, I can ensure a seamless transition with her new doctors."

"New doctors?" Dr. Meek adjusted his glasses, his forehead creasing. "I'm not at all certain—"

"It's for the best," Ra said, his voice ringing with an authority Thor had never heard him use. Meek blinked, the troubled lines clearing. "I'm sure you understand, Doctor. Evelyn is very dear to me. After everything that's happened, and all you've done for her, I wouldn't want to place you in an awkward position with her husband."

"Of course," Meek murmured. "Of course, yes, I do understand. It's very kind of you to consider . . ."

"Just so." Ra smiled his most grandfatherly smile, though the expression was marred by an underlying grief. Thor knew it too well. "Now if you'll just prepare the records for us?"

Dr. Meek busied himself collecting the proper files, and Ra leaned back in his seat, across the desk. His expression was more than grim, his falcon eyes hard as amber. Fury, and barely contained, Thor realized, though he had never seen him betray even the slightest hint of such an emotion before.

"If you'll follow me," Meek said at last, folder in hand. "Evelyn should be back from her shock treatment by now. Convenient for you, really. She ought to be quite docile for the trip home."

"Indeed." The word barely escaped through Ra's teeth, though Meek didn't seem to notice. "After you, Donar."

Thor followed the small man down the yellowed corridor. The tiles he'd cracked hadn't been replaced or mended, and the dust crunched beneath his shoes. If he had not been bound by his father, all of this would have been so much easier. Eve would have been safe in France already, sleeping in his arms. Once the drugs had cleared her system, he could have told her everything.

"Just in here," Meek said, the keys jingling as he turned the lock. "I'll just send an orderly to retrieve her clothes."

Thor ducked through the doorway, crossing the room before Ra had even stepped inside. Eve lay on her cot, curled in a tight ball on her side, her arms over her head showing handprints of blue and purple bruising. She must have struggled, fought with the orderlies when they came to collect her. Perhaps bleeding herself dry had been about more than finding oblivion. Perhaps she'd been fighting against the medication as well. Certainly she had been more lucid since, more present. But today, her skin looked green and sallow. Another dose of the venom, by the stink.

Ra drew in a sharp breath behind him. "God forgive us all. What have they done?"

§

Thor carried her out of the hospital, her head lolling against his shoulder and her body limp. She hadn't so much as stirred when Ra examined her, nor opened her eyes when Thor lifted her from the cot. He hadn't waited for Ra to finish speaking with the doctor. The sooner she left the ward behind, the sooner she could begin to recover, if there was any hope for it at all. And Thor was beginning to fear the worst, in that regard.

By all rights, Ra should have been able to heal her somehow, to bring her back to consciousness at the least, but his face had only become more aged, more lined with pain. His fingers had traced the ragged scabs on her forearms, the skin held in place by neat, black stitches, and he had bowed his head. When the old god had risen from her bedside, his face had been damp with tears.

"She's retreated so deep into her memories, I cannot reach her. And the poison—I fear it has done too much damage to be wholly reversed. Is there some antidote, known to your people? Some treatment, if it is your Jormungand's venom?"

"The golden apples saved my life, but I am not certain what they will do to her. She is so fragile, compared to us."

"Of course," Ra said. "Yes, I believe the golden apples will serve, Elohim willing. If their power cannot help her, it certainly will not do any greater harm."

He would have to send them by way of Athena, for once Eve was returned to her family, he did not dare follow. Not immediately. Perhaps if the circumstances were different, if it were not a god's hand which had done her so much injury—and that too, he would have to see to. Dr. Williams, if he was in fact a doctor at all, must be addressed. Jormungand's venom must be purged from this world, and the god responsible for its use punished. For that much, he would have the Council's authority, though the Allfather was sure to object.

But if Odin knew Loki had returned—and Heimdall must have seen it was so—if Odin had helped him to return, concealed his actions all this time . . .

Thor only hoped he would not be forced to kill his own father.

§

"Well," Meek said, after Ra had left with Eve. "Evelyn is very fortunate to have such a caring family. But I would have thought you would go with them, Mr. Sonnungar."

The car Thor had hired would take them to the hotel room where he'd been staying. Once they arrived there, Ra would transport her to France. Perhaps it was for the best that she was still unconscious. The less Ra had to explain to her later, the better off they would be, and a sudden transition to DeLeon Castle would hardly convince her of her sanity.

"I'm afraid I have other business yet, today. With Dr. Williams."

"Ah." Meek adjusted his glasses, peering up at him over the rims. "He hadn't mentioned to me—that is, did you have an appointment?"

"Oh yes," Thor lied. "If you wouldn't mind directing me to his office?"

Meek frowned. "I suppose there isn't any harm . . ."

Thor followed him once more down the corridors, the ugly, yellow lights flickering over his head as he passed beneath them. Rain had begun to fall again, tapping against the rare skylight. Just a drizzle, really, to allow him to keep his temper. He didn't want to give himself away completely. Not yet.

Meek paused at a heavy wooden door bearing a crooked number nine. He rapped his knuckles against the wood, then twisted the knob, sticking his head into the room on the other side. "Dr. Williams? Mr. Sonnungar is here for his appointment."

Thor reached over his head, pushing the door open wide. But even before he saw the doctor sitting behind his overlarge desk, he knew him. Loki was making no effort to hide himself, now.

"Ah, Mr. Sonnungar. Of course." Loki smiled slyly, removing the glasses he couldn't possibly need to wear. "You're rather late, aren't you?"

Thunder cracked so loudly the windows shook, and Thor growled. "How?"

"What kind of Trickster would I be if I gave away all my secrets?" His smile turned wolfish, a feral baring of teeth. "Dr. Meek, if you'll excuse us."

"Of course," Meek squeaked. "Yes. Certainly."

The door shut. Thor did not so much as glance behind him. By now, Meek was scurrying off down the hall, just another mouse to be played with in the larger game, released when he no longer entertained.

"Did Odin know?" Thor demanded.

Loki lifted his eyebrows, his gaze almost pitying. "Do you truly believe Heimdall would not have seen it all? From the moment Sif hatched her scheme, Odin might have stopped me from returning. But this? Would it help if I told you she was insane long before I arrived? Sif and Lugh had her convinced she was quite mad, outdid themselves, really. Odin sent me to handle it quietly. You were so distracted by the war, you see, and it wouldn't do to have you refocusing your attention here."

Lightning exploded inside the office, the white heat draining all color from the room. The desk smoked, fingers of electricity crawling across the wood, and Loki coughed, struggling to pick himself back up off the floor where he'd been thrown by the blast.

Thor grabbed him by his shirt and pinned him against the wall. "If you think I will not kill you again, Loki, send you back into Hel for whatever role you played no matter how small, you are grossly mistaken."

He coughed again, his pale skin scorched and smoldering. Lightning still danced, crackling across the tile floor. "Then she'll die, too."

The storm roared in his ears, wind and rain and thunder. Just a thought, and he could tear it all apart, stone by stone. Hurricane and tornado, lightning and thunder. He could swamp the whole state, if he willed it, and his eyes burned with the power, barely leashed. The women in the ward would be free of their prison, saved at last. Already the gale tore at the roof, rattling the glass. That a place such as this existed at all—that any people could think it was not horror and nightmare—

"Temper, temper, Odin-son." Loki rasped. "These lands aren't yours to smite. Can you just imagine how Odin would respond if you broke your precious Covenant? No need to hold himself back, anymore. No reason not to destroy Eve, once and for all . . ."

Thor dropped him, stumbling back. *Ragnarok.* Loki spoke of Ragnarok. Another world destroyed, another eternity of war. He shook his head to clear the haze from his eyes. Was that what Odin wanted? To goad him into this rage? With the Covenant shattered, his father would have his way. Eve first, then the angels, then Elohim. The way the gods had fled, there would be no other power to stand against him in the west. Just Bhagavan in the east. Strike a truce, then, and he would own half the world. A billion people to do with as he pleased, to harvest for their prayers, their power.

"No," Thor said. "Not here. Not through me. I won't be used by him again."

Loki climbed to his feet unsteadily, brushing the soot from his jacket. "Then I suppose you'll have to do something about your father, won't you?"

His eyes narrowed. "And what do you stand to gain if I do, Trickster?"

"If Odin falls, the Aesir move on. They leave this world, and so do I. There's nothing left here for any of us, but Zeus and his brothers won't welcome me alone. I've already tried."

Odin gone, with all the Aesir. He could be free. Finally free of his father, free to return to Eve, to care for her in France without fear of what it might cost him. And who was left to call a Council to object, if he chose to reveal himself? Bhagavan would give his blessing, and Ra as well. Who would stand against them, if they spoke in his favor? Anansi would not be able to unite the gods of Africa, and the South American gods, what was left of them, had no will to fight, even if they cared.

And Sif would never torment Eve again.

"Jormungand's venom. I want all of it. And you will leave Eve alone, no matter what happens."

Loki smiled slowly, his lips half-scorched. "Agreed."

§

"Father!"

He stood outside *Valaskjálf*, his father's hall, *Mjölnir* humming in his palm. Loki stood behind him, as Loki had stood a thousand times in the past, before Jarnsaxa had died, and he had nearly lost his sons with her. Before he had realized Loki only used him as another pawn in his games of deceit.

The thought did not give him any peace, now. But he could not doubt himself. Odin would only prey upon it.

"Allfather!" Thor called again. A hush had fallen inside the hall, the sounds of laughter and the clanking of mugs turning to murmurs. The great silver doors, carved with the image of Yggdrasil, his mother's tree, and the nine worlds Odin had won from Ymir, remained closed.

"Perhaps a well-formed insult?" Loki suggested, a smile in his voice.

Thunder rolled, soft and menacing. "Do not try my patience, Trickster, or *Mjölnir* will taste your blood first."

"Did you know he took Sif to his bed, before the Council? I wondered then if it was the first time—or why else would he lie to you about Ullr's birth? Have you never considered that your step-son might be your brother?"

His eyes were hazing white, lightning thrumming through his veins, and if Loki did not bite his tongue, Thor was more than tempted to remove it from his skull. Sif and Odin—Thor had barely been married three years when Ullr was born. When Sif had come to him, weeping, he had not doubted her story for a moment. The Vanir had been their enemies. That she might have been assaulted by one of them made more sense to him than the alternative. But if it had been his father, of all the gods . . .

No. Not even Odin was that great a fool. He had wanted Thor bound to the Aesir, not driven from them. He would not have taken such a risk, nor was he so cruel as to take his son's wife as a lover. Odin had made many mistakes, not the least of which this latest game he played, but always there was a purpose, and taking Sif to his bed after wedding her to Thor would not have served him.

Loki sought to distract him, to anger him further.

Why?

"The coward won't even face you," Loki jibed. "Because he knows he cannot win! Everything he's done to you, to Eve, make him pay for it in blood! Just as Eve did. Over and over. Do you know how often we mopped her blood from the floor? And the miscarriages. Meek only knew of the one, but there were more. Half a dozen children, all lost because of Odin. Just another way he drove her slowly insane, tortured her while your back was turned."

Thor fingered the hilt of the ivory dagger Loki had given him—carved from Jormungand's fang, and the source of the venom he had used to poison Eve. A dagger capable of killing a god, poisoning and fragmenting the soul so thoroughly they would never find the strength to return from Hel in any living form. Capable of taking Odin's life, if need be.

But why did Loki not desire Ragnarok? Half a world in which to sow his chaos. Half a world of men and women to play with, to taunt and tease and torture. Why would he want to move on to another world where he would be bound by oath to peace?

The silver doors opened, and Odin stood before him, armed with his spear, *Gungnir*. He wore no helmet, no armor, and the empty, scarred socket of his eye glowed like jet.

"And so it comes to this," the Allfather said. "You would forswear yourself for her, break all your vows of allegiance, betray your people and your king!"

The vows. Thor had given two vows to Ra, so long ago. His own and Odin's, on behalf of all the Aesir. Because Odin was king. Because no Aesir would dare betray his trust, his honor, by breaking such a binding oath.

But if Odin died, they were *all* free. Not just Thor, to care for Eve, but the rest of his brethren, too, to act as they pleased, to wage any war they desired. And Loki . . .

"He speaks of betrayal, but you have seen with your own eyes what he has done!" Loki said. "What honor was there in driving the poor girl mad? Was that not a betrayal of the Covenant you are sworn to?"

"No," Thor said quietly, meeting his father's eye. He drew the knife, his knuckles aching with the force of his grip.

And then Thor spun, and plunged the blade into Loki's heart.

The Trickster spluttered, his eyes wide and shocked. He sank slowly, first to his knees, then to the ground. The venom hissed and burned, acid devouring his flesh. Thor pulled out the knife and leaned down, gathering him in by the eye.

"You forget, Trickster. If there is one thing I always know, no matter what lies you tell, it is my duty."

Because if Odin had died, Loki was no longer bound by his king's oath. None of the Aesir were. The Covenant was broken, and what stood in Loki's path, then? Only Odin had ever been able to control him, and that much only by the oath which bound them together as brothers.

He looked up at his father. Odin had not moved, his expression grown even grimmer than it had begun. Thor wiped the blade clean on Loki's shirt, and sheathed it.

"Sif must be punished," he said. "And if it is left to me, she'll share the Trickster's fate. But I will leave her to your justice instead, on one condition."

Odin arched a brow. "And that is?"

"She must never threaten Eve again. Never come anywhere near her. Never so much as look at her."

"Is that all?" Odin asked.

"I will not suffer Ragnarok on this world, Father. If the day comes that it threatens these people, I will do everything in my power to stop you."

"I am bound by the Covenant, Thor of the North."

"See that you remain so."

He stopped at his mother's tree before he left. The apples were still Eve's best hope.

EPILOGUE
1923 AD

§

Thor stood with Luc upon the hill overlooking the small cottage. Tempting though it had been to return before now, he had not wanted to risk drawing his father's attention to Eve, not when she had been so weak, so broken by the ward. So he had stayed away, to give her what peace he could, hoping she would heal with the help of his mother's apples. One year, then two. Ra had given him news of her, of course, of her recovery, such as it was. Her mind was still fragile three years later. Fragile enough, Ra had suggested, that she might still believe him a delusion, if he came.

"She spends much of her time in the garden, when she is well enough to leave her bed," Luc said. "The dogs sit at her feet, their flocks forgotten. But if it gives her comfort, I will not begrudge her the lost sheep. Not that there have been many."

At least one of the dogs was a wolf, Thor thought, its head in her lap, but it wouldn't serve to alarm Luc. If Eve was not well enough to control it, Ra certainly could.

"Sometimes, I come to see her, and she thinks I am another ghost, Lord Ryam, or Reu," Luc was saying. "On her good days, she waits politely for an introduction. Horus fears her memory in this life is unlikely to recover, but at least she can care for herself more often than not. It is the things that require more than one day to complete that give her trouble. Reading is difficult, if the novel is longer than what she might finish in an afternoon. Unless it is a story she already knows. But even then . . ."

"Yes," Thor interrupted. "I begin to understand."

She would not remember he had come tomorrow, would not remember anything he told her, even if he revealed himself. Loki's last so-called treatment had all but destroyed her mind, and Sif had her vengeance at last, though she could hardly appreciate it, locked in Asgard and stripped of her power for the next century, at least.

But this could not be what the angel had meant, when he promised Thor's time with Eve would come. Gabriel had said she would know him, and if what Luc said was true, she barely knew her own mind, now.

"Horus says she will be herself again once she is reborn," Luc said after another moment. "But I would not wish the memory of such a life on even my enemy."

"My thanks, Luc."

"She is our Lady, Thor. What are we Lions for, if not this?"

Nothing, Thor thought. There was nothing else.

§

Her forehead furrowed when she spotted him, her hand, absently stroking the wolf's head, stilled. And then she rose, shading her eyes against the sun. "Thorgrim?"

He hesitated, stopping just out of reach, but his fingers itched to touch her, to stroke her hair from her cheek and tuck her head beneath his chin. Even if he could only have her for this one day. Even if she would not remember it tomorrow. *"Ástin mín."*

"Thorgrim." And then she was in his arms, delighted laughter strangled by shuddering sobs of relief. She was so soft, so warm. "My Thorgrim."

"I wish I could stay," he murmured into her hair. She smelled like sunshine again, and springtime. "Someday, I promise you. Someday, I'll tell you everything."

"Shh." She pressed her finger to his lips. "You're here now. We're together, now."

And when she kissed him, her mouth like strawberries and sweet wine, her fingers twining into his hair, nothing else mattered but that.

§

Look for other installments in the Fate of the Gods by Amalia Dillin

TEMPTING FATE

A Fate of the Gods Novella: Book 1.5

Mia's lived in her sister's shadow long enough. Now that Abby is getting married to a Frenchman, Mia scents freedom. In fact, Jean DeLeon, the groom's too-charming cousin, seems like the perfect place to start. But the House of Lions is full of secrets, and what started out as an exciting fling is quickly becoming more frustration than fun. Mia wants answers, or she wants out, and it isn't like she doesn't have other options. Ethan Hastings, for example. Tall, handsome, and gray eyes like nothing she's ever seen before. The fact that Jean seems to hate him is just a bonus. *(This e-novella takes place during the events of Forged by Fate.)*

TAMING FATE

A Fate of the Gods Novella: Book 2.5

Coming December 2013 in **A Winter's Enchantment**: *three novellas of winter magic and loves lost and regained.*

Ryam DeLeon may have saved Eve from burning at the stake, but their hasty marriage is off to anything but a smooth start. As tensions in the town grow, Ryam knows if he and Eve cannot find common ground, their first Christmas may be their last.

BEYOND FATE

Fate of the Gods Trilogy: Book Three

Coming September, 2014

ABOUT THE AUTHOR

Amalia Dillin began as a Biology major at the University of North Dakota before taking Latin and falling in love with old heroes and older gods. After that, she couldn't stop writing about them, with the occasional break for more contemporary subjects. She lives in upstate New York with her husband, and dreams of the day when she will own goats—to pull her chariot through the sky, of course.

Find her online at AmaliaDillin.com,
or follow her on Twitter @AmaliaTd.

ALSO AVAILABLE
FROM WORLD WEAVER PRESS

Shards of History

a New Adult fantasy novel by
Rebecca Roland

"Five out of Five stars! One of the most beautifully written novels I have ever read. Suspenseful, entrapping, and simply . . .well, **let's just say that *Shards of History* reminds us of why we love books in the first place.**" —Good Choice Reading

Like all Taakwa, Malia fears the fierce winged creatures known as Jeguduns who live in the cliffs surrounding her valley. When the river dries up and Malia is forced to scavenge farther from the village than normal, she discovers a Jegudun, injured and in need of help.

Malia's existence—her status as clan mother in training, her marriage, her very life in the village—is threatened by her choice to befriend the Jegudun. But she's the only Taakwa who knows the truth: that the threat to her people is much bigger and much more malicious than the Jeguduns who've lived alongside them for decades. Lurking on the edge of the valley is an Outsider army seeking to plunder and destroy the Taakwa , and it's only a matter of time before the Outsiders find a way through the magic that protects the valley—a magic that can only be created by Taakwa and Jeguduns working together.

"Fast-paced, high-stakes drama in a fresh fantasy world. Rebecca Roland is a newcomer to watch!"
—James Maxey, author of *Greatshadow: The Dragon Apocalypse.*

White as snow, stained with blood,
her talons black as ebony . . .

Opal

a novella by
Kristina Wojtaszek

The daughter of an owl, forced into human shape . . .

"A fairy tale within a fairy tale within a fairy tale—the narratives fit together like interlocking pieces of a puzzle, beautifully told."
—Zachary Petit, Editor *Writer's Digest*

In this retwisting of the classic Snow White tale, the daughter of an owl is forced into human shape by a wizard who's come to guide her from her wintry tundra home down to the colorful world of men and Fae, and the father she's never known. She struggles with her human shape and grieves for her dead mother—a mother whose past she must unravel if men and Fae are to live peacefully together.

"Twists and turns and surprises that kept me up well into the night. Fantasy and fairy tale lovers will eat this up and be left wanting more!"
—Kate Wolford, Editor, *Enchanted Conversation:*
A Fairy Tale Magazine

Available in ebook and paperback!
❦

Beyond the Glass Slipper
Ten Neglected Fairy Tales to Fall in Love With
Introduction and Annotations by
Kate Wolford

Some fairy tales everyone knows—these aren't those tales. These are tales of kings who get deposed and pigs who get married. These are ten tales, much neglected. Editor of *Enchanted Conversation: A Fairy Tale Magazine*, Kate Wolford, introduces and annotates each tale in a manner that won't leave novices of fairy tale studies lost in the woods to grandmother's house, yet with a depth of research and a delight in posing intriguing puzzles that will cause folklorists and savvy readers will find this collection a delicious new delicacy.

Beyond the Glass Slipper is about more than just reading fairy tales—it's about connecting to them. It's about thinking of the fairy tale as a precursor to *Saturday Night Live* as much as it is to any princess-movie franchise: the tales within these pages abound with outrageous spectacle and absurdist vignettes, ripe with humor that pokes fun at ourselves and our society.

Never stuffy or pedantic, Kate Wolford proves she's the college professor you always wish you had: smart, nurturing, and plugged into pop culture. Wolford invites us into a discussion of how these tales fit into our modern cinematic lives and connect the larger body of fairy tales, then asks—no, *insists*—that we create our own theories and connections. A thinking man's first step into an ocean of little known folklore.

Available in ebook and paperback!

§

ALSO FROM WORLD WEAVER PRESS

Wolves and Witches
A Fairy Tale Collection
Amanda C. Davis and Megan Engelhardt

Shards of History
A New Adult fantasy novel
Rebecca Roland

The King of Ash and Bone, and other stories
A Collection
Rebecca Roland

Heir to the Lamp
(Genie Chronicles Book One) YA novel
Michelle Lowery Combs

The Haunted Housewives of Allister, Alabama
(Cleo Tidwell Paranormal Mysteries, Book One)
Susan Abel Sullivan

The Weredog Whisperer
(Cleo Tidwell Paranormal Mysteries, Book Two)
Susan Abel Sullivan

———

World Weaver Press
*Publishing fantasy, paranormal, and science fiction
that engages the mind and ensnares the story-loving soul.*

27344501R00205

Made in the USA
Lexington, KY
05 November 2013